Not Worthy

To Be Compared

by

Ruth Sauder

NOT WORTHY TO BE COMPARED

by
Ruth Sauder
485 Walnut Road
Birdsboro, PA 19508

Library of Congress Number: 00-133295
International Standard Book Number: 1-930353-18-9

Printed 2000 by
Masthof Press
219 Mill Road
Morgantown, PA 19543-9701

Preface

Many people have requested that I publish my stories. Now that *Hidden Man of the Heart* has been published, more persons have encouraged me to print a sequel as well as begin another book.

Not Worthy To Be Compared is fictitious with no names referring to a real person or settlement but rather written in the setting of the Old Order Mennonite Church. I enjoy writing to release my imagination and especially enjoy sharing it with you—the reader!

Yes, I have started my third book—this time based on a girl as the main character. Of course, it will depend on the sales of the first two books as to when the third one is published. Thank you for purchasing this book, making it possible for you to read the third book.

- Ruth Sauder
September 2000

Chapter One

A peaked cloud was hanging in the western sky. It almost looked like a mountain, and it gradually covered the sun as it kept rising higher, hiding the view of the sunset as twilight enveloped the earth. A pale pink narrow border edged one side of the mountain like clouds. Slowly the border changed to lavender, and the breeze felt more crisp since the sun was hidden behind the growing cloud.

The fields were spotted with patches of snow that remained from the fresh cover of snow that had fallen last week. The January temperature remained in the twenties, dropping to the teens during the night.

John Mark Wenger walked across the frozen field, his head bending low rather than continuing to watch the western sky change patterns as the breeze was becoming brisk. When he set out to walk across the fields, the clear, cold air felt refreshing to his dusty, tired body, but the air was beginning to chill through his jacket.

Darkness had settled when he came in view of his home. The lantern in the kitchen cast a glow through the window and spread a small ray of light on the yard. His steps quickened. As he stepped on the porch and eased off his overshoes, the door opened from the kitchen.

Josiah smiled and announced, "John Mark is home!"

John Mark quickly kicked off his overshoes and entered the door that Josiah had been holding open and pulled it closed behind him. The range's warmth enveloped him with a cheery cozy warmth.

Josiah had a wide grin on his face as he asked, "Did the big truck really bounce?" John Mark pulled off his wraps and walked over to the wash basin, with Josiah following after, still asking

1

questions. Mother was putting the rest of the supper on the table and looked up at him. He could see her concern as she watched him walk by. He knew he limped more. It was true his muscles ached. And being tired always made his limping more noticeable.

Dad, who was sitting at his desk in a daze of figures, looked up a brief moment. After John Mark had washed off the sweat and hay dust of the day's toil, he picked up baby Rebekah, who was complaining.

"You can put her on the high chair," Mother said, "and, Delores, you can put water on the table. Also, fetch a pie from the cellar shelf." Mother continued, "Then we want to eat since John Mark is home now."

John Mark was answering Josiah's eager questions as he put Rebekah in the high chair. Questions about the big truck that the neighbor (across a few fields) had used to move loads of hay home from across the mountain. And John Mark had been asked to help load and unload. It had been a long day, but he had a tired, satisfied feeling.

At the table Josiah sat on one side asking questions, and from the end of the table, Delores was trying to tell him something about the sixth-grade English in school. Two-year-old William and one-year-old Rebekah were hungry and tired. As Dad took his place at the table, the volume stilled. Mother took Rebekah out of her high chair and held her on her lap as they bowed their heads in prayer. The meal began with the usual chatter and clatter.

Dad asked, looking at John Mark, "Did you get all the hay moved that Smith wanted?" He asked a second time till he got John Mark's attention, as Delores was relating school news to him.

John Mark nodded toward Delores, motioning her to wait. He wanted to hear the rest of it.

Answering Dad he said, "We didn't get quite all the hay moved. It was more than he figured it was, and once we lost a half-hour when the truck engine was making trouble."

"Does he want to move the rest tomorrow?" Dad asked.

"No, he has a business meeting to attend tomorrow. He said he would say something when he is ready. He will use his own truck to haul the rest as it isn't that much anymore."

John Mark was glad to hear that when he talked his voice didn't squeak every so often anymore. It had a steady sound, although it sounded strange, more low and gruff. He had noticed that first Mother had looked up quickly when he started talking. Mostly when other people were around, he suspected at times she wasn't sure it was him talking. But everyone, including himself, was getting used to it.

As the meal ended, the children were visiting with each other at one end of the table, while Mom and Dad were talking at the other end of the table.

Delores followed John Mark to the small blackboard that was on the kitchen wall. She stood concentrating, watching as John Mark slowly explained each step of the arithmetic problem. Slowly she picked up a chalk and started writing.

John Mark explained, "Now think, how often does 258 go into 140?"

Delores looked at him, then got big eyes and said, "It can't."

"No, that's right. It can't."

"But I did bring a number down already," she argued.

"Right," John Mark stated, "and if it doesn't divide into it, you have to put up a zero and bring down the next number," pointing after with the chalk. Delores obeyed and after another few problems her eyes lit up in understanding.

Minutes later, John Mark looked up when Dad said his name.

"Are you about done helping Delores with her lessons?" Delores looked at John Mark and then back at Dad.

"These are not her lessons," John Mark admitted.

"I was wondering if fourth grade had such problems," Mother said.

Dad got up from the table and said, "Delores, you help Mother either get the dishes off the table or make Rebekah happy. John Mark, you get the chores started. Maybe you'll have to do them all; Josiah can help you some," he said as he patted his hand on his almost-six-year-old son's head. "And I really should go over to Widow Emma's. I should have gone before."

Mother looked at Dad, asking, "Do you really have to go tonight?"

Dad walked to the desk and pulled out some papers and a notebook, saying, "Well, tomorrow we promised to go along visiting shut-ins, and the next day we want to go to the funeral, and the rest of the week is butchering. You know, they tell me Emma's son is in the hospital again. I haven't taken care of the matters from the last time, and I should go over there. She has enough problems."

As John Mark slipped on his wraps and went out the door, he heard Dad talking to Mother in low tones.

"I was going to go over this afternoon, then you know, those people came."

Mother nodded her head with a solemn, tired look. Josiah followed him out the door and to the barn. John Mark's mind dwelled on Dad's responsibility. Apparently Dad had company again, when he said, "those people," a phrase they heard time and again when people came to see Dad about church matters. And the children need not always know who it was, or why they came, or where Dad was going.

John Mark did not mind doing the chores when Dad had to go away or had company. The times he found himself rebelling toward the church work was when it denied them of having a happy family, like times when Dad had company or had been away. The effect of those visits left Dad's mind so burdened that he would hardly respond to the family for a day or so and walked around in silence with a troubled brow.

But tonight John Mark worked in ease since he had no fears that Dad's task was unpleasant. It sounded like it was to help Widow Emma with hospital funds.

As John Mark finished the chores in the barn and took the milk in the house and went out to the calf barn, his heart felt light as Mother and Delores had been working and visiting together while the little ones were happily playing. There were times when Dad went on church errands that John Mark sensed that Mother was tense, and it seemed to affect the little children when Mother wasn't relaxed.

As John Mark filled the water pail in the calf pens, he thought of what Dad had said about them going away visiting shut-ins to-

4

morrow, and the next day going to a funeral. He was wondering if he would be baby-sitting. Sometimes he had Josiah and William to look after when they went visiting sick ones. On a few occasions he had kept Rebekah too.

Pulling on his coat collar more securely with his left hand while with the right hand he guided the horses toward the barn, fifteen-year-old John Mark scanned the bleak February skies. He almost shivered. There seemed to be no warmth from the sun, which now and then faintly came to the surface. But clouds kept hiding its rays. At times you couldn't even see the outline of the sun. The manure spreader bumped on over the frozen field. Everything seemed so silent. No wind, no buds, just a dreary gloom. Clouds had completely hidden the sun.

John Mark put one hand in his pocket to warm it a bit. He drove on down to the shed. They were now done cleaning manure out of the heifer pen. It had been a good job as forking manure had warmed him up. Dad had helped for a few of the loads.

After John Mark had led the faithful chunky workhorses, Pet and Dolly, to their stalls and lifted off their harness, he remained standing at the harness closet. He stared at the cats unthinkingly while they purred in the warmth of the barn. His thoughts turned to Delores telling him how the sixth grade class had quite a time in school learning their new arithmetic problems, and how Teacher Ellen had almost come to the end of her usual strong patience. John Mark was pondering the thought of having the class at the board and explaining an arithmetic problem.

The one number was one-fourth, the other one-half. First change it all to one fraction before starting. He nodded his head to himself as he imagined that they were catching on, too. Delores said that if the teacher had more time she could explain it, but the first graders needed so much help with their arithmetic that they couldn't go ahead alone.

John Mark still longed to be in school. He had enjoyed it so much. He finished eighth grade the year before and was supposed to go to the three-hour school once a week, but since there wasn't so much work to do at home and the teacher and board didn't care,

Mother and Dad consented to his desire. He had gone to school regularly till December when he turned fifteen years old. The teacher said it was of no use to continue since he knew all that was in the books. Now the time seemed to pass so slowly because there wasn't much to do. He had helped some here and there in the neighborhood. He helped move the hay home for the neighbor, and a few times he had helped in the harness shop two miles away. But it was such a dull job. The work was so boring. He sensed Dad was disappointed that he wasn't more enthused about the job, as they had figured bit by bit he would learn the job and maybe be a regular hand when they needed more help. But he didn't like it. He had no interest in it.

Moments later he came into the kitchen. It was so quiet. Two-year-old William was sleeping on the sofa. The others were outside. Dad had been to town, and he saw when he was in the barn that Mother was plucking feathers off two chickens as Josiah and Rebekah looked on. John Mark got a drink and started walking across the kitchen. Then he remembered that he wasn't done reading the *Blackboard Bulletin* yet. He finally found it in the room which they called "the study," a room enclosed from the sitting room between the kitchen and hall where Dad did most of his church work. At times privacy was needed from the family, so they had remodeled a small room off the kitchen. But the entrance led off from the hall. John Mark plopped himself on a nearby chair and was instantly engrossed in his reading.

The story was written by a teacher whose geography classes had become monotonous and how she visited a school where she witnessed an interesting, lively geography class. It went on to explain how she tried the new teaching methods on her own pupils and how her pupils failed to revive. But she wasn't to be defeated. She taught geography as if her class was thoroughly enthused, till she herself was truly enthused. At times John Mark smiled to himself, as the teacher had a good sense of humor and seasoned the story with it. It went on to say how her pupils' interest finally ignited from her flame.

Then there were a few letters that teachers had written of the school year with little amusements, etc., in.

The next story took him right into a school room. It was so plainly written that it put the reader right in the school room with the teacher who discovered that a certain arithmetic answer book was misplaced. It happened a few times till she was aware that someone was at times using it. And the whole class was innocent—John Mark thought he felt the stillness as the teacher called everyone's attention before dismissing the class for recess. Then John Mark heard a voice in the stillness, or did he hear his name? Now he heard his name again.

He listened, and Dad was saying, "I know, I've been looking around a little as to what there is to do this winter, but he doesn't seem anxious at all to help in the harness shop. And Paul said he doesn't seem like the one to learn the job as the interest seems not to be there, and so he doesn't take much hold."

Then Dad said a few sentences a little quieter so that John Mark didn't understand all of it. Something about "Can't be there— would let him take care of calves."

He heard Mother say, "Well, I'm afraid this can't go on. Josiah knows too much of what they are to learn in first grade, and I caught on that Delores feels her lessons are boring since John Mark has been teaching her the lessons of higher grades." She took a long breath, then continued, "Maybe if he had work all day, he would be interested in visiting or reading with the family in the evening instead of teaching them." Rebekah was making noise and he couldn't understand all of the next reply, but heard his parents talking. Then he understood some again.

"Where is he now? Is he hauling manure?"

Dad said, "He was at it when I came home. Guess he's putting the horses away." Then Rebekah made more noise again. He waited a little and then silently slipped out of the study, went on down the hall, and out the door to the outside. Now what could he do? Oh, maybe the mailman had made his round already. He walked out to the mailbox and picked up the handful of mail and brought it in the house.

When John Mark came in, Mother had left her chicken butchering and was getting dinner ready. John Mark passed the kitchen

7

closet already so Mother thought he had hung up his wraps and brought the mail along it.

Mother looked at him, saying, "Did you see Dad? He was asking what you are doing."

"No, I didn't. I guess I was out getting the mail when he went out the front door."

"Will you get Rebekah satisfied till I have dinner ready?" Mother asked, loosening the little girl from her skirts. When Dad came in, John Mark was showing a picture book to Rebekah with William listening, too.

Chapter Two

John Mark tossed the last cakes of hay to the cows that stood waiting for their share while the rest of the cows were munching on their hay. The cow stable seemed quiet after the cows were all milked and fed and were now content, enjoying their hay. He heard George finishing up in the milk house. George was a good friend and a year older than himself. He was doing the milking and John Mark was asked to do the feeding for George while the Martin Horning family had gone on a trip. They were expecting Martin's home tomorrow evening.

John Mark picked up the pail that was standing at the inside milk house door by the barn entrance where George had saved the milk from the cow that freshened a few days ago. John Mark had already fed the cow's own calf, but now he poured an even amount of milk in two smaller buckets and headed out to the calf shelter to feed the last two calves.

The February weather had moderated. The gentleness of the air felt as if there was a hint of spring on the way. While the calves were eagerly licking the bottom of the pail, John Mark saw George leaving for his home.

In a few more minutes John Mark had returned to the milk house and rinsed the pail and walked through the barn to check that everything was taken care of.

Tomorrow evening at this time they would be finished with the job. To him, tending cows seemed so hopeless.

They would scrape the aisle and grates and sweep everything clean. Then they would put the lime on and sweep it evenly. Then the cows would come in and dirty it all up and till the milking was done, you wouldn't know you had scraped and swept at all.

Out in the barnyard Pearl was eager to see John Mark. He untied her, leaped onto her back, and off across the fields they went with soft breezes drifting over them. Both of them were eager to be going home.

Home had a few different meanings already in his life. John Mark pondered on his life as he slowed Pearl down a little to enjoy the ride. He remembered very little of his life before he was at Mercy Home. He just remembered hearing it being talked about years ago, and remembered some of the unpleasant things of being in different homes, but now it was a forgotten dream. His memories of home now were of when Mother took him home and they lived with Grandma Musser. He still recalled the evenings Grandma sat in her rocker by the stove, wrapped him in a bed covering, rocked him, and told him stories. He couldn't clearly remember Grandma's death. He remembered that, when Delores came into their home as an unclaimed baby from the Home, his mind was so overjoyed that it faded the losing of Grandma some in his memory.

That is what childhood memories of home meant to him: Mother, whom they had called Kathleen then, and Delores, and helping with small things in the salvage store they had. Then the time came when Dad stepped in to the family. He wasn't sure how that came about. As he grew older, he pondered these things and had many unanswered questions.

About the first memory he still recalled was the evening Dad came over the yard from nowhere, helped hull peas, and sang for them before they went to bed. But he wasn't "Dad" until quite some time later. He visited regularly in the home till he seemed to be one of the family. That seemed to be the beginning of the rest of their lives: Dad folding into his family, things happening fast.

Suddenly Annie came into our lives, John Mark thought. She was a baby whose parents had been killed, and she needed a home. She was very sick at first. The baby seemed to be nobody. It sort of dimmed from John Mark's memory, but it seemed to him as if that was about the time Dad came to stay with them and he started calling him Dad rather than Clayton. *And then we became a family and it seemed as if a whole new world opened up. Suddenly we had lots of relations, uncles and aunts, cousins, and Grandma Wenger.* He still remembered the heartache when Annie died so suddenly. She had been someone after all, as they had sorely missed her.

By now John Mark had arrived at the barn entrance. He slid off Pearl, led her into her stall, and dipped some oats out of the barrel with the acid dipper with the broken-off handle that was in the oat barrel. Pearl was the horse they had since about as long as he can remember, and she was still their regular horse. There was Huckaberry, the horse that Dad brought along. He wasn't as steady as Pearl and didn't have the power, but Mother used him on short errands, or as a stand-by when Pearl wasn't ready to go, like last Sunday when Pearl had a shoe missing. Dad had talked of replacing Huckaberry, since Pearl was getting older too.

Mother looked up from her ironing when John Mark entered the kitchen. She set the iron back on the stove and reached in the baker oven, pulled out his plate, and set it on the table. Nine-year-old Delores was standing on her low bench, her sleeves rolled up and her hands in the dishwater with suds up to the elbow. She was fishing out a few spoons and forks. She looked up at him when he came to fetch a spoon to eat his supper. She got a wide smile when she saw him. Then suddenly she frowned and said, "You smell like cows."

"Just one more day," John Mark reminded her, sliding onto his chair.

Delores looked at him for a moment, then started wiping her dishwater hands on her apron, saying, "Do you know what? We didn't have our English class today. Seventh grade is having such a hard time understanding their arithmetic. The teacher put in a lot of time explaining it when they were in class. Then later she took them to the board, and they still didn't understand. She had to explain it more, and then we didn't have time for some of the classes."

Delores shook her head hopelessly, then continued, "And little Erla couldn't find her workbook, and after a lot of hunting the boys finally found it. It had gotten in with the social studies notebooks."

John Mark ate a few spoonfuls and said, "It must have been a bad day."

"And we had visitors later," Delores said, brightening up the situation. "Then we sang for them. We tried the new song that Caleb brought along that we were practicing every so often. The teacher looked worried when we picked that song, but it went well. The big girls know it well by now."

"Delores, don't forget to keep at your dishes," Mother reminded her as she slipped a freshly ironed shirt on the hanger.

Delores turned back to her dishes and was soon whirling dishwater and telling Mother what Irene had in her lunch that was so good.

John Mark was musing to himself at Delores's joy of informing everyone what is going on. If she came to the end of one subject, she switched to another one, but she was a ray of sunshine. Although she had hair that curled everywhere, there were always loose ends. She had brown eyes, almost darker than her hair. Eyes that didn't miss much, and her mind never lacked.

Delores was the one who made him feel not quite as awkward, since she didn't resemble anyone in the family either. Now and then when they had travelers, the subject would surface when visitors expressed their curiosity that they couldn't tell who the children looked like, Mom or Dad. Sometimes travelers thought he and Delores were hired help. If it hadn't been for Delores, he would often have felt odd and different from the rest of the family.

Josiah came bounding in the door, exclaiming, "Mother, do you know— Oh, John Mark is home. Guess what?"

"Josiah," Mother called after him, "close the door!"

He backed up and closed the door and caught his breath in gasps, then continued. "Pam, well, she has five little kittens up by the hay bale where we throw it down to the horses." Delores had him repeat his message, then she started washing dishes faster. Maybe she could still go out and see them before Dad came in from the barn.

John Mark pushed his empty plate away and remained sitting at the table as he listened to Josiah and Delores naming the kittens. Josiah was describing what colors they were.

John Mark remembered when Josiah was born. The first two years he looked quite a bit like Dad, except for his brown eyes, but the last few years his cheeks weren't so filled out; they were more narrow. Grandma Wenger said he looked a lot like Uncle Enos did when he was small, but his hair was like Dad's, although his cowlick was more in the middle of his forehead instead of to one side.

It was when Josiah was some months over four years old that baby William was born. He had blue eyes like Dad, but a slender face and frame, and somewhat blonde hair that no one could really place. His hair was lighter than Mother or Dad's but more brown compared to Delores's. He was a very content, quiet boy. Ever since John Mark came in William was playing with clothespins he had gotten out of the wash basket that was standing in the east corner of the kitchen waiting until someone put it away. William was clipping them together making a fence. He seemed a lot like Mother, but rather sober. His smiles on his own were rare. He had to be coaxed into a smile. Mother said he looked much like her Dad did except his eyes were bluer.

William was only a year and some months old when Rebekah, the baby, was born. She was broader and heavier than the boys and had dark hair like Mom's. But her eyes were a mild color, about nearest to brown. She was trying to walk, but crawling was still easier and safer.

John Mark looked around and asked, "Is Rebekah in bed already?" Delores started answering but was interrupted when the door opened and dad came in carrying Rebekah who was rejoicing at seeing everyone. When Mother reached for her, Rebekah smiled easily and let herself fall into Mother's arms.

By now Delores had the dishes washed, and she and Josiah were drawing on the blackboard.

"Is everything still going all right with your chores over there?" Dad asked John Mark.

John Mark yawned and nodded his head. "One of the cows freshened today and all seems well. And tomorrow the Hornings plan to come home," John Mark yawned again. Getting up so early was starting to catch up.

The smaller children were getting ready for bed.

Mother handed Rebekah to John Mark, saying, "Will you entertain her while I put the little boys to bed?"

Josiah stood at the stairway door waiting while Mom put William in his night clothes. Delores had gone upstairs already. Rebekah was looking in Mother's direction and complaining. John Mark steered her glance away from Mother and exercised her in a pat-a-cake session, but she was more interested in standing on his lap and pulling his hair. When he jerked away, Rebekah laughed, thinking it was a game. By the time Mother came downstairs, Daddy had come out from the study and was in the kitchen. John Mark got up and handed Rebekah back to Mother as he headed toward the upstairs door after taking off his shoes.

Dad, who had gotten a drink of water, set his cup down and asked, "Are you going to bed already?"

"I may as well. I keep dozing off. Only one more morning of getting up so early to go feed cows."

John Mark noticed that Mother and Dad exchanged a look that seemed like a command. Mother seemed to be waiting for Dad to speak. Dad sat down on the rocker and brushed his stocking toes over the floor. John Mark sat on a chair near the stairway door at Mother's request.

At length Dad asked, "Do you miss going to school?"

"Oh well, yes, some days I think more about it," John Mark answered with a wondering look.

Dad began again, "Teacher Ellen stopped in here late this afternoon soon after you were gone. Mother and I weren't aware of it, but she says you had helped her a lot in checking papers and answering questions and the like." Dad ended it in a question.

"Well, yes, some days that I didn't have anything else to do, but what of it?" John Mark asked.

Dad continued, "She says she is falling so far behind and at the parent-teacher meeting she asked about having a helper, and they wondered why she is just now getting so far behind. Then she said that she just realized how much you had been helping her, and the board agreed that she could have a helper again. The people suggested she would ask if you would still help."

John Mark gasped and sat up in surprise. "May I?"

Dad and Mother stared at his eager reaction, then looked at each other a brief moment.

"As far as we being able to spare you, that is no problem. I was hoping to find work for you that you have an interest in. But I don't know if this is what you need."

Mother cleared her throat saying, "But we wanted to get you some other interest as you have been teaching Delores lessons beyond her grade and Josiah knows a lot of the things already that he is supposed to learn in first grade. I'm afraid your actually helping to teach won't work out well."

Dad was nodding his head in agreement.

John Mark remained silent for a few minutes then said, "I realize what you mean, but didn't I play more school with them since I quit school than while I was in school? I got my school interest filled."

Maybe that is why it seems it isn't getting better, Mother was thinking.

John Mark continued, "What I'm trying to say is if I am in school all day, then I'm not as tempted to teach in the few hours I am at home."

Dad was looking down at the floor. When he looked up, Mother was watching him with a silent wondering. "Well, if you are interested, we can try it on that reasoning. If it doesn't work out, Ellen has to seek other help."

John Mark sat deep in thought trying to grasp it. At length he asked, "When can I go? I mean, when do I start school?"

Mother and Dad looked at each other and Dad shrugged his shoulders. "I guess you have to arrange that with Ellen—how many days you are to help and the like."

John Mark remained sitting for another ten minutes in a daze. Then he rose and went up to his room and lit the kerosene light. He sat on the edge of the bed and stared at nothing. He wondered if he would soon wake up. He had never really given it much thought that he could be a helper in school. It was such a new thought. He had often desired to still be a scholar.

An urge went through him when he remembered the things that Delores had said about some grades having a hard time with lessons, and that it took up so much of Ellen's time that they missed other classes.

Maybe he would get a chance to drill some grades in lessons too, he thought. Not only checking papers and answering questions.

He was getting carried away in his thoughts. In the next half-hour he had envisioned a few days in the classroom, and then a disturbing thought occurred to him: Tomorrow I have to milk cows. Finally his thoughts settled down enough that he could prepare for bed.

Chapter Three

John Mark came down the stairs and stopped for a brief moment in front of the mirror and quickly brushed his hair to obedience.

Mother Kathleen looked up from her sewing and asked, "Are you going somewhere?"

He walked over to the clothestree, reached for his hat, looked at her, and attempted to say it in a matter-of-fact way, "I'm going over to see if Ellen is still at school." But Mother heard an eagerness, or was it anxiety? She continued sewing, then turned around as John Mark opened the door to go out.

She called after him, "I just now remembered, I need yeast. Maybe you could circle over to the store on the way?" John Mark turned back and walked to the cupboard and opened the door. He got some change and a dollar from the can that stood there to catch dollar bills and change that accumulated in pockets and dressers, etc. He put the change in his shirt pocket and continued out the door.

When he arrived at school, many happy memories seemed to pour out at him as he opened the door. The posters and pictures and charts. Everywhere he looked were things that seemed so familiar. But where was Ellen? He noticed the empty chair at the teacher's desk. Seconds later Ellen stepped out of the storage book closet wondering, then recognizing him.

She smiled, "Oh, it's John Mark. I thought maybe I had heard the door, but I wasn't sure. I'm hunting for reading books for the third grade; I'm not sure I have enough." She turned back to the closet.

John Mark asked, "Do you have another book, or are you giving them the first book of fourth grade?"

"No, they didn't have the last one yet. Martin and Ella have quite a bit of trouble understanding their reading, so we were going slowly and repeating stories," she answered as she stepped back on the chair and shuffled through books. "I think I loaned one book to Center Ridge School last year and now it looks like I should have it again." She stepped down from the chair and had a few books in her hand. She headed toward her desk explaining, "At least I found another seventh-grade arithmetic book. Florence's is worn out, and George lost his spelling book. She shrugged, raising her shoulders, throwing out her hands and raising her eyebrows. She laid the assortment of books on her desk in a heap, sat down on the chair at her desk, and gathered up a few papers and put them on a stack. She was putting some things away on her desk—the scotch tape, a few scissors, and the reinforcements.

Ellen asked, "Did your mom and dad tell you that I was down to see them a few days ago?" she asked as she straightened the scattered piles of paper.

John Mark sat on the bench that was near Ellen's desk and replied, "Yes, I have heard about it, and I wanted to see if you were serious."

Ellen looked up at him quickly, catching his eagerness, although he appeared calm when he asked.

"You mean you are interested?" She was leaning back in her chair, forgetting her array on the desk.

"There is nothing I would rather do," John Mark humbly admitted.

"And your parents agreed?" she asked, nodding her head hopefully.

John Mark tried to remember. "Oh yes, if it works out. Mother is concerned because I teach Delores and Josiah too much at home, and if this makes it worse they won't allow it." When he looked up, Ellen had her head propped in her hands and was studying him.

At length she sat back and said softly, "I think maybe you could get your fill helping the third grade with their arithmetic and the first grade with their phonics so that you might want to relax at home."

18

John Mark noticed that Ellen took a few quick glances at the clock. He gathered all his courage and asked, "When shall I come, on Monday morning?"

Ellen took a deep breath and wiped her hands across her eyes as if she were trying to remove the tiredness and sat in deep thought for a moment. Finally she replied, "Yes, there's always so much to do on Monday. I didn't get finished with social studies. I started writing on the board, and I have to select the March poems. Oh yes, these art pictures," she said, gathering up a stack of papers on her desk.

"Shall I put them up for you?" he asked.

She shook her head, "No, first I have to judge them. We had a contest and there will be a first, second, and third prize." Ellen opened a book, took out a sheet of paper, and looked at the blackboard saying, "If you want to, you can finish putting the social studies quiz on the board."

Ellen chuckled at his apparent hesitation. "What's wrong, John Mark?" she asked.

"I don't know if I can write neatly enough to match your writing without lines on the board."

She caught her breath unbelievingly and said, "Don't you remember this isn't the first time you wrote on the board for me?"

John Mark got up when she handed the paper to him. As he pulled off his jacket and hung it over the seat, he said, "But not a long article like this. Just Bible verses and notices." He walked over to the blackboard.

As he wrote and Ellen graded art pictures, she told John Mark that she was thinking about having him help all day on Mondays and on Tuesday afternoons, since that is when they have German. Then he could get some grades in to review whatever needs practicing. Wednesdays she would try it alone. He could help again all day on Thursdays, and on Fridays only till noon, since the last session was art.

Ten minutes later, John Mark was just finishing the last sentence on the board when he heard the door open. Thinking Ellen had gone outside, he was suprised to hear a man talking. John Mark

19

whirled around to see Ellen looking just as surprised to see Samuel Garman, a board member who lived over on the next road from the schoolhouse, coming in the door.

Samuel said, "I see I came at the right time. It looks as if you have your helper already, so maybe this news won't be as bad as I feared." Ellen stood and stared at him with her mouth open.

Samuel buried one hand deep in his pocket and looked like a mischievous boy as he continued, "We were just informed that the Miller farm next to Ed Ringler's was sold and there is a family of our church people moving in from Ohio. They asked about sending their children to our school.

Ellen seated herself on a desk and leaned forward, asking, "How many children? How old? Who are they?"

"The father's name is Menno Leinbach. I understand they have one in seventh grade, one in fifth, and one in fourth, but I don't know more except it seems to me that they said the one in seventh grade is a girl."

"When are they coming?" Ellen asked in a daze.

"Oh, let me see. I think they said not till the week after next." Then, Samuel continued, "Oh, yes, Menno's wife is a sister to Reuben Hurst." Samuel stood shifting his weight on the other foot, waiting for Ellen to respond.

At length Ellen said, "You sure came at the right time. If John Mark wasn't here to help me, I think I would walk out!"

Samuel gave a low laugh and said, "Why, Ellen, you have been through deeper water than this, and if they are cousins to Reuben Hurst's children, they should blend well."

Ellen toyed with a pencil on top of the desk in front of her, saying, "I haven't planned to drown in deep water again, as far as that goes. And it's not that I fear their characters, but cousins can be very different. It's just that I thought the load was about heavy enough for me."

"I think with John Mark, you'll be able to carry it."

John Mark put on his jacket, set his hat on his head, and started walking back to the door. Samuel was asking about something at the window that needed repairing and Ellen started talking in a more relaxed tone and said as John Mark was going out the door, "Don't forget, John Mark, I'm depending on you for Monday."

John Mark looked back, nodded his head, and went out the door. He was thinking of Samuel's remark, "Ellen, you have been through deeper water than this." He wondered if Samuel meant two years ago when John Mark was in seventh grade and things didn't seem to be going so well in school. One of the eighth grade boys had no respect for Ellen and some more became unruly. Ellen seemed to have no urge to try. After a few meetings trying to iron things out, the families found out that Ellen was hurt. She had broken up a friendship with a boy she had been dating for over eight months. After that was known to the school parents, they put much effort into helping Ellen win the victory. Maybe Ellen was almost drowning then.

When he arrived home and came into the kitchen, the family was eating supper. As John Mark took his place at the table, Mother asked him about the yeast.

John Mark's mouth fell open. Then he said, "I thought I could get it on the way home, as I was afraid Ellen would leave before I got there. And, well, on the way home yeast never entered my mind."

"Well, that means he must fetch some tomorrow," Dad put in. John Mark nodded his head as if to say, *Sure, why not.*

That evening when they were out in the barn, John Mark told Dad what had been on his mind on the way home: a new family moving into the area.

John Mark lit the light upstairs in his room and lay back on his bed to relax for a while before getting ready for bed. He put his hands under his head and stared at the ceiling, not seeing the blue wallpaper border than ran around the room and edged the white and blue design paper on the wall. Instead he was thinking, Was this only Thursday of the first week that he had been helping Ellen at school?

He recalled it was only about three months that he was out of school, but it seemed longer than that. He was no longer classed as one of the boys. He remembered the first morning when they lined up to sing, Ellen had given him a book and motioned to him that he should stand over in front of the boy's group as she stood in front of the girl's group. Otherwise he was going to stand in line with the older boys as he was used to doing.

Just the last morning Ellen had said that the boys were helping better with the singing since he was there as an example or leader for them.

He also realized that his few months' absence had brought a change or difference. He had been slow in catching onto it, but he was becoming more aware of how the eighth-grade girls and a few of the seventh-grade girls seemed to be ill at ease when he answered their questions or helped them with something. They never acted like that while he was going to school. Ellen never mentioned anything about it, but he sensed that she suspected it. A few times when these grades needed help with problems at their seat or at the board, Ellen had assigned him to take the second grade class and she answered questions for the eighth grade. John Mark felt sort of disturbed by this. He wished they could all be one group like they used to be when he was going to school. He didn't like the awkwardness that the girls had built up between them. Still, he felt much more at home in the classroom than in the harness shop. Here was life and challenge.

The first day at recess he walked out on the porch for a little fresh air and watched as the upper grades took up their baseball game. He never enjoyed sports very much. He often was an outfielder or catcher for both sides, and it seemed they all had their places filled. The younger grades were having a little dispute, so he fetched a tin can from the cellar and got them started playing Kick the Can. It worked out well since he wasn't so swift in running. (When John Mark played, the children had an opportunity to get the can since it seemed as if someone their own age played with them.) By now the younger group looked up to him to lead their games.

Next thing he knew, he had almost dozed off and was thinking about school things that didn't make sense, so he prepared for bed and blew out the light. Tomorrow forenoon he was going to school again. How fast the week had passed! Tomorrow was Friday already, and next week the new pupils would be coming to school.

Chapter Four

It had all seemed so simple when Ellen asked John Mark on Thursday if he would be interested in going along to the teacher's meeting on Friday afternoon. School would dismiss at noon and Ellen had asked him, "By the way, would you like to go along to the meeting?" The question had been very unexpected for him.

He had repeated the words, "Me go to a meeting?"

"Sure," Ellen had said, "quite a few people are there that are teacher's helpers. They can also gather ideas and information and share experiences."

It had sounded interesting, and the more he thought about it, the more he got enthused, so he agreed to go along. But already he felt like an awful misfit. They had hired a driver to take all three teachers from the area to the meeting, which was at a schoolhouse in Stony Creek District. This was the area Dad grew up in and where Mommy Wenger and a host of uncles, aunts, and cousins lived. He thought if it was the school right in that area he could maybe go to Grandma's or one of the uncles for supper while all the teachers went to a place for supper.

John Mark sat on the front seat with the driver, now and then visiting a little. John Mark was also taking in the view of the countryside. Spring used to be around the corner, but it had now made its appearance. A lot of fieldwork was being done. Some farmers were plowing; some were picking stones. As they traveled over the countryside, John Mark, without realizing it, wasn't watching the scenery anymore. The talk in the back seat had become interesting. He caught snatches of one teacher who was saying how she had the next year's first graders there the past week for their preschool days and how one child seemed to be so timid.

Ellen said, "Oh yes, she is the oldest of the family."

The other teacher said, "Oh, that doesn't always make a difference. I have had an oldest child from another family, too, and she came all rough and ready and taking everything in."

Then the first teacher shared what she tried to do to relax the timid child. John Mark couldn't understand quite everything. Their talk had now switched to another preschool child that seemed to know no English. The talk continued. Sometimes one teacher talked, then another.

John Mark lost track of the conversation when the driver talked to him. The next time he concentrated on listening, one of the teachers was asking Ellen about how she uses a certain kind of phonics book.

"It takes so much teacher's help for the pupils. I liked the red ones better."

Ellen said how she did it but then admitted, "But I do have a helper now so I think they are very suitable. I used to skip some pages that they couldn't do alone till I had more time to help them."

So often John Mark had something on the tip of his tongue to say if it was about something that he dealt with more than Ellen did. Often he would bite his tongue when he was on the verge of asking something. The girls were so engrossed in their visiting, he felt awkward interrupting. But then there were times he didn't feel at all like them, like when they discussed filling out report cards or talked about finding notes returned with report cards.

Before he knew what had happened, the car came to a halt. When he looked up he saw a schoolhouse, many buggies and bicycles, some cars and quite a few vans, and many people. John Mark almost lost his courage. A handful of girls stood by the teams in a conversation that had never reached the schoolroom yet. A few men stood on the porch. A group of girls were further over on the porch in a half-circle. And there were people walking here and there. The schoolhouse door opened every now and then.

Ellen said, "There's Mildred. I need to talk to her."

One of the other teachers said, "I hope I remember to give the book to Irma." Soon the girls had all piled out. John Mark crawled out, still watching all the people coming and going in and out of the schoolhouse. Ellen and the other two teachers had disappeared already.

A few men nodded a greeting to John Mark as he entered the porch. Two girls came out the door and apologized and excused themselves when they almost ran into him. He went in the door and almost gasped when he saw all the people and activity. There were different small groups standing around. Some were showing something to the others. One group was up at the map studying something. He noticed a few here and there reading the charts and looking at pictures on the walls. One had a notebook and was jotting something down.

As John Mark hung his hat on a hook, he noticed a display on the wall. Wondering what it referred to, he soon caught on that it was a health chart of cleanliness hung near the sink and water cooler and drinking cups. But what was that hanging on the other wall? He walked over and studied it and realized it was a chart to record visitors. It was not a library list like Ellen had. Every time visitors came they wrote their names on a paper designed like a book. Then they displayed the names on a shelf. Looking like a row of books, this chart acknowledged that a house without books is like a house without windows or a schoolhouse without visitors.

Last year Ellen used a picture of a grain field to convey this idea. The grain in the picture is about to form heads. Visitors put their names on golden bearing grain heads and placed them on top of the stalks, making the wheat appear to be ripening as the visitors came. The caption read, "Visitors are the fruit of the school."

The next chart John Mark noticed wasn't really a chart at all, but an illustration of what adjectives are and how to use them. He studied it for awhile realizing that this illustration would likely help the fifth- and sixth-grade students understand adjectives better.

An older girl came up the aisle and paused a moment then asked, "Are you a teacher I haven't met yet?"

John Mark fumbled for words, "Yes. No, I mean, I'm helping Ellen Fox at Chestnut Bottom in Cloverdale, and she asked me to come along."

"Sure, I have a helper here, too. I didn't know Ellen had a helper."

"She didn't at the beginning of the term." She asked if he helped every day, and he explained how their schedule had been set up. She went on to say how she had a few special education people in her school and those were mostly the helper's responsibility. He never did get further down the wall as another girl had moved up the wall and greeted them and they began discussing the charts. John Mark explained what he had figured out.

The other girl asked, "Are you a teacher?"

Before John Mark could answer, the older answered for him. "Oh, he is Ellen's helper," she said knowingly. "I read in a circle letter that she has a helper. Do you plan on taking a school alone come fall?" she asked. John Mark's mouth fell open in astonishment.

She chuckled as she said, "I just wondered, as you can't keep good helpers. They always start teaching on their own."

The other girl replied, "Shhh, don't say that. I want to keep my helper."

Suddenly the bell rang and they all took seats. A teacher was up front and about three or four girls sat on chairs by her side. The men were at the back of the schoolroom on a bench near the door, and some of the women sat on chairs. Supposedly they were parents and board members of the school.

Someone called John Mark's attention to a seat in the back row. He was hoping no one would mistake him for a teacher. Suppose he had to speak, he thought. He felt like a timid preschooler.

They calmed everyone's nerves by singing a few songs that carried a lot of volume. John Mark thought maybe it would be a good idea to continue singing if there was such rich, strong volume, but with the writing on the blackboard and people sitting with notebooks and people glancing at papers, John Mark knew there were things to follow yet.

The meeting had begun. A girl rose from the second chair up front, greeted everyone, and reminded them whose power they were under, etc. For a moment an eerie feeling went through John Mark. *Women don't preach at meetings, do they?* He thought it would have sounded better for a man to make the opening speech, but she soon got on with school business, reminding them that at the last meeting some had requested sheets of the songs they had sung at the other meeting. The sheets were there on the desk for the ones interested in them, and the Iowa test books were here for those that still needed some. If people needed perfect attendance diplomas, they were to ask Helen Wise about them. Lucy Sauder, who was on the committee, shared a speech titled "Having Preschool Children in School, the Do's and Don'ts."

A tall girl rose from the next chair and explained that almost everyone practices having the next year's first graders come to school for a few days or a week, either whole days or half days in the spring to prepare them for the fall. The question of half days or whole days being better was discussed. After the ones up front each took a turn to say how they felt, others in the group were asked to talk if they had their hands raised.

The discussion was well under way. Most encouraged whole days for better transportation, since not all students walked to school. The tall girl continued to explain how she managed to fit the pre-school children into her routine. She shared experiences that brought some chuckles. Some raised their hands to ask for details while she talked.

The overall requirement for preschool children was that they know obedience and English when they come. The rest can soon be taught.

Next the girl on the third chair rose. She introduced herself as Ann Stauffer. The topic was doing something new for a change of scene instead of only regular sessions. For example, in English she would ask the class to each make a list of adverbs. Then she would read sentences and the students would have to fill in a word from the list they had prepared. Then she demonstrated her lesson. She asked the first two rows to think of an adverb. Then she read her story and asked for the adverbs. The class was on. Some sentences sounded a little improper since the adverb selected didn't always mean what it was supposed to mean in that sentence, so it was amusing till it suddenly stopped.

The girl up front said, "What did you say, Mary? Fence row?" She nodded her head. The girl up front with blonde waves looked over her audience and said, "Don't laugh, what is an adverb?" Several people raised their hands. John Mark caught on that the teachers were pretending purposely to see how teachers would handle such a case. She called on those who raised their hands and adverbs were thoroughly discussed.

The class continued. Then the people were told to get their questions ready. A hat was passed around to gather them, and the girls up front took turns opening the questions and answering them. They asked if others had any other suggestions, so some subjects were thoroughly discussed. Quite a few approaches to discipline were explained.

Throughout the afternoon John Mark saw some people write in their notebooks. He was beginning to understand. He wished he had something to take notes. There were things said and explained that he wanted to remember.

One teacher took a group of teachers to the blackboard for a pretend class of subtraction with borrowing.

One of the teachers stood there counting her fingers, then turned around and said, "You can't take eight away from four."

The teacher in charge went toward the board and picked up the chalk and explained, "That's right," she said with all patience and agreement. "You cannot take eight away from four so you have to borrow from your left hand number. You have ten extra because it takes ten to make a whole number. You had four, now you have ten more because you borrowed a whole number, so now you have three. Now you cross that three out and you only have what?"

"Two."

"That's right. So now since you borrowed ten, you take eight away from fourteen and you have?"

"Six," the pretending child answered.

"Whenever you cross out a number, you borrowed ten because a number is always worth ten." The teacher wrote another number on the board and showed each step. The questioning child's face lit up; she understood the meaning.

The next subject of discussion was of the Iowa tests. Should the lower grades stay home those days, play outside, or what? It turned out to be quite a discussion.

At the beginning of the meeting John Mark was afraid he would have to speak, and now countless times he tried hard to be quiet. Sometimes a few questions went through his mind. He wished to ask more about it and other times he felt a question wasn't properly answered. But he wasn't going to speak in the presence of all these experienced teachers.

The tall, dark girl rose from her chair and stood at the teacher's desk. She announced that there were still some questions to be discussed. She silently looked at her folded paper and opened it again. Slowly she started speaking.

"I don't know how familiar this question is or how many people deal with it. For myself, I had only a little experience on this subject. The question is how to help pupils gain respect for adopted schoolmates."

John Mark felt his face color. He hoped no one noticed, or else they might think he had put the question in.

The girl said, "Like I said, I have had very little experience. I did have one adopted child in my class, but I had no problem as far as I know. The pupils respected her fully. I would say, it is the parents' responsibility to teach the child respect toward others if there is a problem. I would advise talking with the parents first, and then if need be, to the pupils."

A girl by the window on the other side of the room raised her hand, "Yes, Barbara."

"How do you talk to your pupils so the adopted one isn't present?"

Someone else raised her hand and she instructed knowingly, "Send the one in discussion for water that morning, and send a pupil along that needs no admonishing."

The girl at the far side of the room asked, "But suppose there are two?"

The tall girl said, "Send them both to fetch water. If they aren't of the same kind, send the one for water, and at the same time send two to pick up trash in the schoolyard, or discuss it before the families arrive, if possible."

The girl at the far side of the room raised her hand asking, "And how do I quickly explain so that they understand?" A girl on the northeast side on the bench raised her hand. The tall girl asked her to speak and they sent a few low messages back and forth. The girl rose and timidly but obediently walked up next to the tall girl. She paused a moment and barely raised her eyes, but looked only at the rows of books on the teacher's desk as she spoke slowly, almost quivering with tenseness.

"It was well said, if the parents have the respect for adopted children, the children won't cause much trouble. But children will be children. I was asked to explain a little since I had some experience. It wasn't pleasant. It was mainly one family that would always throw hints and insults, and soon they had a few followers. But how could I get the leaders to change their behavior? I talked with the parents and they were on my side. Anyhow, while they talked with me, they seemed to agree with me, but matters continued.

"I lost a lot of sleep wondering how it could be solved, since I knew if it were not solved, it would grow to more than that family. They were always ready to blame all the other students' weaknesses and failures on one thing. 'Well, they are adopted.' I punished them countless times the best I could without making a big scene so I wouldn't make the others more aware of the situation.

"One night I prayed and cried far into the night until I thought a solution had been revealed to me. But I shuddered at the treatment. I spent the rest of the night worrying about that; the treatment was as bad as the problem. It was in the fall of the year. I lived at a place where they had a whole row of maple trees along one side of the yard. I invited all the children of this erring family to help me rake leaves one Wednesday evening when there was moonlight, as we didn't get done before dark. And rake leaves we did. While we talked, I brought the adopted family up in conversation. I explained it as well as I could, but I could hear that it was still the cause of all the weakness. I used what I dreaded so much.

30

"The father of the children who were raking leaves for me had a bad temper. He had to work against it to keep it in check, and I started pointing this out. It is a situation they can't help, that their dad gets so angry. They have to live with it, and so do the adopted children. They can't help it. Suppose every time one of you would cry at school, we would say, 'It's because his father has such a bad temper.' Or every time you have many answers wrong, people would just think, well, it's one of those children. That's what you have been doing with these children for things they have no control of at all, being adopted.

"Then one of the children said the parents could have helped it. They wouldn't have had to adopt them. Then I said, 'I guess your mother could have prevented it too, by not marrying someone who gets so upset.'"

The girl's lips quivered; a tear trickled down her face. The room was as quiet as an empty house, until people started wiping their noses.

The girl wiped her nose and softly continued, "Then a child said, 'But Dad has a lot of good points. He is a good father.'"

"I said, 'I know, and these children also are good if only you'd like them and overlook their faults as well as you do your dad's. And if you would love them as much as you do your dad.'

"We had all the leaves raked. We went in the house for hot chocolate and cookies, and I walked home with them. And for two weeks I was shaking in my shoes waiting for the boomerang to come back, waiting until the parents came to tell me what I knew I deserved. They never came. These children have helped me rake leaves every year after that for three years until I moved away to another school. And the parents said they always begged for this outing. 'They must really enjoy it. They don't like raking our leaves so much.'

"As far as I know, they never found out why we started raking leaves. I assume the other children never found out why these children no longer point fingers at them. But it was the most dangerous place I ever walked. It was not in vain, and if anyone can learn from this experience, let God be glorified." She walked to her seat quite humbled.

31

"Does anyone have any questions?" the committee asked. Not a sound was heard. Then one of them said it would be a good time to sing a song before they depart.

The people softly, gratefully sang,

God moves in mysterious ways, His wonders to perform. . . .

John Mark was touched to the depth of his heart. He only blinked at the words the others were singing. He kept glancing up at the girl at the far side of the room who had been asking the questions. He had stolen a few glances at her while the other girl was speaking, and somehow he felt she didn't get what she needed. She stared straight ahead, over the songbook that was under her arms. He felt he should talk with her; maybe she had more questions. But what could he say? How could he remember which was her?

He looked again. She had a medium brown dress on with light brown designs. She didn't wear glasses. Oh my, how could he remember, there were a lot of brown dresses there. Her hair was the usual brown color. *Let's see, what did the girl call her the first time she raised her hand?* If only he could remember, he could ask, "Are you . . . ?"

The songbooks were closed; the meeting dismissed. Supper was being served at a place just up the road.

As John Mark pulled on his coat, he watched a lot of people pass out the door, but then he noticed that girl was still in the schoolhouse. She was talking with another girl. They were looking at something on the wall. He went out on the porch and lingered. He watched the people pass in and out; they were slow to leave. After a while he went back inside. The girl was copying something in her booklet. There were a host of girls around the teacher's desk and here and there were groups of teachers still visiting. John Mark was looking at the things on the wall as he hadn't been over in that corner before the meeting. As he came nearer, the girl looked up at him questioningly.

He asked, "Do you have adopted pupils in your school?"

She lowered her eyes and said, "Yes, I do." Then she looked back at him and asked, "Are you a teacher? I don't remember seeing you at a meeting before."

John Mark fumbled with the pencil sharpener on the windowsill beside him as he answered, "No, I am not a teacher. Only a helper for Ellen in Chestnut Bottom in Cloverdale."

"Oh, yes, I know Ellen. Did you begin as a helper recently?"

"Yes, in February." Then he continued, "You may not know me, but I am adopted and the subject always interests me. I sort of gathered that maybe you wondered about some things that weren't answered. I mean, has the session answered your questions?"

She looked puzzled, then her eyes became a little knowing as she asked, "Is your mother Kathleen who used to work at the hospital?"

"Yes, that's it," he answered. "I recall it faintly from years ago. Is the problem in your school of the same nature as what that teacher explained?" John Mark asked.

"Well, after she explained it I realized that it's a little different even if the pupils don't really show disrespect. The adopted children seem so moody at times. I mean, it's so easy for my pupils to see their weakness because they show it so much. But I thought maybe at times my pupils made remarks that I was not aware of that turned the others sullen."

"I figured maybe you dealt with a different problem. As for myself, I had troubled times, too. But it was not about others accusing me. The real battle was when Mother and Dad married and had a child of their own and people would say it looked like Dad or Mother. Then I felt inferior. I rebelled. I wanted to be part of someone, too."

"I think that is what some of my pupils struggle with, inferiority. But how did you get victory?"

"Well, when Dad found out what my rebellion was about, hearing people say the baby looks like him, he talked with me for a while. He explained to me that he didn't look like his father or mother either. And he told me that he and Mother love me even if I don't look like them. I also have a sister who is adopted. She has very curly blonde hair and Dad said that Mother should have married someone with blonde hair so they would have looked alike. And someone with brown eyes, as Dad was the only one in our family who had blue eyes. So he pointed out that maybe he didn't belong in the family either.

"I was quick to tell him that I didn't want any other daddy. Then he said, 'So we can love people even if we don't look alike.' But the baby would always remind me of everything. When I heard someone say something about looking like someone, then I rebelled. Finally Dad sat down with me and showed me a verse in Romans. You know, I reckon that the suffering of this present time cannot be compared with the glory that will be revealed in us."

The girl nodded her head, "I know which verse you mean."

"Well, Dad reminded me where I would be if Mother had not taken mercy on me. I might be at the Home, or maybe in a foster home where I wouldn't have a nice home life. So now I can be with them even if I have to hear at times that the other children look like Mother and Dad. That is not hard compared to what it would be like if I were with someone else that didn't love me. So Dad told me that every time I get upset, I should always remember that this not looking alike is not worthy to compare with the joy of having a loving family. It would be harder if I was at the Home all the time. Then I would suffer more. Dad never knew how often I had to say that verse to comfort myself. But it helped. And still does, but it doesn't bother me so much anymore."

The girl had been drinking in the words and then scribbled a few lines in her notebook. She sighed and said, "I wish you could explain that to my pupils."

"Maybe you can," he added.

She sighed again and said, "I have to study it awhile. I don't know if I get it at places, but thanks for sharing it."

"I hope your pupils learn to gain victory over circumstances."

John Mark turned and headed for the door. There were only two teachers still in the schoolhouse and a few standing out in the yard. As he arrived at the supper place he noticed the first seating was almost finished with their meal. During supper he learned to know a few more of the teachers and some helpers. They had discussed in what area they helped the teacher.

He had been asked the question so often, "Are you planning to teach by yourself someday?" The question always startled him and more so when he realized he was the only boy at the table.

The table in the next room had a few men who were van drivers.

As they were heading home, John Mark was thinking. *So this is the teacher's meeting that Ellen goes to about once a month.* He never dreamed what all a meeting contained. If he was ever invited to a meeting again, he would take a booklet along to take notes. There were many things he wanted to remember and could only think of a few things just now. Then he almost gasped. He was going to find a way to go over to Grandma Wenger's for supper and have them pick him up there. *When would I have left? There was too much to miss.*

Chapter Five

Through the open window a gentle spring air breezed in, and the birds could be heard singing cheerfully. John Mark paused for a moment, letting the fragrances and sounds of spring flood his mind. He looked back on the table to the papers that he had just finished checking. He picked up the papers, rose from the chair, and took the papers over to Ellen's desk. Ellen was humming a tune as she was bent over her desk, preparing an art project for the lower grades. She looked up momentarily when he laid the papers on her desk.

Then he showed her the two he had put on the top of the pile saying, "I guess Caleb and George didn't understand the second step of the arithmetic problems." Ellen frowned and bit on her pencil as she looked more closely.

He started walking away from the desk when she asked, "Would you please do one more thing for me?"

John Mark turned back and gave a lopsided smile and asked, "Only *one* more thing? Are you going to lay me off then?"

Ellen shook her finger at him, as if to say, "Mind." Then she smiled as she picked up a pile of papers saying, "I was wondering if you'd prepare the first and second grade's penmanship papers before you leave?"

Back at the table he set to work. He didn't think much about it when the schoolhouse door opened, since he was so used to hearing it open and close all day. But he suddenly was aware that the footsteps were heavier than Ellen's. When he looked up, a man was walking in. He wasn't one of Ellen's board members. He was Harvey Bowman from the other end of the district. He teased them good naturedly as to how they could stand being in the schoolhouse on such a fine spring day.

"In another hour I'll be out there too," Ellen rejoiced. John Mark turned back to the penmanship papers while Harvey and Ellen continued visiting.

Later he thought Harvey was talking a little loudly, asking the second time; "What would you say about coming to teach for us at Cedar Lodge?" John Mark looked up to see why Ellen didn't respond. Then he jumped in surprise to see Harvey standing right next to him. No wonder he thought the volume was loud. John Mark thought Harvey was still over with Ellen.

"Oh, are you talking to me?" he asked, surprised.

"I sure am talking to you," Harvey replied.

"Does your school need a helper?"

"No, we need a teacher, and I was sent here to ask you."

"Ask me? I'm only fifteen and won't be sixteen until December."

"I know all that already," Harvey said, sounding as if he was planning to win their conversational dispute. Then he continued, "If need be, we have two people who would be willing to take turns filling in at the schoolhouse until you are sixteen."

John Mark looked at him dumbfounded.

"I'm serious," Harvey said, breaking into a smile. "This board said they could probably get someone else to help Ellen."

John Mark started to say, "My dad wouldn't approve of it."

"I just came from talking to your father and he said he had nothing against it."

John Mark stared at him, then shook his head, "No way."

After another ten minutes' discussion, Harvey said, "Well, you think about it for a few weeks or so."

After Harvey left, John Mark looked up to see what Ellen was chuckling about.

Then she said, "I knew it would happen sooner or later."

"Why?" he asked.

"Because you can't keep good helpers. And it's true what Harvey said. I'm sure they could find someone else to help me who doesn't have so many teaching qualifications themselves." John Mark stared at her and she continued, "Maybe you are not aware of it but

37

you are spoiling me. I don't work nearly as hard as I did before. I'm taking advantage of you."

"I don't feel that way. I wouldn't at all be prepared to take teaching over by myself."

"Maybe you would be surprised how easy it would come if you'd try it."

"I never, ever started thinking about it, ever."

Ellen suddenly laughed and said, "I learned that while Harvey was here. It amused me at the way you reacted as if it never entered your mind."

"It didn't. It comes as a complete shock. At the meeting I was shocked when people asked me if I had considered teaching some day, and since the meeting I didn't take time to dwell on it."

Ellen turned back to her papers saying, half to herself, "If time goes on, someday you will be teaching on your own, and less talented people will be teacher's helpers."

"We'll see once," John Mark replied, as he turned back to the penmanship papers.

*   *   *   *

When he arrived at school, John Mark saw he had arrived before Ellen. Maybe he had started earlier as he had the phonics book to check yet and papers to prepare for the first grade's spare time. John Mark stood for a moment looking at the perfect blue sky, October's bright blue weather. A sound caught his attention. He looked south in the distance. There he saw them, a flock of geese winging their way high in the air, calling as they winged on.

While his eyes swept over the wide countryside, he noticed the brilliant colored leaves. Wouldn't this be a perfect day to take the nature walk Ellen had been talking about for the last week or so? But there always seemed to be something that delayed it. He turned toward the schoolhouse, hunted for the key in his jacket pocket, and unlocked the door. Ellen had given him a key because now and then he arrived before she did. He hurriedly put his lunch pail down and went to the basement to stoke the fire. There were still red ashes there, and with kindling wood and paper, the flames sprang to life, licking at the wood. He put a few heavier pieces of wood on the fire and went upstairs to set to work.

When he walked past Ellen's desk, he saw the seventh- and eighth-grade social studies quiz papers lying on top. Ellen was going to put that on the board the first thing. He decided to surprise her and copy it onto the board for her, as she was sure to be in a hurry when she arrived. He was writing the second to the last sentence when the door opened. He wrote on, waiting to hear Ellen's remarks when she noticed what he was doing.

He heard a pupil's voice say, "Ellen said—" then it stopped abruptly and asked, "How did you know?"

John Mark whirled around. Reuben Hurst's children had arrived. Caleb was putting his lunch on the shelf and Laura was coming across the room to meet him, saying, "Ellen said you shall leave your checking and write the social studies quiz on the board." She stopped and asked again, "But how did you know?"

"I didn't know. I just wanted to surprise Ellen. Where is she?" Junior Hurst stood inside the door listening to see if Laura got her message across.

"She can't come," Laura said shaking her head. "She fell last evening and hurt her leg. She has to go to the doctor."

"She fell," John Mark repeated. "Where?"

"Her leg," Laura reminded him.

Then Junior came up front when Laura looked around knowingly and said, "Ellen's dad came over this morning and said Ellen won't be here this forenoon. Maybe she can come this afternoon, depends on what the doctor says. She was picking pears and the ladder slipped and she fell. She said you should take up classes and get the older ones to help you with things."

John Mark's head was whirling. There were so many things he should do. He went to Ellen's desk and looked to see what was lying on top. The sixth-grade arithmetic book with some papers in it was on top. He looked at them. Jason and Caleb had too many wrong. *She was going to tell me to take them up the board this session.* There were the eighth-grade German books with a paper in and only one question written out. She was preparing a German quiz today. And there were a few stacks of books to check. And there was a paper he picked up. He saw it was Irene's penmanship paper. She needed help in writing "br" and "vi."

The pupils were coming in the door. "Good morning!" John Mark answered them while checking workbooks. He had to work quickly as some grades' arithmetic books had to be checked in order to give them back for the next lesson.

Laura, Bertha, and Edna Mae were at the lunchbox shelf informing all the pupils that Ellen couldn't be here this morning and what happened. Once he heard Edna Mae say, when someone was so shocked with the news, "But it is at least good it's Thursday, so John Mark is here."

Later someone reminded him it was time for the bell. John Mark gave the clock a quick glance. He wondered where the morning went.

So he began classes. They sang so well. He said they could sing another song, but he shook his head when they selected a third one. He helped first and second grades get started on their arithmetic and called third grade to class. One of the second graders had her hand raised already. And a few of the sixth-graders also sat with hands raised.

Then he remembered that Jason and Caleb needed to do review work now or they wouldn't know how to do this assignment for today. He looked at the eighth grade. Clara sat with her desk empty. She looked away when he looked at her.

He cleared his throat and asked Clara, "Are you caught up with your lessons?" She nodded her head. "Would you please come up here and do me a favor?" She rose slowly and unsure. John Mark said, "Jason and Caleb, will you please go to the board?"

By now Clara came to his desk rather embarrassed. He showed her the boys' papers and explained where they had erred and told her to give them practice till they understood it. He turned to the boys, "Clara will help you on yesterday's arithmetic problems as you have the same kind today. She will show you how to do them."

40

By the time fourth grade was called up to class, he noticed the first and second grades all sat with empty desks. He looked at the eighth grade. Jane was reading a storybook.

"Jane," he announced. She looked up from her book in a daze. "I have some papers for you to pass out." She yawned and turned the book upside down on her desk and came forward. John Mark handed her two sets of papers. "Give these papers to first grade. Tell them to mark all the B's in each group, and give these papers to second grade and help them get started if they need help. And answer the raised hands for me."

After checking fifth-grade arithmetic, he turned the page and caught his breath. He saw they had a new chapter, and he had to explain how to do the first few problems. Some seemed unsure. Every time he looked, there were a few hands raised with questions to be answered. Questions Jane didn't know how to answer.

When he called the seventh grade to class, brother Josiah who was in first grade this year, was waving his had.

"What would you like?" he asked.

Josiah looked at the clock and said, "It's time for recess." Sure enough, it was five minutes past already. He collected the seventh- and eighth-grade arithmetic papers and dismissed ten minutes late, with his desk a mess. He put the seventh- and eighth-grade papers in the teacher's arithmetic books of each grade, and gathered up the first grade's papers that they had handed in. There was a corrected paper a fourth grader had handed in, and what's this? Oh, someone had to correct his spelling from yesterday and here was a composition paper that wasn't finished yesterday. And a few penmanship papers.

He had just about all of the papers sorted in piles that had been strewn over his desk with first and second grades' workbooks mixed in. Now he was about ready to correct some books. He hardly had time to listen to the few pupils that stood around his desk visiting with him. Then he remembered he had to check the next subject to see if it was prepared or what they were to do. He glanced at the clock and saw it was time to call the students in already.

As he went out on the porch to ring the bell, he paused for a moment to admire the glowing yellow trees scattered around the countryside. Some showed an orange glow. Others were laced in red and dipped in brown, while others still held onto their green. The sky was such a nice deep, bright blue above the yellow and red blazing trees. They almost seemed to lighten up the sky.

As John Mark came back to his desk, a thought started churning in his mind. Would the nature of autumn stay in its peak for a few weeks yet? Or would it soon be over if rain came? If Ellen hurt her foot, would she be able to go on a hike? Should he go now with them? Would she care? Isn't that maybe why she delayed it? Because she wasn't eager to do it? As he set the bell down, he caught himself thinking, *There are already more books and papers here on the desk than I can check tonight, without papers piling up yet from this afternoon. And when do I prepare lessons for tomorrow?*

It was while they were having lunch that Reuben Hurst dropped in to give them the message that Ellen had been to the doctor and there were no bones broken. But the doctor said it was as bad as being broken. Her ankle or foot was badly sprained and her knee was bumped and bruised. She was having a lot of pain in her right leg. If she comes next week, she will be on crutches for a while. Reuben wondered if John Mark was making out all right.

John Mark told him, "It might go better tomorrow if I have time to get things in order tonight and tomorrow morning."

Continuing with classes, he asked if any of the eighth graders were done with their lessons. Clara, Emma Mae, and Jane raised their hands. He gave Clara and Jane workbooks and papers to check and put Emma Mae in authority to help first- and second-grade students with workbooks and to answer questions. He asked if every one of the pupils was present.

They said, "We are all here." He cut out some of the German classes and prepared for an earlier than usual recess dismissal. He explained to the pupils that autumn would soon be losing its beauty and splendor, and it sounded like it could be a week or more before Ellen was ready for a stroll.

"Does anyone think that Ellen would care if we went on our nature hike today? Gasps of triumph were heard over the classroom. They had the same opinion that he had, that Ellen wasn't enthused about the nature hike. And how they rejoiced when he said they were going to walk in the woods across from Brubacker's sawmill.

They were sort of in groups with Junior and Caleb Hurst in the lead. First came the older boys, then the middle grade boys, followed by the upper grade girls, then the smaller girls. The younger boys walked with John Mark. There was only a short distance between each group, so it really was just a big organized group.

The group scattered somewhat once they got into the woods, but the Hurst boys were in the lead as they were familiar with the woods and knew where the trails led. They followed the trail to an old windmill that some of the boys climbed onto to look around. The girls and smaller children were finding colored leaves. They said they wanted to show them to Ellen. The older girls were gathering leaves for an art project. The Hurst boys guided them to another, steeper path. The younger ones needed help.

Up ahead the boys' voices could be heard, "Look at this high cliff of large rocks. There is a space between the trees, a clearing where we can see over the valley. Some were pointing out buildings or towns; some were carving their names in trees. Others were reading the carvings that had been carved in earlier years. Others rested. They remembered the old hearth oven down on the other path. This was something new for a lot of the pupils.

John Mark explained to the pupils how a fire was built in the ovens and then scraped out. Food was then baked in the oven while it was hot. That was many years ago. But why was there an oven here? They looked around and found part of an old foundation off to the right where a building once stood. They also found part of a stone fence in back of the old foundation. Some of the boys were turning up stones and discovered the remains of an old shallow well that had been covered with stones and boards.

The Hursts saved their greatest joy until last. They led the way to a large tree house they and the Brubackers had built during the summer. (The Brubackers went to school in the next district.)

You had to climb up a wooden stepladder fastened to the tree to get up to the tree house. It had a few rooms.

John Mark was often called "Ellen" during the afternoon hike. The younger ones just couldn't remember to call him John Mark. From all the things they were going to show Ellen, John Mark got the feeling that Ellen must share a motherly love in the children's hearts. They started back to the schoolhouse, and when they arrived, they had only ten minutes until it was time to dismiss for the day. Everyone was busy putting their collection of things away or in their lunchboxes.

John Mark felt lighthearted as he dismissed them. He enjoyed the afternoon more than he had expected. And now he had only a half-day's array of books and papers on his desk to sort and check. The girls had checked some. The long walk had made him tired, but he figured he didn't mind it more than the younger pupils. He decided when he saw them frolicking around with boundless energy that maybe they were more limber than he was. But anyhow, it sure felt good to sit down and rest his legs. Since he had limped because his body wasn't even, walking made him tired. But the hike had been well worth the effort.

Chapter Six

The clock ticked on to keep up with the rhythm of time. John Mark had an urge to go and silence it so he could peacefully rest and relax a few hours and not have any responsibility for a few hours or maybe a day. But unpleasant thoughts tried to creep into his already weary mind. Even the books that lay before him on the desk needing to be checked seemed minor. The load he was carrying came pressing down today. He leaned back in his chair and stared over the empty classroom. Then he closed his eyes for a moment and pretended this was Chestnut Bottom School where he was helping Ellen teach school, and she would handle the responsibilities and the discipline. Then he opened his eyes again. No, this was not Chestnut Bottom.

There was a four-foot-high divider near the entrance door where the wraps and lunches were kept before you entered the classroom through a double opening space. The schoolroom had only twenty-three desks occupied with pupils during the day. He glanced at the calendar on the wall. He studied it for a moment. Today was March twenty-third. It was now about three weeks since neighboring school board members had come over to see him. In fact, they had come over a few times, and they weren't satisfied with only a "no." They wanted a good reason for his not wanting to teach at this school and the reason he had stated of disapproval, they did not accept. So he was almost forced to come over here to Four Acres School to take over teaching for a few weeks or more since Naomi, the teacher, had come down with a bad case of flu. The doctors couldn't agree if it even was the flu; some had called it rheumatic fever.

The first days at Four Acres were hectic, but John Mark thought it was going a little better as he and the pupils got used to

45

each other and he to the schedule. But the last few days he thought he was losing ground, and then a sixth-grade girl had outright talked back to him when he refused her something. On the spur of the moment he had taken action. He ordered her up to the teacher's desk and told her to sit in the chair since she was in authority.

He had sensed some disrespect the last week, and it was this straw that broke the camel's back. He saw the repentant tears, but it wasn't the first time that she had shown disrespect openly. She seemed like a leader, helping others to turn against him. He had to tell her a few times to sit down in the chair. It was only after he went up to the desk and demanded her obedience that she sat on the chair and laid her head down on the desk, sobbing. Then he was aware again of the rest of the schoolroom. He looked around to see if the other pupils were still in the room. It was as quiet as an empty room except for the sobbing girl. He noticed a few tears over the classroom. He read fright in the first graders' eyes, shame in the older pupils, and submission in most of the other pupils.

The rest of the day passed quietly. It was soon after he had continued with classes after the last recess that he told the girl she may go back to her regular seat if she allows him to be the teacher. Ever since school was dismissed he kept thinking of her going home. He tried to imagine how it sounded when her parents were told. Would they understand? He had considered writing a note but decided better of it. If they wanted to know more, they could come and ask for details. He picked up a pencil in the holder before him and noticed that most of the pencil tips were dull. So he picked up the pencil holder and took it over to the little table near the window where the pencil sharpener was fastened.

He sharpened a few pencils and paused, looking out the window. The March winds were playing an energetic game, scurrying any loose leaves and stray plastic bags around.

Far out across the landscape he saw a hill with no buildings nearby and only a few trees further to the side. For a moment he got the urge to be a little boy out on a hill flying a kite in the March winds, with his only worry or concern that the kite didn't get tangled in the trees.

Maybe his real kite was flying so high that it got tangled. Just for a few days he had let the thoughts come, since he was teaching here, about being a teacher on his own. Maybe he needed to be lowered.

Suddenly a sparrow came flying out of nowhere, swooped down to the ground right outside the window, hunted about, and picked up a short piece of straw. He let it fall again, and hopped further over and picked up what looked like a piece of string. He dropped the string and hopped over a little, turned around, and picked up the string again. Then he lifted and flew off to the tree with the string. As the sunlight hit the piece of string, it flashed its blue-green color. Then it dawned on John Mark. It was one of the strings that had been on the children's balloons which a parent who had come visiting a few days ago had brought along for all the pupils. The balloons all had blue-green strings tied to them. A few of the pupils' balloons had burst before they left the school grounds, and now the sparrow selected the string to use in its nest building. A new hope filled John Mark's heart. Knowing the sparrow was building a nest caused him to recognize that there is a tomorrow and summer is on the way.

With a refreshed spirit John Mark turned back to his desk and locked unpleasant thoughts out of his mind. Fifteen minutes later when he heard the rattle of the doorknob, his heart stood still. As the door opened he fully expected to see Karen's parents entering. His mouth fell open in astonishment when a young girl stepped in. She stopped short and stammered for words, and finally she succeeded in getting words together, asking, "Are you a substitute or am I at the wrong schoolhouse?"

"Yes, I am a substitute. Are you looking for a job?" he asked.

She laughed a little and set her bag on one of the desk tops. She explained that she had talked with Naomi at the last meeting and they had things they wanted to exchange and duplicate.

John Mark explained about Naomi's illness.

Suddenly she remembered, "Oh, you are Ellen's helper. I knew I saw you at meetings already and I was trying to remember in which schoolhouse you belonged."

"Not here," he dully answered and with a little encouragement, John Mark poured out all that had happened that day.

The next half hour passed swiftly as they discussed it and some other school incidents, until she looked at the clock a few times and said, "Well, I have a driver waiting out there. We will go over and see how Naomi is doing. I will tell her you are faring well," she assured him as she went out the door carrying her bag. Things looked a lot different since he had discussed his feelings with a teacher. She said he had made the right move. The students were seeing how far they could take him and he needed to them know that there was no more leverage on the reins.

$$* \quad * \quad * \quad *$$

The family lingered around the table, visiting a little longer this morning since it was Saturday. John Mark didn't have to hurry off to school and neither did his brothers and sisters. John Mark had just recognized that Rebekah was no longer a baby; she would soon be two years old. He hardly knew when that took place. It seemed he hardly had time to notice the family anymore. But today he pushed away all school thoughts. Just last evening he had been informed that Naomi was planning to return to her teaching job some time during the following week.

As John Mark went out the door, he was humming to himself a wordless song. He walked around to the upper part of the calf shed, to the end they had built as a storage shed. He opened the door and stood for a moment looking at the buggy. Then he pulled the buggy out into the yard beside the little shop. Dad had bought the second-hand buggy, and they had it in the buggy shop to have some repairs done. Now it was ready to paint. There were times now and then when he needed to have a team for himself like when Dad and Mother went to another district and some of the children stayed home. It would be convenient if he had his own team to take them to church rather than asking the neighbors. And since he was teaching at Four Acres the past few weeks, it would have been handy if he had had a team on the days he needed to drive and Dad also wanted the team.

But as of yet he had nothing to hitch to a buggy. Even Dad had only one horse, Pearl. But he was shopping around. They really needed two horses because some weeks their trips made too many miles for one horse.

While his thoughts wandered about, he stirred the paint and carefully started brushing. He was picturing a dainty, frisky, dark-brown horse. Just the right size and good stepping to pull the buggy.

A half hour later he was roused from his thoughts and painting when a team turned into their lane. He wasn't sure who it was. It looked like someone for Dad, a middle-age man from a neighboring district. It was likely someone who needed help with a hospital fund. As he turned back to painting the buggy, his thoughts also turned back to dreaming about a horse. A little later he jumped when a man started talking right beside him. He had greeted him and John Mark told him Dad was down in the calf barn, but the man, who John Mark now recalled to be Barton Reiff, stuck his hands deep into his coat pockets and continued visiting about the weather and the work and whatever fit into the subject. He was asking whose buggy it had been. The subject had brought up Nelson Stouffer's name since it was their son's buggy and he had gotten a new buggy.

Barton asked John Mark, "Are you going with the young folks, I suppose?"

"No, I won't be seventeen until December, but I could use a team at times."

Barton asked what he would be doing once school was over and John Mark answered that he hadn't many plans. "The barn should be painted and, well, schoolwork doesn't end when school is over. There are things to duplicate and supplies to search after."

"You are a helper, right?" Barton had interrupted.

"Yes, that's what I try to be, but that's why I'm busy, helping the teachers do all the things they haven't time to prepare over the summer."

"Have you considered taking up teaching on your own, not only being a helper?" Barton asked, stepping back a little.

John Mark couldn't deny that he never thought about it. Breaking the silence, he answered, "I might think about it if Ellen wouldn't need my help."

Barton pushed around a few stones in the drive with his shoes until he finally selected the words to say, "Well, I talked with one of Ellen's board members and I talked with Ellen, and they both said everything is going well. And Ellen does need help, but they admitted that they could get by with a helper who is less qualified to teach on his own. Ellen said she would have to learn to manage again."

John Mark stared at him, then asked, "Do you know of someone who wants to help Ellen?"

Barton cleared his throat and replied, "No, well, I mean, the board said that there are some possibilities, but I was sent to ask you to teach for us at Timber Lock School this fall."

John Mark brushed on silently, smoothing the paint carefully on the surface. Barton asked, "What do you say?"

John Mark asked, "Why do they need a teacher there?"

"Well, you know Loretta from the higher church was teaching there and she wants to stay with her grandmother during the nights. So she will teach over in the south district," Barton explained.

"How many pupils are there?" John Marked asked further.

Barton scratched his head, "This year there are nineteen or twenty, so I assume there will be somewhere in that range." When John Mark continued painting in silence, Barton asked him what he was thinking.

John Mark said, "To be honest, I'm thinking how handy it is to help Ellen; it's so near home."

Barton smiled a little and asked, "Aren't you over at Four Acres just now teaching?"

"Yes, that's why I know it's so handy helping Ellen."

"Timber Lock is about the same distance from here isn't it?"

"I suppose so, only that road has one more hill."

"Well," Barton started saying slowly, "if you wouldn't want to go back and forth all the time, there are possibilities of boarding somewhere."

"Don't say that, or I surely will get the idea it's too far," John Mark teased. Then he added in a more serious tone, "But I didn't ask Ellen if I may go for another job. She wasn't too happy that I consented to help at Four Acres for these weeks."

"Well, I have no fear if you go ask her. I think Ellen knew this time was coming."

There it was again. Every now and then he heard the remark that he wouldn't always be helping Ellen. It seemed that every time he was at a teacher's meeting he heard these words from Ellen or someone else. He would be willing to continue as they were, but like Barton had said earlier, or maybe Ellen had said, others could help her who weren't old enough yet to teach on their own. He had been looking forward to the time when Naomi came back to Four Acres so he could hand her the responsibilities and decisions and lead an easier life again.

The discussion continued for another fifteen minutes when Barton reminded John Mark that he would like to know how he felt about it. John Mark paused and lifted his eyes from the partially-painted buggy and looked out in the spring-clad world. Field work was being done, and birds were flying. The world was rushing on. Time will too, and it wouldn't be long until summer was here and soon it would be gone again and September would be here. John Mark looked at Barton, who was waiting expectantly.

Finally John Mark said, "Well, let me think about it for a few days and talk with Mother and Dad."

"Sure, I'd rather you don't be too hasty making a decision," Barton said as he turned away, then he turned back and said, "Also remember that something can be worked out if you think it's too far to always go back and forth."

John Mark stared at the buggy. He had lost the carefree, leisurely feeling. He had planned to relax while painting the buggy, thinking about handing things back to Naomi. Now his thoughts were churning. He couldn't even concentrate on painting the small fine corners. He reached for the rag and wiped a spot that had somehow dripped onto the box of the buggy.

For the rest of the day two forces were raging within him. One wanted to continue helping Ellen. Another force rose to the idea of teaching on his own, doing the things he desired, the way he thought more proper or fitting. Although Ellen and Naomi were good teachers, there were still times he found himself desiring to do things another way.

As his thoughts drifted on, he found himself thinking that if he would teach at Timber Lock School, he would surely have to get the buggy in order and would need a horse, as sometimes he would need transportation if he had to go three and one-half miles daily. Then he thought how strange that would seem to be in school regularly where Josiah and Delores weren't. Even in these few weeks he felt somewhat separated, but in another sense it might be good if he was teaching on his own not to have his brother and sister in the class.

Chapter Seven

The early sun shone clearly, proclaiming a fine summer day. John Mark rested for a moment as he looked back at the fresh rows he had marked in the garden. Then he lifted the row marker and carried it back to the shed. Dad had made the marker with shafts and parts of a cultivator. Turning from the shed, he automatically walked down to the pasture fence that almost came up against the shed.

John Mark's eyes moved along to the west side where Duke, who was eating grass, suddenly looked up to see what movement he had seen. His head rose high and he stepped around with his hind legs and snorted a little.

"Come here, Duke. Come on," John Mark coaxed gently. Duke only snorted, but then the workhorses came striding up ahead of them. John Mark petted them and looked with awe at Duke right before him. He loved that horse. He liked it right from the beginning. And so did Dad. A horse dealer had been trying to sell Duke to Uncle Seranus, but Seranus did not need a horse now and had notified Dad. Then last week the horse trailer had pulled in and Dad and him had both admired Duke. Dad had made a deal that if the horse was what the dealer said he was, Dad would pay him in two weeks. Duke was taller than a buggy horse needed to be and had a little more power. John Mark was hoping that Dad would decide it was not a horse for him so that John Mark could drive him in the buggy for his own horse. But John Mark had gone along a few times when Dad had hitched him and he knew Dad was pleased with the horse. Dad promised him that he would try his best to have a horse for him before school started and if not, he would use Duke or Pearl on the days he needed to drive.

*　　*　　*　　*

Everything was so silent, not even a clock was ticking. But John Mark didn't notice. He put the folders back in the box and lifted the next box down from the shelf. *What could this contain,* he thought. He looked through the box a moment and decided it contained extra art supplies. He looked again, then he looked at his tablet. Yes, he had marked art supplies already in the low cupboard. He put that box aside so he could put it with the rest of the art things. He was marking down all the things he was finding and where so he knew what was available. His stomach growled. He was hoping he could go through the cabinet yet before eating his lunch. Then he would have looked through most of the things. Well no, he hadn't looked through the things in the basement yet.

When his stomach growled again, he fumbled for his watch. Then he gasped, "Surely not?" He held the watch against his ear. Yes, it was still running. Could it be ten minutes till two? No wonder he felt hungry. John Mark left the boxes sit and got his lunch pail and went out on the porch to eat. He couldn't believe where the fore-noon had gone.

He had come to school before eight o'clock this morning and started going through all the teacher's desk drawers, the filing cabinet, and the long, narrow built-in closet. Then the closet in the corner and every door in the classroom, and many times he got carried away. He didn't even start making orders yet. Next week the teachers wanted to come together to order supplies that the three schools needed. Loretta said she would try to come this week to help him look over the supplies. So now he was going through all the things to see what was here and then he could ask her about things he couldn't find or didn't understand. He was hoping she would have a record of the pupils that would be attending this year, so he could begin to make a list of what books and things he needed.

He had eaten his sandwich without even making a dent in his growling stomach. He opened his thermos and was glad to see there was hot soup in it. As he crumbled the crackers into it, he lifted his eyes beyond the school porch. After eating a few spoonfuls of the soup he looked in the other direction, or he thought he had looked the other way. He stood and walked out into the schoolyard. On three sides, fields bordered the schoolyard but all the fields ran up against a bush. Even the small road that went down to the south looked like it ran right into the midst of a bush. John Mark knew there was only bush on either side of the small country lane, and on the other side of that bush was open country. But with the slight rise he couldn't see from here that the trees ended. Only to the west was open scenery like opening to a small prairie. Oh yes, the timber locks off the view. No wonder this is called Timber Lock School. Even the view of Four Acres School that was only a half-mile on the other side of the bush to the east was locked off. As John Mark went back on the porch to finish his lunch he mused, this would be a splendid location for a poet to describe, and he wondered who the poet was that named the school.

It was the first week of August when John Mark had gone with some of the teachers to a few school supply stores to shop for things they couldn't get where they had put in the big order. When they were unloading the things at home, two of the teachers asked if they could see his duplicator. He had gotten a duplicator a few weeks before and it proved to be a little different than what most of them had—maybe a newer kind. They were interested in seeing it work, so John Mark demonstrated it to them in the living room end of the kitchen. Then one of the teachers was more interested in the sheets he had been making for extra work and they discussed the sheets, some asking where he got the idea. John Mark noticed that the family was waiting to eat supper, so he tried to make the details short.

During the evening meal whenever John Mark happened to look at Dad when he talked to him, he noticed a sort of perplexed expression on his face. At times it seemed Dad had his gaze glued on him, but he seemed in deep thought. John Mark felt a little uneasy, like he should feel guilty or something.

Josiah and William had hopped off their chairs and were playing with their toys. On their wagons they were pretending to haul green chop with the old string beans that Mother had thrown out when she had cleaned beans.

Delores had taken the table scraps out for the cats when Dad, looking at John Mark, said, "I don't know about you, John." John Mark looked at him, puzzled. Then Dad asked, "Were they all teachers who went along shopping for supplies?"

John Mark wrinkled his brow trying to remember, "Well, yes, I guess they were."

"Are there no other boys teaching school?"

"There's a middle-aged man teacher in the district where Alpheus lives, but of course he is not often at our meetings. And there is a boy from the Hoffman Church who is teaching, and I think there is another boy from that church starting this year. Why are you asking?"

"I was just wondering if you are interested in teaching or interested in the teachers." Dad's grin disappeared when he saw John Mark's insulted expression.

John Mark said, "At first when I was helping Ellen, I often felt awkward meeting other teachers, but by now I'm about used to the idea that we are all one big family working in the same field."

"You mean all the girls that were in here watching you didn't even thrill you?" Dad asked mischievously.

"Well, no, they didn't because I had to think twice if there were only girls along."

"It's a wonder not more boys teach school for such an opportunity."

John Mark was getting irritated at Dad's teasing and he asked, "Why didn't you teach school then if you think that's why boys teach?"

Mother was returning to the table, gathering up the silverware at each plate and stacking it in the empty potato kettle when Dad answered, "Because I wouldn't have found Mother there anyhow." He looked up at Mother while he spoke the last words softly. Mother looked at him for a brief moment, her face adding more color to its glow.

"Where did you find her?" John Mark asked quickly. He didn't know if he could get him to talk more about it.

Dad and Mother exchanged a quick glance and Dad said, "When I came into the salvage store to get something to eat." Delores

56

came back in spinning the empty bowl. He wanted to ask more but felt embarrassed. He valued the conversation. It was rare that Mother and Dad showed deep feelings in front of the children. John Mark treasured this incident as a more secure feeling of "being one of the family." He felt more as if he had roots.

The whole family welcomed him when he came home on Thursday evening. The little boys had endless rows of information to reveal to him. Some of it of course had taken place before he was gone since children always think you were gone long already. The most important thing that he had taken time to hear was that Grandma Wenger had been here yesterday. William was saying something about Charlotte, which John Mark assumed was a doll. Mother and Father were asking how everyone was in Naomi and John Irvin's family, since he just returned from spending a few days there. Since the annual school meeting was held this week and since it was in the area where Naomi lived, John Mark had spent the nights, mornings, and evenings there rather than going back and forth every day.

Upon Delores's request, asking about Naomi's girls, he remembered that Naomi's girls, Lydia Ann and Virginia, had sent some girls' treasures along for Delores, merely because Delores had sent some along for them.

Mother asked again, "You didn't say how everyone is at Naomi's house."

John Mark shrugged his shoulders. "Oh, mainly busy. I would say Naomi isn't happy to see school starting, as all her girls, Lydia Ann, Kathryn, and Virginia, are going to school, plus John David and Cleason. And I think she said there will still be five preschool children at home yet, and Amanda, of course, is only five. She could use a more helpful baby-sitter with all these younger ones."

"Guess the big boys have to do housework liked we used to," Dad said. "Are the boys at home or do they have jobs?" Dad asked further.

"Joel is at home. Paul Isaac works at a chicken place, and Emory is working as a hired hand somewhere; he doesn't always come home for the weekends."

"I guess Naomi is living up to her word," Dad said. "She used to say when they needed hired help that as time goes on they will have hired help for other people."

"She has to wait long for girls' help, but then she will suddenly have plenty with three girls each only about a year apart," Mother added.

"Anyhow, it isn't like Mother who had only one girl, and when she left, there were no other girls coming, but we survived," Dad said.

John Mark opened his notebook. He wanted to look over some sheets that had been passed out today to the new teachers. And he wanted to look over some notes he had scribbled down before he forgot what they meant. But Josiah was pestering him to go along out to the barn. John Mark pushed the papers back into the folder and promised Josiah he would go out a little to satisfy him. He knew that he would be spending most of the next few days at school.

He walked along helping Josiah feed the few calves that were his to take care of. Then Josiah begged him to go along down to the barn to see his rabbits, to see how much the little ones had grown since he saw them last.

It was while they were walking back to the rabbit pens that John Mark stopped and said, "What do I see?" Josiah stopped and looked at what John Mark saw. He followed his glance over to the horse stable.

"Well, we told you," Josiah said, suddenly running over to the horses. "William told you when you came home and I told you, but you weren't interested. Didn't you see her yet?" Josiah asked. John Mark stood in front of the horse stable looking over the dark, sorrel horse. It was rather tall and its neck was too long. It looked as if the horse hadn't been fed enough.

John Mark finally asked, "Whose horse is here?"

Josiah looked at him saying, "This is the horse we told you about when you came home. This is yours. I thought maybe we had it before you left since you weren't interested in hearing about it." Speechless, John Mark stared at the horse.

Just then Dad came walking up to them and asked, "What do you think of the horse?"

"It isn't as fine-looking as Duke, but where did it come from?"

"On Tuesday, I was over to the guy in Greensburg who deals with horses. He had a few there that I thought you might be interested in, but he talked me into this one. It's a four-year-old mare. He claimed the only reason he had it was because the people moved and couldn't take it along. He said I would regret it if I didn't take her. She seemed gentle, but also had power and spirit. She may not win first prize in beauty, but I thought I would give her a try as the price was reasonable. That man is known for his honesty in dealing with horses. I got papers with the horse, and the papers say her name is Charlotte.

"Did you hitch her already?" John Mark asked.

"No, I didn't take the time. Maybe we can when you are here sometime."

Delores was calling Dad from the house, so Dad went to answer. John Mark stood for a moment longer looking at the horse. It sure didn't look like the horse he had been seeing in his mind for a buggy horse.

Chapter Eight

John Mark watched the last students file out the door. Then he rose and walked to the south window where the dirt road that ran between the two fields was in view. It looked as if the lane led to a forest, but there was only a whole cluster of trees or bushes right where the landscape rose to a hill, thus hiding the open country on the other side of the bush. He saw three groups of children trodding down the lane heading home. In the second group two were walking backwards talking to the group behind them. The front group was moving faster, seemingly eager to get home. Something tugged at his heart. The children were in his care all day and now he had sent them home. He wondered if the mothers were ready for them. *Will they take time to listen to what they have to say about the day?* he thought. He tried to picture the scenes as the children arrived home, but he couldn't very well picture it as he didn't know how every home looked. He had met some of the parents, the ones that had come to visit the school or that had come to pick up their children when it rained.

He walked over to the west window. There the group of children had moved further down the road already. One group had crossed over to the other side where he couldn't see them anymore since that road bearing to the left went down in the hollow. He stood for a moment longer watching the rest of the children walking west, and he also viewed the scenery. When looking out the other window, he got the feeling the schoolhouse was on a deserted little prairie enclosed with timber all around. Now from the west window he could see farms and people working in the fields, but they could only be viewed on the west side and some on the north side if there had been a window there.

Were there twenty-two or twenty-three students in his care all day now? And had it been five weeks? He was beginning to get anxious to meet all the parents. Of course he saw most of them at the meeting before school started, but then he hadn't known the children yet, so he didn't remember them. Now the children almost seemed like part of him. Sometimes he almost felt guilty sending them home, thinking likely the parents weren't ready yet for the commotion of the schoolchildren. But sometimes he was glad to send them home, glad that it was now someone else's responsibility to care for them until the next day.

He walked back to his desk, slowly sat down, and leaned back in his chair still picturing the children arriving in the different homes. He thought of one first grader that walked down the south road. It was nice he could walk most of the way with the Ringler family. His mother was likely happy and waiting for his return. He was the oldest of the family, named Dennis Leinbach. John Mark had met his mother and father. His father once came to pick him up when it rained and his mother had stopped once to tell him to go to the neighbors when school was over, since they were going away and wouldn't be at home when school was dismissed.

Then there was also Ammon Shirk in the first grade. He came to school with his three brothers. The Shirks had all boys in school. Ammon was an eager little pupil. He liked to be doing something at all times. He did his papers a bit carelessly in order to be finished to see what they would be doing next. His brother in the second grade, Benny, wasn't so anxious about papers. Benny would forget to do his lessons and get carried away in cutting paper or cardboard and pasting it together to try to make something. He could handle his lessons if he remembered to stay at them. He was a bit more shy where Ammon would often come up to the desk and tell John Mark things that happened at home and so forth.

Their brother in the fifth grade was a top scholar. He did his work carefully and handed in neat papers, and if he had extra time he would bury himself in a storybook. Therefore, he wasn't often included in mischief, but then there were mostly girls around him, since the other two fifth graders were the Ringler twin girls and fourth grade was all girls. The oldest of the Shirk brothers, Gerald, was in eighth grade. He did his lessons because he had to. He could have had better grades if he had been more interested in lessons. He had a great talent in art, and he was creative. The things he didn't build with paper and cardboard! He was a disturbance to the ones around him as he drew their attention from their lessons, and he didn't take rebukes or commands too well.

John Mark sighed. Did he want to think about it again? There was another boy in first grade. In fact, all three first graders were boys. The last one was Edgar, the pupil he spent most of his time on, even when he was not in school. John Mark often found himself concentrating on Edgar's ability, wondering how to get the best out of him. Edgar came to school with two brothers and three sisters. While the other first graders wrote numbers the first weeks, Edgar was trying to grasp how to write on tablet paper. If he did make a row of numbers, some were backwards; some were lying down. When he came to the end of the line, he started right underneath and wrote on the way back again. And if the paper fell on the floor, he picked it up and started writing, even if it was upside down. But most of the time he wasn't doing anything. Nine times out of ten when John Mark looked up while he was explaining something to the lower grades, Edgar was sitting there staring at him watching every move, listening to every word. It seemed he liked to watch people.

John Mark thought maybe Edgar was too young to be going to school. Since he was having a birthday soon, John Mark checked and saw Edgar would be seven years old, so it was time for him to start school. John Mark had at first rebuked him often; he thought he wasn't trying. But he sensed that the other pupils were beginning to look down on him or ridicule him, and he was beginning to see that the pupils' actions were a reflection of his, so he was trying to be more patient. It seemed to embarrass his brothers and sisters the few times John Mark questioned them about Edgar's ability. It seemed they would rather not talk about it. He was getting more eager to meet Edgar's parents.

Maybe he just hadn't found the right key yet. It didn't matter even if John Mark had just rebuked him; he was so friendly. He was always there if someone was crying or got hurt; he was always first to report it. And if Edgar raised his hand, John Mark was about used to the fact that it was only to inform John Mark that it was raining.

At first John Mark had chuckled about such incidents, but he was beginning to notice that the pupils were looking down on Edgar because he himself was actually mocking him at times. His brother in the third grade, Mark Anthony, was a regular third-grade pupil. He did not have the best interest in lessons, but he was very capable of doing them. However, being mischievous was much more inviting to him. For his fourth-grade sister Mildred, lessons were a breeze. If only she could share her intelligence with Edgar. She had the most patience and compassion toward Edgar than any of the rest of his brothers or sisters. At times she helped Edgar, and John Mark learned from her how to deal more successfully with him. But when John Mark questioned her further about Edgar, she would become shy and shrug her shoulders and say, "That's how he is." Sort of like she thought he chose to be that way.

Edgar's twin sisters Etta Mae and Ella Fay, who were in the fifth grade, looked so much alike that he wasn't always sure who was who, unless they were in their seats. But he knew them apart by character. Etta Mae was a lot neater and had better scores, but both of them seemed rather unfriendly, and he sometimes got the feeling that they were sort of the root cause why the upper-grade girls didn't get along as good as they should.

Then there was Maynard who was in the eighth grade. He would enjoy school if only he allowed himself to realize it. It seemed he thought maybe it was too childish to go to school, as if he was too big. And with Gerald, his classmate, well, at times he had his hands full keeping the eighth-grade boys reined in.

John Mark was hoping for a chance to meet Edgar's parents, the Nevin Ringlers. They never came to visit, and they never sent any note along. He was considering going to see them once about Edgar, but he kept pushing it off.

Then there was Lester Weaver in the second grade. He was a quiet fellow who did his lessons well. He came and went and the school almost forgot he was there. But then that was what the whole

Lloyd Weaver family was like. Lucy was in the sixth grade. She was one you wouldn't forget. You could hear her voice in singing; she had a wonderful gift. If there was no friction among the girls, she wouldn't make any. But because at times the girls sort of divided into two groups, she had to be on one side or the other, but she was no leader in trouble. Lessons came well for her, but she was a little lazy at times. Her sister Sylvia, in the eighth grade, was one who kept the girls in as much unity as they had and Sylvia seemed to do well helping Edgar, or in taking over classes occasionally so he had time to spend with Edgar.

Their parents, the Lloyd Weavers, seemed like concerned people. They had visited the school together, and Mrs. Weaver was very concerned and interested in the children's behavior and progress. John Mark had met the whole family when they invited him to stay overnight to save him one trip back and forth. The whole evening John Mark tried to pinpoint Mrs. Weaver's sincerity and thoughtfulness. He was still wondering the next morning and he finally asked if she had been a teacher once and she so humbly and matter-of-factly said she had taught a few years before she was married. She seemed not at all aware why he asked. They had one girl at home ready to start school the next year. And there was a boy and girl out of school.

Then there was Florence Newswanger in the second grade. The only one of her family going to school, she had some trouble reading, so that made her lessons a bit difficult. But what was more difficult was she had one baby brother at home, a little over a year old, and John Mark suspected that might be the reason that she at times was pretty well set on her own way of doing things. During recess, her self-will showed up many times and John Mark had to settle it.

Leroy was in third grade. He was from the Titus Hoover family. His sister Harriet was in the fourth grade, and another sister, Katherine, was in the seventh grade. They were polite children, and their lessons were average, but they were raised more old-fashioned. It was a constant job to keep that fact in check, so that it didn't come to the surface. But children will be children and at times it rose up.

In response, the Hoover children had the tendency to be easily upset or quick to show anger, and the other pupils knew it.

John Mark had also met those parents and they were very concerned about any problems their children caused. He said that at times it was their quick temper that caused trouble. John Mark thought before he had met the parents that maybe they were proud parents. That pride was the root of the disunity. They were proud of their old-fashioned raising that made the children resentful, but after meeting the parents, he saw that he had misjudged them. The mother had admitted that the children had inherited her nature. She didn't seem high-strung, but maybe a little nervous.

Also in third grade was Roman Reiff, a son to Barton, the board member who had hired him. His daughter Joann was in the fourth grade, and Ida was in the seventh grade. Roman did lessons because he had to and if any mischief was going on somewhere, Roman was sure to be an interested witness, either helping or coming tale-bearing to John Mark with the details a little twisted up. As for Joann and Ida, there wasn't much to think about. If everyone was like them, things would be fine, but they were quick to see the difference. Joann had made many a mountain out of a molehill, but Ida was more quiet. You had no real way of knowing what she was thinking. Sometimes she disrespected silently; other times she was friendly.

Also in third grade was Lydia Ann Kilmer. She was a good example for others. Her brother Moses was in sixth grade. His lessons were a little hard for him at times. And he had plenty of energy, but with Floyd Shirk being the only boy near his age, he was usually pretty well-behaved. Unless his good sense of humor got out of order. He couldn't help it, he was a born—what would you say?—rather comical. The things that he said were usually humorous. He didn't try to be funny; it came naturally. He said his things in such a dry, humble way. Once in awhile it caused trouble when someone couldn't see the funny side of it and it was said at their expense.

Floyd's brother Peter came to the three-hour school. John Mark never really learned to know him. He said very little and just came and went. John Mark was slowly forming the opinion that whenever Peter was in the school, the older girls acted sort of more mature. He kept close watch over them. He hadn't really come to any conclusion yet who it was, but he could feel it every time Peter came. Yet Peter made no fuss, he passed in and out silently, but John Mark was convinced that his coming was very real to someone.

Now all the children had gone home for the evening. Tomorrow they would be entrusted to his care again. So many different natures, so many different upbringings. They were all children, and I am a child and am to lead them. There was always an eager flutter in his heart when the doorknob turned in the morning. He was anxious to see them again, but he always had a sort of helpless feeling of anxiety of what the day may bring. He decided to go home early and take lessons along to prepare. He was thinking too long and didn't feel like going back to studying in the quiet schoolhouse.

On the way home when he was thinking about how he depended on the parents, and the parents depended on him, the song started going through his mind,

I'm depending on Him, he is depending on me. . . .

But then he thought of the real meaning of the words. He found himself realizing more and more his own nothingness and that he was fully depending on a higher hand to lead him as he worked with the many souls entrusted to his care. His thoughts went to the coming Sunday when the young folks would be baptized. He had a deep yearning. If the people were now giving their names in preparation for that, he could be stirred to it, but this summer he wasn't quite able yet as there were things that he did not fully understand or believe yet. But as he attended the class meetings this summer, his eyes were opened. He felt more submissive.

Edgar told John Mark the other day that they were going to church on Saturday and Virginia would be baptized. He asked Edgar if that was also his sister and he said it was. So many times Edgar talked about his sister and usually it was a name that none of his sisters had that went to school. He was beginning to wonder if they were all his sisters or if he sometimes said a wrong name. If he had that many sisters, it was no wonder they had a fabric store. They needed it either for jobs for their girls or so that they wouldn't have to go to a fabric store once a week. Three of Edgar's sisters were in school, but there must be more at home, including baby Mabel, but he gathered she was over a year old. He didn't know the Ringlers very well, since they went to the next district church. About half of the school families did, as the school was at the dividing line of the church districts. Dry Hill ended and West Prairie began, with Cloverdale that many miles in the other direction.

Chapter Nine

"It looks like a photograph," John Mark mused to himself as his eyes scanned the countryside. Fields were covered with pure, white snow; trees had their twigs decorated. But the roads were mostly cleared except for a few spots of snow that remained like patches pressed down hard on the road.

The sky was a light blue with pink hues which curtained or laced where the sun had just disappeared. Likely promising a cold day tomorrow, John Mark guessed. He tucked the buggy robe more firmly around him, but quickly put his second hand on the reins again; Charlotte was anxious to get home. No wonder. He had not blanketed her when he stopped at Four Acres School as he hadn't planned to stay long. He intended to stay only long enough to leave the copies that he had duplicated for Naomi, but she had an interesting project laid out that the class had been working on for art, so John Mark stayed longer than he had planned to and Charlotte apparently was eager to get back to the warm barn.

He smiled to himself when he thought how disappointed he was when he first saw this horse. The first times they hitched her he wasn't impressed, but now and then he took her for a short errand. Sometimes he took her to school, and over the months her reputation and character had blinded his longing for beauty in her appearance.

Her neck was rather long and she had no style for holding her head in fashion. Her body was sort of slender, and she had no perfect markings on her forehead or feet. She was spirited, and at times it took two firm hands on the reins to keep her under control. If allowed, she would pass every team on the road rather than slow down and stay behind. Since he used her more often and knew her ways and traits, John Mark didn't covet Duke anymore. He assumed, though, that Duke could maybe match Charlotte in speed if a younger person was driving him.

Tonight John Mark let Charlotte have the reins. He was eager to be going home, too, as he hadn't been home the last two days. On Wednesday it had been cold and blustery when he hitched up to go to school, so he said if the weather stayed that way he would stay up there for the night, and maybe even the next night if the weather still hadn't moderated.

Then Thursday the weather was dreary and chilly and snow started falling in the afternoon, so he stayed at Stanley Weaver's overnight. His place was west of the school. Stanley had talked with him a few times and said he would be welcome to stay with them anytime he didn't want to go back and forth. He planned to go there on Wednesday evening, too, but when Moses and Lydia Kilmer's parents brought their children to school, they stayed to visit a few hours and when they were aware that he planned to stay in the area, they invited him to come for the night. They had offered earlier to board John Mark any time he wanted, but it was handier at Stanley's and they had no children going to school.

Leading Charlotte, John Mark opened the stall door and the horses neighed impatiently as soon as the door rattled. The cow urgently voiced her impatience as she crowded up to the trough. He had expected that Dad would be feeding already. The calf barn looked dark too. With a happy urge he hurriedly tied Charlotte and tossed a cake of hay to each of the horses and promised them he would be out soon to give them a proper supper. He desired to go quickly in and join the family at the table. He thought he had missed supper, and being away two days made him more eager to see his family. He grabbed the lunch pail and things off the buggy and hurried toward the house.

As he opened the door, he saw some of them still at the table.

Josiah jumped off his chair when John Mark entered, exclaiming, "We were watching for your buggy long already." John Mark stopped in his tracks. Delores smiled, amused. Josiah looked at him questioningly.

In Mother's place at the table sat neighbor Irene. She looked around and smiled rather amusedly, and then asked, "Did you have supper already?"

He was trying to think when Josiah explained, "Irene is here, you know; Mom and Dad and Rebekah and William went on the bus."

Delores saw his blank look and said, "You know, Levi asked Dad to go along to Ohio, then they finally decided to go since they could visit Uncle Apheus."

"Did they tell me that on Wednesday before I left?" Delores shrugged her shoulders and Irene got a knowing look on her face.

"If you weren't home since Wednesday morning, they probably didn't know it yet. Levi's are going on account of a funeral tomorrow and asked your dad to go along, and I think your parents only found out on Wednesday evening or Thursday," she said as she was gathering a plate and silverware for him and making an empty place at the table to set it on.

Delores rose from her chair, her meal finished. She walked to the window and then strayed over to the sewing machine where John Mark had unloaded his armful of school things when he came in.

She was humming to herself and suddenly exclaimed, "What's this? she gasped. "Where does it come from?" All eyes looked up at her as she unfolded a crocheted object with folds of it opening up to reveal its royal blue color trimmed with sky blue and deeper dark blue. John Mark had just taken another bite of bread and nodded his head and hurried up chewing.

Then he explained, "I got that from some of the school parents for my birthday to put on my buggy."

Delores looked at him wonderingly. "Did you have it on Tuesday already? Wasn't your birthday on Tuesday when you brought some gifts along home?"

"I had it already but hardly had room to bring it along home. I told Mom about the afghan. Maybe you weren't there when I told her."

Irene came over and felt the fluffy afghan. She admired the beautiful color combination. Then suddenly she exclaimed gleefully,

70

"You said for your birthday. Are you seventeen now?" She clapped her hands saying, "Maybe I'll have a way to go to the singing tomorrow." She finished, looking at John Mark. John Mark, forgetting his food on his plate looked at her wonderingly at her exclamation. Josiah and Delores looked from one to the other.

At length, John Mark answered, "I remember again that Mom asked me if I was going to go to singings now, and I said I didn't know if there was one."

Irene went back to the sink, getting the dishwater ready and explained, "Yes, there is one over at Mahlon Martin's and I don't know how I'm going to get there."

John Mark finished his supper in silence. He had been so occupied at school that he had not taken any time to concentrate about going to a singing or joining the young folks. He had been occupied in drilling the first-grade pupils on their letter sounds before giving them their reading books. Then he helped them to get started reading, and work on the Christmas project. Also, he worked on ironing out the discipline discord that wanted to wrinkle in first with the upper-grade boys and next with the middle-grade girls.

Sometimes he felt like he was treading water to stay abreast and not gaining the surface. He was flopping urgently only to keep his head above the tide, struggling to keep the next wave from swallowing him up in the sea.

With those thoughts he rose from the table, saying to Josiah, "I guess it is about time we do the chores."

Delores went for her wraps too. Looking at Irene she said, "Oh, now you don't have to feed all those calves."

"I didn't help much," Irene mused as the boys went out the door. It was true, John Mark thought as he went out to the barn, Josiah who was almost nine and Delores who was eleven, could do a lot of the chores if someone watched over them. But later in the evening he gathered that one of Irene's brothers had been helping with some of the chores.

It wasn't until Irene came out while they were feeding the smaller calves, after the chores in the barn were completed and the bigger calves had been fed that John Mark, seeing Irene remembered again the incident in the kitchen over the afghan.

He said to Irene, "I couldn't go to a singing on Saturday as Josiah and Delores would be here alone."

Irene silently nodded her head, but after a while she matter-of-factly said, "I'm sure Helen wouldn't mind coming over on Saturday evening for the night. She isn't interested in going to singings unless the neighbors have one." Helen, Irene's older sister, was in her upper twenties. Irene's two brothers, who were still at home, were just coming out of school. Helen had stayed with the children at times when Mother and Dad went away or else the children went over there.

Thus it came to be that on the dreary, damp, dark Saturday evening, John Mark hitched up Charlotte to the clean buggy which Irene had offered to wash in the afternoon. So in the newly washed and sparkling buggy with the soft, three-toned blue afghan draped over the seat, John Mark headed for his first singing at Mahlon Martin's. Irene was along as his passenger which he was grateful for to help break the ice. It was like taking a sister along.

Once inside at the singing it wasn't as strange as he had assumed it would be for there were Levi and Justus and Chester, the boys he often sat with at church. He sort of missed Paul Ray who was a little younger than himself, but they were good friends. John Mark thought he was neglecting his friends some since he started teaching, as before he was so apt to go over on a free Saturday and visit them.

He found as the songs were selected his thoughts went back to his pupils and school. As page forty was selected and the singing began, he thought of Lucy Weaver who would often pick that song. As they sang number 191, he remembered that was the song they were singing when the group of visitors came the other morning.

It was rather a surprise to him how many memories were stirred up while the songs were being sung. It was almost startling when it was about time to go home and he realized that he had been visiting mostly with the girls. He had met Naomi and just naturally started talking with her to see if she had made arrangements to go to

72

the teacher's meeting that week, and she had asked him how his first grade was doing in reading. Then there was Lena Jane, a teacher from another district whom he saw only at meetings. She had given John Mark some pointers on working with Edgar as she had some pupils, too, who needed extra help or had a handicap in learning. She seemed rather embarrassed when he started talking to her. He didn't know why since at a teacher's meeting it was so common, but he noticed that some people gave him a few glances while he was talking with different ones who were teachers. And he had also met Ellen and they had much to discuss.

Till the evening was over he felt rather confused. He lay awake a long time after he was in bed thinking things over. The singing sort of left him feeling like he was a misfit. There was just no way around it. He had more in common with the girls since they were doing the same work. Their teacher's conversation were just so much more interesting than the deer stories the boys were talking about, how they tracked the deer, and endless stories of hitting them and missing them. He had failed to even hear one whole story just because he forgot to listen.

Then he remembered that once when Dad was recalling memories of his childhood he said that since there were no girls in his family after Naomi married, and since the boys had so much housework to do that he sometimes found himself having more in common with their girls' conversations.

Dad's sister Naomi had once asked John Mark that since he had such an interest in teaching if he knew if one of his birth parents had been a teacher. The question had caused him to do much thinking. He approached Mother with the question, and Mother was taken by surprise that someone had asked him such a question, but he didn't mention who it was. He also wondered now if he had inherited his interest in teaching. His mother was deep in thought, trying to recall what she knew about John Mark's parents.

"I know your mother wasn't a teacher and, like I said, your father I really didn't know. It has been so long since I was connected with these people through other people. I really can't tell when I heard snatches of conversation what his occupation was. I would sooner assume he may have been studying to be one," she had added. "To tell the truth, you have been one of us for so long I keep forgetting that you once weren't one of us."

Those words had been such a comfort and joy to John Mark that he suddenly decided it didn't matter who his parents were. It was so valuable to know he belonged in this family. He sometimes caught himself wondering if since Josiah and William and Rebekah were born, that maybe he and Delores were sort of out of place or in the way, but this conversation reassured him anew that they were definitely a part of the family.

In earlier times he had felt more like a misfit when he was supposed to take an interest in the harness shop and just couldn't. But when he was granted a job that he enjoyed, like teaching, it helped him to feel as if he had found his purpose. And now Dad was working in the harness shop since he had help to do the chores.

John Mark couldn't think of Mother without him and Delores. It had been Mother and Father for so long and it was so complete. He wouldn't have it any other way. One day when he was deep in thought he asked Mother how she could have taken him and Delores in her care if she hadn't known Dad would come yet.

Mother had looked at him silently and got a faraway look in her eyes. At length she answered, "At the time it was the only right thing to do and I often prayed to God for His help in directing us in the way He planned for us. Some days I wondered too how things would work out, but His wisdom was far above mine. Like a verse says,

> *He was better to me than all my hopes,*
> *He was better than all my fears.*
> *He made a bridge of my broken works*
> *And a rainbow of my tears."*

Chapter Ten

John Mark slipped past the people and the noise and disappeared out of the classroom and down the basement steps to check the fire in the furnace. It had burned rather low. Leaving the door open, he put a few shovels of coal on and stood for a moment gazing at the fire and listening to the noise upstairs. If excitement ever rose high, it was today.

Dad had said he thought it was useless for the parents to give the teachers gifts since there is really nothing they know they need, and for the teachers to buy the pupils presents when they don't know what they need either. It was far removed from giving where we don't look for anything in return. John Mark had toiled with these thoughts and then he explained to his pupils that he really didn't need anything. And he knew of nothing they really needed either, but people did give gifts to show their appreciation to others. He suggested that they might give gifts to people who were not looking for things, and people who needed things to cheer them.

With these suggestions, the students quickly caught on. They made scrapbooks for some lonely widows, and the parents shared, too. It was a parent, teacher, and pupil affair. The parents said they would add little gifts to the scrapbooks like homemade bread or apple butter, etc. They suggested that the students remember the family in the other school district who had lost their mother. They could get gifts for each of the children. John Mark also helped to pay for the gifts and there were different shut-ins that they made cards or scrapbooks for and included some gifts.

Now the day had come when everything was brought to school. The parents came, too, to help get everything in order and onto the right piles. As John Mark watched the parents look at the scrapbooks the children had made, he knew the scrapbooks had been well worth the time and effort spent on them. He wondered if maybe the children should also have made scrapbooks for their parents. He could see feelings of gratitude on the parents' faces as they looked at their children's accomplishments. Some of the parents had also offered to make some scrapbook pages.

The parents and the pupils had spent an hour or more singing Christmas songs. The singing was now over, and people were visiting. Tomorrow three school fathers and mothers would help deliver the gifts. They were going in four groups to present the gifts to the people so there wouldn't be so many pupils at one place to disturb the elderly and the sick people.

John Mark was sure the pupils and the parents had more pleasure already than if they were just giving gifts to each other. John Mark sat down on the bottom cellar step. He needed to relax a bit and since the parents were here today, they could watch the children for a while.

In all the excitement he felt a little troubled. He had started talking with Nevin Ringler, Edgar's father, a few times and was making a start in commenting on Edgar, asking if he seemed to like school. But Nevin appeared to be a man who was rather nervous and did not understand what John Mark was trying to ask. He wondered how to approach Edgar's mother. She looked as if she was so kind that it almost made her weary. From hearing her talk to other mothers a few times, he gathered she was a woman of few words. She just calmly agreed to all comments in a gentle way.

Suddenly John Mark became aware of where he was as it suddenly grew rather quiet upstairs. Then he faintly remembered that shortly before he had heard many footsteps crossing the floor above him. Apparently most of the children had run out to the playground. He decided to go back up the stairs. As he came to the top of the stairs, he looked out the window at the children running around in the yard. The parents were still standing around visiting. Across the room he saw a father closing the window. He had been talking to a pupil on the outside. The next instant the schoolhouse door opened and the pupils were pouring in. He was slowly walking to his desk and had stopped and looked at what the pupils were doing when he felt a hand tapping his arm. He was used to it. It was Edgar's way to get his attention.

When he looked at Edgar, his eyes were dancing in excitement as he urgently said, "There's a present on your desk."

John Mark looked at his desk and saw a pile of parcels there. He stood bewildered, then shouts of exclamations came from the pupils as they came pouring in the door.

"Look, there are gifts on the teacher's desk!" In a few seconds John Mark and all his pupils stood around the teacher's desk. When he looked up, the parents sat there so expectantly.

He asked, "What's this?"

"Open them, it's for all of you." John Mark watched as with squeals of delight the pupils tore open the four parcels, about three people to a package. The paper was torn off revealing a game of Bingo in one; another revealed a Bible Bingo game.

"Alphabet Land," the younger girls rejoiced when the third package was opened, and a chorus of celebration was heard when Probe was uncovered in the last package. The parents had gotten the games for the school as they thought they hadn't helped much with the few small gifts they put with the scrapbooks.

John Mark now knew what had taken place while he was downstairs. The parents noticed he wasn't there and had sent the children out for exercise while they put the games on his desk. With the winter coming, John Mark assured the parents they couldn't have done anything that he appreciated more. Some of the pupils didn't know how to play Probe.

Others said, "Oh, yes, we have that game. Remember we played it that Sunday when we had company."

"But what is Alphabet Land?"

"Oh that's an easy first-grade game," another chanted.

With all the excitement it seemed hard to believe that they had another day coming tomorrow to deliver the Christmas gifts to the lonely and elderly people. It almost seemed as if the height had already been reached. John Mark remembered he needed to talk to

Christ Shirk yet about the plans for tomorrow. Thus he walked past the desks and over to the next aisle and in doing so he met up unexpectedly with Mrs. Ringler. She humbly moved out of the way for him to pass. Just as he passed he remembered to take this opportunity to get better acquainted with her.

He turned back and scratched his hand through his hair saying, "Oh, I seem to be doing a poor job teaching Edgar."

She smiled humbly and so easygoing and said, "Oh, I thought it sounded as if it was going good." John Mark dropped his mouth open in surprise.

At his shocked surprise Mrs. Ringler continued, "Edgar seems to like school, and we are pleased how you are working with him."

"But his reading?" John Mark asked in alarm.

"He enjoys his book," she replied so calmly, not at all irritated or excited. "He talks about the stories," she added kindly. He expected to have her understanding and sympathy and discussion about how difficult it was to teach Edgar, but now she assured John Mark that he was doing well.

Before he was able to ask more questions, Mrs. Barton Reiff walked up to Mrs. Ringler and gave her a small bag and said something about, "You know, it's the pattern."

Mrs. Ringler said, "Oh, so you found it?" and soon they were in a conversation. And it didn't matter, John Mark thought, as he realized that the conversation he was trying to make didn't help matters any. He felt disappointed, but he was soon talking with Christ about tomorrow's events.

Making his way back to his desk, he passed Edgar's desk and was surprised to see Edgar sitting in it. He had his activity workbook on top of the desk and then John Mark saw one of his sisters kneeling at the other side of his desk. Edgar was showing the book to her.

Edgar looked pleased as he looked up at John Mark. John Mark asked, "Do you have someone to help you?"

He nodded his head with a happy smile showing and said, "Lavina can help me." With a pleasant smile on her face, she looked up at John Mark. Then suddenly her countenance fell and she looked like a frightened chick, not knowing where to hide. John Mark explained that there had been no one available to help him with the last half of the page. That was why most of them weren't done and the ones which were done were not correct. He really didn't know what he was doing.

"Now I know," Edgar beamed. "Lavina said to put a mark around the smallest animal, here, the one that has feathers. Guess so it can't fly out," Edgar chatted away.

His brother Mark Anthony came hurrying to the desk panting, "Edgar, Mom and Dad are going home. Do you want to go along?"

"Yes, I'm going home with Dad." He leapt out of his desk seat with all lesson pages forgotten. Lavina looked hopelessly after him.

John Mark picked up the book that Edgar deserted and said, "Something like this he can do very well if someone has time to explain it. What has feathers, and what is biggest, and so forth, but what am I doing wrong in arithmetic and reading?" He looked at her hopefully; maybe he hadn't tried the right method yet. Lavina had risen to her feet and appeared to be as a frightened chick too stunned to run and frozen on the spot.

John Mark found himself talking softly so he wouldn't scare her as he said, "I mean, have you had any success in getting him to understand numbers and letters?" She looked at him almost pleading, her lips quivering.

Then she cast her eyes downward as she folded her hands in and out, then she said, "Numbers don't go so well, but acting them out seems to help."

"Like what?" he asked, "how do you mean?"

She took a deep breath as she started talking. She was a little more at ease, seeming to forget herself as she said, "Like when we send him to the cellar to fetch five oranges, he would come with three or so. But if I say 'Get one for Dad and one for Mom, one for Mark Anthony, one for Mildred, and one for Alfred, and one for yourself,' he'll get six, the right amount. And when I'm ironing and need five clothes hangers, I learned to say, 'Get one hanger for all your fingers and thumb on one hand,' and he'll have the right amount. Otherwise, the names and numbers don't seem to make much sense to him." John Mark was drinking in every word he was hearing. Things he never learned at the teacher's meetings.

"Acting out numbers," he said. A new field was opening to him. "Does anyone else in the family have difficulties learning?" he asked, becoming interested.

"No," she answered, seemingly more timid again. "He was sick when he was two years old. He had a very high fever. The doctors are surprised that he does this well." Lavina had been drifting away a little and gradually kept on fading away. John Mark stood grasping the details.

When all the pupils and parents left, he was alone in the schoolhouse. His thoughts were churning and it was almost as if he had just been informed that he must learn to use sign language.

With his eyes staring at the wall, he imagined himself making papers and searching the bookstores for workbooks that had things you could explain and do without numbers. He got a paper and started writing things down. His mind was being challenged. The writing started making sense. He picked up a new sheet, and with his ruler he made columns and blocks and his freehand drawing ability was put to the test. It was being sharpened after not being used often over the years.

He drew three cats, then wrote, "Draw a dish for each cat." Then he drew two boys and wrote, "Draw a hat for each boy," and so he filled the pages. For a while he made papers then he started questioning, *Could we draw that?* He sketched awhile, then finally reminded himself that he could read the story to Edgar, then he could ask him questions to see if he understood, or ask him what he thought would happen next. Suddenly it seemed to be getting dreary. John Mark looked up at the clock. "Oh no! It must be getting dark." It was time to head for home.

As he expected, the ones at home were doing chores already.

Mother looked surprised and said, "I just decided you must be planning to stay with someone for the night. Did you have supper yet?"

"No, I didn't," he admitted. Mother got a few bowls out of the refrigerator and heated things up for him. She asked John Mark about the day, thinking they delivered the gifts today.

"No, the parents were at school today to see the scrapbooks and things the children made and to bring the things they were giving. So we were getting everything ready and singing Christmas songs. But the parents still surprised me, as they gave us four games to play at school when the pupils have to play indoors. It guess it was their joy since no one was looking for gifts and I appreciated it. I was wondering what the students would play all winter when it wasn't fit to play outside or they didn't have the games we had at our school."

The kitchen was quiet, only Mother and Rebekah were there. Delores and the boys had gone along to the barn. It was no longer quiet when Delores came back. She wanted to know all about the day and was very enthused when he said how the parents put the games on the desk when the pupils and he were out of the room. Dad said the parents probably had much more joy in giving the games than if they were to give the teacher a gift from each of them, as was usually expected. This way it was more of a surprise and they didn't give where they looked for something in return.

John Mark sat on the rocking chair, his head cupped in his hands. The heat of the range felt good since the drive home had been chilly. He had been listening to the usual family chatter but had drifted off to his own thoughts. He was thinking about the papers he prepared and how to explain the things to Edgar and wondering if it would not just automatically put Edgar in a grade by himself. He wondered what Edgar's parents would say. Would they approve? They never gave him any clue that Edgar had a learning handicap.

John Mark was roused from his thoughts. Either Delores was asking him something or else William was showing him the blocks he was building things with. Once when he looked up, he noticed Mother watching him with a questioning look. He leaned back in the rocker trying to be alert to the family chatter, but he wasn't very successful. Dad asked him if he was worked up about delivering the gifts tomorrow.

"No, not at all. I'm hoping it will seem real once we start because with all the activities today, it almost seems we did it already."

Another time when he met Mother's eyes, she asked him if he had a headache. Almost before realizing it he answered, "No," and afterward he realized maybe his head did ache some. When the younger children started getting ready for bed he said he was going early, too. He pretended not to see his parents exchange a wondering look and watch him silently as he went upstairs.

John Mark stirred. He felt exhausted, but he was in bed. He felt so tired. He rubbed his eyes. It was still dark. He tried to remember who was teaching school while he was at Uncle Israel's helping in the shop, or was today Saturday? He clicked on his flashlight. It was eleven o'clock and he saw he was in his own room. Why then was it so clearly in his mind of being in Uncle Israel's woodworking shop? A frightened little chick was chirping in the corner. He was under the table behind the sawdust pile and when they had tried to rescue it, it went fleeting over to the barrels. It kept chirping. They had chased it time and again only to have it go under the lumber pile. Well, he was mostly trying to rescue it alone.

Uncle Israel had gone back to work and was singing on and on. When John Mark went to ask him for help, he was at the office desk doing paperwork and loudly singing the same song over and over:

> *I looked in the forest and I looked in the lake,*
> *I looked in the mountain's highest quake,*
> *And in the earth's lowest hollow,*
> *Where no one could ever follow.*
> *But the Word is our lamp and guide*
> *To those that in Him abide.*
> *So if you seek, you shall find*
> *A faithful friend there behind.*

John Mark was getting aggravated at Israel for not helping him; he just kept singing. The frightened chick flew from the dark corner on the stairway and landed quivering on the fifth step. John Mark reached for it only to discover it was Lavina standing there, trembling with downcast radiantly glowing eyes.

Now John Mark was coming to his senses. He was in bed. He must have been dreaming of snatches of things at school. The fearful and trembling look that Lavina had given John Mark at Edgar's desk had become woven into a dream. But what song was Israel singing? He got out of bed, found a paper and pen, and wrote down the words that were still ringing in his ears. He had never heard such a song. He was afraid he would forget the words until morning. Finally, he went back to bed, hoping to relax and sleep soundly.

Chapter Eleven

The clock ticked loudly in the almost-empty schoolroom, but the minutes and seconds passed by unheeded. The clock kept up its duty faithfully. A deep sigh now and then and the soft rustle of papers were the only other sounds to prove that the room wasn't empty. Then the thud of a book closing. In the corner by the window stood the teacher's desk where John Mark sat on a chair bent over papers with his pencil scratching check marks now and then as he sat correcting the English papers. Some had too many check marks on. After checking fifth grade sheets, he put them on a separate pile and reached for the dictionary. He had to figure out a way to get them to understand the lesson.

He was so deeply engrossed in his work that when the door rattled a bit his whole body jumped in surprise, or maybe it was a sound in the room; he was trying to decide. When the door opened, he almost jumped again, for he hadn't known anyone was around. The door opened slowly and there in the doorway appeared Lloyd Weaver and his wife.

"Oh, so you are still here. It was so quiet I wasn't quite sure," Mrs. Weaver greeted him. Lloyd came into the room, closing the door and silently following behind.

Mrs. Weaver came up to his desk asking, "Why the discouraged look when correcting papers?" she asked in a teasing way.

John Mark stretched his arms, yawned, and leaned back in his chair, straightening the tousled hair he had combed through with his hands quite often while correcting papers.

Then he chuckled and said, "By the looks of the papers it is evident that these children should have a better teacher."

"Do you think the pupils are always doing their best?"

"I'm sure they don't always, but this fifth-grade English assignment that they handed in today leaves me wondering if maybe it wasn't explained carefully enough or if they weren't doing their best."

"Maybe it has to do with spring coming," Lloyd offered as he sat down on the bench near the blackboard. Then he added, "Sometimes it sounds as if your children are getting spring fever already."

"Spring fever," John Mark repeated. "Maybe that's what was wrong with me this past week," John Mark said as he gazed out the window and saw, lo and behold, that things were greening up a bit already. He hadn't had time to notice.

He lifted his eyes from the window in time to see Mrs. Weaver give her husband a look of—John Mark wasn't sure what, some kind of command like, "say it now" or "all right." Lloyd brushed his hands over his knees, not heeding the silent command.

Then Mrs. Weaver, almost sympathetically, asked, "What about the last few weeks? Haven't you been feeling up to par or are the children hard on you?"

John Mark chuckled, "Sometimes I wonder if maybe I'm too hard on the children."

"Don't let them take advantage of you. Maybe you have been too easy on them," Lloyd offered without looking up. Mrs. Weaver sat on the empty chair next to the library case. John Mark looked at Lloyd silently wishing he would talk straight out, rather than making him curious. At length Lloyd looked up and then seemed a little uneasy to find John Mark staring at him.

John Mark could not stand the quietness and asked, leaning forward toward where Lloyd sat, "Should I know something?" Lloyd's gaze went beyond John Mark. He was looking at his wife.

At length she drew a deep breath, more like a sigh, and slowly said, "As a whole how do you feel about school at present?"

"A month ago I would have said it was good for the end of February. But now being the end of March, I sometimes wonder if maybe I shouldn't have promised to try it again."

Then Mrs. Weaver began to get interested saying, "That's a very normal feeling for a teacher to get in March or April."

"It is?" John Mark asked hopefully, "Are there any cures?"

"All depends on what causes the feeling," Mrs. Weaver answered becoming relaxed as if she was engrossed in a hearty conversation.

John Mark thought a moment. *Should I confide in them?* He didn't want to make things worse than they were.

Lloyd casually said, "I sense it isn't the English papers that are causing these feelings."

"No," John Mark admitted, "the explaining of lessons I can usually handle, although at times I may lose patience too soon and accuse someone of not wanting to do better when it is that they don't understand."

"Should we know something?" Mrs. Weaver asked.

John Mark honestly replied, "I wish some other parents of this school would give me the opportunity like this to pour out."

"Why not us? Lloyd asked.

"Well," John Mark began slowly, "it's not you or your children who have been making my work hard."

"Who is then?" Lloyd pressed him.

Unbidden tears came to the surface. John Mark tried to blink them back. "Sometimes I wonder if it's fair to Edgar to try and teach him with the rest of the school. It's hard for me and him and for the rest of the children to always understand. He alone maybe I could handle, but sometimes the friction of everything crops up." John Mark cut the words short, swallowing the sobs that were rising.

At length Lloyd asked, "Are you referring to the Titus Hoover family?" John Mark automatically raised his eyes and met Lloyd's kind understanding eyes. *How had he known? He never admitted it to anyone.* The clock ticked on triumphantly, not aware of the silence it was intruding upon.

Mrs. Weaver cleared her throat and softly with feeling said, "If it wasn't for Edgar and the Titus Hoover family, this would be an easy school, right?" This was too much. John Mark got out his handkerchief and sobbed into it. He dropped his eyes and swallowed the excess tears that were coming, as if a fountain had been opened to a strong current.

Then Lloyd, like a strong hand in support, said, "Now don't misunderstand us. We don't feel Edgar and the Hoover children are all the fault. It is also the other children who don't accept them as they are."

John Mark nodded, "You understand exactly what I am trying to say. I have thought it over and over and it always comes to that. If only I could keep a feeling of peace and acceptance in the atmosphere. At times I was tempted to bring the problem up at a meeting, but I got the idea it might stem a little deeper than just the children. But what do you know?" John Mark asked suddenly.

Lloyd motioned over to his wife saying, "She was sharing incidents that Sylvia brought home from school, things you don't find out about, and unfortunately the last while it wasn't getting any better and Sylvia was getting a personality we didn't like. After a lot of talking, I went to see Barton Reiff, wondering if the school board was aware of any problem and he said they had been sensing things. But he said from earlier experiences they learned that things might not always be as they sound. I understand their children, in times past, had things quite twisted up and sometimes it caused more trouble than if they had left well enough alone."

John Mark nodded his head in agreement. "At times I thought since it was now the latter part of March, maybe we could struggle through the term and then decide what to do for another year."

Mrs. and Mrs. Weaver both started talking, "We have been thinking of that too," Lloyd finished. "But I think maybe it would be best to iron out things a little beforehand so that we don't open the new drawer all full of wrinkled clothes."

"Do you mean call a meeting?" John Mark asked.

"I wasn't thinking about that. As you said, I know not all parents would be willing to discuss it. I thought maybe things could be explained to the children in some tactful way like how people are not all alike, but that God loves us all the same, not some better than others, and that each has his share to do, and well, you know in what ways your children can be reached. I would advise you to somehow explain these things a little, as I think with a few right moves our problems are still solvable. And we knew you weren't aware of all the things Sylvia told us about the friction among the girls and that it was spreading over the school. I wanted Barton to come since he is on the board, but he was afraid of making things worse. My wife said of her experiences as a teacher that she always wished the parents confided more in her with things that she knew nothing of but was expected to control and solve."

"Yes, I agree," John Mark said, "and I am glad you voiced your concern. I thought it was only me that felt the friction, and I didn't know if it was only a lot of my imagination."

Lloyd got up and shook hands with John Mark saying, "We stand behind you. We will do for you what we can, and support you with prayers as you are leading these children in the fear of the Lord. We know the utter feelings of helplessness at times just trying to raise our own. If there was no bond of love, we would not have made the effort to come over, but we are all struggling together."

Now Mrs. Weaver was talking. "And don't get discouraged if some of the parents aren't open enough for you to confide in. They still appreciate what you are doing and maybe some are battling in a stronger current than you are. If you have any problems, feel free to come to us to talk. Don't let yourself get discouraged. It may be you have misunderstood us if you start feeling discouraged. We meant well, and we will have to be going home and hoe our own row."

"I thank you for your concern. It sure would help matters if all parents welcomed such an opportunity to discuss things," John Mark said, as the Weavers stepped out the door.

Later he remembered Mrs. Weaver had said that even if other parents weren't open enough to confide in him, they still appreciate what he is doing and it may be that they are battling a stronger current. He wondered if she was referring to the Nevin Ringlers. They were never open enough to confide in. They seemed to brush everything off by saying, "It's going good." Mrs. Ringler was too kind, and Nevin always seemed restless. It was as if he expected the teacher to take care of the school alone. They didn't complain, nor did they come for help.

John Mark went through the motions of finishing a few papers, straightened up his desk, and prepared to go home. But half an hour later he found himself sitting on a chair with his hat still on, staring into space. How his thoughts were racing around in his head! He felt as weak as if he had just completed a very strenuous job or if an unusually difficult task was facing him.

An hour later he arrived home and put Charlotte in her stable and stared unaware into space as she ate her oats. Then he gathered the rest of his things from the buggy and went toward the house. The smell of fresh homemade bread greeted him as he opened the door. Mother looked up at him as she was lifting the golden delicious-looking bread out of the bread pans at the end of the table where the tablecloth was pushed aside because the table was partly set.

She looked up at John Mark for a moment and asked, "Are you hungry?"

"Oh, I don't know—maybe a little." She turned back to her bread, little noticing what a half-hearted answer she had received.

Some time later John Mark was roused from his thoughts when Mother startled him, asking, "John Mark, is something the matter with you?" Mother was standing in front of him wiping her hands on her apron. John Mark had been sitting on the rocking chair in the back part of the kitchen with his jacket and hat still on and Mother was exclaiming, "Is something the matter with you?"

"Why?" he asked, roused from his troubled thoughts to see Mother motioning over to where his wraps belonged on the wall. He had hung his lunch pail on the hook instead of his jacket and hat. John Mark chuckled at his absentmindedness.

"Take your wraps off and eat. I have saved a plate of food for you."

"Did you eat already?"

"Yes, we ate a little early since Dad is going on an errand and he is doing chores before going. The children are out helping."

Moments later Mother roused him again as he sat at the table with his head propped in his hands.

She sighed, asking, "What is your burden tonight, my son?"

He smiled at her for her concern and answered, "I should not have chosen to teach school."

"Chose?" she replied surprised. "I didn't know you chose to teach. Don't you remember that you used to be a helper and when people asked if you were going to teach on your own, it was such a surprise to you. You hadn't considered it. You were asked to do it. It was your lot in life and you have to accept it. Dad also didn't choose to be a deacon. Someone has to be a teacher, and we don't want to rebel against our duty. Don't start thinking of shirking your duty, only work to win the victory. Suppose I would give up being a mother when certain burdens come along—like my son having too heavy a load or my husband struggling to keep faith. When the load gets increasingly heavy I think of the song,

Must Jesus bear the cross alone and all the world go free.
No, there is a cross for everyone and there is a cross for me.

I often think of the words,

Burdens are meant for this life only left on earth when we depart,
there'll be joy beyond all measure when we sit at Jesus' feet."

Just then Delores and William came in the door and John Mark went in search of the plate of food that was awaiting him. Josiah came in through the other door and was eagerly telling him about a chase he and Dad had earlier that evening when a calf had gotten out of the shed as Dad was cleaning manure out of the stables. John Mark assumed it was a lot more exciting to Josiah than it was to Dad.

Later John Mark walked through the calf shed and the barn to make a routine checkup before going to bed since it was awhile since chores were done. He found it refreshed his mind, helping him to think about other things.

But hours later he was churning and tossing in his bed. He had gotten out of bed and tried reading but it did not help. Finally he went back to bed but his mattress felt as hard as ever and he had fluffed his pillows around time and again. The clock seemed to always show only five minutes later. Now he had gotten a dry cough that kept tickling his throat. Disgusted, he hopped out of bed, loosely pulled on his clothes, and tiptoed downstairs to get a drink.

He felt his way around in the dark but knocked over a plastic cup trying to pick up another glass and sent the sound echoing through the silent house. Then he dipped the glass in the water pail and took a refreshing drink. Just as he was about to set down his glass, goose pimples chilled up over his spine. He thought he heard a sound in the kitchen but knew it was only a notion, *the creaking sound of a house at night*, he thought. As he set the cup down and started turning around he thought he heard someone breathe. Then he saw a movement in the shadows of the dark kitchen. He felt all his blood drain from him. He didn't have the strength to run or scream.

As he gasped out loud, a voice came, "John Mark, what are you doing?" John Mark's racing heart slowed down some when he heard it was his dad's voice.

"I came down to get a drink of water," he weakly spoke.

"But why aren't you sleeping?" Dad whispered. John Mark tiptoed over near where Dad sat on the sofa. He saw Dad was fully dressed in his good clothes.

"Likely for the same reason that you aren't." Then he asked Dad, "Did you just now get home? Where were you all evening?"

"I came home about an hour ago and Mother was sleeping so well I was afraid I'd disturb her, so I'm trying to relax before I go to bed."

"It must not have been a very pleasant errand," John Mark said.

"Wasn't your day at school pleasant either?" Dad asked, ignoring John Mark's words.

"I was on the verge of regretting that I ever chose to teach school but Mother explained to me that I didn't choose to teach. It was my lot in life, and she said neither did you choose to be a deacon but it was your lot. Maybe we could change burdens for tonight?"

Dad rubbed his bare feet together, after taking off his shoes, saying, "I would give you all the calves out in the barn if I could sleep on your pillow tonight, resting on your burden. I guess I'm a deacon because Mother is a good deacon's wife."

"But, Dad, if she wasn't married to you, she would be no deacon's wife."

"That's what she keeps telling me," Dad admitted not sounding at all convinced. Dad ran his hand through his hair saying, "If only there were wise men, deacons who have wisdom like Solomon. It's times like this that I sorely miss my father. He always knew the best things to do in circumstances. Such older people who are old and wise should be in a deacon's place."

"What do you mean about Solomon?" John Mark asked sitting down on the other end of the sofa.

"You know about Solomon, the one who asked for wisdom to discern between good and evil, and he was granted it as the Lord was glad he asked for wisdom instead of riches. Two women who lived together in one house who each had a child came to him. The first woman said the other woman's child had died and she had put the dead baby in the first woman's bed and she discovered the dead child in the morning. The second woman said it was the other way around, the living child was hers and the first woman had put it in her bed, and so they argued back and forth.

"Then Solomon said, 'Since you can't agree, give me a sword and I'll divide the living baby; you can each have half of it.' The mother of the living child said, 'No, rather let her have it than harm it,' but the other one said, 'No, as you said, divide it.' King Solomon said to the one that was willing to give it up, 'Give her the living child and in no wise slay it: she is the mother thereof.' He had wisdom to decide weighty matters; the wisdom of God was in him.

"That is in the Old Testament, I Kings, chapter three, from verse ten to the end. We don't use the Old Testament very much."

"I thought I read it all through already. Guess I failed to grasp it," John Mark said.

A soft sound was heard. Dad looked up and Mother, wearing her housecoat and carrying a flashlight, was coming. Suddenly she stood still as if wondering. She saw her husband in good clothes and sitting in the dark kitchen with John Mark who had his clothes pulled on loosely.

She stared in disbelief and asked, "My men, what are you doing? What is going on?"

Dad explained briefly, "I came home awhile ago and was thinking things over before going to bed. John Mark came down for a drink when he couldn't sleep from thinking his things over. And then we got to visiting."

Dad turned back to John Mark saying, "Another place in the Old Testament tells of one who had wisdom enough to show a man his fault and sin without offending him. That was maybe David; no, I guess it was Nathan talking to David. David had more than one wife, but he desired to have another woman who was already married. David desired her so much that he worked it out so that her husband was put on the front line of battle. When her husband was killed, David took her as his wife.

"Then Nathan told David in a parable of two men, one who had many sheep and one who had only one dear lamb. The man with many sheep came and took from him who had only one lamb.

"David listened and angrily said, 'Such a man should be put to death.'

"Nathan replied, 'David, you are that man. You had many wives and yet you took the wife of another man who had only one.'"

"I was sitting here wishing for such wisdom, wisdom like Dad had or William who I used to work for."

"It's so easy to think when the cows get out that making a larger meadow will satisfy them, but it doesn't. You have to keep the fence tight. It is much easier to tighten the fence, then to chase the cows back in."

"Maybe we should go to bed so we can each chase cows tomorrow," John Mark offered.

"But in this case," Dad said, "I'm not sure if we can get the cows back in. We should have worked on the fence before."

"Well, I am starting to feel tired. I will go to bed and see if I can figure out which part of the fence I should tighten," John Mark said, getting up and heading for the upstairs door.

*   *   *   *

The eastern March sky was a deep blue, and a chilly breeze was friskily playing about. A few red streams of clouds decorated the far east, but they were fading as the blue sky came up further. John Mark sat with his head propped on his arm at the breakfast table waiting for the egg platter to come around. Josiah and Delores were trying to guess who was going to bring lunch to their school today. Rebekah was scolding them for not sending the egg platter around. William's place remained empty. He, as usual, was sleeping late. Mother was trying to calm Rebekah down. Dad, at length, picked up his fork and knife and started cutting his toast and eggs.

As the morning light shone in the east window streaming over Dad, one could see his hair was thinning and his figure was becoming more lean than in earlier years. It seemed the afflictions of life was wearing down his earthly body; he was carrying too heavy a load. John Mark thought as he observed Father, *Were he and I talking down here in the kitchen last night when both of us couldn't sleep? Or was that part of a dream?* Dad seemed extra quiet this morning but not disturbed. He looked like John Mark felt, as if he lacked a few hours sleep.

Josiah hopped off his chair to get the saltshaker and asked Dad, "Are you going to plow today?"

Dad looked up and shook his head silently, then he looked at John Mark and asked, "Shall I take Charlotte to have her shoed for you?" John Mark did some fast thinking. *Why would Dad be concerned to have the horse shod when he himself had only noticed yesterday that one shoe was rather loose? And my horse at that.* Then it became clear when he saw Mother look at Father with a solemn but kind look. Abner does horseshoeing and his parents, Christian Brubackers, live in the Doddy house there on Abner's farm. Christian was the bishop of the church and a man who had been a great help to Dad already. John Mark had deep respect for Christian.

He looked at Dad and said, "It would save time for me. Then I'll take Duke today." Dad nodded his head in agreement. Last evening, John Mark was too troubled and weary to concentrate much and this morning he had been too dull-headed, but on the way over to school this morning, he was beginning to see a way through. Dad often said how the earthly body weakens and persists in tribulations and afflictions, but the inward man is renewed day by day.

John Mark opened the school in the usual manner and started classes. But there was a lump in his throat as if a stone were pressing on it. He tried to ignore thinking about talking to the class while school was in session, but at recess he pondered over it, re-weighing it. Repeated times when he looked up from teaching, he found Sylvia watching him meekly as if she was expecting a lecture. She seemed to sense that something was hanging in the air. Mark thought, *If everyone was like her, I would not need to have this talk.* The time had come.

John Mark rang the dinner bell and was nervously arranging the papers on his desk and studying the art project. He took a deep breath and looked out over the classroom. Most of the pupils were getting books out of their desks. But Sylvia watched him in wonderment. *Some people know me better than I think they do*, he mused to himself. He looked over the classroom a moment and quite a few of the pupils looked up to see what the silence was and why no class was started. Edgar was waving his hand but then his paper flew on the floor and he went after that.

John Mark cleared his throat and as he started to speak he heard his own voice quivering in tenseness as he said, "We will be doing something a little different this afternoon. To begin with, I have an art project planned and we will be needing some things and therefore I am appointing Sylvia to take the first and second grades down to the bush to gather things that we need for the art project. So first and second grade, you can get your wraps. Sylvia, I want you to come up here and get the paper of the list of things you'll be looking for." Most of the boys got disapproving looks on their faces which John Mark ignored.

Sylvia was quite reserved coming up and listening to the directions of the things they were to look for. "Go up the bush lane and there at the opening where it goes up to Four Acres School, see if the pussy willows are far enough along to gather." He continued describing the stones and bird's nest, moss and buds, and all that they were to look for. He gave Sylvia the list and explained where they might be able to find different things.

He gave Sylvia the watch and told her quietly not to return until after one-thirty or even a little later. Then he gave her and the pupils each a paper bag to put their articles in.

As the nature party hiked out the door, the remaining ones looked at him expectantly as if to say, "Don't tell me, we have to study stupid health lessons while they are out hiking." John Mark reminded himself. He didn't want Edgar to hear, and the first and second grades really didn't have to hear either for that matter. They will hear enough of the results so they know, and Sylvia is no trouble-maker and she'll hear about results enough to know the rule. John Mark watched as the hikers left the school grounds and then he turned back to his chair. He moved his chair more in front of the middle rows of desks facing him. "Today I will be telling you stories." Every face changed to a questioning expression.

"I shall try and tell you a few stories which may help this to be a better school. We shall begin with how our bodies are made. We all have two eyes, one mouth, two ears, two feet, and two hands. In that way we are all alike. Some people may have only one arm or one leg, but that does not apply to anyone here. Maybe some of our eyes aren't as good as others' as some have glasses, while others do not. How nice if we could be so alike in everything. In what ways are we different from each other?" John Mark paused. No one made a sound.

"Well," John Mark began, "I can tell you how you are different in some ways. Some of you draw better than others, but I don't hold up those who do well in art and making crafts because others are better than they are in arithmetic. We are different from each other, but we still need each other to work together just like we need different parts of the body. We wouldn't think of not accepting our ears because they are different from our eyes and decide we want just eyes and no ears. Ears couldn't do what the eyes do. We need them both for they both have a job to do. I think that it's time we practice this kind of acceptance more in school with the people around us.

"Some of us have dark hair, while others have quite light hair and we wouldn't think of saying, 'Why do you have light hair when you know it's better to have dark hair?' For example, some mothers comb their children's hair and put barrettes in their hair. Some barrettes are more brilliantly colored; some barrettes are shaped differently. Some mothers braid their daughter's hair all the way down while others leave the ends of the braids open. Some mothers sew their girl's dresses with longer hems so they can wear the dresses another year while some mothers sew dresses with rather small hems and have to make new ones more often.

"Some of you come to school with lunch that contains a sandwich made of meat while other mothers make sandwiches of apple butter or eggs, depending upon what they have.

"If we would decide to laugh because someone else doesn't live like us, it would be like the eyes teasing the ear because it is different. If we couldn't be happy unless everyone combs like we do, dresses exactly as we do, or eats exactly the same foods, it would be the same as if we were not satisfied unless we all had ears and no eyes. It wouldn't work. We have to work together. Therefore, whenever we are tempted to tease someone or not play with them because they dress differently or eat different foods, it is like our saying, 'No, ear, I don't need you.' When you notice a difference in someone, rather than teasing them, think, 'I am an ear and he is an arm.'"

John Mark asked the students, "What can we do to show that we feel so?"

Gerald put up his hand and said, "Show that we appreciate them."

"You are very right. That's the same word I had in mind. And what makes us sometimes appreciate a hand and arm much more than at other times?"

The students offered a number of suggestions, but it was one of the twins who finally said, "To be unable to use the arm for a while would make us appreciate it more again."

"Very true," John Mark said, "and now that's what we are going to practice. Whenever someone teases another about food or clothing or combing, etc., I'm going to put a sling on that person's arm for a while so he is reminded of our discussion today. For we need everyone as much as we need all the parts of the body for we are as many parts, the whole body is Christ. I will send notes along home with the first and second graders who have no older brothers and sisters here so they understand what our rule is about."

"Now I have another story which is a little different but still makes the same point," John Mark said to the class.

"It is a story in the Old Testament found in II Samuel 12, the first twenty-three verses. Well, no, it really starts in chapter eleven when it says how David saw a woman that he would like to have but the people told him it was Uriah's wife, and it goes on to say that David so desired to have the woman that he arranged it so that Uriah was put in the front line in the battle where it was dangerous. Then he was killed, and David took the man's wife to be his and it displeased the Lord. David had other wives and this man had only one.

"Then in Chapter Twelve it says, 'The Lord sent Nathan unto David and he came unto him and said unto him, There were two men in one city. The one was rich and the other poor. The rich man had exceeding many flocks and herds. But the poor man had nothing, save one little ewe lamb which he had bought and nourished up. It grew up together with him and with the children. It did eat of his own meat and drank of his own cup and lay in his bosom and was unto him as a daughter. And there came a traveler unto the right man and he spared to take of his own flock and of his own herd to dress for the wayfaring man that was come unto him but he took the poor man's lamb, and dressed it for the man that was come to him. And David's anger was greatly kindled against the man and he said to Nathan, As sure as the Lord liveth, the man that has done this thing shall surely die, And he shall restore the lamb fourfold, because he did this thing, and because he had no pity. And Nathan said to David, Thou art the man. Thus saith the God of Israel, I anointed thee King over Israel I delivered thee out of the hand of Saul; I gave thee thy master's house and thy master's wives . . . and I would moreover have given unto thee such and such things. Then David saw his sin.'

"But I'm not talking about wives; I'm talking about talents, things we can do well because God has blessed us. We who are here can learn all the numbers and letters, and we can write them. We can learn everything we try to. We are like the rich man; we have many talents. But there is one of us who has only one talent and sometimes we try to take that talent from him when we tease him and talk about

98

him or fight with him. We are trying to take the one talent he has. Yet we have so many, why should we take his?"

Then John Mark asked, "Who am I talking about? Who is with us that has only one talent?" The students looked at each other. The twins looked embarrassed or insulted.

Kathryn put her hand up half way and said rather uncertainly, "Edgar?"

"Yes, that's right. I'm referring to Edgar. God made Edgar without as many talents as we have, but he has a talent."

Moses Kilmer asked, rather curiously, "What talent does he have?" putting an accent on "does he." A few people chuckled, but they straightened out when John Mark gave them a firm look.

John Mark asked, "Can someone tell me what his one talent is?"

Lucy Weaver asked, "Contentment?"

"Well, maybe we could say he has two talents. He is rather content, but I was thinking of compassion. Does he ever tease others to hurt their feelings? I have never heard him mock anyone, and when someone is hurt or frightened, he is always the first one to tell me. He has a talent for compassion, and when we tease him it's like we are trying to take that talent away, for he could lose patience and compassion and we would be at fault.

"So when you are tempted to belittle Edgar in the few things he can do, always remember we would be like the one with a lot of sheep who came and killed his one little lamb. We don't want to be stealing lambs or wearing slings and if we have to wear a sling and the others tease, some others will also be wearing slings. Now I will pass out the construction paper and show you what we will be doing for art."

He was in the midst of explaining the details when Sylvia and the first and second graders came pouring in the door with their treasure bags. After a calm recess, an interesting art class followed.

After the pupils left, John Mark was overwhelmed at how the pupils were touched. He trembled and wanted to scream, "It wasn't of myself. I just told it as it was being revealed to me." A lot more had come to him than what he saw on the way to school.

He picked up the Bible and paged through it, trying to find something soothing to calm himself down. The speech left him feeling weak and he feared the children would go home and tell their parents and have things all mixed up. He hoped the parents realized that he excused the first and second graders so Edgar wouldn't hear and so the others wouldn't get confused with things they didn't understand, and Sylvia sure didn't need admonishment.

He hoped the Titus Hoover children didn't feel hurt listening to it. *At least they now know that I love them as well as the others and that I care if the others mock them.* As John Mark was scanning through the pages of the Bible, his eyes fell on the words, "For whom the Lord loveth He chasteneth, and scourgeth every son whom He receiveth. If ye endure chastening God dealeth with you as with sons, for what son is he whom the father chasteneth not?" He closed it. He couldn't read more. It said how the father chasteneth the son and I am only a child. *What right have I to correct other children. How can I ask God to lead me when I'm not serving Him?*

He fell on his knees and poured forth only sighs and sobs and promised God that he would surrender his life to God. He cared no more if the other boys were older or that he felt too ignorant. *I don't want to be a father or a master, but only a son.* Earlier he had asked Dad about surrendering his life to God and Dad said he must know if he is ready to submit himself and also remember that it wouldn't be an end to struggles and temptations only the start, as it was *after* Jesus was baptized that Satan came to try him. And like Dad repeated at times, everyone's work shall be made manifest for the day shall declare it because it shall be revealed by fire and the fire shall try every man's work of what sort it is. For other foundation can no man lay than what is laid, which is Jesus Christ.

Chapter Twelve

As the mild July breezes whispered through the heavy-leafed trees, John Mark's heart was light and carefree. He was whistling as he pulled the buggy out of the shed, checked to see if the lights worked properly, and fixed his afghan which had drooped over the seat. He always thought of his pupils and parents when he saw the afghan. It was a gift he really appreciated. It looked so good in the buggy, like the final touch-up. Then he headed for the house to get dressed. The sun sinking was a reminder that it was about time to be leaving for the supper place at Charles Shirk's way to the north, so he'd start in plenty of time.

Reaching his room he opened the closet and got out his shoes. He reached up for his blue shirt on the hanger when he noticed Mother had finished the new shirt. He had known Mother was working on it. A few weeks ago Mother had said if he got material she would make him two shirts, a white one and a blue one. And he had found the material he liked, a light blue with narrow silver lines crossing the blue very near together and every other little square was whitecapped. All dressed, he went in the kitchen and took his hat off and ran the comb through his hair, moistening it down and combing it up and back with a twirl. He carefully set his hat on his head. In doing so he saw the rest of the family resting out in the yard. Dad and Mom were on lawn chairs and Delores was sprawled on a blanket with her nose in a book. William had climbed on Dad's lap, and Rebekah was having an ordeal with her kitten family. Maybe that's what Josiah was doing up the tree.

It was rather rare that his parents were at home on a Sunday afternoon. There was usually visiting to do some place or another.

As he opened the door to go out to the yard, Delores asked him where he was going.

Mother looked up and said, "Oh, do you have the new shirt on? Does it fit all right? One sleeve didn't want to get right."

John Mark stretched out his arms. "Feels all right, but guess I forgot to tell you to make the back a little broader. It is a little tight."

"Oh yes, I think you did say something. I should have changed the patterns right away."

Father reminded him, "Don't forget to come home earlier. It will be a long day tomorrow."

"Yes, I want to if my passengers agree."

"Passengers?" Mother questioned with an emphasis on the "s."

"Yes, sometimes Elizabeth comes home with us if Earl's hired boy isn't around."

John Mark brought Charlotte up from the barn, hitched her to the buggy, and took off down the road a piece, turning into the lane to the south as usual to pick up Irene. He clucked to the horse, turned around, and stopped by the gate.

When he looked up after hearing the door, Helen was coming out to the walk. Rather hesitantly she asked, "Are you looking for someone?"

"Isn't Irene going?" he asked matter-of-factly.

"You mean to Charles's?" she asked.

He nodded. Then she said, "The girls were at Walter Weaver's for dinner and they were going on from there to Charles's."

"Oh," John Mark said. "Maybe she did tell me now that I think of it." While Helen was speaking to him, she blinked her eyes and suddenly an interesting look that John Mark couldn't have named crossed her face.

He waited to hear more but she remained silent, so he thanked her for the information and gave Charlotte the word to go. As she trotted briskly down the road, soft warm breezes swept across John Mark, since the buggy top had been flipped back, letting the breeze drift over him. Here and there the perfume of mown hay filled the air. As Charlotte trotted on, her feet singing on the macadam, he remembered Dad's orders to come home early, as tomorrow they were heading for Dad's home settlement. That settlement had some high winds last week and it did some damage to Uncle Israel's shop and Seranus's barn, so they were going with some others to repair the buildings. They were going to start early and maybe come back later that evening, unless they were needed another day.

As he continued on his way, his mind kept wandering back to the sudden expression that had come over Helen's face. It had made him feel a little uncomfortable, but maybe it was just because he had forgotten that Irene wouldn't be there.

The way was a little farther than he thought, so he was one of the last ones to arrive.

Paul Ray asked him, "Where were you this afternoon? I thought you were coming over to go fishing?"

"I was thinking about it, but then I fell asleep. Where are Chester, Justus, and Levi?" John Mark asked.

"Some of the guys walked to the dam in the back pasture to try out the boat."

In another fifteen minutes, the table waiters, wearing their white aprons, were lined up on the porch, calling everyone to supper.

With the number of boys who started heading for the house John Mark decided he'd let the people who were here before him go for supper first. The remaining boys sat down under the two big shade trees where the other boys had left their chairs empty. Eugene and Joseph were telling the boys about the bicycle ride they took earlier in the day and how they turned off the road and weren't sure where and had biked about fifteen miles until they realized they were on the wrong road. Suddenly a big black dog came silently charging at them. They hadn't noticed him until he was within inches of their legs.

"It's sort of funny now," Eugene said, "but at the time it wasn't funny. We had nothing to defend ourselves. I reached down and picked up a few stones off the side of the road. The dog hesitated, then Joseph slapped his hands together like a shotgun and cried 'Go!' The dog slinked back, and we took off as fast as we could. There was a car coming further back, but we were going too fast to look in our mirrors. Suddenly we heard the tires screech."

"You mean for you or for the dog?" Melvin chuckled.

Eugene said, "We weren't sure. Joseph turned in front of me at the side of the road, so I had trouble controlling my bicycle. Joseph pedaled on down the hill and I followed, slowly gaining control of my bike. When we reached the bottom of the hill, we stopped to look back, but the hill was in our way.

"I stopped the next car and asked if a dog had been hit back there. They said they didn't know. They saw a black dog rising out of the dust at the side of the road, heading quickly across the road, and never looking back. They almost hit him when he ran in front of their car."

Elmer drawled, "Soon the morning paper will read, 'Two young men held hostage by big black dog.'" Elmer always saw the funny side of things.

Then past experiences of narrow escapes were shared. It made you wonder that Elmer was still here to talk about it. They hadn't even noticed that the ones at the table had filed out.

Soon the call rang out, "Supper! Last call for supper!" Just then they spied the boys coming in from the meadow lane and extended the call to them.

As John Mark came into the house, the table waiters ordered them to sit at the table in the living room since the tables in the kitchen were full and waiting. As John Mark came to the end of the kitchen table he noticed Irene and Emma sitting at the end. Remembering his fruitless trip to pick her up, he had to smile. He lifted his eyes and at the same time with a rather startled look she lifted hers. When she recognized him, she blushed and her eyes dropped. He felt—well, he didn't know how he felt. This wasn't Irene's way. She was always friendly and outgoing and seemed like a sister to him. *I wonder why she acted uneasy,* he thought. *She acted as if she heard something about me and it reminded her when she saw me. Well, maybe I will find out this evening on the way home, unless she won't go with me.*

From the living room he couldn't see her end of the table, so he dismissed it from his mind and ate heartily.

He had forgotten the episode and after supper was watching the boys play a lively game of croquet when Levi came to him asking, "By the way, are you leaving early?"

"Who, me?" John Mark asked.

"Yes, you. Are you leaving early?"

"I sure would like to if I can. If it suits Irene."

"Sure, shall I tell her you want to leave early?"

"I don't mean yet. But just earlier." Levi stood nodding his head. He was Irene's cousin. John Mark wondered how Levi knew of his plans tomorrow, but Levi was off before he had a chance to ask.

Later Annie Beth and Frances made remarks to him that he didn't understand. He asked, "What are you saying?"

They chuckled and said, "Never mind." Later as they were sitting on the porch swing a group of girls came around the corner of the house. He recognized Irene, but she avoided looking up.

A few hours later while some of the boys were playing pitch and catch on the lower outside yard, couples were leaving one after another. Sometime later when John Mark checked his watch, Paul Ray came and asked if he was ready to go.

"Yes, I would be if Irene is."

Just then Levi came up behind Paul Ray and overheard the last sentence and said, "Irene is ready anytime." Going up past the house toward his buggy in the back yard, he told some girls to tell Irene he was leaving.

As he hitched up and hopped onto the buggy, he heard girls whistling. He looked around to see who else was hitching up, but he saw no one. Maybe they saw some couple walking.

As he stopped at the gate there were short whistles from behind the house, up the tree, and out by the windmill. *People must be feeling gay tonight*, he thought. When Irene emerged from the group of girls on the porch, it seemed almost as if a flock of whippoorwills had suddenly appeared or if the fireflies started whistling instead of blinking. It was mostly girls' voices, although some boys could be heard further away. The volume increased as Irene stepped on the buggy and the chatter could be heard over the group, but luckily only a few boys were around.

John Mark had just cleared his throat to ask what had come over the girls when halfway out the lane a shrill whistle rang out right beside the buggy and the whole bunch of boys jumped out from behind the hedge of pines. Charlotte took one leap to the other side of the lane. The buggy wheels turned sharply at the bank where it went down steeply into the pasture lane. He heard Irene gasp and she stiffened in her seat. The hold back had unhooked and Charlotte started backing up. Suddenly a few boys were at the horse's head and side and fastened the harness and helped get them headed properly on the lane. Charlotte was stirred up and when she was released she took off running, but John Mark had control and the buggy swept swiftly out the lane. The boys' cheers faded out as he came out to the road.

He spoke to the horse, "Easy, Charlotte. Easy does it," and she relaxed at the sound of his voice. Soon they were out on the road. John Mark chuckled to himself. Irene hadn't said anything yet, so he said, "I'm not chuckling because we almost drove down that steep grade sideways, but it struck me funny how the boys seemed not to be around, then suddenly they exploded out like a blast from behind the pines."

At length she said, breaking the silence of the evening, "I'm glad you can chuckle over it."

Then he chuckled again, "Why wouldn't I?"

"I was afraid you may be insulted."

"Insulted?" he questioned, "At what?"

"By the young folks tonight."

"I deserved it; for had it been someone else, I would have been right there joining in. So I have to take it too. I should feel honored that they even think such a thing," John Mark reasoned. "But what was going on? I mean, were they just silly or did Levi misunderstand me about leaving early?" he asked further.

"Did you really say something about leaving early to Levi?" she asked curiously.

"He came and asked me if I was leaving early and I said I would like to if you wanted to, as we are going away early tomorrow morning. But how Levi knew that, I don't know."

"Oh," she gasped, "it's starting to make sense."

"What makes sense? What did Levi tell you?" John Mark said, looking at her. Had she blushed again?

"He just asked me if it was all right with me that you wanted to leave early, and I said I would be ready anytime you were. But I wondered if you were leaving early. I didn't trust Levi."

"Didn't he tell you why I was leaving early?"

"No, did he ask you why?"

"No, I assumed he must know something about my plans for going down country since he asked me about leaving early."

"That was the only thing I didn't quite understand, but then he just asked you teasingly if you were leaving early and you said you would like to if it was all right with me. That's all Levi needed to hear," Irene said, satisfied she got it figured out.

"I don't catch on," John Mark shrugged. "What's behind all this?"

"Never mind, the young folks were only looking for excitement. I guess it had something to do with the dress I have on," she said meekly.

John Mark squirmed to get his flashlight out of his pocket, saying, "Well, what dress do you have on, a gray wedding dress?" Then he beamed his flashlight right on her. Irene squinted her eyes at the bright light, but watched his face as the truth finally dawned on him. The dress was light blue with narrow silver checks and every other tiny square white-capped. Then he looked at her sincerely, and they both had to blush.

John Mark put his flashlight back in his pocket and said, "This is fun." At length he asked, "Is this the first time you had the dress on?"

"No," she shifted her eyes, "I have had it about a month already."

"And you thought I knew it?" he asked.

"I didn't know; I thought maybe you didn't as I wouldn't expect you would have had a shirt made out of the same material if you had known. But why did you look at me like that when you came in from supper as if you knew something? That's when I noticed it and I thought you did too."

"Oh that," he chuckled, "I have to tell you about that. This evening I drove up to your home to pick you up and Helen came out and wondered what I wanted. She told me that the girls all went somewhere for dinner and wondered if you hadn't told me. Well, I faintly remembered that you did, but I had completely forgotten. When I saw you, I was thinking how foolish I felt, and that I wanted to tell you about it before Helen did."

"Well, that's when I and some girls noticed what shirt you had on and they thought you planned it and they thought I knew about it too. To be sure I didn't say the wrong thing, I didn't say much of anything and they got carried away."

"Now I better understand the expression that came over Helen's face when I was talking to her. I was so innocent. Mother told me she'd make me some shirts if I got the material and this was the material that caught my eye."

Irene took a deep breath and said, "I think maybe we will have the last laugh yet. I have a feeling there will be some boys like Levi and maybe some girls stopping in at my house tonight. Levi wasn't sure what this was all about and since I didn't say much, he thought he knew more than I did."

"Well, I wonder how old they think I am?"

"You wouldn't be the first boy to date before eighteen if that's what you are referring to," Irene said.

"But the first of Clayton Wenger's boys," John Mark answered assuredly.

"I felt sort of bad," Irene admitted, "because I knew that this would be just how I would have acted if I had noticed this about someone else. Then you have to take it too."

"It was fun if you want my honest opinion. Now I know how to do it if I ever want to ask a girl out and don't know how. I order a shirt to match her dress and it happens automatically," John Mark teased himself.

"But," Irene reminded him, "don't forget to make plans about going home early and make sure the boys know it. By the way, where did you say you were going tomorrow?" she asked.

"We are going to Stony Creek settlement where most of Dad's brothers live. They had storms there last week and they damaged Uncle Israel's woodworking shop and Seranus's barn. So we're going down to see if we can help, and Dad wants me to get to bed as we are starting early and likely coming home late in the evening."

"Just drop me off here by the lane," Irene said, slipping out from under the afghan. "So long," she said, "thanks for the ride."

"It was much farther going up than coming back," he admitted as she stepped from the buggy.

Chapter Thirteen

John Mark paused at the door and looked out at the bush in awesome wonder at the color the leaves had taken on in the past weeks. They looked like seven colors of red with gold intermingled with yellow and brown and a tint of green here and there. He had come to school to straighten out the book closet and some of the cabinets, or that is what he ended up doing. He really had come to hunt a master copy that Ida had asked for at the teacher's meeting and in hunting for it, he ended up cleaning out the cabinets that he had never finished before school started.

But now the beauty of the autumn woods was beckoning him. He checked his watch. It was only 2:30. He went back in and got his hat and light jacket and started down the dirt lane. Then he strolled over the newly cut cornfield to the thick part of the bush. He looked up in wonderment. The color of the leaves was so brilliant it almost seemed like a light was shining on them. Already some of the leaves had fallen on the ground, making a colorful pattern, but for the most part, they were still on the trees displaying their beauty.

High above the trees was October's clear bright blue autumn sky. Where could there be more beauty found here on earth than in this thickly wooded area in the midst of autumn's brilliant colors?

He knew this beauty would soon vanish when dreary November days came and the leaves lost their hold, when the light of the colors faded out to brown and came tumbling to the ground. Our life is also ever-changing just like the beauty of these leaves, so soon the wintry time sets in. He walked along deeper in thought, recalling last Sunday's sermon about our life being changeable, today in bloom, but tomorrow the flower falls off and fades. He could not quote the exact words.

As he walked John Mark came to a tree that had fallen over with the branches sprawled across the ground. He sat on the thick part of the trunk and let his mind wander and ponder. He had stored up his thoughts that were pushing to be re-examined, for last evening it was late until he went to bed, and he had felt too tired. Then this morning there were other things to do, and he hadn't taken the time to exercise his thoughts. He looked at the tree where he sat, and thought about what the minister had said a few times lately in church. "As the tree falls, so it will lay" and "As we live, so shall we die," and how the minister had compared these sayings to our lives. Beauty was but for a season; soon it would fade, and so it is with out lives. Blooming today, but the grass withered, the flower falleth off, and so forth. What is important is that we serve our Maker, so we might bloom in eternity.

He had realized his own nothingness and now that he had completed the instruction classes, he, along with the rest of the class, was looking forward to sealing his faith with baptism, the seal of a good conscience.

At times he dreaded the thought of the day when he would be surrounded with so many witnesses, but he passed the thought on. He wouldn't start fearing today. Then his thoughts turned to the day before when school had dismissed early and he had gone to the first teacher's meeting for the new term.

There he saw how time had a way of bringing changes. He met quite a few new faces, people who had been teaching their first year, and some who had quit teaching that were not there. He had been used to meeting them every month. He thought of the experience that the teacher's meeting held for him. They left him with some troubled thoughts. Some of the teachers seemed ill at ease in his presence when he discussed certain things with them.

Others he noticed had been looking his way and before he could give a smile of recognition, they had quickly shifted their gaze. It happened quite a few times that when he looked up, Nancy or Eva had been watching him but always steered away their glances suddenly. And when Eva had asked about how to cope with pupils who never had their work done on time, he tried to share a little advice that another teacher had shared with him once. But Eva had seemed to be in a flutter, not relaxed, the response he had been used to in discussing things with other teachers, and she was no new teacher.

Nancy studied him in silent wonderment. It had made him feel uneasy. He sensed to these few he wasn't just another teacher, and it bothered him. He wanted to be friends with everyone. Once without thinking, he had smiled when Eva had been absentmindedly looking his way. He had not realized until her eyes suddenly lowered and a glow flushed over her complexion that she was uncomfortable with his smile.

But then there were teachers like Lena Jane and Ellen. When he talked to them he could be perfectly himself and get engrossed in deep discussion with satisfying results. They treated him like a brother.

His startling experiences with Nancy and Eva reminded him of something his Dad had asked him: Was it the girls who lured him into teaching school?

Eva was a decent girl and appeared to have many good qualities, and she was a good sport in helping with activities when classes were demonstrated at teacher's meetings. It made him think it would be enjoyable to slip into her school on a regular day and watch her teach. But he felt no admiration, which apparently she was struggling with. The truth was, when he came to meetings he felt like coming home to his big family where they all spoke the same language or they were in the same current. He had no respect of persons and he desired to keep it so.

Nancy, he really didn't know very well. She was rather quiet within the group. he guessed Nancy didn't even admit it to herself that her thoughts were drawn to him.

While thinking about Nancy and Eva, his thoughts turned to that summer evening in July when the young folks made such an uproar when Irene and he left the supper place because the shirt he had on matched her dress. Irene had sort of apologized that evening for the fuss, but he had taken it as a joke. He sort of sensed it had left some scars. Irene had never mentioned it again, not even when he wore that shirt, and he had come to realize that she only wore that dress to church anymore. First he thought she had quit wearing it, but he later discovered she wore it only in church, never to evening gatherings. Maybe because she knows I don't wear the shirt to church. And with that scar it had seemed to change the character of Irene somewhat. Before they would visit openly as a brother and sister, completely relaxed while driving to and from singings or supper places. But now she was a little more, how should he say, she was a little more like some of the teachers he mingled with. More aware of him, as if a little ill at ease or regarding him too highly.

Sometimes he thought of her as more than just Irene, but he didn't like the feeling. He wanted her to be just Irene. When they took Elizabeth along, it was as the pleasant times in the past. The girls in a lively conversation and he commenting on it every once in a while, finding things out he had not known. He was aware that if you had a sister with the young folks, you would find out more interesting things.

He got up from the tree and slowly started retracing his steps with his head bent down in deep thought. He no longer noticed the tri-colored leaves that had been beckoning his attention. As always when he shut off his mind from wandering over the teachers who surrounded his life, when he shut off the churning there was a thought that flowed in unbidden. Freely. It was of the meek timid face that looked up at him when he had stopped at Edgar's desk last December. In his mind he saw the round face with rosy cheeks and the medium black hair neatly combed back. The double natural wave edging the hairline. Her hair had looked freshly watered. And the pleasant smile that had suddenly vanished in timidness. Pale brown eyes that looked soft, almost pleading. But pleading for what? She was one of Edgar's sisters. She looked so different from the twins who were not so friendly and at times a little vain. And to think they were only in sixth grade. Neither did she resemble Mildred who was tall and slender and darker complected and who had an outgoing personality. Edgar said it was Lavina.

What was beyond those pleading eyes? Her smile had looked so sunny but had vanished as a cloud blocking out the sun. He hadn't known where Lavina belonged in the family. He had a time trying to place all the Ringler family. He learned to know Virginia and Mary Ethel whom he had met at times with the young folks. They went to church in the next district. But the young folks usually had their singings together. Once in a while the gatherings were only for the home district. He assumed Mary Ethel was about his own age. She was just now joining church. Virginia had joined the year before. Edgar had informed him of this. Maybe Lavina was just under Mary Ethel, but on second thought, there was Priscilla. She hadn't joined the young folks yet. He had met her a few times when she drove the schoolchildren when it rained. She was early and had tied the horse and had come inside. She resembled her mother a lot, but had lots more energy. She had about the same shade of hair as Lavina, but she displayed it more.

Mary Ethel was somewhat like her father, not so relaxed and, well—he didn't know how to describe her—but Virginia had a smile for everyone. She was gentle like her mother, but not weary at all. She had been dating Reuben, one of the older boys, for a while. John Mark didn't know him too well.

Suddenly a thought struck him. He remembered a while ago seeing Lavina in church and realized with which girls she sat. He decided she had to be older than Priscilla but apparently not old enough to go to singings yet. He tried blocking those gentle, pleading, fragile, brown eyes out from his mind, but he could not. It was looking at a price tag and knowing he could never afford what it was attached to.

*   *   *   *

The time for John Mark's baptism had come. The chilly autumn skies remained clear, and the colored leaves still held their beauty. But this morning the many teams that traveled the road to church didn't take much thought to the beauty of the leaves.

The church house was full as John Mark with the rest of the class filed into the church. It was a sea of faces. John Mark felt himself trembling, but as the forenoon wore on, he relaxed and drank in the words that were coming forth in the sermon. A few visiting ministers were present for the occasion, maybe one was a deacon.

The home bishop, Christian Brubacker, was standing before the congregation expounding the sermon as the Spirit led him. He made mention of the passing beauty of the leaves. "Soon winter will come, the leaves will lose their hold, and the trees will become bare. Likewise one generation comes and another goes. Here a class of young people sits before us today to take the Holy Baptism of water, an outward sign of an inward change." He explained that unless the young folks take hold, the church will not stand for long. "Just as the leaves come into their prime and then die off, so do we older folks die off and younger ones take our place.

"But what I am now thinking of is a writing I came across when I myself was young. It wasn't from our area, but it still left an impression on me. Since the year I joined church we had an experience and thus I was able to better grasp the idea of the second birth. The year I joined church there was one in our group who found it hard to give up the things the church asked her to give up, even thought it was explained that if she died to the old nature and was born again, it would be easier to give up these things. The writing gave details about a girl who stubbornly resisted every plea, and the bishop was about at his wits' end on how to persuade her. He looked out the window and saw an oak tree still clinging to its old leaves. He called her attention to the tree and told her to watch daily and see what would shake the leaves from the tree.

"Maybe my class here isn't aware that even though in the next few weeks or a month most of the trees will shed their leaves, but not all trees will be bare. If you notice, the oak trees cling to their old leaves long after all the others are bare." The bishop compared this to the girl in the writing. "She clung to her old ways and didn't want to give them up. She wasn't giving the second birth a chance. The writing went on to say that all the winds and stormy blasts of winter were powerless to make the leaves drop, but on nice warm spring days when no winds were blowing, she noticed leaves rapidly falling to the ground. New life was coming into the tree and it was budding so it loosened its grip on the old leaves.

Grasping the lesson, she became a penitent and obedient member in the church.

"And so it is today, the baptism cannot help unless there is new life budding in the heart. When new life comes in, it loosens the grip of the old nature and a change comes forth." The bishop then took up the text and many more pleadings and admonishments fell. To John Mark it was mostly a blur when the class was asked the questions and were baptized in the name of the Father, Son, and Holy Ghost.

It was when the bishop beckoned his hand while he was on his knees, saying, "To a new beginning and a new walk of life, give me your hand and rise up." The bishop kissed John Mark and said, "God bless you in your new work. Testify the truth and the truth shall make you free." An overwhelming feeling was settling over John Mark. The few words had suddenly taken on a new meaning he hadn't grasped before.

While the congregation sang its closing song, tears spilled out of his eyes as the truth was sinking in.

On the way home from church, driving alone, John Mark tried to get control of his emotions so he could enjoy the company they had been expecting. Grandma Wenger wanted to come to church, and Uncle Israel came along with her, bringing their whole family.

It sure was good Uncle Israel had a woodworking shop as he had plenty of help coming. The Wenger clan was known to have a majority of boys, but Uncle Israel and his wife Emily were the only ones that had all boys, seven of them. They were always an interesting bunch. The oldest at fourteen was a real young gentleman already, neatly dressed and mature just like Emily had been, and pronouncing some of his words on a different accent. They also had interesting names. The oldest one was Reuben James, then Ralph Jacob, and Roy Justus, Raymond Joel, Ray Joseph, and Rufus John. Each one had the initials R. J., except the youngest one was R., Jr. The "R" stood for Roman, but no one called him Roman, Jr., because his father's name wasn't Roman. The Jr. stood for Israel; his actual name was Roman Israel, but they wrote and called him R. Jr.

116

In the afternoon Dad and Israel had been outside walking around. John Mark had been in another room watching the boys play a game, but they had since run outside. He had been sitting there idle, when he was suddenly aware of Grandma Wenger walking past the door. She must have been resting in Mother and Dad's room. She stopped at the door, and when she saw him sitting there, she carefully stepped inside and with some effort walked nearer to him. He hadn't realized that her walking was so tottery. He saw her eyeing the rocking chair in the corner, so he got up and placed the rocking chair close to her.

"Thank you. My steps aren't so good anymore," she explained as she sat down.

"I didn't know you were having trouble with your walking," John Mark said.

"I thought my arthritis was getting worse, but the doctor thought it was a little more than arthritis." She put her hands on the rocker arms and said, in a calm voice, "I guess I am getting old." She went on to say that she was going to Seranus' for the winter as she can hardly keep house anymore without a lot of Emily's help. "And since Emily has no girl help and she could use the extra rooms, we decided to do so for the winter, as Seranus has two girls out of school and three more in school and also three boys out of school, besides the little girl yet."

She paused a moment and then asked him, quite concerned, "Have the events of the day been hard on you?"

"No, I wouldn't say hard. It was almost more joy than I could grasp," he said with the last words coming out in a tumble but leaving a lump in his throat and tears in his eyes.

Grandma Wenger looked at him a moment, sort of as if doubting him, then asked, "What joy? The work hasn't begun yet."

John Mark cleared his throat and leaned back on the sofa saying, "I mean the thought that was revealed to me as the bishop said that I shall rise to a new beginning and a new life. I just realized then that I now have the same chance everyone else has. I mean I was always an adopted boy, and it just came to me as he told me to rise to a new life and a new beginning that I had the same

117

birth that the rest had. Now it does not matter about my natural birth."

When he looked at her she sat listening intently, leaning forward and spellbound, her mouth half open. He noticed a tear slip down her cheek behind her glasses.

At long last she nodded her head and said in concern, "Hold on to that thought always. There will be times you need that to comfort you. That's why it was revealed to you. Just as Satan came to Jesus after He was baptized, so he also comes to the rest of us to try us, to see if he can get us to fall. But never forget, although Satan is mighty, God is almighty. The afflictions of the righteous are many, but the Lord delivered him out of them all."

Just then Dad and Uncle Israel came in the door. Another conversation was soon going when Dad asked Grandma how it was with her. John Mark tucked the precious counsel in his heart. He wanted to remember her words, and there were a lot more things from today that he wanted to remember.

Chapter Fourteen

The days were getting shorter, and the November air felt quite crisp. It almost felt like snow. It seemed the day was slow in dawning this dreary November morning.

As John Mark drove in the barnyard at Stanley Weaver's, Stanley was coming out the walk toward the barn.

"Why, hello, John Mark. So you haven't forgotten us," he greeted John Mark.

John Mark got out of the buggy and chuckled, "No, I guess you'll have to put up with me this week and maybe more as it's so near dusk going both ways."

"Sure, sure," Stanley said as he pulled on his overshoes that were at the end of the walk. "I was just telling Erma maybe we should say something to you again, that you should just come whenever you want to because we're always glad to see you. Even Walter was wondering where you were."

John Mark smiled to himself at the thought that little Walter remembered him. As he unhitched Charlotte and put her in the barn, he was still thinking of little Walter. Last year he was only a little over two years old, and he couldn't converse much with him. But John Mark enjoyed playing with him and listening to his chatter. But this year it was interesting to visit with him, and Walter was quite willing to talk. Since he was the only child in the family, he got a little bored at times, so he enjoyed anyone who took the time to play with him.

Earlier this fall when he had stayed here a few days when it was raining, John Mark had played hide and seek with Walter in the barn while his parents milked. Minutes later John Mark walked up to the schoolhouse and as usual, everywhere he looked, there were things he wanted to do. He checked a few assignments and then went down in the cellar to check the fire. Coming up he saw those books again that he had laid on the filing cabinet. They weren't using those third-grade reading books this year. They had gotten other ones so he would now take time to pack these away in the closet next to the cellar stairs where they kept the extra books and things. He took the books and carried them to the closet and stood on the chair to put them up on a higher shelf.

He moved a bag away to make room. Then he suddenly wondered what was in the bag. He opened it—white cloth, like diapers! He was puzzled, then he pulled it out. Now he remembered it was the slings he had brought along last year at the end of March when he had that talk with the pupils. A slight smile spread on his face as he remembered the incident. The first day quite a few people had to wear slings. Sometimes one had to have it on only a short time because someone else needed it and he had only a few. But they learned fast. The second week not many were used. They learned to think before they talked and avoided mocking each other. Until the third week was over, none were used. Then he chuckled to himself as he remembered that once the pupils had quickly reminded him that he had to wear one. It was when one of the second graders had come to him at noon to open their jar.

If he remembered right, it was Lloyd Weaver's Lester, and John Mark had eyed the jar and asked, "What is this? It looks like sand." Not to make fun of people's lunches had been part of the rule, so John Mark took his punishment and wore a sling for one session. How handicapped he was!

He took the bag along to his desk and put it on the shelf underneath it. He wanted to take it home. They had no use for them. That term had been so near to the end of the school year that the reminder lasted the remaining days. As he put the bag under his desk, he thought of this new term. It was almost December, but there was not much danger of that problem cropping up again. There were only girls in the eighth grade this year and Lucy and Moses in seventh grade. Lucy was more quiet, and Moses was no troublemaker if he didn't use his jokes at the wrong place. Well no, there was a boy in eighth grade. He kept forgetting, but he was sort of a tonic for the school.

A little before school had started, the Stephen Weaver family moved to the area from across country somewhere. (They were no relation to Lloyd Weaver's.) John Mark expected all kinds of trouble when he met the family for the first time, as they were quite talkative and were dressed in everything top-notch and in order. They were ever so polite, but they just stepped in and made themselves at home. And they were so easygoing. If someone laughed at them, they laughed right along. First he thought the Ringler twins would turn the others against them, as he sensed their politeness rubbed them the wrong way. But the Stephen Weaver children had something about them that drew the pupils to them.

How happy he was when he saw the Ringler twins' reserved way melt away and they began to mingle better than they had ever before. Marilyn was in their grade and somehow she was a tonic to those girls, and Eli James, who was in the eighth grade was a good sport if there ever was one. He coaxed everyone else to be one, too. He lured everyone into games and then rejoiced heartily at his classmates' success. The Hoover children were doing things that they could never do well before.

"Good morning," a group of voices blended, interrupting John Mark's thoughts. The Ringlers and Leinbachs and Shirks were spilling in the door. And right behind them came the Hoovers. He answered their good morning and watched them as they placed their lunch boxes on the shelf and chatted and started the day greeting each other.

A feeling of gratitude swept over him as he realized anew that there was just more happiness and interest in the pupils this year. Stephen Weaver's children had something about them that drew people together. And it seemed to serve as a tonic to the school as this school at the present had the tendency of splitting up into groups. The Weavers weren't ones to just have a few special friends.

He had met the father, Stephen, at a meeting, and he was everything Eli Jonas was and then some. It was the nearest thing to flattery John Mark ever received from the pupils' parents in regard to his teaching. Stephen made John Mark feel as if he had the most important job and was doing it very well. He had seen the mother already but hadn't really met her. She came only twice to the meetings, but hadn't spoken publicly. She didn't have to ask about her children as her husband had touched it all.

At the summer meeting John Mark had asked about how to get time to visit with all the pupils. The smaller ones wanted to visit with him, and then often he didn't get all his work done that he wanted to do before bell time. It was then that he learned that some teachers had a little visiting session right after devotions, taking a ten-minute period when the pupils could reveal events, news, and happenings, and it was worthwhile.

But it took awhile until the pupils got used to going out and playing and waiting until visiting session to visit with him. But by now it was the highlight of the day. And this morning was no exception. Sometimes a pupil would confide something to him that wasn't practical to speak in front of everyone, but usually they waited and visited all together.

The songbooks were put away and the pupils settled into their seats and some raised their hands. Leroy was happy to tell the class that his grandparents were coming for Thanksgiving dinner. His sister Harriet joyfully informed everyone that they were going to kill the cross turkey for Thanksgiving dinner. Then that reminded Roman how his uncle's turkey once attacked him. Mildred said where her family was going for Thanksgiving. Dennis said that the vet was coming to his house because their horse was sick. Florence said that her grandmother had been at her place when she got home last evening. Little Margaret, in first grade, said her father fell down a few steps in the barn and was using crutches; then more questions were asked. Eli Jonas explained that he had twisted his ankle and it was badly sprained. He walked a little on it this morning but went for the crutches again. Bennie was waving his hand. John Mark was looking at the clock; time was running out.

Bennie asked, "Can you stay in the area tomorrow night?"

"Yes, I'm planning to stay at Stanley's for a few days, maybe all week. Why?"

Floyd and Bennie both talked at once. "You are invited to come for supper. You can stay for the night if you want to."

"Tell your mother, thank you for the invitation. I plan to come for supper. What time?" The Shirk boys had a time deciding what time they eat. They ate after chores, but no one knew what time that was. They finally decided it was sometime between six and seven.

It was time to begin classes and another day had started at Timber Lock School. It would be another busy day with six first graders; a lot of time could escape unnoticed. And with Edgar, well, it was like having nine grades. But in some ways he took part in his grade's lessons. He could help discuss the reading story if someone had read the story to him.

It was the next evening when he had dismissed the pupils that Bennie reminded him, "Don't forget to come for supper." He said it as he went out the door. John Mark had momentarily forgotten. Just thinking about supper made him hungry. There were still some hours until six o'clock, he thought as he looked over the stack of papers and workbooks to check. The eighth grade had a difficult time with arithmetic problems and then there were essays to check for English class, so the checking piled up while he had helped the pupils with some of their essays.

He reached for the workbooks and settled down with his red pencil and answer book. But before the checking was all done John Mark was going through files getting papers ready for first and second grade for the next day. Then he found an art paper on his desk that was handed in late. It reminded him that he had promised the pupils he would put up the new art pictures by the next day. Soon the ever-racing clock showed a little after five. He quickly straightened up his desk and fixed the fire. Then he went to Stanley's to get a bicycle and to tell them he was going away. He had forgotten to tell them.

Arriving at Christ Shirk's, Norman, who had started first grade that year, met him at the barn entrance saying, "I was watching for you long already. Gerald is here in the barn feeding."

Just then Gerald came with a wheelbarrow of silage and grinned at him saying, "Norman was watching a whole hour for you already." Then he added, "Dad and some of the others are down in the pig barn." Norman pointed down to the pig barn and led the way, but half way down they met Bennie and Ammon coming toward them.

Ammon asked him eagerly, "Want to come to the shop to see what Gerald is making?" Bennie went on ahead and lit a lantern in the shop where Gerald soon joined them. John Mark could see that Gerald now played with wood, saw, and nails instead of scissors, cardboard, and paste.

John Mark studied the structure. It was some kind of weather vane on a round board. Tin cans, which had been cut in half, were fastened to the bottom part of the round platform and were supposed to catch the wind. He was working at cutting out horses that he wanted to paint and put on the top of the platform. Thus when the cans caught the wind, the platform went around, making the horses march in a circle.

Gerald came over and explained, "I saw one at my cousin's place in another state. They had it on top of the wash line post. I wanted to see if I could make one that worked. The first one didn't, so I had to write to them. Now I'm trying again."

Suddenly Bennie said, "Listen. I think Dad's calling us for supper."

"Oh," Gerald said in surprise, "I thought he was still down at the pig barn."

Minutes later they gathered with the rest of the family around the Shirks' stretched out table which served their growing family.

The meal had begun and Christian asked while looking at John Mark, "I suppose Gerald was showing you his project in the shop? I saw the light on in there." John Mark nodded and Christian went on explaining how the hub of the weather vane was made, part of it was the inside hub of a bicycle wheel. John Mark listened with interest while he took a piece of homemade bread from the plate being passed around and spread butter on it slowly while listening to Christian. He then spread on homemade apple butter and looked at Christian's wife who was helping the little ones fill their plates.

He said, "This looks good. I haven't had apple butter for a long time."

Christian's wife looked up saying, "I too think it's good for a change again. That's why we have Lavina here to get some things finished. I just wasn't getting bread baked and the boys complained that there was never any cake or cookies around, yet it seems I bake something about every day." John Mark was only half listening while Mrs. Shirk continued explaining that they did the butchering and mending and were baking now and cooking apple butter. "Soon we might get to clean house and do some sewing while Lavina is here. The boys have been asking for a while that we invite you to come, and I thought now was a good time when we have a little more good things around to eat." John Mark reached for the plate that Floyd was handing him.

Floyd held it while asking, "Mother, may I have more than one liver patty?"

"I guess another half," Mrs. Shirk answered, looking at him as if wondering where in his stomach he would put that yet.

John Mark picked up his fork and guided a tender rich liver patty onto his plate. Then came the sliced potatoes with cream and butter, but his mind was also trying to listen to Christian as he talked about the corn he was still husking. John Mark began to wonder what Mrs. Shirk had said. It sounded like their daughter wasn't home regularly, but Lavina didn't sound quite right. The boys had at times talked about her. He thought it was something like Ella Mae. He dipped out some baked beans and took a quick glance down the table to the left, and then a lump came in his throat that made him cough.

Lavina Ringler? The food seemed to stick in his throat and wouldn't go up or down. Seconds before he felt so hungry. He hadn't looked around at the family as they were waiting on them when they came in, and then he had been visiting with Christian or rather Christian was visiting with him. Now he looked around the table. He saw all the boys that went to school, plus Gerald who was out of school this year, and Norman who just started this year. Then he saw a little boy about three years old and two little girls, one who probably would go to school soon and then one who just grew out of babyhood.

Floyd suddenly said almost urgently, "Teacher, here?" John Mark awoke back to life and took the cheese dish that Floyd had been trying to hand to him.

Mrs. Shirk looked at him and Floyd wonderingly, then said, "Floyd, you must be more patient. John Mark, were you looking for something?" John Mark felt embarrassed. He wanted to know something but now. The volume had become lower, and it suddenly was almost quiet.

Without looking up he said, "I guess I'm a little confused. I thought you had an older girl yet," he motioned over to the two smaller girls.

"No, just Ruthie and Lillian here," Christian said, as he brushed his hand over Ruthie's disheveled hair. Then he looked at Lillian, the oldest of the girls, saying, "The boys are trying to get her to eat more so she is soon big enough to wash dishes three times a day."

In a lower tone John Mark asked Gerald who shared the end of the table with him. "I thought you had a sister that was named Ella Mae or something like that?"

"No, no. That is our cousin who comes to help us at times."

"Who is our cousin?" Ammon piped up, hearing some of the conversation.

"Ella Mae," Floyd quickly answered. "Teacher thought she was our sister."

"I wish," Gerald said wistfully, "then we'd graduate from washing dishes and ceilings and—" he faltered for words.

Then Floyd added, "—and folding wash and cleaning upstairs."

"No, Lavina can bake better cookies than Ella Mae can," Norman said seriously from behind the table on the bench next to his smallest brother. Everyone laughed at his serious expression. Christian himself had a good chuckle. John Mark, still smiling, took a glance at Lavina, wondering if she heard the praise. She had a humble, surprised look on her face. Then suddenly, as if feeling everyone's eyes on her, she lifted her eyes, but for only a second. Then the amused little smile dropped from her eyes, and she looked as if she wanted to disappear under the table.

John Mark managed to force down a little dessert. He lifted his eyes a few times but Lavina never looked up. She was again fading away, like that day in school, hoping the boys would soon file out in silence again, letting her be unknown.

Before John Mark left the table, Mrs. Shirk brought a box of books to him wondering if he was interested in any of them. They had gotten them at a sale and the boys thought they would be good library books.

While John Mark and Christian looked at the books and read some and discussed them, John Mark was very little aware of what else was going on until later when Ammon came and was almost pulling him saying, "Come, teacher, here."

John Mark looked up and said, "I'm only a teacher in school. Here I am John Mark." He had been listening to Christian while rising up to Ammon's beckoning. John Mark started following him. Before he realized what had happened, John Mark was led into the living room and a stack of Dutch Blitz cards was handed to him.

"Yes, yes," Floyd cheered. "Now maybe someone can beat Lavina," he said while moving over to make room for John Mark.

But Gerald said, "Don't sit too close. I need room to move fast." Thus the Blitz game was on.

Roman, who wasn't helping, said, "Teacher, here, put your nine out. Here, there is a two on your Blitz pile." Gerald was standing up and handing out cards as if his life depended on it.

Ammon took a quick look at Lavina then asked, sort of unbelieving, "Your six?" Bennie clapped his hands victoriously when Gerald announced, "Blitz!"

"That is the first time Gerald beat Lavina in a long time." The second game followed with John Mark winning. How the boys rejoiced!

John Mark sensed that Lavina was usually a very swift player, but now she seemed sort of in a daze like some pupils were when visitors came and it became difficult for them to concentrate. Floyd and Bennie silently looked her way.

Then Bennie said a bit alarmed to Lavina, "Are you tired?" She never lifted her eyes, only took a deep breath.

Roman put another game before them, pushing the Blitz cards aside. John Mark read, "Chinese Checkers."

"Don't you know how to play it?" Ammon asked.

"Not really. I saw it played already in school, but I didn't help in a long time."

"Here, you watch," Bennie instructed. "You can help the next time." Such a confusion of jumping over marbles. The next game he tried to help but even then the boys kept giving him orders, "Here, jump over these before she moves them away," or "No, take the back one first; that takes you further." It did not help. Sighs of displeasure rose when Lavina won the second game.

"Here, give me the blue marbles," John Mark said. "I think I understand now."

The next game was quieter; the boys seemed to be holding their breath. John Mark was getting his marbles home as quickly as Lavina was. The boys even missed some of their good moves because they were watching John Mark so much. It was John Mark's move. He saw a route that would get his second to last marble right next to home. Then he suddenly realized that if he moved that one, it would take away the one Lavina probably was planning to jump over to get hers almost home. Seeing it was the nearest route, he moved that one.

Lavina picked up her hand to move a marble, then got a questioning look on her face like "Let's see, how was I going to move?" Then she looked up and saw his knowing look. Her pale brown eyes smiled tenderly. For once they didn't look pleading but rather gentle and understanding, but only for a moment. As a cloud covers the sun, her glance dropped and wouldn't lift again.

A few more moves were made and John Mark landed his last marble home. Gerald had two more to get home, and Lavina had only one more move. The boys rejoiced heartily but were soon interrupted when Bennie came with a handful of chewy oatmeal cookies.

Ammon said, "Bennie, we may not have more than two at a time." Bennie shrugged his shoulders unconcerned as he showed his pile of cookies in each hand. Norman begged some from him, and Gerald grabbed one and with a few big bites, he had it in his mouth before Bennie could protest.

Then Floyd came with a filled doughnut. "Here, where did you find these?" Gerald asked, quickly swallowing his cookie.

"It's my secret," Floyd said.

Bennie said, "I don't care; the cookies are better. I hope she bakes twelve hundred dozen before she goes home."

"Bennie!" Lavina exclaimed, alarmed, as Bennie looked at her mischievously.

They were laying out the marbles again, but John Mark stood up and said, "Well, I will have to be going. Thanks for the evening. I haven't played games for a long time."

"Are you going all the way home tonight?" Lavina asked.

John Mark looked up at her surprised. It was the first time she had spoken to him directly that evening. He said, "No, only back to Stanley's." But before he was half done with his answer, her glance fell without rising again.

John Mark went out to the kitchen and thanked Christian for the invitation and slipped out the door. There were scenes that were deeply imprinted on his heart tonight. Were they shared? His thoughts were tumbling over each other on the way home. The road had a fine covering of snow on it. Now and then he felt a little wetness on his face. When he looked up, he faintly saw the moon but quickly the clouds covered it again and he felt more wetness on his face.

Back at Stanley's he quietly went upstairs and prepared for bed. It was time for his usual evening prayer, but his heart was so full he couldn't concentrate. He went over to the window and looked out into the night. He saw a dim circle where the moon was barely hidden. Then it got brighter, but when he thought the moon would become visible, heavier clouds came and covered any sight of it. For a full half hour he sat there on his knees looking out the window, reliving the evening. *Why did Lavina ask if I was going all the way home? Did she care if I would have had a far way to go? Why does Lavina always drop her glance instead of smiling? Why do those pale brown eyes seem to hold fear? Why do—?*

John Mark wondered many things, some he didn't form into words, only pictured them. He remembered how the boys looked at Lavina when they were playing games. He sensed that was not

129

how the game had been going before he was dragged in. Suddenly he saw the clouds had passed and the moon shone beautifully. But already another cloud was edging in and starting to hide the moon.

The clouds reminded John Mark of Lavina's face this evening. When he thought she might smile, her eyes clouded over. He thought of those few precious moments when she had looked up at him after he had destroyed her path of marbles. And when she asked if he was going all the way home. Both times it seemed she had done it unaware and then turned away when she realized what she had done. Warm circles wrapped around his heart when he thought of these moments. Were they shared? He looked out at the sky again. The moon was nowhere in sight. *I may as well quit longing,* he thought. Here he was again looking at a price tag he knew he couldn't afford. And she must be so young yet. He thought of his own eighteenth birthday a few weeks away.

Then his thoughts turned to Irene. It seemed uninteresting. Then he wondered how it would be to have a chance to take Lavina along to the singing and visit all the way there and home again. *Maybe some day I can find out.* He looked at the sky again. No moon in sight. He could see it was lightly snowing. Maybe tomorrow the clouds in the sky and in his life would roll away, he thought. He knelt by his bed to pray but no words came.

He finally uttered, "Lord, You know what I have need of even before I pray. Help me to see Thy will."

After he was in bed, John Mark kept thinking of the unexpected turn of the day's events. He had no anxious thoughts of going to Christian's for supper. *If only I could always walk so trustingly and rely on a stronger guidance,* he thought. As he lay there in bed the thought came to him again. Did it mean anything to Lavina? How could it? It was only him. He felt so worthless. While dwelling on what her thoughts may have been, he remembered that the Shirk boys' expression showed that the game wasn't going like it usually did. He remembered that one of them had asked if she was tired. His train of thought continued. Sometimes he found that he was more dreaming than thinking. It didn't make sense anymore.

Suddenly he jerked. He thought his heart was beating too fast. Maybe he was sick. First he felt light, as if he had no strength. Slowly he felt his muscles responding, but what had awakened him? He looked at the clock. It was only 11:30. He felt all sleep was gone. It was dark, but he thought the sun was shining brightly. What actually had happened? It must have been a dream. He thought he was at a school meeting and was sitting out in the schoolyard watching a busy road. People and vehicles were going past. It seemed he was waiting for a driver. It was school meeting but still it was in Aunt Naomi's yard. He heard singing; and when he looked, there were a group of girls walking over the rise of the road below Naomi's house.

They were singing, "And the clouds should roll away." He knew some of the girls: Ellen and Irene and Lena Jane and Nancy. Then there was one whose face he couldn't see. The group kept walking and passed under a tree which shaded the sun and suddenly he saw. The one girl was Lavina! That was when his strength left him. Then she softly said, "John Mark, have you come all this way?" Her eyes never shifted or fell, just softly, kindly looked at him. When he tried to ask her where they were going, he awoke. He just couldn't recall the picture that had been so vivid. He got up and looked out the window. "Yes, the clouds have rolled away." The moon was shining.

Chapter Fifteen

The January day, though a bit nippy, seemed cheerful after the cold, dreary weather of last week. It seemed cozy inside with the sun shining through the window. The sun created a lot of warmth and it felt like a greenhouse right at the window. But when the door opened, one could feel the crisp winter breeze. Never-the-less, the pupils donned their caps and coats and ran out to make up for when the weather had forced them to play inside on those damp, dreary, shivery days.

John Mark paused for a moment in the warmth of the sun's rays that were streaming in the window where he stood sharpening his pencils. He took a moment to watch the activity out on the playground. The younger ones stood in a circle playing Drop the Handkerchief. The merry shouts and laughs and rosy cheeks were a telltale sign that the students were enjoying themselves to the fullest, breathing in the fresh air again after days of playing inside.

The older ones were playing Four Corners with renewed energy. For a few minutes John Mark wished he was the age of those children. Ever since Stephen Weaver's children came to school, Four Corners was the favorite and most lively game for the upper grades.

Slowly, John Mark turned back to the schoolroom. He wanted to hunt poems for the lower grades. Then he saw the figure at the blackboard. He had almost forgotten that he wasn't alone in the schoolhouse. Edgar was still at the blackboard, drawing pictures to amuse himself. He had been absent two days, and yesterday he returned but was still quite listless. Today he seemed a little brighter, but John Mark could still tell he had a cold. Earlier in the day John Mark saw Edgar had been resting his head on his desk. He didn't go out to play with the rest of the children and John Mark was glad, as his cold still seemed rather persistent.

When John Mark walked over to the filing cabinet to hunt for his folder of poems, Edgar came toward the table where a puzzle was sprawled out and started concentrating on it. It was while John Mark was selecting the poems that Edgar walked up to him and started talking about a sled they had just gotten at a sale and then he started talking about a shirt Mary Ethel was sewing for him. Maybe he could wear it tomorrow.

John Mark closed his book and asked, "Do you feel better or are you still feeling sick?"

"I don't have to cough so much, but I feel tired and my throat feels better when I don't go outside," he said meekly. Then he added, "Mother said I should bring my books along home to do the pages I didn't do when I was absent. Maybe the girls can help me."

John Mark took a deep breath, nodded his head, and said, "That would be all right. Do you like your sisters to help you?"

Edgar nodded. Then as an afterthought he added, "Lavina isn't at home and Mary Ethel must sew a lot of things."

"Where is Virginia?" John Mark asked.

"She doesn't like to help me with my books," he answered.

"What about Priscilla?" John Mark asked further.

"She works in the store we have," he answered.

"Where is Lavina that she isn't at home?" John Mark asked pressing the matter.

"Helping to butcher the cow."

"Helping who?" he asked. Edgar shrugged his shoulders, not knowing.

After a moment John Mark asked Edgar, "How old is Lavina?" He shrugged his shoulders. Then John Mark remembered that he must act out numbers for him. After a moment he asked Edgar, "Who is the oldest in your family?"

Then he answered, "Dad."

John Mark tried again and said, "Who was your father and mother's first baby?"

Edgar replied, "Lavina was the first baby; when she got big, Virginia was a baby, then Mary Ethel and—"

"Oh, I wonder," John Mark cut him off, "I guess Virginia was the first baby?"

Edgar shook his head disagreeing and said, "No, no."

"Well, why do Virginia and Mary Ethel go to singings and Lavina doesn't?"

Edgar propped his arms on the table, leaned his chin on the palm of his hands, and looked blankly out of eyes that were bleary from his head cold.

At length, as if he had just heard what John Mark asked he said, "Virginia goes to singings with Reuben. Sometimes Mary Ethel and Lavina take Sandy, but when it's dark they go with Elton." Then he started talking about Menno and his horse that always causes a scene when starting off. But why was he talking about Menno? Then John Mark remembered that Menno had recently started going steady with Mary Ethel.

"You say when it is dark they go with Elton?" John Mark questioned.

"Yes, you know, Cousin Roy's big brother Elton." So, Elton Newswanger was their cousin. There was no other Elton with the young folks. At first he didn't know why they would go with Elton as he did not live along their road. He would have to drive farther, but then he was related. But things still didn't make sense. He talked as if Lavina was the oldest and went with her sisters to singings. But he didn't know if Edgar knew what he was talking about, as blank as he looked with his cold or maybe more dull than blank. He might not have things quite clear as John Mark never saw Lavina at a singing though her sisters were there.

*　　*　　*　　*

As the January days lengthened, the cold strengthened, Dad had always said. Thus the buggy wheels creaked as they drove over the frozen cold snow as John Mark was driving to the singing.

While he waited until the horse was more cooled off before blanketing her, John Mark saw other buggies arriving. As he was blanketing Charlotte, he saw Menno's horse acting up as he stopped to let off his passengers. He saw Mary Ethel and Virginia going toward the house. Later he noticed Elton pulling up at the walk. John Mark watched a girl climb off but it wasn't who he was looking for. He wasn't sure who it was, but then another girl followed. His heart leaped. Yes, in the shadow's light he could see it was Lavina. He stared as they walked briskly toward the house and disappeared in the door.

He felt nervous as if he was at his first singing. As John Mark filed into the house with the rest of the boys, the cozy warmth from the room seemed to welcome them. The small stove in the room drew the boys and they warmed their fingers. John Mark looked around the room and greeted some of the boys by their names.

Justus scratched his head and made his way over to him saying, "You're the guy I am looking for."

"I hope it's something good," John Mark answered, trying to sound scared.

"We need a few more drivers for tomorrow, as there are some Indiana young folks around who want to visit the community."

"Are they here tonight?" John Mark asked.

"No, I don't think so. They'll be in church tomorrow."

John Mark shrugged his shoulders. "I really don't have much planned for tomorrow." As Justus continued with the plans for the travelers tomorrow, the door opened and a few boys came in. John Mark gasped in surprise.

Justus looked at him and asked, "Is something the matter with you?"

"Oh no, nothing, I didn't hear what you said. I was just surprised to see Cousin Anthony come in."

"Oh, didn't you see him outside? He's been here ever since I came."

"Are there more folks here from Stony Creek?"

"Not that I noticed," and then he continued talking about the plans for tomorrow.

From out in the kitchen the feminine voices singing "Sweet hour of prayer, sweet hour of prayer, that calls me from a world of care," rose and blended making the boys gather their songbooks and run combs through their hair. They became quiet and filed into the kitchen, filling up the rest of the table. Others stood behind the table while the remainder sat on chairs farther away.

John Mark managed to get next to Anthony who was standing behind the table. Once between songs, he asked Anthony if he was coming for the night. But he said that Mark, a cousin from the other side, had told him to come along for the night. Later John Mark asked him to come to the dinner place where the Indiana folks and some more of the young folks would be, but Anthony had shrugged his shoulders and said something about not knowing if he was staying all day.

When they rested awhile between songs and people were getting drinks, John Mark gathered that Anthony had come up with a guy in a truck who was coming this way and that he brought his bike along and would go home on the bicycle.

Anthony, Uncle Seranus's oldest boy, was some years older than John Mark. Some months ago John Mark had a singing at home and some of his cousins and others had come from Stony Creek. Then in December, Anthony had come again with a group of young folks to a supper place. John Mark enjoyed having one of his cousins, one of Dad's relations, among his friends. Although Anthony's brother Cletus was nearer his age and they had had many enjoyable times together, he was more talkative than Anthony was.

It wasn't until they were almost finished singing and John Mark happened to see Mary Ethel that he remembered about Lavina. His heart started fluttering, remembering the eagerness earlier in the evening. At the other side of the table Virginia sat with Irene. When the next song was selected, he took another glance over the kitchen. Now and then one of the girls met his glance as he swept it over the kitchen; some of them gave him a slight smile of recognition. But he could not spot the face he was searching for. *She might be in back of me,* he thought, but then he remembered there were boys sitting on the chairs behind him.

When the singing died down and refreshments were set out, people gathered around to visit. Jay Paul and Justus continued making plans for hauling the travelers around tomorrow. John Mark gathered that Elizabeth would be going along and one of Justus's sisters and they now were supposed to pick them up at the Martin's and take them to church.

An hour later, as John Mark was heading home with Irene and Elizabeth riding along, he was thinking of the events of the next day, going up to Martin's to pick up the travelers and take them to church, going to Abner's for dinner where most of the young folks would be going, and then making a call or two in the afternoon before the supper place. He couldn't remember if he had heard where the supper place was. The last he heard, they weren't sure. Now his thoughts were on the conversation he had shared with Anthony. He said Mommy Wenger wasn't so good. Her walking was poor, her eyesight was failing, and she was having a lot of pain in her knees. John Mark jolted back to life when a car, crowding them off the road, barely missed them. After some gasps from the girls and speaking assuringly to Charlotte, they continued on with John Mark being a little more alert.

The girls continued the conversation that John Mark had been deaf to while he had been having his own thoughts.

Now he heard Irene say, "I know, that's what Mary and I discussed already. People could even think she is stuck-up."

"Anyhow toward Virginia and Mary Ethel," Elizabeth said.

"I know," Irene put in.

"She is so pleasant when we girls are together," Elizabeth said.

Irene added, "I've wondered already if any boys even know her? Sometimes I wonder if she is as bashful as she lets on."

"I've wondered too, but when I really got to know Lavina better I found out she really does have struggles. She lets her fears, or whatever you call it, master her, and—well, she should forgive," Elizabeth said.

"But we don't know how it would be."

"I know, but we have to accept it. We haven't walked in her shoes."

"But to think what a relaxed interesting person she can be when we girls are all together."

"I know," Elizabeth said, as she struggled out from under the blankets as John Mark pulled up at her yard gate.

Silently, John Mark and Irene headed out the lane traveling home. At length John Mark asked, "Did I understand you and Elizabeth say that Lavina's quite bashful?" For a few seconds John Mark thought Irene wouldn't reply.

Then she slowly, as if it was a difficult matter, said, "Depends on who she is with. We girls know her as a naturally interesting person, but inferior to life."

When Irene didn't continue, John Mark asked, "She goes with the folks—or doesn't she?"

Irene looked over at him in silence and he stammered, "I thought she did, or I mean I thought she—she may be too young, but I gather maybe she is older than Virginia or Mary Ethel?"

Irene gasped and said, "I didn't know it was that bad that the boys didn't even know she was there."

"Was she there tonight?" he asked.

"Yes, Elton sees that she has a way, since Mary Ethel and Virginia are dating." John Mark had a lot of questions, but he didn't ask any more. He had enough to think about. And Irene seemed lost in her own thoughts. She hadn't done much more than answer his questions.

As they pulled in at Irene's drive, she asked, "What about tomorrow? Are you going to Abner's where the Indiana folks are going and whoever else wants to come?"

"Oh yes, I am supposed to help haul them. I guess I didn't tell you. Are you also helping?" he asked.

"No one said anything," she replied.

"I am to fetch some at Martin's and take them to church. Elizabeth and Justus and his sister and Jay Paul are some of the ones that are helping and going along. If you need transportation to get to Abner's from church, you have to talk to Elizabeth. I have no idea if there's extra room."

"Don't worry, I can always find a way," Irene said as she got off and thanked him.

It was while the young folks were at Abner's for dinner that in the afternoon some were singing. Others were scattered around visiting and John Mark had asked Mark where Anthony was.

"Oh, I think he left for home right after church. After Irene refused him he lost interest around here." John Mark stared at him open-mouthed. When Mark remained quiet, he finally asked, "Do you mean Anthony asked Irene for a date and she refused him?"

"That's the way I understand it," Mark answered matter-of-factly, as if it was an everyday event. So Anthony had been coming to the area on account of girl interest. He was twenty-one and never had a girl as far as John Mark knew. Irene was a year or so older than John Mark; surely she wouldn't have turned him down. Well, she just didn't know him; that's all there was to it, he reasoned to himself.

Later Justus roused himself from his stupor. "We better get moving with our people if we want to make a visit to Weaver Martin's before supper." John Mark had one of the Indiana boys and Elizabeth in his buggy to go to Weaver Martin's. He really wanted to ask Elizabeth if it was true about Anthony, but now wasn't the time.

As the afternoon wore on, the question dimmed from his memory. The travelers were an interesting bunch and as the day continued on, John Mark learned to know them better. John Mark had his team ready and the girls were waiting at the end of the walk at Weaver Martin's, ready to be picked up. John Mark asked Justus, "Where did you say we were going for supper, to Ammon's?"

"No, the plans got changed. We are going up to Nevin Ringler's. That's the area they will be visiting tomorrow."

If John Mark thought his mind was churning before, it was nothing compared to the tumble his thoughts were doing now. His hands didn't even want to stay steady. All the thoughts and memories returned to his mind of what Elizabeth and Irene had been discussing on the way home from the singing. One of the Indiana boys hopped on his buggy, and when he stopped at the walk, Justus's sister Esther climbed on and they were on their way with the rest of the buggies following behind. The Indiana boy, who John Mark by now remembered as Leon, struck up a conversation with

Anna. John Mark tried to stay alert, but a strong force ruled his mind.

Amid the anxiety and turmoil his mind was battling, he suddenly became more conscious when he heard Leon say, "Oh, he doesn't say anything; he must be getting tired of us."

"Have you been talking to me?" John Mark asked innocently.

Anna laughed heartily and Leon said, "Never mind." At the same time they came up the west road toward Timber Lock School. They turned down the south road where it goes toward the thick cluster of bushes on either side which make it look like a woods, the road where some of his pupils walked down every day. The sight of the schoolhouse almost made him gasp. He had completely forgotten his school and his pupils, and he wondered if he could act like a teacher tomorrow. He didn't know which he dreaded most, the supper tonight or school tomorrow.

Suddenly, as if an idea had just struck her, Anna exclaimed, "Oh by the way, John Mark, aren't you going to tell Leon that this is your school?"

Leon echoed, "Your school? Did you get your education here?"

John Mark chuckled, "No, it's where I am supposed to teach education."

"Oh, no wonder the sight of the schoolhouse silenced you. Were your thoughts good or bad? I mean are you glad to see Monday morning coming?"

"Usually, I come to school to relax, but this weekend has been so full, I have forgotten I am a teacher and it almost scares me," John Mark truthfully admitted. Anna and Leon laughed, thinking it was a joke.

At Nevin's they had no more than unhitched and taken off their wraps when they were called to supper. Some of the neighboring young folk were there, and the girls' partners and a few cousins were also invited for supper. So the table was full before everyone was seated. Mrs. Ringler and most of her daughters weren't at the table. Priscilla and Mary Ethel graciously waited on the table. Virginia was washing the dishes. John Mark took another look around the table. Maybe Lavina was at the table after all. Oh no, maybe—well, maybe she wasn't at home as she often worked as a hired girl somewhere. He gathered this from Edgar's talk in school.

Mrs. Ringler was bustling around clearing the dishes off the table. Edgar gave him a warm smile as John Mark looked around the table. The twins pretended they didn't know him. Edgar was surprisingly quiet, but missed nothing and almost forgot to eat. He watched intently as the boys visited back and forth, enjoying every moment. At that moment the cellar door opened and Lavina came through carrying a spoon and disappeared into the little corner where the cooking was done. Later, as they were leaving the table, John Mark caught a glimpse of Lavina going across the built-in porch. The few glimpses he got of Lavina were brief, but they were long enough to leave their effect on him. He got out his handkerchief and blew his nose, and blinked his misty eyes.

Rising from the table, most of the boys went into the parlor. But Chester, who was also there for supper, had shared with John Mark his desire to go out and look at the German Shepherd puppies that Nevin's raised. So they went out the closed-in porch. Suddenly and unexpectedly they met up with Lavina who was coming out from the wash house with a bowl of fruit salad.

Chester stopped in his tracks and put up his hands saying, "This is what we call a head-on collision." Lavina jumped a little in surprise.

When John Mark lowered his eyes wondering how Lavina would react to this, he was startled to meet her soft, pale-brown eyes, looking rather apologetically. A sudden, shy smile spread across her blushed face. As suddenly as she appeared, she fled. Chester was still chuckling as they went out the door saying something about a bowl of fruit in your face.

Later Chester and John Mark came into the parlor from the outside door passing the other boys who were going out.

Chester said, "Good, I take the sofa." He sprawled himself on it, pretending he would take a good, overdue nap.

John Mark picked up a scrapbook that was on the end table beside the sofa and took it over to the chair to read. He found it to contain news clippings of familiar people from the area that had appeared in newspapers long ago. Some of the accidents and events were of things John Mark had heard Mother talk about already. A few of the events had happened in his time. He looked up to say something to Chester about one of the articles and realized that he truly was sleeping. He heard the girls having an enjoyable time out in the kitchen. While he was reading the next article, he looked up when there was an outburst of laughter in the kitchen, and when he looked up, he thought he saw movement in the room. He looked up again and saw that when he looked at the mirror on the parlor wall, it reflected part of the activity from the kitchen.

The cluster of girls were sitting in a crooked half-circle, visiting back and forth. A handful of them got up and grouped around Anna who was showing them something. Later Mary Ethel was holding everyone's attention. It must have been a story that held them spellbound. He couldn't hear much of the conversation.

Then Lavina and Lorene, one of the Indiana girls, stepped in the group. A few of the girls jumped, and Lavina's face showed some kind of command and motioned for them to wait. He couldn't hear the conversation but the gasps and chuckles he could hear and see from their expressions. John Mark sat spellbound. The scrapbook was laid aside. Lavina, by all appearances, was relaxed. Sometimes her expressions looked rather mischievous, but mostly her eyes, which normally were often covered by shyness, were gentle and serene. Once he thought she must have glanced into the parlor as it seemed she had looked directly at him, but apparently not, as her expression didn't change, and her relaxed manner continued. The door, bumped from the outside, flew open and three boys came pouring in.

Reuben was saying, "Well, you have to open the door first."

Kevin, the tall guy from Indiana, said, "I suppose you know pretty well how to open this door by now."

Reuben said, "Oh no, she opens it for me." Kevin gave a low whistle and Chester jumped up from the sofa. After watching and listening to the boys' good humor, it was a little while until John Mark remembered the scene he had been watching. Then more boys poured in and some of them stopped at the kitchen doorway. After the doorway was cleared, John Mark looked at the mirror again. The girls were still active, but at least one was missing. Where had she disappeared to? Then the thought occurred to him. She was probably somewhere further in the background since the boys came in so noisily. She likely thought the boys were all outside and she was like Irene said, "enjoyable to be with when just us girls are together."

John Mark checked his watch and got up and walked to the kitchen door. The girls looked up and a few asked him who he was hunting. When Elizabeth looked up, he said he was going home since the travelers were going to walk to nearby neighbors for the night and their suitcases were there already. Elizabeth nodded and glanced at the clock. When John Mark turned around he saw Lavina and Rhoda halfway down the hall with their back turned and in deep conversation.

By now most of the snow was cleared off the road but there were still patches of packed snow that made the wheels creak as they glided over them. It was another frosty night. High overhead the stars were twinkling brightly as John Mark picked up Elizabeth and headed out the lane. He noticed some more boys were getting their teams ready. Now and then Elizabeth made a remark about something, but mostly they drove in silence.

As they crossed Route 10 they remarked about the accident that had been on that corner the other week. Then later Elizabeth reminded him, "You are pretty quiet tonight. Are you sleeping?"

"I should be. I can't believe that I have to teach school tomorrow. This was a full weekend. Usually not so much is going on over the winter."

"Full?" she questioned. "You mean a dinner and supper place."

"And a singing. It seems like longer ago than just last night that we came home from the singing," he replied, as he was thinking of the conversation that Elizabeth and Irene had on the way home.

Then Elizabeth said, "There's more to look forward to. Irene has a singing in two weeks."

"Irene has?" he asked. "Then I can just about walk to the singing." Thinking about Irene brought thoughts back to John Mark that he had momentarily forgotten.

Out loud he said, "Wasn't that a jolt, or isn't it true that Anthony asked Irene for a date and she refused him?"

"It was a surprise to me that Anthony asked her, but I wasn't surprised that she didn't accept him," Elizabeth said quite calmly and assuringly.

"Why not? Doesn't she know him? He is twenty-one already and a decent guy and was up here a few times already. He must have been considering it. I thought she would at least give it a try."

"It was a hard decision for Irene. That's why she didn't give her answer till in church. She was very undecided."

"Wasn't she expecting it? I didn't know it, but I thought maybe she had caught on."

"I assume she hadn't expected it, the way she talked."

"Maybe I should have given a good word to Irene about Anthony. I think she must not know him." Elizabeth chuckled and took a deep breath as if to say something but remained silent.

"Well, don't you think I should have given a good word about my cousin?" John Mark asked seriously. At length Elizabeth spoke in a serious tone. John Mark felt a few goose pimples go up his spine at the change of her voice.

"John Mark, I am afraid you may be the cause of her decision."

"Am I that bad that she would turn my cousin down?"

"You are hopeless," Elizabeth stated and then continued, "I— I mean—I'm afraid a lot of the indecision was—" Elizabeth held her words, then under a low breath she continued, "that she may be waiting to see what you do."

"What do you mean, what I do? You mean how I turn out?"

She groaned, pretending to be at her wits' end. "I mean, waiting to see what you do now that you are eighteen."

Without thinking John Mark pulled on the reins and Charlotte stopped. "Elizabeth, you can be so funny. Even if she wondered, she wouldn't refuse him for me! Just what proof do you have?" John Mark asked, urging the horse on. "You're teasing me," he added.

"I'm not. I am serious and I already said more than— than— " she fumbled and swallowed words that wanted to come. Finally she finished, "—more than I should have."

John Mark wondered what words she wanted to say and shouldn't. He wasn't surprised that maybe Irene had such thoughts. He detected at times that she had pretty much respect for him, but surely Anthony's qualifications far exceeded his own.

At length Elizabeth said, "Life wouldn't be so difficult, if we could see further ahead."

"I doubt it, because if we could see further ahead, we would start worrying what is yet before us. I'm afraid it would be more difficult," John Mark concluded.

"Well, yes, in a sense. But what I mean is when a boy asks a girl, it is a big decision for a girl if she isn't sure what the Lord's will is or if it includes His blessing."

"But it must have been hard for Anthony when he prayed about it and felt led to ask and was refused," John Mark replied.

"To be sure, it was also hard on Irene." By now John Mark had pulled up to the walk at Elizabeth's home.

John Mark headed home, his already full mind had one more load to think about. Was he responsible for giving Irene such thoughts? Did he have any such thoughts? Maybe he did at times. Did he still have them? Not after a weekend like this, but—

That evening, as he went to bed he left his mind wander. *If Irene would ask me, would I turn her down in hopes that maybe Lavina would ask? If Lavina would ask me, would I turn her down thinking suppose Irene asks me?* He shook his head no. *But if Irene would ask me, could I refuse when I wouldn't know if Lavina would ask? Would I wait?* He was beginning to see Irene's side of the situation. When he closed his eyes, he saw the pale brown, gentle smiling eyes that had brightened for a moment over the usually sober, serene face and then vanished as soon as it had appeared. He also saw the reflection in the mirror again, Lavina as her natural self. He ached to know her like that.

Now that he finally was at home he could let go of his emotions and let his struggles and turmoil loose, he gave way to

145

tears. It relaxed him enough that he started feeling tired. What a joy it was for him to actually look forward to a week of school to keep his mind occupied.

Chapter Sixteen

John Mark had looked forward to this day for quite a while. He had been to many teacher's meetings and always looked forward to them. Quite often he was called upon to give a speech or demonstrate a class, or he was asked to lead in a discussion. At first he dreaded it, but he had gotten used to sharing, and he always got so refreshed with renewed strength and wisdom at teacher's meetings that it was worth the sacrifice. Often he learned from listening to others who were discussing things that he hadn't even realized he also needed help with. He was being called to help instruct but he always gained more instruction than he was able to offer. At the last few meetings he and Lena Jane, Ellen, and Doris had a little private meeting by themselves with others who had things in common listening in. Now Lena Jane had announced a special education teacher's meeting since there were a few more teachers who had some pupils who needed special attention, like Katie and Mary Ann, who hadn't included themselves in the circle at the other meetings.

Lena Jane had invited them all personally. John Mark had hitched up and took Ellen along on this Saturday forenoon. Lena Jane planned the meeting for Saturday so they wouldn't need to find substitute teachers. John Mark decided he could drive with the team if he had plenty of time and Ellen agreed. The meeting would begin at noon. This was the first year Ellen identified a pupil as a special education pupil. Ellen poured out the story of little Richard who had been in grade one last year. She thought he was slow in catching on or maybe lacked interest. But she didn't get far into the September term until she realized that he was not a pupil who had just gotten rusty over the summer. There was a deeper problem. She had tried to just put up with what she thought was a lack of interest in first grade, but that was not such an easy solution.

The time had passed unnoticed while Ellen and John Mark shared and compared their experiences of teaching a special education pupil. Her frustrations were those that he had experienced the first year with Edgar, the frustrations of trying to grasp the fact that Edgar couldn't be taught with the rest no matter how much time you spend trying. John Mark understood that now. It was easier once you accepted the student's limitation and did not try to force the pupil to learn what he wasn't able to learn.

The drive up was only an appetizer to what he feasted on in the afternoon. The meeting was very informal and there were no prepared speeches. They had pushed the desks back and sat in a big circle. The teachers took turns pouring out their most challenging experiences. When one explained that what she learned by trial and error was helping her pupils and herself, another teacher was sure to say, "Why, that would never work out for me."

Once Lena Jane laughed heartily and one of the others asked what they had missed that was so funny.

She chuckled again saying, "It's just struck me that our circle reminds me of a bunch of mothers on a Sunday afternoon lamenting the behavior of their trying children with each mother thinking she had a worse example."

"Maybe you are referring more to disobedient children," Katie replied. "Sometimes it is so hard to determine the fine line between disobedience and a learning disability."

As the afternoon wore on, Lena Jane and Katie were leading the discussion. They had more experience because their special education pupils were older. The rest sat drinking in the instructions and warnings like mothers with only seven- and eight-year-olds, listening to the woes of mothers with fifteen-year-old children. The others revealed to them as gently as they could that the burdens wouldn't become any easier as the student got older. The younger mothers asked a few casual, hopeful questions, hoping it was not going to be the same for them.

John Mark was spellbound as he looked over the books and papers that other special education pupils did to keep them occupied and to challenge their minds to increase knowledge. John Mark, though much enthused, kept glancing at the clock, but Ellen was spellbound and paid close attention to the subject being spoken by Katie.

Once when Ellen for a moment seemed to drift back to the present, John Mark said, "I too hate to leave, but it looks as if it's about time. Ellen, are you going with me?" She eyed him as if she were a child awakening from a deep nap, then she looked at the clock.

Her mouth fell open in disbelief saying, "I guess we should be going." While Ellen was getting her wraps, Lena Jane and Katie were still showing her papers and explaining how to use them. John Mark was waiting at the door, wondering if he should unblanket Charlotte while Ellen was still gathering information.

She asked Lena Jane, "Where did you say I could get this book?"

"Here, I'll write down the address," Lena Jane said, going for a piece of paper. John Mark thought he would then ask Ellen for the information about the material.

Later as Ellen and John Mark were heading home, Ellen said, "I prefer this over a regular teacher's meeting."

"Oh, I know. I was thinking this afternoon that this was the value I used to get out of the first teacher's meetings I attended where you could not grasp enough of the things and you needed it so much."

"My first meetings are so far in the past I don't remember if they were ever so refreshing and challenging as this was," Ellen said as if talking to herself.

Then she suddenly became more alive and asked, "But I still don't understand about that chart Katie had."

"You didn't understand it because the subject was changed before I could explain further?"

"You mean with the letters?"

"Yes, what was that?"

"You didn't hear the beginning of it. She also had a pile of pictures, and . . ." John Mark went on explaining and so the meeting continued on the way home.

As they were nearing Ellen's home, she said, "Well, at least you don't have far to go to the singing."

"Singing?" John Mark echoed.

"Don't tell me you forgot that Irene is having a singing tonight!"

"Oh, I sure did forget," John Mark answered. Then he added, "But that's not so near for me anymore. I moved up to Stanley's home."

"You mean you are living there even over the weekend?" Ellen questioned.

"Yes, as it so often was on a Monday morning that the weather was rough that I wished I was nearer to school. And it was so confusing; Stanley's didn't know when I was coming and my parents often thought I was coming home and then I didn't. It was sort of a worry to Mother as she said, if something would happen, no one would know because they and Stanley would both think I was at the other place. Some Sundays it was so mild and then till Monday the weather had changed so unexpectedly that I decided to move to Stanley's for the winter months. Anyhow, so I'm not sure once I get to Stanley's tonight that I will go back down for a singing."

"Not even at Irene's place?" Ellen questioned with a hint of doubt in her voice.

"No, not even at Irene's house."

After dropping Ellen off, he headed on three more miles toward Stanley's. Only for a moment did his mind dwell on the singing. Then so soon he was thinking of the events of the day. He had gotten new ideas on how to work with Edgar. He got out his pocket-size notebook as already some things dimmed from his memory. Reading the notes he had scribbled in the booklet suddenly took him back to where the afternoon left off. He was thinking of a few supplies he would need to get in order to try some of the new things he learned.

Putting the booklet back in his pocket, he glanced up and saw the view of Edgar's home. Of course, he wouldn't go past; he would turn here. It looked like the little boys were sledding on the upper field leading down to the barn. It was the only activity he could see. Making the second turn off to the next road, there was suddenly a buggy approaching him from the other direction. In a moment's time, he was trying to recognize the passengers, but they quickly had met and then passed. The driver waved good-naturedly, having a ready smile of neighborly friendliness. Lavina, a passenger, had for a brief moment stared, rather wonderingly. Priscilla was driving and was dressed in her everyday clothes. John Mark had bid the time with his hand and nodded and maybe looked just as wonderingly. Lavina was a little more dressed up, likely Priscilla had gone to fetch her home from a hired job.

When John Mark reached Stanley's, he realized that all school matters had vanished from his thoughts since meeting the Ringler team. After putting the horse away he stood staring for a moment, trying to decide if he wanted to go to the singing. No, he probably would come home disappointed. He just saw more of Lavina already than if he went to the singing.

He was still in time for supper at Stanley's.

Rising from the supper table, Stanley said, "Oh, there is a letter for you. I almost forgot till I saw it here." Then he reached for the letter and handed it to John Mark.

At a glance John Mark saw it was from home. He sat back on the sofa reading it. Mother had written a letter, nothing of importance, just the everyday things. Quotes from some amusing things the little ones said, and what everyone was working on, enough to almost make him yearn to be at home. Mom had said she thought she would write just a little since Dad was writing.

Then there was a letter from Dad. John Mark unfolded the sheet and read:

Dear Son,
A few lines your way this evening above the little boys' clatter. They can be quite noisy at times. But even with all our noise and commotion, we still miss your presence. I wonder if

you miss us too. The other day I had Fred haul some hay for me that I bought that was advertised in our weekly circular. It's a nice grade of hay. Yesterday I and Mom were down to visit my mother at Seranus's, so we also got to visit with Seranus and family. Mother isn't very talkative. She doesn't complain, but one can see that she isn't well. She always asks about all the children. And she mentioned again of something she talked about earlier that has slipped my mind again. She keeps asking me if you ever told us what you told her the day you got baptized. She seems to think it was a "valuable" thing I should know about. She can't get it together anymore, and she feels she won't get any better. She is concerned that if you haven't shared it with someone else beside her, it would be necessary to do so. And I'm interested in learning about it, so I thought I'll let you know before it slips my mind again. Since I don't know when you'll be home again, or maybe I'll see you before this letter reaches you if you come home from Rufus's singing?

Father

While John Mark was reading Mother's letter, Stanley and his wife Erma and small son Walter, went out to the barn to do the evening milking. Alone in the house, John Mark relaxed and leaned against the sofa back and recalled the incident Dad had written about. He thought for a while. Then he started recalling that the Sunday he was baptized, Uncle Israel and his family and Grandmother had come to church and then came home for dinner. Grandmother had asked about the experiences of the day, if they were hard on him. He recalled telling her how it had overwhelmed him when he was told to rise up to a new life and a new beginning; God strengthens you for your new life; know the truth and the truth shall make you free. It had been a joy that couldn't be measured as he realized the truth of these words that had suddenly been revealed to him. He was now starting a new life; he was no more adopted; he had the same new birth the others in the class had. He now dwelled on his life since then. Would recalling this incident make the future path any more clear? His thoughts went back to the team he met a little before coming home earlier in the evening.

He meditated deeply for ten minutes or more, then he shook his head thinking, *No, I guess even if I wasn't adopted, a smile still wouldn't replace the pale half-fearful eyes.* Then in his memory he thought again of the evening at Nevin's when he and Chester met up with Lavina unexpectedly on the closed-in porch in front of the wash house. Just the thought of the rare, priceless smile that met his glance when he lowered his eyes to see how she would react was still enough to make him tremble. But he was sure he had not returned a smile. He must have looked rather startled. He thought, *I would have been just as startled if I accidentally met up with Stanley's yellow cat that lives in the shed if she was cornered, and instead of hissing and dashing away as she normally does she would suddenly purr and let you stroke her.* Then he smiled to himself as he thought of the next moment when Lavina disappeared as fast and silently as the yellow cat does.

He had often desired to be gentle to the yellow cat and make friends and show her that he meant no harm. She would look so pleading but always scamper away in fright. Pleading? Where else had he been thinking of using that word? Then he thought of the pale brown eyes, serene and sober, wanting to trust but yet showing only fright. Yes, pleading was the look. He sighed remembering that Stanley said the yellow cat was raised under the rain shelter in the meadow and was never around humans till she was over half grown. She never learned to trust humans. Walter chasing her didn't help at all, and Stanley himself never had the patience to win her confidence.

Then the half-fearful but pleading look of the pale brown eyes appeared in John Mark's thoughts again. *Why was Lavina so timid? What were her fears? What was the pleading for? Confidence? Confidence in what?* He thought of her Father Nevin. He was rather nervous and uneasy. Did her home life leave something to be desired? Then his thoughts came back to the words, "A new life, a new beginning." Oh yes, that is what he had started dwelling on. It was beyond him how his thoughts had strayed so far.

Suddenly, he got up and went to his room to get a tablet and bring it along down in the kitchen where it was warmer. He wondered why Grandmother was concerned about what he said. Why should Mom and Dad know? *I guess maybe I never told them.* He realized that Grandmother felt her time on earth may not be so long anymore, and she somehow sensed that no one beside her ever shared that comforting thought. *Would I need it someday and there would be no one who could remind me if I failed to remember? Well, anyhow, it wouldn't hurt to share it with Mom and Dad.* And he decided to put it on paper while it was fresh in his memory. *Maybe I can give it to Dad tomorrow.* The clock ticked on unnoticed, as John Mark wrote.

Dear Mom and Dad,

Concerning your question about what Grandmother asked, I had to think a little about that day when I was baptized. The bishop beckoned my hand and asked me to rise to a new life and a new beginning and wished God's blessing on my new walk of life. Overwhelming joy pressed around me as the words revealed the truth that I was in a new life and a new birth just like the rest of the class. I was no more the only adopted one. I had the same birth as the rest, born again in Christ. It was now a new beginning. I had the same chance everyone else had. I was ashamed of how my tears fell after we were seated again, but I could not help it. It was such a joy I had to cry. Then in the afternoon when I met Grandmother alone, she asked me if the events were hard on me. I told her how it was, but I remember she was rather startled and reminded me that it was too soon for joy. The work had only started. I wonder why she's now thinking about it and why she thinks you should know.

John Mark

John Mark laid the pen and tablet on the stairway and had only for a moment gone back to the sofa when the kitchen door opened and Erma and Walter came in. A few minutes later, Stanley came too.

Stanley stopped in his tracks. "Are you still here?" he said when he saw John Mark. "Isn't there a singing somewhere? We saw some buggies going."

"Yes, there is a singing down near home," John Mark said lacking enthusiasm.

Stanley looked at him a moment and asked, "What's wrong? Aren't you feeling well?"

"I feel better already," John Mark answered, realizing that his head was feeling rather weary from sitting here thinking too long.

154

John Mark saw Erma taking a quick look at him and then at Stanley with a hint of mischief showing in her dark eyes and then she said, "Don't worry about him. Remember he was with a group of girls all afternoon. Why does he need to go to a singing yet tonight?"

Stanley looked from one to the other, then his eyes twinkled as he looked back at him saying, "Hey, not bad. I never thought about that. You have it pretty well made. Maybe for all we know, there was only one other teacher there, ah?"

"There were more there than one, but I drove one home," John Mark chuckled.

"See, I told you, now he is even personal about it," Erma said, her eyes speaking volumes.

"And who was that? Stanley urged.

"Not the one I would have liked to drive with," John Mark answered truthfully, carefully omitting the word "teacher." Erma and Stanley exchanged glances that showed they doubted he was telling the truth any of the time.

After another half hour of visiting, John Mark excused himself and headed upstairs hoping to sleep without thinking everything over again.

Chapter Seventeen

With pencil in hand, John Mark sat at his desk with the third grade workbooks before him. He should be checking them so he could get some work ready for Edgar, but other things were weighing on his mind. The last few weeks, or so it seemed, everyone in school was rather listless. The children played heartily at recess, but something seemed amiss. He almost had to coax the children to talk during their visiting period which used to be so interesting. Often he had to quiet them down before everyone was done telling their events. He himself felt a little restless, or as if he was dragging himself along. This morning when he walked the short distance to school, the winter air seemed sort of cruel, or, well, discouraging. He longed to feel a gentle breeze, with a hint of spring. The February calendar page had been torn off a week ago. Now John Mark was longing for a gentle breeze and scents of spring, the color and life of spring. *Maybe the children feel the same way, or maybe my boredom has worn off on them,* he thought.

The door opened suddenly and a few students spilled in and said in unison, "Good morning." On the spur of the moment, John Mark sat up and replied, "Good morning, Lydia Ann and Emma." They stopped in their tracks and looked at him in wonderment since he had spoken their names with interest; he usually said good morning without looking up or saying more. He pretended this wasn't unusual and asked, "Where is Moses?"

Lydia Ann said, "He's coming. He was helping Dad bag feed, and they went to get the wagon ready to pick stones, but they had to unload something first."

Then Dennis came in and John Mark also greeted him with

156

"Good morning, Dennis," and he greeted everyone by name that came in. Most of them looked at him the second time, wondering what had come over him. Edgar took it as an invitation to come up to his desk to talk, carrying his lunch pail with him.

Later as he was checking workbooks, John Mark heard the girls visiting with each other near his desk.

He heard Mildred say, "Oh, I wish I had some. I'm so tired of sandwiches. I wasn't going to pack any but Mother said I had to."

Then Joanne said, "Our bologna is gone and the new batch isn't ready yet, so my parents bought some and it's so much better that I now like my sandwiches."

Someone said something about apples and another one said, "Well, I started peeling mine and put peanut butter in the center. That is good for a change." And so the talk continued and John Mark checked a few more pages. Then a thought started working in his mind. Why hadn't he thought of that before?

The morning discussion after singing was as it usually was lately, so half-hearted as if the children thought there was nothing worth sharing.

Then when the time was about up, John Mark said, "Well, suppose we exchange lunches once this week?" It took a few seconds for the pupils to grasp it; then their faces lit up.

They answered, "Yes! Yes!" They planned to exchange the names later in the day and then exchange lunches on Friday.

It was in the second session that Bennie raised his hand and asked, "May we make things to put the lunches in?" John Mark looked over the room as the pupils raised their heads when they heard the question. A few dreaded expressions were seen, but mostly there was the look of "Dare we?"

John Mark was thinking out loud, "I wish we could make it as an art project as I have nothing planned for art yet. But that wouldn't do, the other people would see it." Then a thought clicked in his mind. "For something different we're going to dismiss at last recess on Friday, then you can take your art project home and work on it if you haven't already finished it. Then on Monday, we'll exchange the lunches. Tonight before we go home we'll exchange names." Pupils automatically rose out of their seats in eagerness. Only a few remained sitting normally. They finished the rest of the day with renewed enthusiasm.

Just before they dismissed, they exchanged names to make lunches. Now the schoolhouse seemed quieter after the excess volume of excitement only minutes before, when they were finding out whose name they had. John Mark himself had to pick again, as he had picked his own name the first time.

He opened the narrow drawer in front of him and looked again at the small folded paper which said "Lucy Weaver." So he had to make a lunch box for her. It was beyond him what a seventh-grade girl would like. He'd rather make something for a second-grade girl. "A seventh-grade girl," he said to himself. "Let's see."

Then he thought of his sister Delores. *She was eleven or was she twelve? Was she in seventh?* Then he started thinking about the rest of his family at home. He did miss them since he didn't get home anymore, often not even over the weekend. What would amuse Delores? What were her interests? You couldn't pack lunch into a mouth organ. Next to mouth organs came her fondness for playing with babies. But he was to make something for Lucy. She topped all the girls in jumping rope, but you couldn't pack lunch into a jump rope. He often secretly predicted she would be a teacher someday, but what could he make her? He had just started forming plans when he thought he saw someone pass by the window in the schoolyard. The door rattled and opened suddenly.

It took a few minutes to collect his thoughts. He recognized Enos Nolt coming in the door, looking at him with a half-hidden grin. Then he turned to close the door properly. He only lives across a few fields from home. Was there a message from home? Fear gripped John Mark. But as Enos looked up and strolled toward him, he decided his expression didn't look as if he was coming with an urgent message.

"You don't look very busy," Enos finally greeted him.

"No wonder," John Mark chuckled. "I was just trying to decide what I could play."

"You mean with the pupils?" Enos asked.

158

"No, we are to make lunches for each other," John Mark admitted, "and I was trying to decide what to make." Enos helped himself to the chair at the table and sat down facing John Mark. At the same time he took off his hat, put it in his lap, and brushed together his hair that didn't want to cover the middle of his head anymore.

Then he said, "Don't you miss your family down our way? It seems I don't get to see you going past anymore. You must be staying here."

"I admit I miss them, but winter weather and four miles away from school, well, I got tired of that too." Enos looked at him for a brief moment and then paused. John Mark still couldn't determine the expression on his face.

At length Enos drawled, "Well, it might help to teach nearer home, I suppose?" He ended with it sounding like a question.

"I see no opportunity," John Mark replied.

"That's what I am here for," Enos admitted. Now it was John Mark's turn to scratch his head. He did some fast thinking and remembered again that Enos was elected to the board of the school back home last year.

"Why? Do you want to put Ellen out of a job?" John Mark asked, becoming interested.

"I don't want to put her out of a job. She wants to," Enos corrected him. John Mark knew he couldn't be hearing right.

"You don't mean that she refused to teach another year?" John Mark asked, almost excited.

Enos sighed lightly and said, "I thought she had promised to teach another year back in January, and now suddenly she talks as if we need to look for another teacher."

"Is she having problems, more than her pupil that needs special help?" John Mark asked.

"Not in school, as far as I know. I talked with the others on the board and we had a meeting this week. Everything seems to be going fine."

"Where will she be teaching then?" John Mark asked, trying to get Enos to talk faster.

"I don't know. She wouldn't tell me. My wife stopped in at school one day, and she said it seemed something was bothering Ellen. She didn't seem like herself." John Mark continued asking questions that Enos had no answers for. Then Enos reminded him that he didn't come to try and figure out Ellen. He came to ask John Mark to teach at their school.

For a fleeting moment, John Mark thought of teaching at Chestnut Bottom, his home school. He would be home every morning and evening teaching his brothers and sisters, which had some advantages and disadvantages.

But then he remembered and shook his head and said, "I can't leave my pupils. For sure not Edgar, and if someone misunderstands Moses's intentions, he or she would think him mischievous. And Florence is easy to handle if you know how to persuade her before she sets her little mind. And then there's Joann. If a strange teacher stepped in here, Joanne would probably make many a mountain out of a molehill before the teacher noticed it." He felt like he was driving a twenty-horse hitch and he knew which reins to hold firm which to hitch beside each other to keep things in check. Suddenly handing them to a stranger might make them run away.

Enos looked at him and said, "So, what do you think?"

"I feel responsible for my students. My guess is Ellen will get her wits together again."

"I thought so too," Enos said, "but I am about convinced she is serious." Enos got up and said, "Don't you want to think it over?"

John Mark shook his head saying, "I was thinking it over. I can't leave them."

"Well, I thought I'd give you first chance being it's so near home," Enos said, getting up and heading to the door.

John Mark's mind was busy. He still thought probably Ellen and Enos didn't understand each other right, or maybe Ellen had a low week and threatened to quit teaching and Enos took her seriously. He was eager to talk with Ellen sometime soon.

There was no singing on Saturday evening. He did see Ellen filing into the church with the rest of the girls. He found out that Lloyd Weaver's were having the young folks to dinner, as some of her relations from another county were around. He looked forward to going to Lloyd's since it was one of his pupil's parents. He had once been there for supper after school and this now would seem a little special. They almost seemed like part of his family since he knew the children so well.

John Mark didn't get to the table until the last setting. The kitchen was noisy. Some of the girls were washing the dishes; others sat here and there in groups, biting on their toothpicks and catching up with visiting. Half of the table was filled with table waiters who waited on the other tables. They were visiting with the girls who were now doing the dishes.

Some of the boys at the table had joined in their conversation only it sounded more like an argument. Esther wasn't agreeing with Elizabeth. Elmer and Elton had taken Esther's side, and it was getting interesting because Elmer wasn't to be out-done.

John Mark hadn't understood what Levi said, but one of the girls urgently declared, ". . . and for that, Elmer is going to wash the plates on the table." Elmer looked around cross-eyed and whispered something to Elton. Elton chuckled and raised his eyebrows. John Mark could hear that it was all in fun. They were just pretending to be insulted.

When John Mark looked beyond the activity around the table, he happened to see Ellen. She was sitting facing toward the window, but she wasn't even looking out the window. Her gaze was lower and she looked quite concerned or troubled. Anna and Virginia came walking past, and Virginia happened to bump Ellen's chair. Ellen looked up. Virginia smiled at her then continued walking past. Ellen went back to thinking. Then, as if she sensed she was being watched, she raised her eyes and looked up at John Mark. She studied him for a moment, then seemed to recognize him and gave him a weak smile. He smiled encouragingly back to her. Whatever her concern was, it couldn't be that bad. She looked like she was carrying half the world's burdens on her shoulders.

Minutes later, when they left the table, John Mark made a special effort to walk past her chair. She was sitting with a downcast gaze looking quite burdened. He bumped the leg of her chair. She looked up suddenly.

John Mark said, "Cheer up. Better days are coming." She suddenly looked humiliated. He thought she even blushed a little; therefore, he passed by and didn't ask her any more questions. He was hoping to get a chance to discuss the matter, at least to find out if she wanted to talk about what was bothering her.

As he passed through the parlor, he stood for a moment at the window. Then he saw Lavina and Rhoda standing by the yard fence sharing a happy conversation. He watched a moment longer, catching glimpses of a few priceless smiles that weren't meant for him. He slipped away before being noticed.

Just then Paul Ray and Elton came in the door with songbooks. Soon a group of boys gathered around and started singing. You couldn't stay uninspired if Elmer was singing. He had great talent and a voice for singing and he gave his whole heart to it. But at times he was so involved in other activities that he didn't get started singing. Apparently Earl, one of Mrs. Lloyd Weaver's visiting relations, was a talented singer, so they had naturally started singing.

After an hour or so the boys tossed the songbooks aside and visited. Some sat nodding their heads, napping. John Mark wasn't sure if maybe he hadn't dozed awhile. Paul Ray asked him to come along for supper.

"What's up?" John Mark questioned.

"Nothing much. My sister is having some of her friends for supper so I'm asking a few guys to come, too."

Just then Elmer walked up to them. He heard Paul Ray's reply and had such a shocked look on his face.

Paul Ray looked at Elmer rather peeved and said, "Now don't get smart. My sister asked her friends to come over and have supper with us.

Then Elmer looked relieved. "Oh, I was just going over to say I hope you don't eat the girls!"

Menno, who stood listening, said, "Which one shall we leave for you?"

Elmer cocked his head and wisely replied, "The best one of course."

"It's too late Elmer. I have her already," Menno replied.

"Eh?" Elmer said, winking at them mischievously, as if he was about to reveal some wonderful news. "Have you seen what they have in the cradle now?" Most of the boys in the room broke out in a chuckle. A few had a hearty laugh. John Mark was pulling on his wraps. He wondered if Elmer was serious. Menno was dating Mary Ethel and Priscilla was going with the young folks now. He wondered if Elmer was waiting on her.

John Mark went out the parlor door, and as he came around the house near the steps that led to the lower yard and to the barn, he met up with Priscilla.

She looked at him for a moment and John Mark looked at her questioningly, then asked. "Are you waiting for someone?"

Priscilla responded with "I was just wishing I had a ticket to give you."

Suddenly John Mark caught on. "Do you mean to fetch your horse out of the barn?"

"Yes, would you please?"

"I'm not sure I know your horse."

"Well, I don't know where it is either. Lloyd unhitched for me."

"Did you come around the same time Reuben did?"

"Oh," she was trying to think, "yes, I guess he was behind us. Why?"

"Well, I was putting my horse away when Lloyd brought a horse in and then Reuben came with his horse."

"And," she added, "there is a yellow vinyl tape on each end of the neck rope for marking."

"Okay, I think I should be able to locate it."

John Mark entered the barn. Charlotte snorted to him. He checked the second horse next to her. Yes, that was it. The yellow tape was on each end. As he untied the horse and led it outside to the water trough, John Mark met up with Elmer. He seemed not to notice John Mark.

Then John Mark asked him, "Elmer, do you know whose horse this is?"

Elmer turned around and looked the horse over. Then he looked at John Mark and said in a slow, low tone, "Well, not yours." Then Elmer disappeared in the barn.

Oh, now where was Priscilla's buggy? He had failed to ask her. He looked around the barnyard and over at the chicken house. Then at the upper end near the windmill he noticed her waving her hand.

When John Mark finally came up to her with the horse, Priscilla was holding the shafts of the buggy and trying to back it up. Quickly John Mark took in the situation.

Lavina was pushing at the wheel saying, "Not so far, there's another buggy here in back." At the same time she looked up and saw the horse and John Mark. She looked questioningly at Priscilla and John Mark.

With the neck rope in hand and handing the horse, he said to Priscilla, "If you hold the horse, I'll help you get the buggy out." He inched the buggy forward, then backward and turned sharply, then Lavina looked at him.

Mercifully she said, "No, this is our buggy. We are trying to get it out." John Mark smiled as he passed by and pushed the other buggy further over and inched their buggy forward with Lavina's help. Priscilla came with the horse and Lavina grabbed one shaft; John Mark grabbed the other shaft.

Priscilla said, "I think we can manage now." As John Mark slipped the shaft in the harness, out of habit he then went around the horse's head to the other side to hook that up, and there was Lavina hooking up. She raised her eyes for a moment and said thank-you, and although her smile was faint and brief, the warmth in her eyes that brief moment she had looked up was valued over any smile he had ever received.

When he came back to the other side, Priscilla had almost finished hitching up and she said, "Oh, for a brother!"

John Mark asked, "This isn't Sandy, is it?"

"No, Dad's using her. We've had this one about three months or so," Priscilla said as she looked up at the horse and hurried in at the driver's side with the reins in her hands. Lavina was seated already and in a moment they were off.

At the same time, John Mark noticed someone hitching up a few rows over. He looked more closely and there stood Elmer, all hitched up and watching him. John Mark had to smile to think that Elmer was watching him get Priscilla started off. He didn't look very jokingly now, John Mark mused. He went down to the barn to get his own horse and all thoughts of Elmer vanished from him. A strong force was overwhelming him. He fled up the barn stairs and sought refuge in the hay mow, and gave way to his tears as a brokenhearted child and poured out his heart to God in unuttered words. How could he ever ask Lavina for her friendship? The few and far between smiles and affectionate glances he received made him cry and he seemed to be getting worse.

He returned to the lower part of the barn and got out his horse, hitched up, and was off to Stanley's, taking the long way around. He had things to think over before arriving there.

Stanley's were already milking when he arrived. Coming up to his room, he saw the cardboard schoolhouse he had made for Lucy. He had forgotten there was something to look forward to tomorrow.

John Mark rested awhile upstairs on his bed, till sounds from the barn alerted him that Erma and Stanley would soon be in. Then a thought suddenly struck him. He would surprise them. He went downstairs and checked to see if there was popcorn here yet. Yes, there was a bag full. So he set to work and got the corn popping and mixed a pitcher of Tang. Then he made some grilled cheese sandwiches. He hadn't even started setting the table when the outside porch door opened. He waited to hear Erma or Walter exclaim.

First there was silence. Then it was Stanley's voice that said, "Are you in a hurry to go somewhere?"

John Mark looked at him. "No, I just thought I'd surprise you."

"You sure did. I didn't know you could cook," Stanley grinned.

"I didn't cook anything," John Mark admitted.

"Well, it smells good. Walter here was afraid we wouldn't get any supper," Stanley said, stroking his hand over Walter's head. Little Walter was keenly interested in the activity.

"Well, let's set the table," Stanley said, grabbing a few glasses. John Mark looked at him, wondering. When Stanley noticed his silence, he looked at John Mark and said a little softly, "Didn't you talk with Erma?"

"Erma?" John Mark asked, "Is she in the barn?"

Stanley shook his head and said, "No, she's in the bedroom. She hasn't been feeling well since this morning, so I appreciate this, and Walter even more!"

They sat down and had a simple supper, munching popcorn and sipping drink and taking time to visit about their day. John Mark's trouble seemed small. He pitied Stanley as it sure didn't seem right not to have Erma by Stanley's side. Once when no more food was being eaten and they had pushed their chairs away from the table and for a moment had been silent, Stanley rose and went to the bedroom. After a while he came back and filled a drink and made a piece of toasted bread saying, "Erma said the good smells out here made her hungry."

John Mark had put most of the things away when Stanley came back out again. John Mark was watching as Stanley entertained Walter, trying to keep him occupied. When he looked up and saw John Mark watching him, Stanley asked, "Do you want something?"

"No," John Mark answered in a daze, "I was just wondering or thinking; the house seems so empty."

Stanley looked at him almost surprised. Then he answered him in a husky voice, "It is the better half of me who is missing that makes our home. It's almost as if my right hand isn't here. I wish everyone the blessing of a comrade friend. I thought I understood this all in my young years while I was dating, But I realize it was in a childish way. I did not realize the full value and need of this relationship and how it gets more valuable with time. There's one out there for you too," Stanley finished. John Mark looked at him silently. He wanted to ask him some questions, but the words stuck in his throat. Maybe if Erma couldn't hear from the bedroom he would confide in him, but he wasn't ready to reveal any personal thoughts.

* * * *

There was much excitement the next morning in the school-house as each group of children arrived with their prize art in all forms except lunchboxes. John Mark kept busy at his desk but heard the oohs and aahs as each group of children arrived. Once in a while he looked up for a brief moment, but he thought he would go see the things once everyone arrived.

When it was nearing bell time, he walked back to the lunchbox shelf and joined in the children's excitement. His eyes scanned the shelves and table where the things were displayed. He saw some of the girls admiring his schoolhouse and Lucy was among them. His eyes moved on down the row of crafts. Then suddenly his eyes stood still. There it was, a buggy made from cardboard. Everything as real-looking as possible. He could have known the Shirk boys would make things that no one could match. Probably Gerald had even made it for them as he doubted Bennie could have done such a proper job of it. He made a quick survey of the rest of the things. Then he glanced back to the buggy, taking a closer look. When he opened the lid of the storm front, there inside sat the lunch. Most of the boys seemed more interested in the hay wagon. Others liked the tree with a tree house up in it where the lunch was, but to John Mark's taste, the buggy took first prize.

The real excitement came when the students were dismissed for first recess and the lunches were delivered to the pupils. Lucy's admira-tion showed on her face as he delivered the schoolhouse to her.

John Mark was watching Edgar receive the doghouse and al-most missed seeing the buggy being placed on his own desk. It was so sudden he looked quickly at the Shirk boys who were in their seats. He only saw Dennis walking away, and just then Dennis turned around and smiled at John Mark. He was so surprised; he was sure he looked perplexed. He thought maybe the buggy was for him, but not from a second-grader. He was sure the Shirk boys had made it; maybe they made it for Dennis or maybe one of Dennis's parents was creative?

It was not until last recess that he got to talk with Dennis when he was helping him find his boots that he asked him if Mother had helped him make the buggy.

He shook his head and said, "I didn't make it."

"Did your mother make it?" Dennis looked at him and smiled, pleased, and then shook his head "no."

"Oh, did your father make it for you?" Then suddenly he laughed and said, "No, not Daddy!" He stood silently with a smile on his face, enjoying the thought that he knew more than the teacher this time.

Then in his usual slow, practical way he said, "Mother and Daddy went to visit Uncle Ben's, and Lavina stayed at our house to milk the cow and stay with Adam and me; only Leroy went along. They came home the day I got your name, but Mother didn't know what to make. Then she asked Lavina if she could make something." John Mark stared at him as Dennis was about to go outside.

John Mark suddenly asked, "Do you mean Edgar's sister?" Dennis smiled and nodded and cheerfully went on his way outside. John Mark stared at the empty place where Dennis had been standing. He almost wished he didn't know it.

When the children left after school, he looked over the buggy again and for the first time really noticed the handkerchief-size afghan in the shades of color to match his real one that was draped over the small seat. He sat thinking deeply, wondering if it was made because of affectionate feelings or if it was made as a merciful deed soon forgotten.

He decided to keep the thoughts and deed to himself, hoping to get it home to Stanley's without them noticing. If Erma was still resting in the bedroom, it would be easier to do.

Chapter Eighteen

John Mark came up the basement steps after putting a few shovelfulls of coal on the fire and came back into the classroom. Even if the classroom was empty and silent, John Mark could still feel the presence of his pupils who had ten minutes ago all bounded out the door and scattered to their own homes. The half-finished puzzle sprawled out on the card table seemed to speak for the fourth-grade girls who had gotten a notion to put puzzles together lately. The number game that was sketched on the blackboard was left by Cynthia and Florence who had failed to erase it when the bell rang. The Tinkertoys that were lying on the table half constructed into some kind of big earth-moving machine were left by Edgar and Dennis. As he walked to the window he noticed the stack of art sheets on the low filing cabinet and was reminded of Lucy and Kathryn who had started putting up the art on the wall and never finished.

Everywhere he looked there was a reminder of some of his pupils. It seemed they were still all there. The lone English workbook on his desk was a reminder that Roman had to do his work again because of a low score. The books on the other end of the library shelf were a reminder that he had to get that errand done one of these days. He looked out the window and saw that the sun was still high. Days were getting noticeably longer. He was going to finish putting up the art pictures, wash off the blackboards, write up the health quiz for third and fourth grades, and get sheets ready for the preschoolers.

Preschool! That's right! Nancy asked for some of those duplicated sheets for her preschool ones and she will need to have them next week. With a lick and a promise he whirled around, picking up a few scraps of paper around his desk that had missed the wastepaper can and picked up a library book that had fallen down when someone pulled out another book. He pushed the erasers over the blackboard and picked up the seventh-grade geography book and eighth-grade arithmetic book with papers in it. Tonight he could make a geography quiz and also check the eighth-grade papers to see which steps they had failed to understand and correct those they had wrong.

So, off he was to Stanley's to fetch his team. He told Stanley that he might not be back for supper, as he had to take supplies to Nancy's school. Thus he was on his way, driving across the ridge to Nancy's school. Nancy was getting two new families in her school and was short in books, and he had some extra ones. He had meant to get them over before now. Maybe the one family had moved in already. She also asked for some of the preschool sheets that he had demonstrated at the last teacher's meeting.

*   *   *   *

Back at Stanley's things were back to normal again. Erma's mother was there for most of last week and now Erma was housekeeping again, but it sounded as if maybe Stanley himself had done the laundry on Monday.

As he traveled over the miles, John Mark thought of all that had happened recently. Three months or so ago he might have felt a little nervous going to Nancy's school, knowing that at times she had not been able to hide her feelings and showed something more than a teacher's interest in him. But that had passed. He still remembered the surprise he felt when his friend Justus started dating her. So many things seemed to be changing. He didn't get to see Chester, who was also with his gang of buddies, so much anymore, as he often went down to Dad's home settlement since he started dating Ella Grace, who was from there. And Levi surprised everyone when he started dating Justus's sister Esther, who was somewhat older than he and Justus.

He got to see his cousin Anthony about every other week as he was coming to the area pretty regularly. By now it was a fact that Anthony and Irene were dating. Anthony had even spent several nights with John Mark at Stanley's the other weekend.

There were things taking place everywhere. Rhoda and Warren had been published on Sunday and were getting married in three weeks. Now and then some young ones started going with the young folks. If it weren't for Paul Ray, John Mark would at times feel sort of left out with Justus, Chester, and Levi having plans in connection with their girls.

When John Mark arrived at Nancy's school, she bounded off her chair when he opened the door, saying, "You have come! In another day or so I would have come and gotten the things myself." She received the sheets and books like a child being handed a box of toys and a bag of candy. She opened the bag with the preschool papers in and seated herself on top of a school desk in the back row and rejoiced over them. She scanned the sheets and asked a few questions, then went on to explain how the Brubakers had already arrived at her school yesterday, but the Eberly family wasn't coming until next week.

It was interesting to hear about her experience with the new family. John Mark and Nancy had to take turns talking. He could visit with her as easy and relaxed as with Ellen and Lena Jane. He was glad that Nancy no longer felt self-conscious or ill at ease around him. Not until on the way home did he start thinking about the fact that Nancy was Justus's special friend. He wondered what they had in common since Justus wasn't a schoolteacher. But tonight he found out that she could be interesting and fun. When John Mark first learned to know her she had been quiet and reserved.

He almost made up his mind to stop in at home and then decided against it as Dad would likely be out doing chores and until they'd get in, it would be time to drive back. The sight of Ellen's schoolhouse brought back memories of how Ellen trained him as a teacher's helper, starting a future he had never imagined. Just as he was almost past, he happened to notice she was still at school. Now was a good time to talk with her.

In another few minutes he came to the door to find Ellen scrubbing the wash bowl and tidying up the cups. First she looked t him, almost as if she was expecting him, but then her mouth dropped open, and she caught her breath.

"Don't look so shocked. It is just me," he said. Ellen looked at him still wondering, then he explained, "I was up to Nancy's with extra books and preschool papers, then we got to talking and on the way past here I noticed you were still here. So I had to drop in."

"You almost scared me. I didn't hear anyone drive in."

"Do you keep such late hours regularly?" John Mark asked.

"Now and then," Ellen answered and shrugged her shoulders.

"How's Richard doing with that matching picture puzzle?"

"Some days it goes well but the next day I can't get him started." Ellen herself seemed sort of restless and strange this evening. Usually the questions he already asked would have opened a floodgate of conversation, but tonight the conversation wasn't flowing freely. By the look of Ellen's desk she was all ready to go home. Everything was tidied up.

She sat on the bench-type chair that was in the back of the room for visitors and waited for John Mark to talk.

He gathered his courage and asked, "I would enjoy hearing about your low week or weeks. Do those with many years of experience get those too, that you want to give up teaching in another year?"

Ellen didn't look up as she said, "We all get those times. It doesn't matter how long we have been teaching." He mentioned Richard again, the one who was in special education class, but she didn't respond. She said something about sometimes older pupils can be more trying than the younger ones with learning problems.

What she talked about was a little above John Mark's knowledge. She was saying something about "neglect" when not treated can lead to rebellion. She mentioned the name Wilmer a few times and John Mark nodded his head without realizing and thus she continued talking, but he was getting confused.

He asked, "Oh, who is Wilmer?"

"You know Wilmer Good."

"Wilmer Good?" he repeated, then looked at Ellen questioning, "Doesn't he go to Four Acres?" Ellen nodded. "I thought when I took Naomi's place those days that those children went there. Is Naomi having trouble with him?" John Mark asked.

"Lately she hasn't said much," Ellen finally answered after taking time to choose her words. Every time John Mark thought he had a conversation started about school, it always drifted back to Wilmer again.

Her concern was that at such a tender age of thirteen he was so discouraged already. Ellen had mentioned a few times of misunderstanding sorrow and taking it as neglect. John Mark was trying to understand. It was in November a year ago that Mrs. Lloyd Good had died so suddenly. He remembered it was the first year he was teaching, and they had made a scrapbook and gift for the family at Christmas in school.

He asked again, "Did you say Naomi was having trouble with him in school?"

She rubbed her hands over her eyes and said, "Some, but people are saying he was causing more trouble at home with the rest of the family." She went on to explain again that he felt neglected and it turned to rebellion. Wilmer didn't realize that the rest of the family had gone through just as much sorrow. John Mark's heart went out to the innocent boy.

He thought of his difficult years and then said, "It may be that the incident of his mother's death gets blamed too much, when it is more likely the difficult age he is. I was once his age too and had no mother and father. Well, yes, I had someone I could call my mother and father, but they weren't mine and it was long before I was Wilmer's age, but it came more to the surface when I was his age."

Ellen wondered, "Why so?"

John Mark went on to explain how it was mostly after Josiah was born and people said the baby looked like Mother or Father that I felt I really didn't belong.

Then Ellen asked, "Would it have been easier, do you think, if your mother hadn't married then?"

173

"Yes and no. It would have avoided having brothers or sisters with real parents, but I hate to think how I would have coped with the difficult years if Dad wouldn't have been in the family. He helped me more than the extra burden it caused. It is hard to realize at times that he isn't my real father."

Ellen sat drinking in the words like a plant that was so near wilted that it couldn't absorb the water fast enough. Ellen kept asking questions that no one had ever asked him before, and he took a lot of time to think about his answers as he hadn't thought it out in words before. She asked if his reaction to the difficulties of life ever made his mother think maybe marriage had not been the right move or wished she hadn't led your father into such burdens.

"I don't think so," John Mark finally said after thinking a few moments. "I once questioned Mother about how she could take me and Delores in when she didn't know then that Dad would be stepping into the family and she said, 'At that time it seemed the only right thing to do.' She depended on prayer and then she quoted a poem,

He was better to me than all my hopes;
He was better than all my fears.
He made a bridge of my broken words
And a rainbow of my tears."

Then he looked at Ellen and said, "But in Wilmer's case there was no choice about Wilmer's mother's death and after all, maybe Wilmer would have encountered problems during these difficult years anyway. But his mother's death takes all the blame; I know a little how he feels." Ellen had been deeply interested in their conversation, but now she kept glancing at the clock. Time and again John Mark said, "But you haven't answered me yet; I thought I heard that you weren't teaching again. I was hoping to hear about that. I thought maybe you had a few low weeks or so?"

"Did someone say so? As far as I know, I'll still be teaching children. There are more places to teach than here."

"Where then?" he asked.

"I didn't say I wasn't teaching here, did I?"

"Not to me."

"And through a few mouths, things sometimes sound different," Ellen said, taking another glance at the clock.

John Mark said, "I figured when Enos asked me to teach here next year you two probably misunderstood each other and that maybe things sounded different after they were through a few mouths."

"Did Enos ask you to teach here?" Ellen asked.

"Well, that's what I understood him to say, but he himself seemed unsure of things." Then he added, "Well, I'm sorry to keep you so long. I must be going."

"Thanks for taking time to talk," Ellen said and added as John Mark was going out the door, "Sometimes I let myself get too upset about the things I hear."

Dusk was falling over the countryside; it would be nearer to go home, but Stanley would wonder what happened to him, so he headed back up there.

It didn't seem like Ellen to let herself get so worked up about something that wasn't in her own school. And she even admitted that Naomi wasn't complaining much about it, but still his heart went out to Wilmer. He was trying to understand what Ellen really had said about neglect. It must be that Wilmer feels neglected since there is no mother at home. Then when others fail to understand him, he believes that others don't like him and it causes rebellion.

Maybe he never stopped to think that the others in the family have given up just as much and his father so much more. Lloyd Good must have a heavy load to carry. John Mark started to think about his own past difficulties. He had to read over the verse again that Dad showed him. Maybe he could explain it to Wilmer.

John Mark was deep in thought, trying to imagine how he could open a conversation with Wilmer, never giving any thought to when he would get a chance to talk to him.

Suddenly, around another curve, a bicycle came gliding toward him. John Mark quickly guided his horse to the right side as he had drifted to the middle of the road. As the ray of his light shone on the bike while it passed, John Mark didn't know if he could believe his eyes as he thought the figure on the bicycle resembled Lloyd Good. Maybe his eyes were just seeing things since he had been talking about and thinking about Wilmer, his son. After all, where could Lloyd be going at this time of the evening away from home?

He wondered if things were really that bad that maybe Lloyd was going over to see his dad for counsel.

Then John Mark's thoughts drifted to his father's work, ordained to work for the Church, helping to keep peace and lighten the burdens that others found too heavy, ordained to help keep house in the church, to see that the weak and poor were supported. Maybe it was no wonder that Dad was showing his years more. Such were his thoughts as he arrived at Stanley's, but as he put the horse away and got ready for bed, he found himself thinking about Wilmer. He was tossing and turning, trying to shake off the responsibility he felt, but he couldn't. It was like a task handed to him that needed to be carried out.

Chapter Nineteen

John Mark walked back to Stanley's on Friday evening, breathing in the gentle April breeze, beckoning spring.

After supper he put on his jacket and sat out on the porch to prepare the geography questions for the seventh and eighth grade, but he wasn't succeeding well. He kept hearing birds proclaiming spring. He almost felt like a prisoner being released for the evening. After the air began to get cooler, he moved inside and bent down over his books.

Later in the evening when he went upstairs to prepare for bed, he opened the closet door to put some things away that he hadn't put away last evening. Then he spied the well-constructed cardboard buggy. His resistance that was weakening earlier as he was walking home from school, and while he was concentrating on the magic of spring, now broke altogether.

Although the last few weeks didn't bring too much encouragement, he didn't let it affect him very much. Maybe Lavina was timid or maybe she was too cautious.

He fell to his knees to pray for strength to continue, but no words came forth. He was at the end of his strength. He was submitting himself to the mercy of God. Past any words he could utter, a few tears came forth after some moments and then an unseen power strengthened his good will and spent spirit. He rose up and went over to the bureau with the little drawer and pulled out his tablet. He almost shook but something drove him on. He pulled the chair over to the window and slowly wrote: "Dear Lavina, This evening I will unburden the spirit in its leading, which I cannot quench." He read over his partly written sentence, and he started shivering. It sounded too demanding. It revealed too much of his long, great struggle. He tossed the paper aside. Maybe he would tell Paul Ray to do the errand at the singing tomorrow evening. He dwelled on that thought awhile. Then he thought, *No one else need ever know. She need not tell anyone face to face.* He would write a note and send it off Saturday. That way she would get it in the beginning of the week and could think it over all week and answer him privately. He hoped he could word the note in such a way that her reply would be God revealing His will to him.

He got another paper and his hand moved as the words formed: "Dear Lavina, This evening as I submit myself to the guiding spirit of the Higher hand in requesting if He sees it good that we—" Then he couldn't word it further. He realized that the word "we" was what didn't sound right. Another paper was cast aside. He started sweating. It was a temptation to let it go. He took a deep breath and carefully guided his pen over the next sheet.

Dear Sister of the same faith: I lean on the strength of a higher power to guide my weak hand, giving up to the submission of His leading. After much prayer, it seems I am led to ask if God is leading you to my company to become more acquainted. I leave it up to you and trust that the higher power will reveal His will to you and let me know if I am to see you in your home on Sunday evening, April 10. I wish you strength in acknowledging the will of the Almighty God. An unworthy brother, sharing the faith, John Mark.

He had crossed out a few words here and there and copied it twice. He reread the note, put it in an envelope, and sealed it before he could change his mind. The sweat stood on his forehead but a great task had been finished.

On Saturday he noticed a few envelopes tucked in Stanley's letter holder to be mailed. John Mark offered to take them along to the mailbox when he went over to school for a few hours. So he safely carried the third letter along, too. It would now be in someone else's hands.

Saturday evening passed without much happening. John Mark did notice Lavina in the back corner of the kitchen near where Walter Horning's were seated during the singing that they had held for the young folks.

178

It seemed to him that often Rhoda would be somewhere near Lavina, but not tonight. Then he remembered again that Rhoda was soon marrying or maybe was married already. He couldn't remember. He wasn't invited to the wedding.

On Sunday morning in church, John Mark worked his way over to where the half-grown boys had gathered, waiting to go into the church house. He pretended to be walking past and just happened to notice the boys. He couldn't locate the face he was looking for. Then he noticed Wilmer, who had just arrived and was parking his bicycle.

John Mark matter-of-factly moved over that way and said, "Hello, Wilmer." He looked at him bewildered and more so when he noticed who he was. John Mark doubted that he could look more surprised if a robin had started talking.

John Mark stepped closer to Wilmer and commented on his bike, asking if he had it awhile already.

Wilmer looked at him for a moment and then looked at his bike saying, "Since my last birthday." John Mark took a closer look and noticed it was a new bike. He hadn't noticed before.

He had just said something to open up a conversation. "Oh, do you mean it's a new bike?" John Mark asked, wiping his hand across the bike seat.

"Yes, it was in September." The conversation continued as John Mark inquired more and he found out that Wilmer's father promised him a new bike for his thirteenth birthday. It was the first new bike he had. John Mark commented that he must have a good father, as he himself had to wait two years longer for a new bike and then it wasn't such a good one.

Then John Mark added while still admiring the bike, "And you are also lucky to have your own father. I don't remember much of my own father."

Wilmer looked at him, half dumbfounded, and then sort of in a daze as if talking to himself he said, "But I have no mother."

"I don't either," John Mark replied sympathizing. He then continued. "But the mother who took mercy on me treats me as her son, and the man she married treats me as a son." Wilmer looked at

179

him, like a frightened puppy who was longing to trust a new master. John Mark could feel he was softening but that he was still holding something back.

John Mark looked at him, tenderly waiting. Then Wilmer said softly, "Can someone else fill the place of your mother?" Wilmer's voice ended unsteadily. John Mark noticed that the other boys Wilmer's age were watching them, and it soon must be time to go into the church house. He had so much to say to this boy, but not here. He selected his words carefully.

"Wilmer, there is a way, and I want to tell you about it sometime. But it's about time for church to begin. I wish you'd come over to my school one evening this week after school is out. I want to tell you about it."

Wilmer was shaking his head, "Spring work has started. I am always busy since Father bought this other farm, so we have that yet to farm and the heifers to feed there."

"Do you feed over there?" Wilmer nodded.

"What time in the evening do you feed them?"

"Usually around five."

"Maybe sometime I can come over there and see the farm and we can visit more." Wilmer looked pleased. Then John Mark remembered to ask which farm, as he hadn't been aware that Lloyd bought another farm. He had just nodded without thinking in order to keep Wilmer talking.

It was hard for John Mark to keep his mind wholeheartedly on school the following week. Every evening he left school rather early, hardly able to contain his anxiety wondering if there was a letter waiting for him. His anxiety was growing with each day. He had sent the note Saturday already and it was now Thursday.

He cautiously asked, "Was there any mail for me?"

"There sure was," Erma replied, "*The Blackboard Bulletin* came!" A sense of depression overwhelmed him.

He said, "Is that all?"

Erma looked up in disbelief; at length she asked, "Can spring even dampen your school interest?" putting a hard accent on "even" and "your." She no doubt was remembering the times when it was said, "The *Bulletin* has come" and he went instantly to snatch it up before taking off his wraps and scanned over it eagerly. When he looked up, Stanley was silently watching him as if he was able to read his thoughts. Stanley remained silent. Erma looked first at John Mark, then at Stanley with a questioning look on her face. Something in Stanley's expression seemed to tell her that it was best not to ask any questions.

Arising from the supper table John Mark leafed through *The Blackboard Bulletin* a little and then said, "I am going on a spin to do an errand yet tonight."

Until John Mark got over to the farm where Wilmer fed the heifers, Wilmer had most of the chores already done. He seemed surprised to see him, and John Mark soon sensed that Wilmer wasn't very talkative. He had made attempts to get a conversation started asking about the cattle and so on, then he made the mistake of asking how his day was in school. Wilmer seemed more sullen. John Mark asked a few questions about his teacher, Naomi, but he didn't get much of a response. John Mark never remembered just what had burst the bubble, but it came about while John Mark stood against the wooden feed bin in the feed entry while Wilmer was reaching over in the heifer pen closing the water faucet.

Wilmer's pent-up feelings suddenly opened. He talked disrespectfully about teachers. John Mark had been listening in silence, too shocked to answer. Sometime later John Mark became aware that Wilmer was using Ellen's name. Without thinking, John Mark quickly defended Ellen, so John Mark was now talking and Wilmer was listening.

John Mark recalled the good that Ellen did in his own life, how he had an interest in school work and Ellen asked him to be a helper. As she worked with him, he gained confidence. Over the years without realizing it, he was being prepared to take his own school. "She had the patience to teach me and now teaching has become my future." He went on to explain, "Teachers are often looked upon as bossy and as if they desired to punish children, but in truth we are like children. That's why our desire leads us to work with children. If the pupils loved us as much as we did them, our work would be so much easier."

Now and then, Wilmer asked a few questions which kept John Mark in a sober conversation. Somehow they got off the subject of school, as Wilmer was asking again about how John Mark learned to cope with a mother and father who were only step-parents, if it was that.

John Mark explained the verse that his father had shown him and said, "For I reckon that the suffering of this present time is not worthy to be compared with the glory which shall be revealed in us. It must mean that the things that are hard here are not worthy to compare with the joy that awaits us." His father explained that it seemed to refer to the things that now seem hard, things that we cannot accept.

"For example, I found it hard when Father and Mother were married and had their firstborn, and people said he looked like his father or mother. It made my lot more noticeable that I didn't look like them, and I got depressed. Dad explained that I had to remember even if this was hard, how much harder it would be if I wasn't adopted. If I had to stay in the Home or be pushed from one foster home to another, I would have had heavier burdens to bear. They would not be worthy to compare with something as little as not looking like the others in the family."

John Mark caught his breath and took in a fresh breath to continue when Wilmer cut him off saying, "Do you mean that maybe there could be a thing like accepting a stepmother and finding that it could be more pleasant than having no mother?"

"Of course," John Mark continued, hardly even knowing himself what he was saying, "That certainly would be more of a blessing than if your father had to carry the whole load of the family by himself. He could be much more forbearing with you and the rest of the children if his load wasn't so heavy. That would surely make life easier for you. There would still be times of discouragement, but you would also have times of discouragement if your mother had lived, only now you always blame everything on her death, but it isn't always the cause. We just tend to always blame it on that. Yes, I am sure that if the time ever came, you could not compare the present suffering to the joy it would hold." Suddenly Wilmer seemed sort of uneasy and alarmed. John Mark asked him if something was wrong.

He said, "I just remembered the ones at home may be wondering what happened to me. I am usually home long before this and—"

"Oh, I am sorry," John Mark said, standing up straight. "I didn't realize how long we were talking. I don't want to keep you. I have to be going too."

Wilmer looked at him and said, "Thank you," much like an innocent child who meant it so much that his appearance showed it even if words failed.

That evening as John Mark retired for the night, he kept tossing and turning. He had to sort his unsettled thoughts first. He had some unwinding to do. When he thought he had reviewed everything in his mind, his thoughts drifted into dreams. He suddenly jerked awake again, as the disturbing thought crossed his mind that things did not add up. He was trying to remember how they got started talking about Ellen. He thought Wilmer had first mentioned her when he seemed so critical about teachers. It hadn't occurred to him till now that Naomi was his teacher. What had he against Ellen? Then he remembered it was Ellen who told him about Wilmer's bitterness in life.

It must be that Naomi and Ellen share a bit with each other. After another half-hour of tossing, he relaxed enough to go to sleep.

When the spring birds sang him awake the next morning, anxiety again ruled John Mark's mind. The thoughts of the evening before had dulled. This was now Friday. Tomorrow would be Saturday. Would he have any desire to go to the singing? Would he have to go to get an answer to his note to Lavina since no answer was coming in the mail?

Arriving at school, he was soon occupied with the work and activity. That made him able to continue the day with not much time to think of the disappointment he had been tasting. In the afternoon he decided he wouldn't borrow more disappointments by leaving school early in hopes there was an answer.

After checking a few stacks of workbooks, he saw the letter that Katie had written asking about some of the material he was using for Edgar. He gave the clock another glance as he reached for the envelope and re-read Katie's letter. Then he got a tablet and started answering, explaining about the new company he found that had some sort of game-like things that were a good challenge to Edgar. He explained in what areas it was helpful for him and in what ways he responded.

John Mark was so deep in thought that he had been separated from all else. Thus he was roused from a dazed state of mind when the schoolhouse door opened. He stared in silence as a girl entered, looking at him and smiling cheerfully, then stopping to pull the door closed behind her.

John Mark's mind could not register; he was in a stupor. As she made her way up the middle aisle to his desk, she looked up again and he said out loud, "Rhoda?"

She looked up again, sort of embarrassed, and said, "Yes, you act like you don't know me."

"I almost don't in a schoolhouse," John Mark admitted, still wondering if he was seeing right.

"A schoolhouse always fascinated me," she said, lingering at the desk right in front of John Mark's desk.

"You have never taught, have you?" he asked.

"No—well, yes, I have substituted quite a bit but I was never a teacher. I always found enough to do without getting involved in teaching."

"And now you have Warren to keep house for. The wedding took place already didn't it?"

"Yes, yesterday a week ago," she mused.

"Where's Warren? Is he coming in too?"

"No," she smiled, "he was working on the hog barn. He is getting a bunch of pigs later tonight."

She paused and then lifted her eyes, and in a low, kind voice said, "John Mark, has the week been long for you?" John Mark was a little startled at her change of voice. He could almost feel sympathy in the tone of voice.

John Mark looked at her for a moment. "Er, well, maybe it was a little long, or else a full one," he said, trying to remember if it was just last Sunday he had first talked with Wilmer.

Calm Rhoda suddenly seemed a little flustered as she said, "I mean were you looking for a letter all week?" How those words made his heart tremble and stirred his thoughts! Suddenly, he remembered that in times past the few times he saw Lavina, Rhoda was usually connected. They must be close friends.

Rhoda broke the silence by saying, "I hadn't known until last night when Lavina came and I had a long talk with her. I pleaded with her. Oh, well, she has been my close friend for many years and I have on countless times had to carry messages to boys who asked for her friendship. I don't know what form of a letter she received from you, but I know it has touched her deeper than anyone else ever touched her."

John Mark was watching in full attention. He had thirsted so long for a response and now he wanted to grasp it all.

When Rhoda stopped to catch her breath and stole a glance at him, John Mark leaned forward asking, "Are you saying she has been asked for her friendship before by others?"

"Yes, John Mark, more than once," she almost sighed.

"Is there a problem?" John Mark asked when Rhoda hesitated.

Rhoda looked at him briefly and said, "I trust that if you have been considering this, you then know her well enough to know she has a problem."

"Well, I am sort of in the dark. I have realized some, and I heard a little bit in snatches, but I never was able to find out the cause or reason. Maybe she is more than bashful?" he asked.

Rhoda nodded, "Her feeling of inferiority has caused her to be shy."

"And what causes her inferiority?" John Mark pressed the matter now that someone was finally opening up.

"I guess you'd say boys make her feel inferior. She shouldn't hold herself up so much about it; her parents failed and that's in the past, but it left a scar with her. And so far I haven't been able to reach through to her in that sense."

John Mark was trying to keep up with Rhoda's outline, but she left so much to fill in. If his pupils had made such a scant outline, he'd count it as unfinished.

John Mark swallowed tears and said in a gruff voice, "I'm sorry you had to carry this out for me. I pushed it off for awhile, but it seemed to be the thing I was led to do. But please understand me, I don't want to coax anyone. I wanted to know if she had any leading in that direction, that it might be God's will that we become better acquainted. To me it seemed so, but I kept doubting it, and I tried to ask in a polite way and hoped that she would feel free to answer. I thought I'd do it privately so that no one needed to know, as I sensed it may cause her to feel embarrassed."

"Like I said," Rhoda sighed, "I did this more than once, but never like this before. We talked way into the night. To me it seems she felt you were earnest in your undertaking, and yet she is convinced she can't accept it. Well, she is strange, I admit." Rhoda sighed again.

"I wouldn't call that strange, someone not accepting my company. I felt unworthy asking her. If I had known she had refused more qualified boys, I would not have asked, besides being a little handicapped with childhood polio, and the fact that I am adopted I—"

Rhoda cut him off as she held up her hand and started talking in earnest. "That's just it. That's why she is so broken up. She is concerned that you will take it like that. It isn't that. Then I told her, 'Well, then accept it and give in once.' But she had for so long resolved not to get involved that it seems her decision cannot be broken. I tried to tell her it might be more rebellion than inferiority, but like I said, she is not refusing your offer in joy. She is in more anguish than I have ever seen her before. Warren and I were over this morning to talk with her, trying to get her to see things differently for her sake, or asking if she wanted to think about it another few days before refusing, but she said it would not help."

John Mark shook his head, "Don't coax her anymore. I wouldn't have wanted her company if I thought it was forced. I just wanted to know how she felt; now I know—"

Rhoda blew her nose and said, "I doubt that you fully understand, and neither do I. I doubt she even does, but please, John Mark, don't let it discourage you. Don't ever think that it was because of your background."

"I understand that. I gather more than you realize. I want to respect Lavina for her concern and her goal. I hope this won't make her scars any deeper."

Rhoda looked at him in wonderment, then said, "I dreaded coming to talk with you more than I ever dreaded anything before. Thanks for making it so easy. I didn't expect you to understand; I am not sure that I do."

"I think I now know how David felt when he sorrowed while his son lay ill and would not be comforted and would not eat. Then when his son died, the servants were afraid to go tell him the news, but David asked and after he was told, he rose and washed his face and ate. Then he knew God's will and what he had to do. I feel a bit like that."

Rhoda thanked him again and left in silence. When he saw the buggy disappearing, he went down in the basement and let the tears come until his face was washed in submission. Then he came back up and got his things to go home to Stanley's. He was glad it was Friday so that he had time to recover and also to get hold of himself another day before meeting the young folks. But he felt a sense of submission like a child with his will finally broken.

When he went to Stanley's the family was out milking. There was a plate of food reserved for him and he was hungry.

He was reading *The Blackboard Bulletin* when the family came in. The *Bulletin* was almost too interesting to put down, but it turned out to be an interesting evening just visiting. He guessed it was just a regular evening, but he knew he had been a poor visitor lately. When Erma went upstairs to put Walter to bed, Stanley praised John Mark for his cheerfulness.

"I was getting worried about you. I hope things work out for you. We ourselves have been through times we couldn't understand and lately again when Erma wasn't well, but there is always joy if we hold out. I was praying things would also be good for you again."

"Thank you. I didn't realize other people prayed for me. It

was not in vain." When Erma came downstairs, John Mark and Stanley were talking about the season of spring and its beauty and the longer days.

John Mark said, "I might move home again since the days are longer."

"Well, you must know we would miss you," Stanley said.

"Yes, Walter would too," Erma said. "He was just telling me how John Mark told him the Three Little Pigs story and then he asked me if he may say in his prayers, 'Thank you that John Mark is happy.'"

"You said Walter asked that just now upstairs?" Stanley asked. Erma nodded. Stanley and John Mark looked at each other, each grasping the value of the faithfulness of a child.

Chapter Twenty

John Mark checked his watch. It was a little early to go to the singing, more so since he didn't have far to go. But he wasn't anxious to go. As if delaying would help matters, John Mark opened the closet door and began packing some more of his things. He had done a little that morning and now continued the job. Then he came to the well-constructed cardboard buggy that his lunch had been packed in at school. It no longer seemed so special. It must have been made as a favor to Dennis's mother. Should he keep it? Of course he would. He would always say Dennis gave it to him when they had the lunch exchange.

He thought he heard something. He looked out the window and saw it was raining a little. He looked at his watch again and decided he might as well start off. When he came down in the kitchen, Erma was standing at the window and looked at him sort of surprised.

Then she asked, "Are you going to a singing or have you other plans?"

"I plan to go to the singing at Jacob Weaver's. Why?"

Then she looked out the window again and said, "I just noticed your father is here. I didn't know if you were expecting him."

"My father?" John Mark repeated. Then he walked to the window where he could see Dad and Stanley standing in the wagon shed talking. John Mark noticed that Dad was rather dressed up, and he hurried outside. As he walked up to the wagon shed, Stanley excused himself.

"I thought I'd stop in to see if you were still here. I thought maybe you left already for the evening," Dad greeted him.

"I have only two miles to go down the road to Jacob Weaver's," John Mark explained. Then he added. "Where are you going?"

"I am not going away; I am coming home," Dad said rather wearily. John Mark waited. He could tell that Dad had more things on his mind.

"We took Mother to the hospital this morning," Dad began, with pain in every word. "The baby was born at home and things weren't going well." Dad took a quick look at John Mark when he had gasped. Then Dad continued, "Mother had emergency surgery and I was with her all day. Things looked a little better the last two hours."

"Is Delores alone with the children?" John Mark asked.

"No, Helen is there. The baby might come home tomorrow. We took it along in, but the baby seems to be doing well."

"Oh, then it isn't very small?" John Mark asked, surprised.

Dad looked at him and said, "No, it is around eight pounds." The way Dad looked at him, John Mark could tell that Dad gathered he had not been aware of hearing this kind of news.

"Did you say Mother is better?" John Mark asked.

"Yes, better, not well, but stable again. She was quite low when she came to the hospital. Not in shape for surgery but there was no choice." John Mark told his father that he was packing his clothes to come home Tuesday evening.

As Dad turned to leave, John Mark asked, "Is it a brother?"

"No, a sister, didn't I say? It makes three of each. We called her Lavina."

"Lavina!" John Mark gasped as if he had been just severely shocked.

Dad turned around and looked at him asking, "What's wrong with that name? What do you think we should have called her?" John Mark stood open-mouthed and couldn't speak.

"That's the name of mother's only sister, the one who died when she was two weeks old. But why are you so shocked? Do you have a mischievous pupil by that name?"

John Mark shook his head and said, "It's a name you don't hear very often. Guess I thought only older people were called that," John Mark replied rather weakly.

"Oh, let me see, isn't that the name of one of the Ringler girls?" Dad asked. John Mark pretended to be thinking, then nodded his head without looking up. He was hoping his face wasn't as warm as it felt.

Dad turned to go and said, "Well, we'll be looking for you on Tuesday."

It pulled hard to leave Stanley's, but as soon as he arrived home on Tuesday evening the stakes were all dug in again. It was good to be home. Delores was growing. He almost had to look twice, and Josiah had even lost some of his childlike blabbering. He seemed quite well-mannered. William still hadn't much to say, but his smiles were much appreciated. John Mark soon saw that William's alert eyes didn't miss much. He often knew more than you expected he would. Rebecca was so chubby and life was such a joy to her.

John Mark was grateful for all the times she made a smile appear on Dad's face when otherwise Dad said little and looked heavy-laden the time he was at home. Every day he was at the hospital part of the time. Helen played the role well of being a mother, seeing after the little ones, having meals on the table and clean clothes for the family. When the baby came home, she thrived on tender loving care. It caused Helen to feel a big responsibility to be the mother of a newborn. Her mother came over a few evenings to relieve her and assure her.

As little as the baby was, John Mark marveled at the power she had of being able to better fill the emptiness that Mother's absence had caused. The baby filled it better than anyone else could. At times as John Mark bent over his books in the evening, when the younger ones were in bed, he found himself automatically distracted from lessons as he watched Dad caring for the baby and expressing himself to her. There was a deep bond there, partly filling the vacancy Mother's absence left. It was during these times that Dad seemed more like his natural self.

*　　*　　*　　*

There was the usual shuffling sounds of putting away the songbooks when the last words of the hymn were being sung at Dry Hill Church. It had seemed good to attend the home church again. The people paused a little, waiting until Bishop Christian dismissed church with the usual benedictions and everyone grew quiet.

Christian first made an announcement. "I have yet to announce that a brother and sister desire to step into matrimony and this falls on Lloyd Good and Isaac Fox's Ellen; further, I will not keep up the services."

The church house remained deathly still until the truth soaked into the minds. Then you could hear the rustle as people started breathing again. It seemed everyone held their breath. It took John Mark longer to recover.

Most of the boys had filed out of church before he came to his senses and realized that filing out was the proper thing to do. John Mark thought he should ask to have the announcement repeated. Did he actually say Lloyd Good and Isaac Fox's Ellen? Teacher Ellen? Marrying widower Lloyd Good? Lloyd Good who was Wilmer's father? When he came outside, he heard Justus saying something to Mark about "Well, Anna was saying that Ellen wasn't going to teach again, but we didn't know why." And the subject was soon changed.

John Mark was unwinding his thoughts on the way home. He hadn't even thought of it till he heard Justus say that must have been why Ellen changed her mind about teaching. On the way home, he was thinking how he should have caught on. Ellen was so troubled about Wilmer, and Wilmer was bitter toward Ellen. Now it was starting to make sense why he was bitter toward Ellen when she wasn't even his teacher. She was planning, instead, to take his mother's place. He had thought Naomi was sharing her teaching experience with Ellen since she seemed to know about Wilmer's struggles. John Mark still remembered how he had defended Ellen to Wilmer. But he couldn't remember what he had said to Ellen when she talked about Wilmer.

His thoughts were still in a tangled maze when he reached home. The announcement was the main topic at the dinner table. The children all began talking about Teacher Ellen getting married.

Delores was proclaiming that Marietta would like Ellen for a mother. Marietta was next to Wilmer and was about Delores's age, and Susannah was only a year or so younger. Then Delores had more to say. "Hey Mom, how old are Lloyd's twins? Weren't they the babies—I mean the youngest?"

Mother nodded her head in agreement saying, "That's right. I had momentarily forgotten. Yes, let me see. They were about three months old or so when Lloyd's wife died. They must be nearly two years old. I guess Lloyd's sister and husband live nearby and have the twins most of the time. At times Lloyd's had hired help, but not always."

John Mark had been wondering on the way home why when there were other older girls around did Lloyd have to choose Ellen who was such a gifted teacher. But he now realized that it would take a gifted person to fill that role. He thought of the past week when Mother was in the hospital. What a joy it was when Mother came home on Saturday afternoon. Although she was usually in bed, it still was good to have her at home. On Saturday evening John Mark had heard Dad singing to himself when he was doing the chores. It was then he realized that it was the first time he heard Dad singing since he moved home. And it was something Dad would often do, singing while going about his work.

When the children left the table, John Mark lingered while Mother and Dad were visiting.

Mother was asking some questions about this unexpected marriage and John Mark heard Dad say to Mother, "Aaron said that Lloyd and Ellen have been courting at Ellen's schoolhouse in the evenings through the week."

Dad looked at John Mark asking, "Had you been aware of Ellen's plans? We heard that she wasn't teaching again, but I didn't hear more. Then I thought it was only a rumor."

"I heard it a few times but I never figured it out. I was even asked to teach at her school, but when I asked Ellen she didn't say she wasn't teaching again. In fact, she said she will still be teaching children, but she didn't say where."

Dad said, "Well, I guess you know where now."

John Mark was thinking deeply about what Dad had said about Lloyd and Ellen courting at Ellen's school in the evening during the week. Had he looked back on that evening he could probably have seen it. John Mark mused as he remembered the evening he had stopped in at Ellen's school to talk with her. She looked up as if she was expecting him, but then was surprised when she saw him. He remembered how Ellen kept watching the clock and had the schoolhouse all cleaned up, and then on the way home he had met Lloyd down the road. Now it all fit together. Naomi didn't have to be involved for Ellen to know about Wilmer's struggles. Ellen had said it showed more at home than at school.

As John Mark sat back on the sofa and watched Helen put the dishes away, he heard Mom and Dad discussing the ages of Ellen and Lloyd. Dad figured Lloyd to be about ten years or so older than Ellen. John Mark guessed Ellen to be about twenty-four or so, and now she would have a boy in eighth grade.

Chapter Twenty-One

As the echo of the horse's hooves singing on the blacktop grew fainter, an ache grew in John Mark's heart. The horse's echo on the road was growing fainter because Justus was leaving. It had been a good evening. Paul Ray's parents had invited the young folks for supper and since the day had been so pleasant, they hauled all the food and people up to the woods that bordered their back fields, and they ate there. Most all had walked through the woods, exploring the different paths. Now the evening was far spent and departing teams could be heard going in several directions.

Chester, Justus, Levi, and all the guys were present and together like they had been in earlier years. But now one by one they left the group. They had sent someone to tell their girls that they were ready to go. Chester must be seeing Ella Grace at her married sister's place as her home wasn't in this area. John Mark's friends weren't as carefree as they used to be. They now had responsibilities. But the boys didn't call it that. They were eager. Their relationships with the girls exceeded the friendship that the boys had had with each other. Paul Ray was still somewhere. Likely up at the barnyard, seeing that all the couples got started off.

John Mark felt rather carefree all day since school was closed for the summer. There were no school thoughts looming in the background, trying to interrupt when he let his mind wander a bit. But even if there were no school thoughts disturbing him, there were still clouds closing in, marring the peaceful clearness of his day.

He thought of earlier in the day when they were eating supper in the woods, he had seen a group of girls eating down by the pool under the big elms. He recognized Lavina with two other girls.

But he had only seen a few glimpses of her since that fateful day when he had written that letter and Rhoda came to bring the answer. Her presence didn't affect him quite like it had before he knew she was denied him. But there was still a scar. Part of a song came to his mind when he saw the girls by the cool, shady place, eating. "*By cool Siloam's shady rill.*" Then thinking of what was denied him, his thoughts went to the words further in the song. "*Whose secret heart, with influence sweet—*" He couldn't remember what came next, but so his offer must remain a secret; it can't be shared. He noticed when Mary Ethel walked out to Menno's approaching buggy, Lavina was with her. Maybe that meant Priscilla had no other way home. It was no secret anymore that Elmer had an interest in Priscilla. Now and then he took her along when it was convenient.

John Mark started walking toward the house to get his hat. He decided he would go home early since most of his friends had left already. As he came walking around the corner of the house a few girls were sitting on chairs on the lawn, watching the croquet game that was just coming to an end in another part of the yard. He started walking past when he noticed Katie was in the second chair.

He asked, "Well, what are you going to do now that school is over for the whole summer?"

She turned around and looked up to see who was speaking, then she said, "Huh, I thought it was only other people who thought that a teacher's work ends during summer vacation."

"Why? Are you planning your speech already for the August meeting?" John Mark asked, kidding her. She took a long breath and looked at Naomi who was sitting next to her. John Mark hadn't noticed who was sitting next to her.

Then Katie explained, "I was just telling her how much iron I have in the fire."

Naomi looked over at her and said, "You mean you will if the fire ever gets started?"

"Yes," Katie said, "every time I think I have a flame burning on the west side, then a west wind blows up and puffs it out so I start on the east side—" She held the last word, making it sound like a hopeless story. Just then Kathryn came and tapped Naomi on the shoulder and they exchanged a nod. Naomi bid, "So long" to the rest. Apparently Marcus had sent his sister to tell Naomi that he was ready to leave. John Mark thought the couples had all left already.

John Mark looked at Katie, who was still yelling something after Naomi, then he took the chair that Naomi had vacated and said, "You make me curious as to what fire you are trying to start?"

Katie looked at him a moment as if trying to remember. "Oh," she took a deep breath, ending by asking, "didn't you hear?"

John Mark shrugged his shoulders saying, "I don't think I did," beckoning her to continue.

"Oh well," she started saying, then shook her head as if erasing her thoughts. She started over, "I had a few letters from my cousin Miriam in the past months." She looked at him expecting him to understand.

"Miriam who?"

"You know, she teaches in Missouri," Katie explained.

"Oh, yes," John Mark tried to recall, "I guess I heard already. Let me see, she doesn't teach the eighth grade. Isn't she just helping or something?"

"She used to be a helper in school," Katie corrected. "She was helping a few pupils who were rather slow in learning, and then the other year she also had a deaf pupil. Last year she had her own little room where she taught the two slow learners and the deaf child. But around February one of the neighboring schools sent another pupil over to her who had a speech problem, so she had to have a helper because in special education, you are allowed to have only three pupils per teacher. This coming year they will have five pupils and—"

John Mark quickly cut her off by interrupting and saying, "And you are going to Missouri to help her teach?"

"No, but you are coming on the track. Reading her letters just made me more aware that it's not fair to teach my pupil Suetta with the rest of the pupils. She doesn't get out of school what she would if I had more time or if I had a helper, and the ones who can learn by themselves learn to depend more on me for help. But I don't blame Ivan's if they don't want to send Suetta to the special education class

197

in town. Doris feels much the same way about Calvin. Calvin wouldn't have much further to come over to my school . . ." Katie was getting out of breath.

John Mark nodded his head, "Oh, so you are trying to tell me that you are starting up a special education class."

"I've lit the flame many a time, but—" then she sighed.

"But what wind blows? No one to teach your regular school?"

"Oh, yes. Erla will as she's not teaching at Rock View again because Anetta Horning wants that school. It is a smaller school for a beginner to start. But Edward's are having a hard time submitting themselves to the idea that Calvin can't be taught in the regular school. The biggest problem is, where will I teach them? It is too expensive to build a school for a few pupils, and the basement in my school wouldn't be suitable for a schoolroom. The empty end of Luke's house would suit fine, but it would almost be too far for Suetta. We are having a meeting again this week."

"So school didn't end for you?" he asked.

"No," she chuckled, "I have many things to prepare, books to gather. I feel like a first-year teacher. Just the other day I found out there might be a third pupil. There was a first grader supposed to start in my regular school this fall who is very shy and sensitive, but the parents were confident that I could handle her. Now they are upset that I won't be teaching there."

"So will they send her wherever you will teach?" John Mark guessed.

"Well, maybe. You are a much better listener than Naomi was." Then Katie quickly added, "Maybe Naomi is losing interest in school talk."

John Mark said, thinking out loud, "I heard that Grace will teach at Four Acres."

"Oh yes?" Katie asked, and added, "Naomi didn't say she wasn't teaching again."

"She plans to help order the supplies, which we will do tomorrow," John Mark added.

Now and then the porch door opened and whistling broke the

twilight stillness. Then suddenly from somewhere behind the bushes, more whistles echoed.

John Mark looked around and asked, "What is everyone up to?"

Katie answered softly as she got up from her chair, "I don't think the people realize this is a teacher's meeting." Everyone else had cleared out of the yard. "Guess I should go see where everyone else is," Katie said.

"Oh," John Mark said in surprise, "I didn't mean to keep you." He hurried to the house where he was greeted with congratulations and good-natured pats and remarks that didn't mean anything to him. Just as the commotion died down an awful uproar started up in the kitchen. It sounded like an opossum attached a house full of chickens. Apparently Katie had just then entered the kitchen. He wondered if Katie was insulted. He didn't know much about Katie other than her teacher activities. It wasn't often that she was at the singings in the home district as she came from Elm Grove, the area where Dad's sister Naomi lives, but there were some more here from Elm Grove this evening.

*   *   *   *

When the dawn of the new morning peeped into the window through the half-raised curtain the next morning, John Mark rested awhile, musing over the evening. He wondered what Lavina would have thought if she had been there. Then he thought of Baby Lavina and of Mother, who was about back to health again, except for maybe tiring sooner. It seemed the whole family was closer knit since they had come so near to giving up Mother. For a while John Mark was trying to pinpoint the feeling it had caused to grow in the family. He then gradually realized they were taught in truth and example that earthly work was only a secondary matter or maybe a third. Family ties and serving God was the goal. The deacon office came next, then work, and finally, earthly cares.

John Mark realized it was Monday and the teachers of that area were gathering at his school to order supplies for the new term.

Coming downstairs John Mark smelled the bacon and eggs that were about ready to be served. When he came into the kitchen, Dad was sitting in his chair leafing through the Bible. He was dressed up like it was Sunday. Mother was putting breakfast on the table. Only Delores and Josiah and the baby were awake yet. While John Mark stood silently looking at Mother dressed up too, she lifted her eyes and looked at him a moment. Then she looked at Dad who was paging around in the Bible. Something wasn't right. A stone seemed to come in John Mark's throat where hunger had been minutes before.

Father looked up and said, "I'm depending on you to be home today. We will leave the children in your care. Late last night we received the message that Grandma Wenger died and we are going over for most of the day. We'll take only the baby along."

Unbidden tears formed in John Mark's eyes, "Not Grandma Wenger!" She had seemed so concerned about him. In silence, John Mark and Dad looked at each other in a daze.

At length Dad said, "It was her desire. She longed for rest. She was often uncomfortable. I knew it would come sometime, but I didn't think it would be so soon. We don't sorrow because she went; we sorrow because we can't go with her."

Just before his parents left, John Mark remembered to tell them to stop in at Naomi's place to tell her to let the other teachers know that they wouldn't be coming together to order school supplies today, likely not until next week.

Chapter Twenty-Two

The blue October skies were cloudless and the breeze seemed so gentle and mild now after the chilly, frosty mornings of last week. The trees were changing to their autumn array of red and gold.

As John Mark paused and gazed out the window, he didn't see the autumn display that the view offered. For a moment he stared; then slowly he reached for the next envelope and pulled out the report card. There were three more to fill in. He didn't quite get done on Friday evening so he took the last six along home, but before he had finished them, Martha Ann had stopped by as she was having a struggle with Richard. They had discussed their special education pupils, compared them, and sympathized. Apparently, she had gone to see Ellen, and Ellen had sent her over to him. Ellen was now a busy mother.

In another half-hour the last report was completed. John Mark thought about the past week of school. His thoughts were troubled. Every year Edgar fell further behind his age level. He still wasn't able to get him back up to where they had left off in May. He thought he would have more time to spend with him since he had only two first graders, but somehow it didn't work out that way.

John Mark looked up when the bedroom door opened. He thought only Mother and Baby Lavina were in the house and Mother was cleaning the kitchen. Dad passed slowly out through the kitchen. It looked as if he had just awakened and didn't feel very energetic. Usually Dad was in his study when he was in the house during the day. John Mark heard Dad sigh, as he sat down heavily on the rocker. After a few minutes, John Mark heard Mother talking in quiet tones and Dad giving her a quiet answer without many words.

When he finally understood some of the conversation it was about a dinner invitation for Sunday, and John Mark started thinking about tomorrow—Sunday. Stanley's had invited the young folks for dinner so he was going over in that district for church and for dinner. He was looking forward to it. He hadn't seen Walter for a while and well—he buried his head in his hands. He should not even think about it, but he did. (He was anxious, although most every time he was disappointed it still caused anxious thoughts.)

John Mark heard the door open and close. Then he heard Mother continue the cleaning. John Mark came out from the living room and sat on the sofa. Mother looked at him a moment and then continued washing off the windowsills.

The complaining sounds coming from the daytime crib were beckoning but not urgent, and Mother looked at the clock, walked over to the crib, and gathered Baby Lavina up in her arms. She soothed her and deposited her into John Mark's lap saying, "Here is something for you to do if you want something to do." That didn't suit the baby at all. John Mark held her more upright and talked to her. Mother put the pacifier in Lavina's mouth and she quieted down.

Mother turned back to the cleaning saying, "Guess Delores will soon be finished mowing the yard."

As Mother continued cleaning, John Mark asked, "Isn't Dad feeling well? I noticed he took a nap again instead of spending the noon hour in his study."

Mother washed the woodwork around the window as if she hadn't heard.

Then as she rinsed her rag out in the pail, she answered softly with feeling, "He isn't resting well at night, so at times he sleeps a little during the day."

John Mark pressed the matter further. "I thought with communion being over things usually went better for a while again."

"Yes, my son," Mother said without looking up, "but he has a hard battle. He says he is losing spiritual strength. He misses his mother's prayers."

"What about me?" John Mark finally asked after grasping the fact.

Mother turned around and looked at him shocked, "John Mark, we do pray for you."

"I know, but you're not my own father and mother, and since they aren't around there are other people praying in their stead, and I am sure there are many fervent prayers made for those who lead the church."

"I know," Mother answered. "I keep reminding him, but he says he can feel he lost spiritual strength."

"Doesn't Dad remember how the bishop from Elm Grove explained that earlier this year when they were here in church?"

"Was he here this year?" Mom asked.

"Yes. It was when you and Dad were in Ohio because I remember there was only him and Christian there that day. It was while old David Levi lay so low. They had been visiting Levi and a minister from another state was making a call there, too. That minister said when his father lay lingering so low, someone wrote to him saying that we have to be patient as God never takes a post away from the church until he puts another post there first. He explained that's why the church does not lose strength because God does not take away until another support is in place. And sometimes a person has to linger if another one is slow in fulfilling his duty. He said maybe this brother has to linger because one of us isn't faithful enough yet in praying and supporting the church like this brother did."

Mother just stood watching and listening in silence drinking in deeply, and then she picked up a paper and disappeared into the bedroom. By the time she came out, William had seated himself at the table and was looking at a book. Mother continued washing the kitchen furniture.

John Mark suddenly asked, "Mother, I wonder—I mean—Ah . . . I was at Dennis's place last week for supper, and I held their baby. She was a . . . well, she didn't like being a baby. Lavina lies so cozy and content against me—" John Mark finished as he fondly enjoyed her and brushed her hair out of her face. Her hair was becoming thicker and longer. She looked so like a doll.

John Mark was unaware of the silence that followed until he realized Mother had blown her nose twice. When he looked up she was wiping tears from her eyes, but more tears came. John Mark quickly lowered his eyes pretending he had not seen.

Then Mother came and gently talked saying, "Yes, just the other week when we were in town the doctor told us that she will always remain our baby. How small a one we don't know, but help love her. I had been wondering; I thought she was slower than some other babies. She'll need special care and love. The doctor thought so from the beginning, but waited to tell us until he was sure."

"Is that part of Dad's burden?" John Mark asked.

"It doesn't make it easier. But maybe if he sees how you adore her as she is he will see it differently."

She was such a cute doll, but it took a few moments for John Mark to grasp the truth. Then a fresh pain crossed his heart when he thought *Why does she have to be named Lavina?* He often wondered what Lavina Ringler thought when she heard the baby's name. It still almost humiliated him. But as far as he knew, no one but Rhoda, Warren, and Lavina herself knew that he had asked her for her company and was refused.

*   *   *   *

The afternoon at Stanley's was far spent. Stanley served a delicious meal to the young folks, and most of the boys had walked through the woods and spent their time looking at the neighbor's sawmill.

Bit by bit, the boys started back to Stanley's in small groups. Paul Ray was lingering behind and John Mark waited around. The rest of their gang had supper plans here and there. The girls usually had many plans; it seemed as if the others were often going places since they had girlfriends.

Paul Ray poured out his wounded heart. For a long time he admired Verna who was a few years older than himself. He waited until he was a little older to ask her for her friendship, and now he had been refused. He was quite discouraged.

He said, "I should have known I wasn't worthy of her. If only I hadn't asked." He continued to grieve.

John Mark sympathized with him and said, "I know the pain. I was also a victim."

"Of Verna?" Paul Ray asked, muffled and surprised.

"No, not Verna, but it hurt just as much." Then he added, "Maybe there is someone she is watching or waiting on who won't receive her. Then she will consider you again."

"Is that what you are waiting on?" Paul Ray asked, blowing his nose.

"No, I guess she is too pure for any guy. I'm waiting until I feel a leading elsewhere or maybe I'll be called to walk through life single."

Paul Ray was gathering up a handful of leaves and arranging them in the form of a fan when he looked up and gazed at John Mark. Then he asked quite wonderingly, "Guess you know that Judith respects you highly and seems to enjoy your presence?"

John Mark felt his face get warm and he asked surprised, "Did you notice?"

"Yes, I've been noticing. What are you waiting on?"

"I admit she seems to understand me. At first I responded to her smiles and gentle glances, but I started sensing that it was more than a friendly concern and her affections were growing deeper, but mine weren't. Then I could understand a little better why I was turned down by the other one if there just weren't any special feelings there."

"Maybe you don't allow them to grow. Maybe once you forget the other one, feelings for Judith could grow. Isn't that what you were telling me about Verna's feelings once she stopped dwelling on someone else?"

"Well, maybe an admiration can grow for someone else, but not Judith." John Mark shook his head and added, "She is just too hasty. She hasn't looked elsewhere yet."

The boys continued to reason with and encourage each other as they slowly made their way down toward the building. As they rounded the field lane between the heifer shed and meadow, they heard shouts inside the shed and then two boys came running across the lane, disappearing into the shed.

Paul Ray stopped for a moment and said, "Sounds like the horses are stirred up."

"Or then the boys," John Mark added. "Maybe the boys are helping Stanley chase in the cows and they got the horses stirred up." They met more boys in the shed all looking one way.

Paul Ray asked, "What's going on?"

Mervin turned around and said, "A horse got loose and some more were tearing back." Just then a few boys jumped over the trough to give aid. They viewed the scene. A horse was still laying; the boys were loosening the horse beside it and tying it elsewhere. Stanley loosened the horse that was down, speaking gently to it. Some gasps could be heard as the horse struggled to get up. It flopped down; the front leg hung in an odd position. Instantly John Mark was up over the partition without realizing that he went over. He spoke soothingly to Charlotte. She whinnied. The boys backed up a little.

Elton asked, "Is it your horse?" Stanley remained silent as John Mark nodded, but his eyes showed deep sympathy. Anthony explained that a horse was loose and the others tore around crowding each other.

"Some had bruises but this one . . ." he said as he kneeled beside John Mark, but John Mark didn't hear. He was comforting Charlotte; she was starting to shake and whine.

Stanley came over to him and said, "There's no use. We have to put her out of her misery." But no one offered to do it. The vet was called. Paul Ray and John Mark stayed for supper to wait for the vet, and John Mark gave permission to put her out of her misery. Paul Ray, a faithful friend, took John Mark home, but not many words were spoken between them.

At length Paul Ray asked, "Whose horse was it that was loose?"

John Mark replied, "I don't know. I am glad it wasn't mine."

Chapter Twenty-Three

Steam rose from the warmth of the calves' stable when Josiah opened the stable door to the cold, frosty December air, after he had helped John Mark feed the calves. John Mark could hear Josiah and William as they played in the light snow that fell during the night. How happy their spirits sounded.

John Mark was also a bit delighted to see the first snowfall that stayed laying, for he knew his pupils would be rejoicing. He felt his spirits dampen at the thought of cold and miserable weather. Maybe things would be different if spring was coming with the sun shining cheerfully and the wind gentle and soft. He took a brisk walk to the barn. When he opened the door, the horses neighed and snorted, welcoming him. As he scooped oats into the second trough, he watched the slender sorrel horse come forth and hungrily eat the oats. Yes, Chief it was. Chief had been taking him to church over a month already and to school at times. Stanley had loaned him the horse since the loss of Charlotte. Stanley had gotten this horse just this past summer. He said he didn't need a second horse so much over winter.

Chief was a horse that held his posture well and trotted in the same manner. He exceeded Charlotte in looks, but didn't have quite the traveling ability that Charlotte had. He was still a good horse, but not his. John Mark still felt the loss of Charlotte, not just for the good horse she had been, but because it was something that had belonged to him and was taken from him.

A gust of cold air greeted him as he opened the barn door and headed for the woodshed. Dad had chopped a lot of wood and told John Mark he could stack it in the shed. As his hands busied themselves stacking the wood in the shed, his mind was churning. He was sure Dad would have much rather stacked the wood himself if he could choose his work. But last night Bishop Christian was here to talk with Dad and this morning Dad was so pre-occupied, he didn't join the conversation at the breakfast table, and then he left on a church errand.

John Mark straightened his back and rested for a moment looking over the cold, empty fields, capped in white. Troubled thoughts continued to weigh on his mind. Earlier in the week he had reached his nineteenth birthday, but what was the use of being nineteen? It seemed as the years passed, disappointments gathered more thickly. Grandma's dying had left an emptiness; she had always showed concern for him. And her death had been a great loss for Dad. It affected Dad spiritually, mentally, and physically, but he had slowly recovered again. It seemed to leave him more aged.

Then John Mark thought of Baby Lavina. Facing the truth that she would never grow up healthy and would always need special care weighed heavily on his mind. A tear dropped at the thought of Lavina. If only she hadn't been called Lavina. John Mark found himself often calling her Baby and rightfully so, as she continued being a baby. Just as the sound of her name made him think of Lavina Ringler, so did her gentle but fearful light brown eyes that couldn't be reached and the natural uneven wave that formed her hairline.

When had he seen Lavina last? Maybe three weeks ago. Hadn't she been at the last few singings? He hadn't been able to spot her in any back corner.

More tears came when he thought of Thanksgiving, three weeks ago, when he decided to go visit Warren and Rhoda in the afternoon. A few teams stood around the yard when he entered the sitting room. He found two men with Warren. As it turned out, they were married to Rhoda's buddies.

There was a group of girls in the kitchen who were the rest of Rhoda's buddies; most of them were single. So naturally Lavina was there. It had stirred up his emotions. It was when he was about ready to leave and was standing in the hallway visiting with Warren that some of the girls came down the hallway stairs and there he met her face to face. Her face showed a smile of embarrassment. When she recognized him, she halted and took a sweeping second look. Her eyes dropped the instant they met his and she quickly disappeared. He thought he had accepted her refusal and was able to meet her without overwhelming emotion but found out he hadn't achieved that yet. Then he sighed at the thought of her refusal and his disappointments: Charlotte, Lavina, Grandmother, the weight of Dad's heavy load, and the acceptance of dear Baby Lavina, so much giving up. His fingers were getting cold, so he went in the house. He would work on the schoolbooks he had brought home.

Mother was finishing the cleaning with Delores's help, and the younger ones were playing outside. Upon settling down with the schoolbooks, John Mark had more troubled thoughts, thoughts of Edgar. What was the use? If only he could spend more time with him. It was an everyday battle to try to keep the other pupils from looking down on Edgar. They made fun of him without thinking, not really mocking him, but they seemed to think he could help that he was created like this.

It seemed each step of the way was getting sharper and harder. He felt his shoulders sagging under the weight. Wasn't there any escape?

Father's voice brought him back to reality. He heard Mom and Dad visiting in the kitchen. It sounded like Dad was more his usual self again. What would Dad do without Mother to talk things over with?

An hour later at the dinner table, Dad helped more with the conversation and responded to the little boys' usual talking, or rather Rebecca and Josiah, as William didn't offer much on his own. John Mark guessed Dad's burden was eased. John Mark sort of sensed that he himself was too reserved, as a few times he realized Father had been watching him when he looked up. He could have well survived without eating dinner. It seemed where hunger should have been there was a knot. Troubled thoughts continued to rise up and weary his mind most of the evening.

*   *   *   *

When the winter sun shone cheerfully the next morning, John Mark did not feel rested, as he had slept fitfully and felt lightheaded. When he turned around, it felt as if his head just kept on spinning, so that he could almost not walk straight. He admitted his desire to stay home from church to sleep.

Dad had given him a silent, long look, then asked, "If you haven't slept well last night, why would you this forenoon?" Then he added, "I'll harness up Chief for you." When John Mark was upstairs getting dressed, he saw Dad even hitched Chief to the buggy for him. If only his mind wouldn't feel so clogged. He flopped on the bed to rest his aching head. *No wonder sick children sometimes come to school if the parents insist they go,* he thought.

His head jerked up. Was someone calling his name? Then his name was repeated more urgently.

"John Mark, are you coming?" It was Mother's voice.

He jumped up and answered, "Yes!" He quickly combed his hair and grabbed his hat and jacket. When he came downstairs he realized Mom and Dad were waiting. The baby was all wrapped up and the others were waiting at the team.

When he met Delores going out the door, she asked, "May I ride with you?"

John Mark stopped in surprise, and stammered for words and then said, "Of course you may. It's just that since you never ask I didn't think of offering a ride to you."

John Mark could pretty well guess that she was told to ask. But she was good company. Her carefree spirit and chatter was a tonic for him to not brood over troubled thoughts. She noticed a squirrel going up a tree. Adam's farm reminded her that they were coming for dinner next Sunday and who else was coming. The rank of wood in someone's yard reminded her of a story the teacher was reading, and that brought on something that Richard said, and then John Mark asked how Richard was doing in reading. And so the school discussion continued of visitors they had and a project they had planned for the next rainy day.

Suddenly they were at church, and John Mark felt better than he had when he started off. But during the service, he found his mind wandering and too often on unpleasant things. Sometimes he found himself with his head nodding and realized he was falling asleep. He may as well have stayed at home to sleep. He made an effort to be alert and concentrate on what Christian was admonishing to the congregation, but quickly his mind was on other things again.

Later, without trying he was sitting up, alert and listening as Wayne stood before the congregation. First he explained that he felt rather empty and did not know what further would be revealed to him, but said that the brother had mentioned about Jonah.

Wayne said, "I was thinking over Jonah's . . . oh—what would you call it? His voyage? His running away? His assignment? Let's just review Jonah's story. Remember the Lord told Jonah to go to Nineveh, that great city, and cry against it for their wickedness had come up before Him. But Jonah rose up and fled from the presence of the Lord to Tarshish. Now what does that say again? Jonah was told to go one place and then on his own decided to go some other place, away from the presence of the Lord. He was afraid to do what the Lord asked him to do. He found a ship going to Tarshish, so he paid his fare and went the opposite direction of where God told him to go.

"We think we wouldn't disobey God as Jonah did, but what do we do when God tells us to carry a burden or chastens us? Don't we sometimes instead flee from it and not do what God asks us to do? We go another way. But getting back to Jonah, the Lord sent out a great wind in the sea so that the ship was about to break apart. The people on the ship were afraid and started casting their wares into the sea so the ship wouldn't sink. Jonah had gone down to the sides of the ship and was sleeping when the shipmates awoke him and asked him why he was still sleeping. They asked him to arise and call upon his God so that God would think on them that they would not perish.

"Then they cast lots to see who was at fault that this evil came upon them. The lot fell on Jonah and they asked him what country and people he was from and he said Hebrew. He told them how he feared the Lord and fled from Him, jumped on a ship to sail away from where the Lord told him to go. He was running away from God. They asked Jonah what they should do to calm the sea and Jonah told them to cast him into the sea. Then the sea would become calm, for Jonah knew it was because of him that this storm was upon them. They tried hard to bring their ship to shore, but they could not and cried to the Lord, 'Let us not perish for this man's life,' so they cast Jonah into the sea. Then the storm ceased to rage.

"Let us consider this. Jonah thought God's request was too great to carry so he jumped in a ship to flee from God. Then the storm came upon the water and Jonah had to be thrown overboard. According to man's reasoning there was no chance for Jonah anymore. We, too, think at times there is no other way. We despair and faint and yes, lose our trust and doubt God's almighty power. There is always a way. How do things look today to you? Do we think our burden can't be solved? Are we ready to give up in despair and run away from God? Jump into the sea so to speak because we think there is no other way out? It would be impossible on our own ability."

The tears that had been misting up in John Mark's eyes were now coming freely.

"Satan is mighty, but let us always remember God is *almighty*. God was not done with Jonah yet. He had prepared a whale in the water to swallow Jonah, and Jonah was in the whale's belly three days and three nights. Then Jonah cried to the Lord saying, 'I cried by reason of mine affliction unto the Lord, and he heard me.' And Jonah meditated to the Lord about his running away saying, 'For Thou hadst cast me into the deep in the midst of the seas; and the floods compassed me about: all they billows and they waves passed over me. I am cast out of thy sight; yet I will look again toward thy holy temple. The water compassed me about, even to the soul: the depth closed me round about, the weeds were wrapped about my head. I went down to the bottom of the mountains; the earth with her bars was about me forever: yet hast thou brought up my life from corruption, O, Lord my God. When my soul fainted within me I remembered the Lord; and my prayer came unto thee, into thine holy temple.' Jonah also says that with the voice of understanding; ' I will pay that that I have vowed.' Then the Lord spoke to the fish and it vomited Jonah out on dry land. Yes, once Jonah gave himself up completely and acknowledged that God is almighty, and when he was willing to be obedient, he was helped. Jonah did what God asked him to do; he went to Nineveh and warned the people.

"So we see if we shy away from what God has called us to do, we have yet more afflictions to endure. Jonah was running away from God, jumped into a boat, and headed in the opposite direction. Then a high wind came up and it was his fault that the boat was about to sink. Then he was cast in the deep waters. How do your afflictions sound? Maybe each day there is another disappointment or harder traveling, but God is almighty. Just as he had a way for Jonah, he has a way for you and me. Jesus wept the tears of sorrow. If a legacy of love, yesterday, today, and tomorrow. He the same doth ever prove, and now I want to turn to the text that was read so heartily."

After the services, John Mark couldn't remember anymore what was brought forth in the text, but he was glad Mother and Dad did not let him jump in a ship this morning to sail out the opposite direction to be thrown into the sea, going further away from his duties.

Chapter Twenty-Four

John Mark urged Duke on against January's chilling wind. He was glad this was Friday. He was getting tired of going back and forth every morning to school in such cold temperatures. At least the roads were bare again. He had taken Duke today as he needed exercise since Dad was away. Sometime tomorrow Dad and Mother and the little girls should be back. That's why he didn't move over to Stanley's yet for the winter since Dad and Mother, Baby Lavina, and Rebekah had gone to Kentucky on Monday to attend the wedding at Naomi's. Their daughter Elizabeth got married on Thursday. John Mark had been invited but decided to miss it as he didn't feel he had time to get ready for a substitute who would also need to learn to tend the fire. Dad was glad as that way John Mark could help with the chores at home. And there weren't so many calves right now.

The warmth of the barn felt good as John Mark led Duke inside. He hung up the harness and walked further back to get hay down for this evening. Just as he was ready to go up the steps he stopped. Was he seeing things? There was a horse in the box stall where Pearl used to be. John Mark walked to the front of the box stall. The horse stepped around beckoning, wondering what was going on. *Does Helen have company?* he wondered. Helen came over and helped Delores with supper and stayed for the night and helped get the morning started while his parents were away. It was quite a horse, somewhat bigger than Chief and it looked like a horse that any boy would desire. John Mark liked his dark black color and his front legs had two white socks on. He had more than enough muscle to pull a buggy.

Maybe someone was driving past here, he thought, and their horse got lame so they left their horse here and borrowed ours. But no, Chief was here too. When he came in the house, supper was about ready.

He asked, "What is the horse doing in the barn?"

"What horse?" Josiah asked.

"What horse? Was no one here since you came home from school?"

"No. Helen did you see anyone?" Josiah asked slipping on his jacket.

Helen looked puzzled, "I just came over a little before the children came home. I didn't see anyone." Josiah was out the door and Delores was close behind him.

Delores was soon back and saying, "It's just a horse." When Josiah came back in the kitchen he was talking before he was inside. His eyes were as wide open as they could go.

His voice was filled with excitement, proclaiming, "There were no trucks here. There are tracks of a team turning around at the barn, and it looks as if there was a horse behind the team."

John Mark looked at him saying, "Oh, now come on. You are probably imagining things." Josiah encouraged John Mark to follow him outside. John Mark studied the tracks that Josiah had described to him. John Mark decided that Josiah's imagination was filling in some of the details to complete the story, but John Mark agreed there were no truck tracks around.

After supper John Mark finished feeding the calves and filled up the water trough. Then he lifted the lid off the oats barrel and dipped in the bin. He saw something, reached in and pulled out a paper, a typewritten paper. He unfolded it and read it, noticing the paper referred to the horse. He read it was a five-year-old horse. The name had a few initials in front of Ranger, Du. Pt. Ranger. But where did the horse come from? That is what he most wondered, but apparently the horse didn't just happen to be here. He must have been put here on purpose. As he folded the paper together he noticed there was a little paper stapled onto the first with handwriting on it. The note said, "All yours, John Mark, from us." This mystery should be easy to solve, as whoever doesn't act surprised that I have a new horse must be the one who provided it.

John Mark liked the name Ranger but he liked the horse even better. He hitched him up on Saturday, and was driving him around, first in the barnyard and then out in the road on several short trips. Then he drove over to Stanley's with him. He had a hard time convincing Stanley that he was serious about the story of how he became the owner of the horse. Stanley hopped on and went along for a short ride.

"I guess you won't want Chief anymore if you have this one," Stanley said almost as if he was a little jealous.

"I really like him and I haven't even let him at the reins yet."

When John Mark returned, Mom and Dad and the girls had arrived home. As John Mark was unhitching, Dad came walking up to the buggy, pulling on his everyday coat.

John Mark took a quick look at him, asking, "What do you know about this horse?"

"Nothing except what Delores and Josiah were trying to tell me. What's all this about? This is quite a horse, not the ones you find beside the road."

"It wasn't beside the road. It was in Pearl's box stall," John Mark exclaimed. Dad stood silently looking the horse over.

He stepped back and adjusted his hat on his head after he had scratched his hair saying, "There's got to be more to this horse being here than this."

"There is, Dad, we got papers," John Mark explained excitedly.

Later as Dad scanned over the typed paper and then at the little note stapled to it, he said with feeling, "Well, son, the night has been quite dark at times, but this proves that the sun shines through again, making so much warmth that we don't remember the darkness anymore."

Then John Mark remembered that he hadn't had time to think any depressing thoughts since this unexpected joy.

But Dad wasn't finished yet, "And this is only an earthly thing. There never entered into a man's heart what is prepared if we hold out through our temptations, where we exchange the cross for a crown."

*   *   *   *

On Sunday, all the boys wondered whose horse he had.

"Mine," John Mark replied.

"Yours?" they echoed. "Where did you get him?"

"I found him," he admitted. The boys all had a hearty laugh.

"No, seriously, which one of you was it?"

"Was what?" a few asked, while the others stood with big questioning looks on their faces. When most of the boys had arrived, John Mark finally told them the whole story. Elton admitted it was his horse that had torn loose, "But I know nothing about this."

"I'd gladly tell you if it was me," Elmer confessed and the others all laughed and agreed saying, "I wish it was me."

"I never even thought of being so generous. After all, I thought you had a horse," Anthony said.

"I thought so too," a half-dozen others remarked. John Mark said he had been only borrowing that horse from Stanley.

*   *   *   *

John Mark pushed back his chair from the table after supper was over at Stanley's and they lingered around the table visiting as they usually did. Erma got up and started gathering the dishes together.

Then she handed a few envelopes to John Mark saying, "Here is your mail." Oh yes, he had forgotten to ask if there was mail for him. There were a few business envelopes, one from the bank and another one of an advertisement for some books, and there was a letter from Katie. He wasted no time opening it. At school meetings this term, John Mark always had a lot of questions for Katie since she started her special education school. The more he heard, the more stirred up he became to be able to teach Edgar that way. Then maybe he could take Richard off of Martha Ann's hands.

At the last meeting, he had a special discussion with Katie. First when Katie got her school started, she had four pupils so that she had to have a helper. Besides Suetta and Calvin and timid Marie, a neighboring school sent a slow learner, Philip, over to ease the neighboring teacher and at the last meeting Katie wasn't so enthusiastic about how things were going. John Mark had written her asking more questions as to what was involved to get such a school started, so he quickly tore the envelope open and sat back and drank in the words.

Katie had much to say about how she convinced Marie's parents that Marie should now be able to go with a regular class as she had come a long way, and that it would be good for her to mix more with other pupils. She wrote an account of Marie's experiences the first day in the regular school and of the surprised parents who were now grateful to Katie for her accomplishments and also her patience with them. Now Katie got rid of her helper and her school was all she dreamed it would be. Every time he read how she was working with her pupils, he thought of Edgar and then of Richard. Sometimes for a fleeting moment he wondered about starting up such a school. Then he thought of what Grace had said lately about her one fourth grader. She just won't be able to handle fifth grade and is undecided what to do about it. Would special education help her? he thought.

Katie had more to say and it sounded like they had an enjoyable time at the supper place on Sunday evening. It sounded like some Glenn was a happy and lucky fellow. Not everything made sense to John Mark as he didn't know all the people she wrote about. He was hoping she would write more about Lawrence, whoever he was. She hadn't really finished that. It had sounded sort of as if he had a problem, but to what extent she didn't explain.

Reading Katie's letter gave John Mark an urge to go visit the settlement. That was the settlement where Dad's sister Naomi and family lived. It would be interesting to see Emory and Joel again. At the end of the letter she had written her name in a design form like a trade mark: Katie, with the end of the "e" forming a swirl, swinging it up close to the whole name with the tail of it used to cross the "t," and then dropping down like a star to dot the "I."

John Mark retired early to bed. He had many things to think over. And he thought over the things for most of the night. In the morning he felt there was a lot of work to be done.

*   *   *   *

As the days passed into February and moved toward March, John Mark hardly was aware that they were passing. He had written to Katie a few times and once went to visit her school. He had made several attempts to try to talk with Edgar's parents. He ended up going in the house and talking with Mrs. Ringler as his father wasn't very helpful. But talking to Mrs. Ringler wasn't very successful either. As usual, she seemed unaware that John Mark wasn't doing a good job with Edgar. He had made another attempt to talk with his mother. This time John Mark had asked her directly; if he started up a school for pupils who needed more help, would they send Edgar. She had looked at him almost as pleadingly as Lavina did those few times they met.

Mrs. Ringler said, "If you leave Timber Lock, I suppose Edgar will too. He wouldn't have any other teacher. You understand him so well."

Then he talked to Richard's parents and his teacher, and they agreed if it wouldn't be too far, they would send Richard. He hadn't even talked to Martha Ann yet about Pauline, as he heard of some other students who might be attending if such a school was started. Then there were the numerous times he had talked to board members and other people who were interested in starting up such a school. Every time one problem was ironed out, a new one bloomed somewhere else. A board was finally organized of people who had mercy for less fortunate children.

As the snow melted and the earth was changing to spring, the problems weren't ironed out yet. Everyone had a different idea as to where such a school should be located. John Mark was almost convinced there should be two such schools in order to suit everyone.

219

He was beginning to realize that his own school was being neglected since he had so many other irons in the fire. Occasionally, he wrote a letter to Katie asking for more information about starting such a school. The board asked him so many questions that he didn't know how to answer. Once Katie had referred him to Cousin Miriam whom he then had written to for some information.

On one of the letters from Katie he noticed that when she had written his name, she also used cursive to write John with a downward flourish on the "n," running it under the length of John and using that end to begin the "M" of John Mark, then using the end of the swirl in the "k," swinging it up over John to the top of the "J." And she had signed her name the same way as she had earlier.
He sort of liked how it made his name look like some kind of proper signature or trademark. Once in a while he wrote his own name like that if he remembered.

*　　*　　*　　*

It was a mild April weekend when John Mark found himself in the Elm Grove area visiting his uncle and aunt and cousins, the John Irvin Horst family. He had made mention to Katie that he planned to be there. On Saturday afternoon he dropped in to see Katie's school. She said she would be there catching up on schoolwork. It was an educational afternoon for John Mark. He was supplied with many answers he had been searching for. He was ready to leave when he made mention about going back to John Irvin's to get ready to go to the singing.

Then he asked, "Do you have a way to go to the singing?"

"Yes, I suppose Joel will be around to pick me up."

"You mean Joel Horst?"

"Yes, I usually go with one of them."

"Well, I'll be at the singing too if one of their teams has room for me," John Mark said as he left the schoolhouse.

John Mark pulled up at Katie's house and waited a good five minutes. Then Katie came hurrying out the walk and hopped on the buggy, apologizing for not being ready.

John Mark matter-of-factly said, "Maybe I kept you too long this afternoon."

Katie looked at him bewildered and asked, "What's this?"

John Mark chuckled, "It's Paul Isaac's team. He told me I could have it if I took their passenger along. He and Joel had planned to go to one of their friend's house for the night. Some boys are batching at their farm."

"Oh you mean to Clyde and Lewis's? Then you were stuck with me," she added.

"I'm not stuck if you know the way to the singing."

Then she explained the singing was at Henry Kulp's, a few miles beyond the church next to Ivan Musser's. The talk soon switched to the Musser boys and that led to some more talk of the young folks. John Mark admitted that he knew only a little over half of the young folks.

"You'll soon know them all. We are all one group and belong together." The talk naturally switched to a few school subjects. Then John Mark asked, "Oh yes, before I forget, I wanted to ask you, do you practice cursive writing in your school?" Katie started explaining about getting the second graders writing and John Mark said, "No, I mean the way you write your name lately."

"Oh, that's just for fun. It gives it a different flavor."

"I thought maybe you had a book where all the different names were listed and how to write them."

"No," she laughed, "I like to dress up my name at times. It's such a common name."

"How do you keep your pupils from writing that way if you write it in school?"

"I don't often in school," she said slowly.

"But I thought I saw a book on your desk and you had written your name inside the cover like that," he reminded her.

"Well, I do at times, and once in a while we have a special art class when I and the pupils use our imagination to see in what way we can dress up the names in our schoolroom."

"With you practicing theirs first?" John Mark asked.

"Well, yes," she tried to remember. "I practice them first, but often they come up with some ideas I like better. I enjoy that."

There was a few minutes silence. Then John Mark teasingly asked, "Is there a John Mark in your class?"

"Oh, no, no. . . ," she stammered, "but there is a John Adam and it is about the same, both no "i's" or "t's" involved. Why? Did I write your name like that?" she asked doubtfully and sort of apologizing.

He looked at her wondering if she was serious and said, "Yes, first it struck me funny. But now sometimes I write it that way too now and I'm beginning to like it. It looks like some kind of proper trademark. Well anyway, not homemade."

Katie admitted she was named after a great-aunt and she didn't like her common name. She thought her sisters had prettier names, so she got the craving to decorate it. John Mark went on to say he was thinking if he had a business he could use the name as a trademark but then he said how Father wouldn't like that as Dad's father was firmly against using your own name to name a business on account of somewhere in the Old Testament it says that it was evil to use our name to name the land, and with that the talk had switched to church matters.

John Mark began sensing that he was doing most of the talking, so he asked, "Did I say anything that insulted you?"

"No," she answered, "why?"

"Well, you aren't as talkative as you were when we started off."

"Oh, I didn't realize. I guess I was thinking of meeting my friends soon."

"I thought maybe you would rather have come with Joel."

She started saying, "It doesn't. . . ," then she quickly checked herself and said, "I'm glad I had a way to come," she finished as they drove in the lane of Henry Kulp.

There were a few teams ahead of them leaving their passengers off.

Katie slipped out from beneath the buggy spread saying, "I might as well get off while we are stopped." In that instant she was gone. John Mark was beginning to wonder what Katie's true feelings were for him bringing her along. As for himself, he hadn't felt nervous or deeply overwhelmed.

By the time the singing was over and he heard the boys talk with each other, John Mark soon learned which one was Glenn whom Katie talked about. Bit by bit he learned to know more of the boys. There were a few boys who were sort of quiet and reserved. When John Mark looked up, the boy in the plain blue shirt was looking his way. John Mark naturally smiled, but the boy just stared at him. Then to John Mark's surprise, the boy asked who he was. When John Mark explained, the boy just kept the same blank look.

Then Emory (Naomi's oldest boy) said, "He is all right; he's my cousin." Then a partly knowing look crossed the boy's face, or was it a trusting look?

When that boy and a few others walked away, John Mark asked Emory, "Who was the guy in the plain blue shirt?"

Emory replied, "That was Lawrence. He is the one who lives here."

"Lawrence." John Mark was trying to think. That was a name Katie had written about, but what had she written about Lawrence? It was Glenn who was cheering everyone. Something about Glenn was a tonic to keep things from getting dull. But what was it about Lawrence? Maybe Lawrence could be happier and help others from discouragement if he could make a decision. Is that what Katie had said? Well, she really hadn't explained it well.

John Mark kept glancing at Lawrence. He and another boy were in a deep conversation. Suddenly John Mark realized he wasn't watching Lawrence anymore. A bunch of girls were in the other part of the room where the big divider was and he realized that he was watching Katie. She would occasionally lift her eyes and study the boys for a moment, at least the ones on the left side. He didn't mean to be watching Katie, but he was wondering whom she was concerned about. Katie didn't look up often enough so that he could say for sure whom she directed her glance at. It wasn't himself; only once their eyes met and she gave him a faint smile.

It was after the girls were in quite a lively discussion that John Mark took notice that Lawrence was studying Katie, or so it seemed. Then Lawrence rested his head in his hands, studying the floor as if there was a weighty matter on his shoulders.

All of a sudden everyone was leaving for home. John Mark expected Katie to be reserved on the way home like she had been the last stretch of their drive to the singing, but she proved otherwise. She was quite talkative and mentioned their plans for the next two Sundays and shared some of the things the girls had been talking about. Once when there was a lull in the conversation, John Mark mentioned that they were still trying to decide where to locate his little school, and thus the school subject continued on until he dropped Katie off.

*   *   *   *

It was a warm, humid day as John Mark was cleaning up sawdust and fine pieces of wood, and at times he had to wipe sweat from his brow. He stood for a moment looking the compact room over. It seemed like such an accomplishment, but it had become reality. At times it seemed as if it wouldn't ever work out. It was almost supper time until he reached home.

Rising from the supper table, John Mark started unlacing his shoes to get ready to wash up for the weekend. Then Mother handed his mail to him. It contained a teacher's circle letter and a letter from a company that requested a donation for poor people in a distant country. What was this envelope? He took a closer look and saw it was from Katie. Guess she was anxious to hear how his school plans were coming along. He stuck the other two envelopes in his shirt pocket, opened the circle letter, and quickly searched out a few letters he was anxious to read since he wondered how Lydia Mae in Indiana was faring. She had a problem school and he wondered if she had ironed anything out by now or if she was ready to give up. In the last part of her letter, Lydia Mae wrote an interesting comment on Cora's letter. Then he had to read that one. He began to wonder why everyone was giving Lucy such a hard time. As he was reading, Delores came and tapped on his paper, wondering if he was going to the singing as there was a buggy leaving already. He made a hasty exit upstairs.

After he was dressed, he remembered the other letter he hadn't opened yet. He stuck it in his pants pocket and decided maybe he would read it on the way to the singing at Four Acres.

John Mark felt happy as he walked into the horse stable and led Ranger out to be hitched up. It had been such a blow to him to lose Charlotte, but Ranger was all he ever dreamed of in a horse. He never did find out who had given Ranger to him. It filled him with joy to know that someone cared about his loss enough to replace his horse. Yes, there were disappointments, but "Blest be the tie that binds our hearts in Christian love, the fellowship of kindred minds . . ." he couldn't remember all the words, but they expressed his feelings better than he could express them himself.

As Ranger trotted easily out to the road, the cool evening breeze floated lightly in the buggy. John Mark wasn't quite as carefree as the evening summer breeze. He remembered the letter in his pocket. He was going to read it on the way to the singing, but on second thought, maybe he would wait to read it. Lately he wasn't sure how Katie's letters made him feel. There was no denying it. Their letters didn't share only school subjects anymore. They always included some school news; maybe about half was school interests since he was now starting his own special education room. But a troubled thought remained. He enjoyed Katie's letters and the weekends he spent in that area. Maybe he was to that area more often than he would have to visit Aunt Naomi and her family because of Katie and their interest in special education classes, but school wasn't their only interest. But what kept him from getting more involved? He didn't have to wonder; he realized that for a while already.

At first he couldn't express his own feelings, but they soon became more apparent. Although he didn't meet Lavina often, the few times he did, he felt guilty. He felt as if he was mistreating her, or not being true to her. But why should he feel so? Lavina had refused *him*. He was free to make his choice. Or was he? He thought of a certain verse that said, ". . . When thou wast young, thou girdedst thyself, and walkedst whither thou wouldest: but when thou shalt be old, thou shalt stretch forth thy hands, and another shall gird thee, and carry thee whither thou wouldest not (Psalm 21:18)." On a few occasions John Mark thought Katie, too, wasn't her usual relaxed self, as if something was bothering her. Lately, though, she was always relaxed and shared freely but—Lavina's pale brown eyes, timid and serene, always came to his mind

At times John Mark saw a glimpse of Lavina in church. But not at singings yet this summer. Twice he saw her working over in the yard at a small dwelling along Triple Ridge Road. It was where Edgar's grandfather used to live, but he had died a few years ago. John Mark never heard who lived there now. Once he was going past there when he met Lavina walking up the road. By all appearances neither of them recognized the other until they were even with each other. She was picking wildflowers along the roadside and wasn't aware of the team until it was upon her. She had actually smiled, but John Mark was so startled that he hadn't returned her smile and was past in an instant. That smile touched his emotions. It had produced many free-flowing tears, even now they were near at hand just thinking about it.

It was after he had joined the group of boys standing beside the schoolhouse and a group of girls walked up from the swings toward the school that he took a second look. Yes, Katie was with them. Immediately he remembered the letter he hadn't opened. He was going to leave it closed until Sunday was over. He wanted to see what the day held. But now, maybe he should know. What if he was supposed to pick her up somewhere? He suddenly knew he should read the letter before the evening was over, so he wandered off from the boys unnoticed. In fact, the boys had just started to walk toward the schoolhouse, since it was about time to begin. John Mark quickly tore open the letter and read it hurriedly.

Dear John Mark,

Well, I wonder how things are faring in your plans. I haven't heard anything for a while. The last I heard I thought it sounded as if maybe things were working out to a decision where you will have your school. Did things work out now for Four Acres? Will you have only Edgar and Richard? I thought you were talking about another pupil. I now have those folders where the new workbooks are listed which Miriam uses. I was eager to see them. Miriam tried to tell me about the workbooks, but I can't really picture them. Do you need more duplicate sheets of the work pictures? The more papers I get ready, the more eager I am to get another term started. Oh, yes, here is the address you wanted from Special Education, Inc., Short Attention Span.

He read Colorado, and well, he would look later. He was reading fast because he could hear the singing had started. He skipped over the paragraph of school business. The last few lines read,

> A few of our folks are talking about going to Dry Hill for singing and then staying for church and I was asked to go along. I'm not sure how I will get to Uncle Wayne's for the night. Would that be on your way home? Oh well, guess it'll work out.
>
> Katie

John Mark hurried back to the schoolroom where he heard a good volume of singing. A few of the boys looked at him quite puzzled as he took his seat. Likely they remembered that he had been at school already before the singing had started.

John Mark was ready to leave. He had his hat on and was lingering near the door. Only a few people were leaving. He was trying to get Katie's attention. She was engrossed in conversation with Grace. Suddenly he decided this must be teacher talk and walked over to where they were seated.

"Oh, here he is. Are we going to Lydia Beiler's for supplies on Wednesday or must I send for those books?"

"I didn't ask Martha Ann where she needs to go, but maybe you could stay at Lydia's store while I go on up to Morgan Trade Company, since you hardly need anything there and it will take me awhile."

"What about the Books and More Books? Are we going there the same day?"

"Guess it depends if everyone has their order ready. I don't know if Hannah and I will get time to go over our order before Wednesday," John Mark replied.

"Then will Hannah take over Timber Lock for you?" Grace asked.

"Yes, haven't you heard?"

"I didn't know she had given her final answer."

"You don't mean Hannah from Lone Prairie?" Katie asked doubtfully.

John Mark nodded his head, "She had a chance to teach at Lone Prairie, but she told me awhile ago that she won't be teaching there again."

To Katie's bewildered look Grace answered, "I have a feeling it's some connection with her co-teacher. I sort of gathered she was hoping for another co-teacher."

John Mark nodded his agreement and then said, "Well, anyhow, I'm heading for home, Katie. Do you want to hitch a ride to Wayne's?"

She looked at him and shrugged her shoulders saying, "I guess it's up to you. I suppose I could find a way."

"Well, suit yourself. I'm going now," John Mark said as he made his way to the door. Katie quickly got up and went for her wraps.

They were soon on their way. John Mark was explaining how they had remodeled a shop into a schoolroom located almost right across the road from Four Acres. It was a building that wasn't being used anymore. The other farm buildings are farther in the lane. The shop is nearer to the road.

"What are you planning to call your school?" Katie asked.

"Well, I wasn't going to call it anything, but people started calling it 'John Mark's School' and then I knew if I didn't give it a name it would be called that, and Father is against using our name to name things. I didn't want it to be mixed up with other special education schools as there are some with higher churches. So I will call it just what it is, 'Just More Worthy.'"

Katie looked at him asking, "What? Nothing about special education?"

"No, aren't these pupils just more worthy? Why would we spend so much time with them if they weren't worth it?"

"I guess in a sense," Katie said at length.

They had started talking about the singing when John Mark added, "If you think the name I gave the school is different, I'll tell you something. If you use just the initials of it, you have my initials."

"Oh," Katie gasped. "Does your father know what it represents?"

"Not if you don't tell him. This is the first I told someone."

"So you had something to go by. I had been wondering if you had the knowledge to think up such a proper name."

"It helped anyway," John Mark admitted.

There was a short pause in the conversation when John Mark was twisting around with the lines and finally as politely as he knew how said, "Oh Katie, I was wondering how you felt about our sharing our school interests and the like?" Katie squirmed but remained silent.

John Mark took a deep breath and started over, "I guess by now you know as well as I that the interests that we share aren't only school matters. I mean for myself I admit it had been only school things or to visit my aunt and uncle that brought me to Elm Grove. I likely wouldn't have shown up quite as often otherwise."

"To be honest, I haven't formed any serious opinion. Why do you ask? Are you telling me you have been thinking things over? I'll listen if you want to talk about it," Katie invited.

"Well, Katie, I don't know how to say it but there were greater interests than school that led me at times and I thought of seeing into the matter further. But . . . but . . . oh—" John Mark stammered for words, then continued, "something keeps me from it. I sort of feel as if I have wronged someone even though she refused me. But I can't help it, I just can't go against it with a clear conscience. I feel guilty, and therefore, I wanted to let you know that I have enjoyed what we shared together, the information that helped me get the school going and, well, our getting acquainted. But I will not continue our friendship further like I had hoped I could." When only silence followed, John Mark suddenly felt bad; had he hurt her deeply?

Finally John Mark said, "Katie, I wish you'd say how you feel. I want to know."

"Oh, I'm sorry. I didn't realize that you couldn't see that I was thinking. It seems you were thinking about us more seriously than I was, but apparently there were two of us."

"Two of us what?" John Mark asked.

"Well, oh, let me see . . . there were times that I was discouraged about waiting and when nothing happened and you were around, I enjoyed our times together more. I had been dating and then quite suddenly he felt doubtful. He wanted some weeks or months to think it over and we are still tearing off pages and at times I talked to you as a tonic. I began to wonder but then when I met him, I felt I had been misusing him so I guess there were two of us."

"Is this in connection to that Lawrence you wrote about once?"

"Did I write it to you?" she gasped.

"Well, you wrote something about a Glenn who makes everyone cheerful which keeps things brighter, and something about maybe Lawrence could be happier and keep others happier if he could make decisions. I was trying to piece it together."

"But why did you think that it was Lawrence?"

"Well, when I was up in Elm Grove the last time, or I guess it was the last time, I made an effort to find out who he was. I sort of got the feeling that maybe he was a little alarmed about my coming there. Or maybe about the people I took along."

"Well, I have no idea how he feels," Katie admitted. "And thanks for the visit," she said with feeling and she hopped off the buggy as he pulled up to Wayne's yard gate.

Chapter Twenty-Five

John Mark felt a joy in his heart as he scanned Edgar's paper. It sure was "just more worthy." His work was improving since John Mark had more time to teach him. But sometimes he wondered where all the hours of the day went. He looked at the five desks in the room.

Edgar's desk was in the back. Louella's desk was in front of his. He hadn't really been aware of Louella's handicap. She had been going to the public school since there was no private school near enough to walk to. Then the second year she had been put in a special education class in public school because of her hyperactive condition. John Mark looked for a moment at the desk that stood beside Louella's. It was Adam's desk. Adam's parents had come to talk to John Mark only a few weeks before school started. They were of the Hoffman Church and had just found out that he was starting up such a school.

Adam was going to a school in town where mostly retarded pupils attended, and they were desperate to have him attend a school with more normal pupils. Adam's I. Q. was bright. It was because he was deaf and quite bashful that he was more or less in his own little world. That was the beginning of John Mark's challenge. In two weeks he had to learn sign language and find someone to help him teach. The board left no stones unturned hunting for a teacher while John Mark practiced sign language day and night.

Farther over in the room stood two desks, Richard's and Pauline's. Martha Ann had planned to try Pauline another year in regular school since a special education class allowed only three pupils, but since they already had to have more than one teacher,

Martha Ann encouraged Pauline's parents to send her, and Velma Sensenig, a girl in her upper twenties, had agreed to teach Richard and Pauline. Velma was with the five pupils over in the schoolyard with the Four Corner pupils since it was right across the road. The pupils most often spent the recess over on the big schoolyard so the children could associate with more pupils and Velma often joined them.

Velma was quiet-natured, but as the days and weeks passed into months, John Mark learned that she was quite interesting and very motherly. The five pupils soon found her mother-like heart. But Velma looked up to him as if she was only a substitute helping him teach.

He did work for hours after she went home. Often she stayed only a half-hour after the pupils left. She often took her schoolwork home because her mother was an aged widow and she wanted to be home as much as she could. Adam was John Mark's challenge. Never before did John Mark realize how much a child learns from hearing what was said to others. Adam had to be told everything. It would help some if he was more inquisitive, but he was somewhat shy and tried to figure out things for himself. At times he had the wrong answer and John Mark kept forgetting to always sign when others were hearing.

John Mark sensed that Velma often watched when he was signing to Adam. She sometimes asked him what sign to use for certain words. To practice, John Mark at times signed to Velma instead of talking but Velma often answered in words. She did sign to Adam more freely when she thought John Mark wasn't around. When he was staring out the window, he at times saw Velma signing to Adam as they walked over to the other schoolyard. Somehow she didn't do it freely in his presence.

He found out that Velma didn't talk as freely as he and Ellen used to. She was rather reserved with him, somewhat like the seventh- and eighth-grade girls were when he went back to help Ellen after being out of school only a few months. Sometimes he found himself comparing Velma to Lavina Ringler, but they were somewhat different. He often longed to win her like the pupils did. She kept the terms with him all on school-related subjects.

It happened a few times that one of Velma's friends dropped in at school and John Mark had almost stood with open mouth, speechless at the person she became. Like the evening Helen came before Velma left in the afternoon, and John Mark soon found himself unable to keep his mind on schoolwork. John Mark found out Velma had many things to share. It sounded like her mother got a lot of company and she talked about different experiences and a lot of different subjects had been brought up. Helen drew him into the conversation.

After a while, Velma had excused herself and Helen stayed visiting with John Mark for a while. He wanted to ask Helen about Velma, but he couldn't think how to ask properly so it wouldn't sound as if they weren't getting along. Helen could hear how much Velma was enthused with her pupils. He sort of knew Helen would say he was the person who wasn't freely sharing with Velma. She didn't seem like Lavina as she never seemed flustered or embarrassed when he talked to her.

She seemed more like a daughter, too shy to communicate much with her father, but she was quite a few years older than he— almost eight years.

*　　*　　*　　*

It was a dreary November day. John Mark had a cold and wasn't feeling so peppy and Louella was especially hyper today. He couldn't get her settled down to anything. As soon as she tried, her pencil would fall on the floor. When she picked that up, she knocked her schoolbooks down, then she bumped her head picking them up and that caused some tears. That reminded her that her handkerchief was in her jacket pocket and she couldn't do anything until she had her handkerchief. Then her pencil lead was broken when she was ready to try lessons. By the time John Mark found a sharp pencil for her, she couldn't find her papers anymore.

John Mark was sure what the next request would be and she soon proved it by asking permission to go to the restroom. That always followed an extra-hyper spree. As always, Edgar tried to find her things or help her solve her problems. The others were watching with amused looks, wondering what the next scene would be. Even Adam caught on that something was going on. This wouldn't do. John Mark set his lips firmly after nodding his head giving her permission to go to the bathroom, but he decided to make her sit still for ten minutes once she came in, to get her settled before trying to get her started at something. Adam raised his hand and signed a question about his workbook.

John Mark was occupied helping Adam. It took so much time trying to explain things in sign language. Suddenly, John Mark realized that it was extra quiet when Louella came back in. Hadn't she made it in time? Wasn't her dress down properly? At the same time Velma left the blackboard where she was helping Richard, and she hurriedly walked back toward the door. John Mark stood up straight and turned around to see Louella walking happily to her desk. Velma was greeting three girls who had apparently entered with Louella. The last in the line was Lavina Ringler. The next girl he didn't know and the first one was . . . oh, he saw that girl before. Maybe at a teacher's meeting. Why did he think of Katie? Velma welcomed the girls to the chairs near the entrance. They were expecting to watch them teach the pupils! John Mark had no idea what he had been doing.

He straightened up some papers on his desk only to push a book on the floor. When he picked that up he saw a scrap of paper on the floor and he picked that up. He looked at the clock. It was ten minutes until recess time. Suddenly he felt like Louella. He couldn't settle down to anything and when Adam raised his hand signing a question, he couldn't remember the right sign quickly enough.

Velma went back to the blackboard drilling Richard as if these girls entered the schoolroom every day. Louella was stirring around at her desk, maybe trying to find her paper. Then he remembered he had been dealing with Louella and was going to command her to sit still for a time.

John Mark walked up to her desk saying, "Let me help you clean up your desk a bit." Louella looked at him quickly, then she threw all the contents of her desk on the floor; papers scattered, col-

234

ored pencils rolled, scissors clanged on the floor. By the time he helped her pick up her things and arrange them in order on her desk and then answered Edgar's waving hand, he was informed by Edgar that it was time to dismiss for recess.

As soon as class dismissed, Edgar came to Lavina beckoning her to come to his desk. John Mark was introduced to the other two girls. One was Miriam from Missouri, Katie's cousin who also taught at a special school. No wonder he thought of Katie when he saw that girl. She bore no resemblance to Katie, but it was Katie who had introduced him to Miriam. The only other time he had met her was at a school meeting. The other girl was Amanda, the one that was a teacher's helper in a school where they have some pupils who were all in regular classes but they needed more help.

John Mark and Miriam were soon engrossed in conversation as he described each of his pupils, and she showed him books that she had brought along which might be a help to him. Then John Mark was talking about a book with a set of picture cards that he had gotten for Edgar. He had learned of it through a catalog. Miriam had never heard of it and was very interested. Together they walked over to Edgar's desk deep in conversation. When they reached Edgar's desk John Mark was startled to see Lavina kneeling by his desk. Edgar was showing her his pencil colors and the new eraser he had gotten that week. Edgar looked at John Mark and Miriam rather bewildered. John Mark had momentarily forgotten about Lavina. Miriam was seemingly unaware of Lavina and Edgar's presence. She was eagerly waiting to be introduced to this new book-game combination.

When John Mark looked down at the desk to get the book, he met Lavina's eyes for a moment. Miriam stood waiting. John Mark felt himself trembling.

Miriam looked at John Mark. "Oh, maybe I haven't explained we were at her neighbors, the Jacobs," she said, looking at Lavina. "We asked her to bring us over." Then she added, "Oh, that's right, Lavina. This is your brother. So you already know her," she said, looking at John Mark. John Mark reached into the desk to get the workbook and the pictures that went with it.

Lavina arose and said, "Yes, this is my brother. He often wanted me to come to see his little school." John Mark looked up while handing the book to Miriam in time to see the smile on Lavina's face that was meant for Miriam. It warmed his whole being and he felt a smile spread over his own face. Miriam took the book and started studying it. She was rather interested. When John Mark looked up again in Lavina's direction, she was headed back to Velma and Amanda.

John Mark couldn't be sure but it seemed that Lavina's smile had extended when he looked up. They had a longer recess, since there was so much that Miriam was interested in.

Chapter Twenty-Six

Warren and Rhoda had invited the young folks for dinner. It was overcast and damp but not a real cold temperature for January. The dampness seemed to go through to the bone. Inside the house, the stoves made the rooms feel cozy.

After most of the boys had left the table and were in the other room, and while the last of the girls and table waiters and Rhoda were eating, John Mark noticed that Lavina was also at the table. Of course she would be there. She and Rhoda were close friends. Lately it seemed he could not spot her anywhere among the young folks. Well, yes, usually in church. Maybe she felt old now that Virginia was married.

Later, as he glanced out into the kitchen, he saw the little son of Warren and Rhoda was the center of attention.

They had sung awhile in the afternoon and when the singing died down, half of the people left and more were making preparations to leave which was the reason the singing had died down. The circle of people was disappearing.

It was while John Mark was searching around on the table and countertop for his other songbook that Rhoda said his name and when he looked up she said, "We want you to stay for supper."

"Supper?" he questioned. "Is anyone else staying for supper?"

"No one else that I know, but I hoped you would," Rhoda said heartily.

And so, an hour and a half later he joined Rhoda and Warren at the supper table with little Jonathan in the high chair where he was giving away smiles at random. John Mark enjoyed the conversation of community news and activities that they were sharing and relating with each other while enjoying the simple supper of leftover mashed potatoes and noodles fried together, topped with ham gravy and cold sliced ham for sandwiches.

While they lingered at the table and finished up the cake and ice cream, Jonathan became impatient in his high chair. Warren picked him up and Jonathan rejoiced happily in his father's arms. Rhoda was asking John Mark about his "Just More Worthy" school. While the school talk continued, Rhoda seemed quite interested. Warren took Jonathan over to the living room end of the kitchen where they were tussling on the floor. Jonathan got a joy out of pulling Daddy's hair.

Rhoda looked over and smiled at their enjoyment and cleared her throat asking softly, while unconsciously cleaning her fingernails, "Maybe I shouldn't ask, but I was wondering, have you asked Lavina for her company again?"

John Mark took a deep breath but no words came as Rhoda looked at him and when he saw her questioning look he at length said, "Why should I?"

Rhoda changed her posture, as if preparing to settle down to have a long talk and then said, "Aren't you still interested?" she asked, half begging. John Mark felt his face get warm. Rhoda sat patiently waiting for an answer.

"What would it help if I was?" John Mark asked honestly.

"What could Lavina do if she regretted that she refused you?" Rhoda asked just as honestly. Now it was John Mark's turn to think in silence. While John Mark waited for words to form, he saw Jonathan come crawling across the floor and after begging at her feet, Rhoda picked him up.

At length John Mark asked, "Has anyone asked her since I did?"

"Oh—?" Rhoda studied looking over at Warren, who had begun reading *Family Life*. Rhoda remembered, "I guess once or so, though not for awhile, but it doesn't matter who asked her before. It must not have been the right person, as they all have other partners." John Mark looked at her questioningly.

238

Rhoda smiled and explained, "I meant that the others have all gone their way and found other friends. I wondered what you were waiting on?"

"I guess the right girl," John Mark admitted.

Rhoda said, "I am surprised you didn't become interested in some of those capable teachers." John Mark brushed his hand over his head, then brushed the hair in place again after ruffling through it. He longed to tell Rhoda about Katie and how he desired to be led further, but the memory of Lavina didn't allow him to. He wondered to himself if he could become interested in Katie whom he hadn't talked with very much since he discussed it with her.

"Boy, what I wouldn't give to hear those thoughts," Rhoda said, rousing him from his deep thoughts.

"What did you ask me?" John Mark asked.

"Oh, I'm not sure what I asked last. I guess something about asking another girl if you didn't plan to ask Lavina again."

"Would you advise me to ask Lavina again or what were you referring to?"

"Well, I wouldn't want you to be disappointed, but at times I wonder. I haven't talked heart to heart with Lavina for a while, but since her sister was married and, well, since we had Jonathan, I sort of sense that maybe—, oh, well. I don't know how to say it, just seeing her unspoken expression makes me think maybe she longs for things that she wouldn't admit. But like I said, the other boys have found other companions."

"Maybe she is waiting for the right one," John Mark said, and then he noticed Warren pulling on his chore coat and looking at the clock.

John Mark got up and said, "Guess I'll go along when you chore."

John Mark followed Warren to the pig nursery and watched as Warren went about his routine checkup, setting up one feeder and putting more feed into it. One pen had rather damp sawdust in one section, so Warren checked the water line and put more dry shavings on the floor.

Later as they walked to the barn to do the regular chores Warren asked, "Has anyone ever told you the root of Lavina's inferior feelings?"

"Oh, yes, oh—no, well yes, I guess she is sort of shy of men," John Mark stammered. Warren threw a shovel full of silage in the cow's trough and put a scoop of ground feed on top. He got the milk pail and settled down to start milking.

As the milk foamed in the pail, Warren admitted, "I don't know if this alone is all the reason, but it's a fact that her parents failed and didn't marry within the church. And since she is the oldest in the family, maybe it made her feel inferior." John Mark drew a deep breath. It was like finding what you have long been hunting for. This must be what the girls were talking about one evening on the way home from the singing. They said something about she should forgive, etc.

"Hadn't you known?" Warren asked, looking out from behind the cow when John Mark remained silent.

"No, I haven't known for sure what the problem was. I sort of gathered there was a problem connected with it, but what about Nevin? I had her father as a school parent and well, he was like— I couldn't start anything with him, and his wife, well, I couldn't get her to complain about anything so I couldn't discuss any problems."

"Nevin," Warren stated, "is an 'each man for himself' kind, and his wife is very timid as if she is too unworthy to claim her rights. If it wouldn't be for their children in school and young folks, they would be sort of unknown people."

"So maybe Lavina's nature is more inherited than from circumstances," John Mark reasoned. Warren was stripping out the last milk and getting up and putting the milk stool in its place.

"Well, yes, it would appear so, but from what older folks say, Nevin hasn't always been like that. It was a long hard pull for them to come back to the church and it left scars. If it hadn't been for the goodness of his wife, Nevin would have stayed bitter at himself for his own offense. The way people talk, he sure isn't the Nevin he used to be."

240

John Mark walked over to Ranger and said, "Well, I will head back to Stanley's. Thanks for the supper and the visit."

"Then you still board at Stanley's even if you aren't teaching at Timber Lock?"

"Yes, over the winter months. You know Four Corners is just across the bush from Timber Lock."

Warren set the pail of milk down and helped John Mark hitch up. John Mark started on his journey back to Stanley's. He held Ranger to a slow pace. He had many things to think over.

Coming to Stanley's, John Mark found them just coming from doing the milking. They were relaxing in the kitchen and Erma had made some popcorn and served orange juice with it. They were snacking on it while the happy hours passed. Walter was on the floor giving toys to little Ella who was in the jumper, taking the toys and throwing them down on the floor again. Walter enjoyed showing Dad what Ella did. Erma was trying to write but was mostly watching the children's fun. Little Ella was such a sunbeam in Stanley and Erma's home and much treasured by Walter. She was such a welcomed baby.

John Mark thought back over the years when there were black days for Stanley and Erma. Erma had not been well at times and the joys they looked forward to were denied them. But they kept faith and the sun shone again.

John Mark thought over the words Rhoda had shared him with him, why he didn't ask Lavina again. On the way home he was reweighing the things that Warren told him and now he was trying to recall what Rhoda had said. But then he remembered that Rhoda didn't truthfully know. She didn't want him to be disappointed. She didn't want to give him too much hope only to disappoint him. He was trying to imagine himself going to visit Lavina, but somehow the picture always disappeared before he came to her door, as if no such thing was possible.

Suddenly Stanley broke out into a hearty laugh and John Mark looked up and saw Walter looking around, rather shook up, but with a half grin on his face. Emma sprang up from her chair and picked up Baby Ella who had toppled over. John Mark failed to see what happened to cause the excitement or accomplishment, whatever it was.

Stanley looked over at him, still chuckling and then he said to Walter, "Go get the Bible storybook. It's about time for your bed-time story."

Suddenly Erma looked at John Mark asking, "Did you have supper?"

John Mark nodded and said, "If I didn't, I could have made supper with this," he said taking another handful of popcorn and emptying his glass of orange juice. John Mark felt joy seeing the sun shining again for Stanley and Erma's home, knowing there had been clouds of disappointment already. It encouraged his own faith.

Chapter Twenty-Seven

A strange feeling was gnawing in John Mark's chest as he listened to Bishop Paul asking in earnest, yet solemnly, "Will you take sister Ella Grace Witmer as your helpmate, to love and stand by her in all care and sickness, in whatever the good Lord lets come over her and take the heaviest load on you?"

Chester announced, "Yes," clearly without doubt. Then Ella Grace was asked the same about Chester, but taking the lightest part of the load.

She answered a soft and serene, "Yes." The time had come; they clasped their hands and Bishop Paul knotted them together. Chester was now a man. He would be starting his own home and would be missed among the young folks.

John Mark realized that this was only the beginning. Nancy wasn't going to teach another year, so likely until fall Justus would also spread his wings on his own.

Later as John Mark was seated at the table enjoying the delicious wedding dinner, a sudden lump formed in his chest again when he saw the rest of his buddies, Levi, Justus, and Paul Ray, at the table with each having his girl by his side. He took another glance at the far side of the table where Paul Ray sat with Cousin Matilda by his side. Matilda was listening to the girl across the table from her. Then she laughed softly and looked at Paul Ray and Paul Ray nodded his head as he smiled at her knowingly.

A strange feeling stirred in his heart as he remembered the talks he had with Paul Ray when he was grieving for Verna and would not be comforted. He had seemed not to have any further interest in girls.

John Mark had shared his feelings of being discouraged and brokenhearted. Their sharing experiences had caused a closeness which exceeded that of the rest of their group of boys. Paul Ray had gone with him a few times when he went to Stony Creek for the weekend for some meals or nights spent at Uncle Israel and Uncle Seranus's. They had good times like that one Sunday when there was no gathering in the afternoon and they had stayed at Seranus's and visited with the whole family. They had an enjoyable time playing Skip Bo. He still remembered how the following week Paul Ray convinced him to go to Stony Creek again for the singing at Eli Hurst's, a neighbor to Seranus. John Mark gave in, even though he had wanted to attend the home gathering that weekend.

Just a little before they arrived at the singing, Paul Ray said, "Would you ask Seranus's daughter Matilda if she is interested in my company?" John Mark was astonished. He had never given it a thought. He thought Paul Ray was still waiting on Verna or else doing without. He realized that Paul Ray was rather quiet on the way home the week before, but John Mark thought Maybe he was half sleeping or out of sorts.

The joy had increased, John Mark remembered, when he asked Matilda. She was taken as off guard as John Mark was.

She had gasped, "But we haven't been entertaining him for that. We took him just as if he was your brother."

"That doesn't matter," John Mark replied to her.

"Tell him . . . tell him . . . er—" Matilda stammered, then with a laugh finished, "that I didn't even clean the parlor!" John Mark dashed off without giving her time to say more.

Later that evening John Mark sat in Seranus's kitchen snacking after returning from the singing before going to bed, while Paul Ray spent the night with another acquaintance.

When Matilda asked, "What did he say?" John Mark told her, "He said it doesn't bother him. He said maybe he could help clean one corner up."

"Is he coming?" Matilda asked, anxiously.

"He made plans to use Allen Weaver's buggy to bring you home from the supper place."

Matilda blushed slightly and said, "He wouldn't have had to bother borrowing a team. I could have come with Brother Cletus. He goes right past here."

John Mark answered her, "The way it sounded, it wasn't being a bother, but he is looking forward to it."

John Mark looked their way again. It didn't look like he was a bother to any of them, he mused. Recently he had asked Paul Ray about Verna, and he said he didn't care about her, that he just hadn't known everything. He said he thought God was cruel, but now he sees how good God is. John Mark wondered if he himself just hadn't given himself up completely yet.

In the afternoon during the singing, he wondered how Priscilla was making out substituting for him at school. With Velma there, things should be a little easier.

Later in the afternoon, he was rather restless, and on the spur of the moment, he decided to leave for home with those who weren't staying for supper, even if it was Chester's wedding day. Maybe he could go to school yet and straighten things up.

As he stepped up on the small porch at his "Just More Worthy" school and fumbled for the key, he stopped when he noticed how much the sun was sparkling against the window. The late March sun had power. But not that much more. Oh, maybe Priscilla had washed the windows. He studied the door a moment and noticed the wood around the doorknob had also been scrubbed. He looked around. Yes, the porch had also been swept. With the March mud, things got dirty easily. Maybe Velma had stayed longer and was doing housecleaning. As he turned the key, he discovered it wasn't locked. Maybe Priscilla left last and forgot to lock. He opened the door and found Priscilla at the water cooler with Ajax in her hand ready to scrub the washbowl.

"Are you still here?" he asked surprised. She looked up startled. John Mark stopped short seeing it wasn't Priscilla. It was Lavina!

She fumbled with the Ajax can and asked, "Are you back already?"

He explained that he hadn't stayed for supper and then asked, "Since when are you Priscilla?"

"Oh," she said, still interested in the Ajax container. "They wanted someone to help haul travelers from Ohio and Priscilla said she would if I could fill in for her at school."

"How did you make out here?" John Mark asked. Seeing she was having trouble with the Ajax can, he asked, "Is something wrong with the cleanser?"

She looked at him innocently saying, "I wonder too." He stepped closer, as she looked at the slot cut in the top of the can where he had cut it open to get the cleanser out.

She asked, "Why is this cut open? Was it lumpy?"

"No," John Mark said, "I cut it open to get it out. How else could I use it?"

Lavina studied him, hardly aware of his presence, while he was starting to be aware of the awkwardness. Silently she glanced down at the can again and started to scratch at the paper where the price was stamped on. As she pulled it off, it exposed four or five holes purposely put there in the can to shake out the cleanser. John Mark stared for a moment, then looked up to see Lavina watching him. But she looked down as if she were in a daze and her eyes didn't lift again. She seemed in deep thought.

Then he asked, "Does it say anywhere on the can that you pull off the price tag to open it there?" He read over it and found nothing. Lavina was still deep in thought.

Then she raised her eyes slightly and smiled sort of apologizing and said, "I never gave it a thought. But I guess it doesn't say to peel that off. See here, it is not the price tag you pull off. The price is also on, but here is a bigger sticker underneath." Lavina seemed to have forgotten about the sink she was going to scrub as she set the can down. He asked her how she made out but she kept glancing at the clock. As she pulled on her coat she said that she was a little amused at Louella's restlessness. He asked her further about Adam and she said they made out good. She had learned some sign language through Edgar, she explained as she stepped back a little bit at a time, until she was at the door and slipped out.

John Mark walked to his desk and looked around to see what needed to be done. He discovered he couldn't even think. He walked back to the window to see how Lavina was traveling. He saw her walking slowly across the playground of Four Corner School. She stopped for a moment and then walked slowly on with her head bent low. Then she headed for the shortcut through the woods. Suddenly he felt simple, almost hating himself. What would Lavina think of him, not knowing how to use a cleanser can. He could almost read her expression, what she was thinking in silence. But then he remembered that a new light sort of dawned on her face when he said there were no directions saying to open it there. It had never occurred to her that someone wouldn't know. Her look hadn't been mocking or shocking, it was—he couldn't quite describe it, maybe sort of pity, but he felt like a fool all the same. The thought of hoping to win her was even more humiliating.

* * * *

On a mild Sunday evening as the May breeze gently floated across the countryside, John Mark sat in the backyard near the perfume of the lilac bush, relaxing before bedtime, re-weighing his thoughts. It happened again. The young folks were at Justus's parents for dinner, and in the afternoon while he was sitting in the yard visiting with some other boys, he happened to glance up at the porch where some girls were sitting. Lavina was watching him. He hadn't even known she was there. Lavina's eyes dropped as soon as he looked up and they didn't rise again.

It had happened before, over a month ago, when they were at Luke's for supper. It was while they were eating and still lingering at the table visiting with Luke that his sixth sense roused him. When he raised his eyes, he saw a few girls sitting on the stairway. The others were visiting together while Lavina had been intently looking at him, but then her eyes shifted before he could smile. What were her thoughts? Why does she watch me?

He recalled what Rhoda had said to him about Lavina. But he wished he knew a little more of the circumstances before he reconsidered. He feared since their meeting at school that it was not a dmiration. *Maybe she was just wondering what all else I lacked yet.*

Why had he been noticing her silent studying of him since she found out his ignorance at school? But, her expression carried no trace of scorn the fleeting times he caught it.

Chapter Twenty-Eight

Although "Just More Worthy" school closed for the summer, there were still school duties arising that needed to be worked out. Velma decided not to teach another year. Priscilla had shown much interest in the school and John Mark was working on getting her interested in teaching. But he was losing ground. The last time he talked with her, it sounded like her friend Elmer was discouraging her from it. Why would Elmer care? Surely they weren't thinking of marrying already, although they had been dating awhile and Elmer was somewhat older than she was. One could expect anything.

Jason Eberly's had come to see him a few times. Their son, Martin, was sort of in a class of his own in school. He had heard his teacher, Bertha, talk about him a few times. He was in the next school district. John Mark knew Martin had a problem in reading, but he didn't know that it was serious. Martin's parents already knew of transportation, so they could send him to "Just More Worthy." These school matters continued over the summer.

It was the beginning of August, one warm evening, when the young folks were invited to the Four Corners' area for supper. Then Alvin Reiff's daughter, Alta, asked if she could catch a ride home with John Mark as her brother Earl had other plans that weekend. Sarah had gone up in the morning already and she wanted a way home.

Alta was friendly and outgoing and had asked about his school, and he had poured out his frustrations as he would to a sister. John Mark shared his frustrations about Velma quitting and not being able to find someone else. Alta was a good listener. She not only listened; they had quite a conversation on the way home. She seemed much interested and concerned, and he had finally asked if she would be interested in helping teach the other three pupils. She said she always dreamed about such things since she had an older brother who was already grown who would have needed such a school but spent his school years in public school with more severely retarded children. He didn't always learn up to his ability. His parents had helped him at home but since he was the oldest, his mother was busy with the family and couldn't spend much time with him.

In the next few weeks, Alta had come over to his school a few times on appointments and John Mark showed her the material and books they used. The school board got a sudden notion to enlarge the room a little and put a wall between the rooms with each teacher having three pupils. John Mark liked the idea as the undivided room was sometimes disturbing last year. In fact, the school board members had put in another partition also making a room for storage or for the pupils to play inside when needed. John Mark gathered they were thinking ahead, thinking the school would keep expanding.

Thus, "Just More Worthy" school opened for its second term with things more organized. Alta was so different from Velma. Although there was a partition between the two rooms and a door that led from one room to another, it was not too long after three o'clock until Alta would come through the door and tell him about her day and ask about his day. If she didn't have time to come over, John Mark would go over to her room and discuss the day. The subjects they discussed sometimes led to talk of things other than school matters. Often after ten or fifteen minutes of sharing, they would go back to their rooms, sometimes of course their discussions extended to a half-hour.

Once in a while in their conversations, Alta would mention Lavina's name and bit by bit he gathered she and Lavina were maybe about the same age and associated together sometimes. He never dared to ask any questions for fear of showing interest, but he did ask her once if she meant Lavina Ringler.

Sometimes he purposely steered the subject to young folks and weekend activities to try and see if she would talk more about

Lavina so he could find out about Lavina's doings. He did find out that Lavina's brother Maynard was going with the young folks, so Lavina had a way to go. John Mark hadn't been aware that Maynard was with the young folks. He tried to remember if Maynard was in ninth grade or eighth grade the first year he taught. He could hardly grasp it that his pupils would be starting to join the young folks. But then he reminded himself that his own twenty-first birthday was coming up in December. No wonder his pupils were growing up.

Every time John Mark reached for the cleanser can to clean the washbowl, memories of Lavina would start stirring. He would ponder deeply for a time. He just couldn't get used to it. No matter how often he used the cleanser can, it always stirred memories.

Once while he was scrubbing the washbowl, cleanser in hand, and Alta came over, he asked her, "Did Lavina tell you that she substituted here one day last year?"

"No, did she? I wouldn't think she would ever teach school." Then Alta went on asking a question about some papers she had brought over to ask about. John Mark felt relief that Lavina didn't go tell the other people how ignorant he was.

The minutes ticked on, turning into hours as the late evening time was passing. These were the hours when man was meant to rest from his labors, to grow renewed strength for the day. But in the east upstairs bedroom at Stanley's, a lamp was burning, casting a light on the little table where John Mark sat bent over his tablet, writing a few lines, then resting his head on his hand, combing his fingers through his hair. He was waiting for more words that would not form. Every so often he tore a sheet off, crumpled it together, sighed, and started writing on the next sheet. But the words weren't forming any better. Maybe he should tell Rhoda to ask Lavina. But then again, no one else needed to know.

He crumpled another sheet and started again.

Dear Lavina,

I've tried to find words to say what's in my heart,
But thoughts won't settle into words to help me start.
And so I sit and think, and deep inside I start to pray,

251

That you feel the warmth of the thoughts I cannot say.
I don't wish to offend you, but it seems I am led
To ask if you would consider me as a friend;
And would you open your little room so we can talk a spell.
Reminisce of happy days and share the thoughts as well,
Of the present days, its daily afflictions and troubled care,
As we cast our eyes on the future knowing not where
The path will lead us, through sunny or stormy days.
Though we trust our Lord to lead us through all the ways,
And ask Him to choose the path that "seemeth good to Thee."
If it is His will that a friend walks with me,
I ask if you would care—
If I'd ask that you, your friendship share?
If you do not feel led in this way,
Send me a message by Saturday.
If you consider it a good thing,
I only ask that you welcome me in
When I come knocking at your door
On Sunday evening of October twenty-four.
If the youth are asked to a dinner or supper place,
I would say we'd go our own ways.
And I would meet you at your door at seven,
Or if we eat away, at eight or a little more.
Unless Maynard tells me to bring you along home,
Then I won't have to drive alone.
I'll sign my name and nothing more;
I am John Mark from the school of worthy more.

Now the load was off of him and he went to bed and slept good to make up for the lost hours. He awakened on Friday morning, read the poem, and decided to mail it before doubt settled in. Then she would have it by Saturday and have all week to think it over.

John Mark saw a glimpse of Lavina in church but saw no shadow of her at Mahlon's on Sunday evening when the young folks had supper. Somehow he had to live through the days. Sometimes the suspense was quite disturbing. But as each day passed and no letter awaited him in the evening, he felt more relaxed and the days glided on with his feeling lighthearted at times.

The peace came to an abrupt halt and waves of stormy passage raged on Friday just as he was ready to dismiss for last recess.

Warren, Rhoda, and Jonathan walked in the schoolhouse. John Mark's heart dropped to his feet. As class dismissed, John Mark made his way back to where Rhoda was amusing herself with a picture story on the wall and studying charts and looking at some of the books that they used. They also looked at Alta's room. Then they came back to John Mark's room again. Rhoda was saying Warren had supplies to pick up at Rich Lark, so she decided to ride along if he wanted to drive the two extra miles around here. Rhoda seemed so calm and ordinary.

She kept glancing at him questioningly, as if not wanting him to be aware, and then casually asked, "Are you feeling all right?" John Mark wished she would tell her message.

He said, "Should I?"

"I thought you looked a little pale."

"Maybe we scared him," Warren said, rather humbly. Rhoda laughed lightly over it and soon they were talking of community news. It was time to call in the students, so John Mark rang the bell and classes resumed.

Later there was a slight stir and John Mark looked up to see Warren and Rhoda pulling on their wraps and leaving.

Warren said to him and the pupils, "Continue on as you are doing." The pupils chimed their good-byes. The release of strain overwhelmed him. John Mark hurried over to the wall cabinet and opened the door and pretended to be getting something as the tears of tension released. He blew his nose and dabbed his eyes; then he went to the cooler and got a drink of water to flush the salty tears that he had swallowed before he reached the cupboard door. But he must not get his hopes too high. There were still two days that he could receive mail before Sunday.

His heart stood still on Saturday when he pulled an envelope out of the mailbox with his name on. He tore open the envelope out by the mailbox. It was from Katie. She and her helper were bringing down their schoolchildren sometime within the next week, whenever it suited their schedule.

*   *   *   *

When church was about to be dismissed, Deacon Ralph had an announcement to make. Mary Ethel was published but the deacon had more to say. Priscilla and Elmer were also published. John Mark couldn't believe his ears.

John Mark tried to enjoy himself at John Wenger's, where the young folks were for dinner, but he felt restless. Even though they were singing in the afternoon, it failed to calm him. He wished he would have arranged it differently so that Lavina had to answer if he was to come. Then he would know. Suppose there was a misunderstanding and she wasn't expecting him. Suppose he went there and he was not welcome. He decided to go home to his family for supper in case the letter had been sent there, although he had given his return address for Stanley's.

When he got home for supper, he found Indiana company there and he joined them in an interesting conversation at the table. One man was a minister who shared different experiences and happenings. John Mark kept watching the clock.

When he shook hands with the men to depart, Dad asked, "Are you leaving already?"

When he came to talk with Mother, he asked, "Is there any mail for me?"

Mother looked up from where she and the women were drying the last of the dishes, "You aren't leaving already!" she exclaimed and then said to Delores, "Go check if there's any mail in the holder for John Mark." Delores came back with a few sales envelopes and a letter. He stepped further back in the kitchen and opened it. It was a circle letter that Miriam was trying to start of teachers of special education schools.

Mother came over asking, "Why are you leaving already? We will have an interesting visit for awhile yet, before the travelers go to their night place."

"I know, it would be tempting to stay, but I guess I better be on my way."

The Indiana minister who was sitting nearby said, "Don't mothers know long already that boys have to be on their way on Sunday evening when seven o'clock is coming up?"

Dad said, "This one doesn't bother with that." Mother looked at him as if a light dawned on her. He saw the question in her eyes, even though she remained silent.

As he slipped out the porch door, Mother came hurrying after him asking, "John Mark, won't you tell me who it is?"

John Mark smiled at her anxiety and said, "I didn't say it is anybody. If there is, I'll tell you someday." And then he was out the door, leaving Mother with a puzzled look. As he headed out the road with Ranger trotting briskly, he was thinking he would have gladly told Mother, but first he wanted to believe it himself.

His heart was doing strange things as he made his way up the narrow walk. As he rounded the corner to the small porch where the parlor door entered off from, he saw the big maple tree that stood in the corner of the yard, blazing in his autumn colors against the last rays of the sun as it was casting its final rays of the day beneath the golden western skies.

John Mark looked for a moment, then just as he reached to knock, the door opened wide and Lavina welcomed him, asking, "Have you come?" She gestured to him without raising her eyes far enough to meet his glance. She stood waiting with open arms while he pulled off his jacket and hat, which she hung on a low hook that he hadn't noticed. She then invited him to have a seat, motioning toward the array of chairs. He took the rocking chair which stood right next to him.

As his fingers toyed with his watch, he asked, "Were you maybe waiting? I guess it's a little after seven. I was home for supper and they had travelers from Indiana for the meal, so I didn't get started off in time," he explained.

Returning from hanging up the wraps, Lavina took a seat on the platform rocker that was a little off to the right saying, "It need not be a certain time. I thought maybe you weren't finding your way in or then maybe I missed hearing your knock."

"I was finding my way," John Mark admitted, "until I came around the corner at the backyard and noticed the maple tree silhouetted against the western sunset skies. I was watching that and hadn't knocked yet."

"Maybe you want to sit out on the porch until it gets dark?" she asked.

"Sure, why not." John Mark got up and pulled on his jacket while Lavina got her sweater from a hook on the south wall.

There on the east side of the porch was a glider where they sat and could view the western sky as it was displaying the reflection of the sun that had just slipped beyond sight. The orange glow was brilliant, wavering like steam evaporating to red and blue lace edging, surrounding the rays of golden flame-like red-orange, then tapering off to red and purples as it touched the October blue skies.

"Maybe you often watch sunsets from here," John Mark said as he was watching the changing scene, now turning to more blue and red furrows with purple edges.

"Yes, many," she replied. "Have you a good place to watch sunsets?"

"Oh, well, not at home. Only down by the barn, but at Stanley's there is a good view from the front yard if I take notice, but I guess often I'm too busy with school work and thoughts."

"Are you at Stanley's already for the winter?" she asked.

"Not really for the winter. This year I decided to come to Stanley's right away. It's so handy to be near school and have my things in one place."

"Edgar says the school has gotten bigger and has more rooms." The talk continued of school and its activities, and then it changed to Edgar and to the other pupils and its challenges. The sunset faded and a clear blue stretched over the sky leaving only tints of the colorful array. The air became quite cool and Lavina suggested they go back into the house. At one point John Mark mentioned that he was sort of taken off guard when they published Mary Ethel and Priscilla.

Lavina chuckled knowingly, "I thought you could be. I was thinking of warning you, but well, I thought better of it."

"I'm glad you didn't," John Mark replied after thinking it over for a moment. He thought how it would have affected him, receiving a letter when he was afraid of getting one. Until he would have read its contents.

Lavina smiled seeming to realize his thoughts and then he added, "It was difficult enough when Warren and Rhoda dropped in to visit school on Friday." She looked up suddenly without realizing it. It was the first time she had raised her eyes far enough to meet his glance.

But she lowered them in a moment as she asked, "You didn't ask Rhoda anything, did you?"

"Not quite," John Mark admitted.

"I didn't tell anyone," she said softly and then added, "except this evening I told Mother. If Priscilla and Mary Ethel's boys had been here today and hadn't left by now, we'd have had to share a room with one of them until the others went to bed, unless it wouldn't have been too cool on the porch."

Somehow the subject had been directed to school again and then John Mark asked her what she did during the week. He learned that she was staying with an older woman in the country a mile from them. She had broken her hip and she was still confined to a wheel-chair. She had three children. Two lived in towns nearby and they stayed with her on weekends. So Lavina was there day and night through the week. The woman was of the "higher" Mennonites. The children were respecting their mother's wish by allowing her to stay in her home and not putting her in an old people's home. Since Lavina's other sisters were getting married, they sold their dry goods store to a neighbor down the road a few miles, a widow with a daughter still at home.

When John Mark asked about seeing her a few times at the home along Triple Bridge Road, she explained that her father had bought that home from his parents and they were remodeling some. A few of them had stayed there a few days, about a week rather than always going back and forth. They had been wallpapering and painting besides what the men did.

The visit had turned out to be interesting. John Mark couldn't believe that the whole evening was spent already.

He asked her if he could do the same next Sunday evening, and she had shyly said, "I don't care, if it's worth your time."

"Worth my time?" John Mark echoed. "My time isn't worth anything, but it sure goes fast here."

257

On the way home, John Mark remembered that Lavina had only once raised her eyes to meet his during the whole evening they visited. She had cast a few glances his way when he wasn't looking but quickly shifted her eyes when he had looked over suddenly. It reminded him of Rebekah when she had put a veil over her face as she came toward Isaac. Lavina also sort of seemed to be hiding behind a veil.

They had not discussed why he was accepted this time, or why not the other time. In fact, they had not talked about "we," or maybe once when she mentioned about had the girls not been published, they would have had to share the room until the kitchen got empty.

The next morning, John Mark remembered his promise, and he dropped a line to Mother saying that Lavina Ringler kept his company on Sunday evening and he was looking forward to it again next Sunday.

Chapter Twenty-Nine

Once again, John Mark had bid "so long" to Lavina "till next Sunday" and was heading home to Stanley's in the hint of the March spring breeze. Each Sunday evening it seemed more as if he tore half of himself off and left it there and went on home with the other half.

Lavina had become so much a part of him. How he looked forward to the hours. He tried to explain it to her one evening and she said she knew just how he felt, but he didn't believe her. How could she know? Then she said it was just how she has been feeling for a while.

"Just on account of me!" he had exclaimed, shocked. "I fail so much and don't come up to what I want to be and, well, I am just John Mark." It had struck her funny and he was almost insulted that she agreed, just to flatter him. He still doubted that she really felt like he did.

Each evening there were so many things to discuss and share and confide. He was finding out more about Lavina's past life, and it was like reading new chapters, going deeper into the book. By now it seemed like he sort of belonged to her family. He knew the happenings of the family and by now had memories of the place and the little parlor. Five months had passed since he first started keeping her company.

When she confided in him, he also confided in her things he never imagined he would share with her. One evening, they had taken a walk back of the house to the orchard and down to the creek edge. At the edge of the yard, Lavina pointed out an apple tree. Its trunk, near the roots, was rather deformed, like scars formed from being broken off and regrowing years ago. On a closer look he could see it once had been hindered, once had to fight for life. But it had sprouted out again and grown and was just a little deformed. He would never have noticed if Lavina hadn't called his attention to it.

She told of the memories the tree held. When it was just a young tree trying to survive growth, she had two pet goats just for entertainment or something to do on her own. The goats had gotten out of their pen and had eaten some of the bark off and some of the roots were damaged then. It looked like the tree wouldn't survive and her dad had been rather upset with her since it was her goats that did the damage. She told of the struggle she had not to get bitter toward him for being upset with her about an earthly thing like a tree.

John Mark asked her if maybe she had lacked respect for her dad before, as he had sensed it a few times in her conversation through the months, that maybe her respect wasn't too high for her dad. Then Lavina had sort of meekly, but sort of half hurt, asked if he had a close relationship with her dad while teaching school, having him as his pupil's parent. John Mark just looked at her as the truth dawned on him, but surely he wasn't so distant to his own children.

He said, "No, he never gave me a chance. He shrugged his way away from me."

And Lavina had said, with tears choking down her throat, "I don't have any better chance." He hadn't pressed the subject more that evening.

Tonight they had taken a walk out to the field lane and then down the single, rarely-used train tracks to Timber Lock School. They had walked up to the schoolyard and sat awhile on the swings and were visiting. During the conversation, John Mark pressed the subject that maybe lowering respect for her dad through past circumstances had caused him to be distant, things which we should forget and forgive.

There was a long silence, and at length John Mark added his experiences of how he had been making it hard for himself and the others around him, and how his Dad had explained to him to be glad for how things were towards what they could be.

260

Then Lavina sort of weakly started explaining that Dad's relationship to the family always left much to be desired. But she wasn't so aware of it until she got older and saw other family ties and then she questioned their background and was informed of her parents' history.

"I admit, I too often let my imagination make things worse for me," she admitted, "and it doesn't help matters."

On the way back home they continued talking on deep subjects. He asked her if it was family circumstances that caused her to not accept any boy's company she had been asked for earlier. Was that why she hid from the presence of all boys in a group or individually? She admitted it was. But then he had wondered about her sisters. Was there more respect shown to them or what?

Lavina slowly said, "Well, I guess you would say they accepted it better and didn't let it bother them, and it didn't help that I was the oldest. Maybe they had more unity and I guess they didn't have as much fear," she finished. She had worded it correctly; she was living in fear of men. John Mark heard enough from Warren that he did not need to ask what fear.

"And you weren't ever going to let yourself get involved in a man's friendship?" John Mark guessed.

"That's very true," Lavina had answered honestly.

"Then why didn't I receive a 'no' with the second letter?" he casually asked.

When she remained silent, he asked her, "Should I have written a poem the first time?"

She chuckled a little and meekly said, "That wouldn't have helped." Then she asked, "Did you make up the poem yourself?" John Mark admitted he had used a real poem for the first four lines or so. She said that she thought she had read some of the words in a scrapbook somewhere. Then they got off the subject as they walked on. John Mark reminded her again that she hadn't answered the question properly.

She took a deep breath and asked him, "Why didn't you just go and ask another girl when I refused?" The memories flashed through his mind of Katie and the struggles he had.

Then he remembered that Lavina couldn't hear what he was thinking and he suddenly asked, "How could I?"

"There are plenty around," she answered, "and some who would accept you."

Suddenly he felt mischievous and asked, "How do you know I didn't?"

"At one time some people made me believe you did, but I doubted it," she admitted. Then he explained about Katie, and to his surprise, she had gotten some wind of it.

John Mark laughed when he asked her, if he had asked Katie if she then wouldn't have accepted him, and Lavina had soberly and dryly said, "You wouldn't have come back."

John Mark laughed heartily and Lavina said, "It is true. I didn't want anyone who would take just anyone. I wanted someone who wanted me." John Mark asked about some of the other boys who had also asked her more than once. She explained further that the ones whom she refused soon had other friends and one who asked twice had others in between and soon after again.

They were back at the house and seated themselves in the little room. Lavina admitted that she was surprised to hear from him for she knew that likely he and Alta would come to an understanding.

"Alta?" he had questioned as if he hadn't heard right. "Why her?"

"Why not!" she exclaimed. "She is everything I wish to be," she said wistfully.

John Mark admitted, "It never occurred to me that I could."

Then she admitted, "Alta was teased unmercifully." After a while Lavina admitted that even if he would have asked her again, had it not been for a little incident she would have refused him again. The incident had helped her see things differently. John Mark guessed it was because her sisters and most of her friends were married.

But she shook her head and then said, "You are going to laugh. But I don't care. It was, well . . . ," she said rather seriously with downcast eyes. She began telling him about the time she found the cleanser can cut open and then Lavina stopped when he gasped. "I mean it," she said with feeling.

"But I don't understand," he said puzzled and added, "That day I gave up all hopes. I was sure you found out I am not even normal."

Lavina raised her eyes softly and held them gently, something she rarely did. She still often avoided looking directly at him. Then her voice had quivered when she said, "I realized that man does need a helpmate in a lot of ways regardless of how knowledgeable they are. They were not meant to keep house alone."

*   *   *   *

As John Mark put his horse in the stable and went up to bed, he thought of what Lavina had said. She came very near to saying that a man needs a woman more than just for the lust of the flesh.

He was glad she didn't ask him why he had asked her again if he gave up all hope that day. He didn't want to tell her that he was aware that she was actually watching him. Before that, he could never spot her. But tonight he found out the thing that most deeply humiliated him was what made their friendship possible. "God moves in a mysterious way, His wonders to perform."

Chapter Thirty

The afternoon thundershower cooled the humid August air considerably, but it was still warm enough. John Mark came home in time to eat supper with the family. After supper Mother told him the mail delivery truck was there that day with a box addressed to him. It was still on the porch. Josiah ran and got the box for him. He saw the company name and knew it was the workbooks he had ordered. He set the books in the corner. He didn't want to see more books today. He had been at school all day, going over things and running here and there. Since another family of plain folks had heard that he was teaching a deaf person, they asked about sending their eight-year-old deaf daughter. That meant either he or Alta had to get a helper or try to locate another pupil and open up the next room. He had planned to have a helper with four pupils, but then Earl Leinbach's had inquired about sending their boy who had to repeat fourth grade last year, which had left him with an emotional problem. Now it had to be decided if they were to have two extra pupils, did he need to hire another teacher or could Pauline maybe by now succeed in a regular school again.

Benny Leid's Lois had agreed to be John Mark's helper but they weren't sure who would teach whom. But John Mark had to think about something else. He had enough school responsibilities for one day. His mind was full and overflowing. He didn't need to overload it.

He went out behind the house on the slope of the yard beneath the tree to breathe in some fresh air and to unwind, or maybe rewind.

On Sunday evening he and Lavina had made the final decision. They would marry in December. That would be the same week as his twenty-second birthday, while Lavina was twenty-five going on twenty-six. They weren't sure yet but it sounded as if they would have the opportunity to move into that small farmette on Triple Bridge Road that Lavina's parents owned if the renters could find a place to move to by then.

He secretly thought maybe Lavina would be his helper once they were married. He had to see how things worked out with Lois by then. How would he get Lavina's initials in the school name. The clouds passed lazily overheard. Far above he saw some birds winging their way east. Oh, to be so carefree. Oh, if I had wings like a dove.

September rolled around not waiting for any unfinished plans. The school had made a decision to send Pauline to a regular school that had a helper. Alta took Edgar to her side so John Mark had Adam, Louella, Beverly, and Wayne with Lois as a helper.

*   *   *   *

"I wish you would tell me what is bothering you," Lavina asked the third week in October when they were having their weekly visit in Lavina's home.

"Did I say something was bothering me?" John Mark asked.

"No, you didn't. But you can't hide it. I can see you are troubled. You were rather quiet last Sunday evening already. Is it about school?"

"No, school is going fine since we have gotten organized, but I have trouble getting my mind to function. It just wanders.'

"I can see that. You haven't been hearing everything I said, but why don't you tell me what is bothering you?" Lavina asked kindly but concerned.

"For one thing, I'm not sleeping like I should. If I don't get my sleep, the rest of the things don't go smoothly."

"Why aren't you sleeping? Do the December plans have some-thing to do about this?" she asked.

"I'm afraid too much," he admitted.

"In what way? Would you rather put it off for later?" she asked hopefully, adding, "We don't have to go ahead right when we planned."

"I'm afraid putting it off for later wouldn't clear up matters. I wish it were that easy." He had put an accent on "later."

"Are you telling me that you are finally realizing that I am not worthy of you?" Lavina asked with a tear slipping down on her royal blue dress.

John Mark broke out in sobs, releasing a flood of pent up frustrations. There was a long silence.

John Mark dabbed his tears and wiped his nose with the wet handkerchief and said in a broken, contrite voice, "I hate myself to ask you to tie your life to me. I don't think I can do it."

"Is something the matter that I should know?" Lavina asked trying to stay calm. John Mark shrugged his shoulders. She was becoming desperate. She moved near to him and put her gentle hand on his rough one and sincerely asked, "Has something happened that is making you doubtful or are you this nervous? Let's talk about it."

"I read something in the *Budget* a few weeks back that keeps haunting me. Haven't you read it?"

"I don't know. I have no idea what you are talking about."

"Didn't you read of that adopted boy who just out of the blue, up and molested one of his family and then killed his parents and his adopted sister and no one knew he was bitter toward anyone? He had been so happy and had just come home from a birthday party where he had enjoyed himself so much."

Lavina's mouth dropped open as she looked at him pitifully and said, "John Mark, I can see you have been tormenting yourself with fears. I now remember that I did read such an article but I couldn't even say that it said he was adopted."

"Why did you think he did it if you didn't even notice he was adopted?"

"Well, maybe I read he was adopted but I forgot it right away again. I was dwelling more on the thought that he was only fifteen and going through a difficult age and maybe he was bitter about something towards his parents."

"But he said how he was so happy and it was so unexpected. They have no clue or however it said."

"I know," Lavina said, "but you know the papers don't print the whole history. Other people were saying he was a little rebellious. You should not compare yourself at all with him. You've had a new birth. He was so young; maybe he had not given his life to the Lord. You must not lay your hand to the plow and look back. You also said how you went through trying times at a younger age when your father explained things. Did the paper say if the boy was a member of the church?"

"Their church. I think they likely join at a younger age, you know."

"I don't remember what it said. I haven't bothered myself about it. I read it and forgot it, except when I heard people talking about it." John Mark remained silent. He felt hurt that Lavina wasn't sympathizing with him.

Then she said, "Do your parents know about this?"

"Yes, they made me go to the doctor to get something to help me sleep. But it isn't working. I thought when I talked with you and told you everything and discontinued coming here, maybe I'd feel better." Lavina turned pale.

She weakly asked, "Do your parents want you to break up our friendship?"

John Mark shook his head, "No, they don't understand me any better than you do."

"What does the doctor say?"

"Well, it was the medical doctor and he just prescribed the medicine. I am going to the nerve doctor this week. Father is sort of upset with me, as earlier when I was discouraged about being adopted, he explained to me how it says in the Bible I reckon that the suffering of this world is not worthy to compare with the glory that shall be revealed to us, or whatever the words are. He had explained that even if there are trials because I don't look like the rest of the family, that it is not as hard a trial as if I had never been in the family and would live in foster homes and would have a home where the people wouldn't accept me as part of a family. He told me to always repeat that verse to myself when I got discouraged until the tempter goes away, and it has helped me a lot in my childhood. But Father is upset that he can't make me win over my doubt with that."

"I don't blame him. You should have shared your fears before they haunted you so much." They had been going in circles all evening with John Mark raising doubts every time Lavina thought she had him a little convinced.

John Mark wanted to break up their friendship for the time being, hoping it would bring him some relief as that was what seemed to make him feel fearful. But Lavina was at a loss as to what good that would do. She had encouraged him, saying that if he saw the doctor that week who was educated in helping disturbed minds, he would soon feel better. He should wait to see what the doctor suggested, since John Mark's parents also didn't feel breaking off their friendship would be the thing to do. She urged him to bring the clipping along. She wanted to read it again.

She went on to say, "Something in the article might reveal something that you haven't noticed that could be a cause. You just grabbed up the word 'adopted' and all your fears and doubts let loose. I trust you kept the clipping as I sense you read over it pretty often?"

"Yes, I have cut it out," John Mark admitted. He was rather surprised that Lavina could tell so much about him without even knowing. She was sharper than Mother was.

"I want you to come on Sunday evening and bring the clipping along. I want to read it."

"What would that help? I already told you all it says," John Mark said a little disgusted and feeling embarrassed as the part he sort of skipped over when telling it to Lavina was about how the boy had molested his stepsister first, and she couldn't read that in his presence.

But Lavina broke into his thoughts saying, "It makes me think of a story that was in *Young Companion* years ago about how some girl—oh, I don't remember how it all was. It was, I think, about a girl living alone and one lady thought this was so terrible, saying it was not safe since another girl had been kidnapped at work. This girl who lived alone wanted to see the writing that the woman was so worked up about. When the girl read the article it said the other girl was working at The Open Door Restaurant, which sounded like a questionable place to work, and it was in the evening. Then it said she wasn't missed until the next morning at ten o'clock, which proved she had a history of not coming home from work. She must have been leading a questionable life. The woman thought that one incident would make it unsafe for any girl to live alone. Just like your fear because one adopted boy would go mad, all adopted boys would. You're comparing things that don't have the same dangers."

John Mark shook his head, "But this boy was adopted and seemed happy and it was completely unexpected."

"I still want to read that article," Lavina confirmed, sounding a little weary in being contradicted so often.

John Mark left somewhat discouraged and confused that Lavina didn't agree on breaking up their date to see if he could get relief, and that she insisted that he bring the clipping along.

Until the next Sunday evening came, he wasn't in shape to go anywhere. On Friday he had stayed home from school, and he hadn't attempted to go to church. His parents didn't allow him to stay at Stanley's the last week so he had been at home. He was to the doctor a few times but was getting more confused, getting only some forced sleep with pills.

Warren and Rhoda had come in the afternoon with their two little boys. Rhoda was in the kitchen visiting with his parents. Warren sat by his side where he was resting on the living room sofa. He talked about community news and so forth. Then he asked John Mark how he felt by now and John Mark poured out his frustrations, that people didn't let him make a choice. "Maybe if I could, I could feel better; people just don't understand."

Warren questioned, "I hope you aren't going up there tonight?"

"No, I am not going anywhere."

"Then you are going to have off. You can see how it makes you feel once, but people do understand. I believe breaking up with Lavina is one of the worst things you could do. You need your friends. Do you remember another time things looked bleak when a girl refused you? You were in sorrow over losing your grandmother and disappointments in the family, and then your horse got killed." John Mark nodded his head.

"Well, God made things work out then and He will again. I thought we showed you we did care by giving you a horse. I would gladly do it again if it was so easy." John Mark looked puzzled. He didn't understand what Warren meant.

Then Warren said, "I saw your struggles earlier that life was getting rather difficult. The least I could do was to replace your horse to show that we cared and sympathized with you."

"You mean you gave Ranger to me?" John Mark asked sitting up. Warren nodded his head.

"You never told me," he said surprised.

"You never asked me."

"I figured it was the whole community; that's quite a horse. Where did you find such a good horse?"

"I know it's quite a horse. I searched long to find it, but I wanted you to have it. I was glad I could do something for you. That is what friends are for, so you don't want to leave your friend Lavina. She is a better friend than I am. I just hope she can hold out. You cannot imagine what she is enduring. She is taking the blame on herself for refusing you and making you suffer earlier. Now she feels that's why she has to go through this."

John Mark felt a sense of joy he hadn't known for weeks, finding out where Ranger came from and grasping how much Warren cared. But he felt disturbed about Lavina, the thought that she was having a burden and trying time had not entered his thoughts. He thought she wasn't very caring, since she didn't agree to discontinue their friendship.

In another half hour his heart warmed when he saw Lavina entering the room where he was resting. He was sort of confused that her arrival had sent a joy through him. He thought that's where the weight of the load was from, dragging her into his hopeless life. He asked her, "How did you know I wasn't coming tonight?"

"Your parents sent me the message through others."

"You wouldn't have needed to come down."

"I know, but I wanted to. And you look more cheerful than you did last Sunday evening." Then he told her how Warren was here and confided the secret he had kept through the years, and he shared with her what all he had said about giving John Mark the horse. Lavina was overwhelmed and rejoiced with him. John Mark

270

was trying to grasp her joy. She seemed to care so sincerely, not only because she should be interested.

Lavina looked at him trying to guess his thoughts and then she asked, "What are you looking at?"

"Just thinking," he said.

"It must have been rather deep," she said.

"I was thinking you seem to care more for me than I do for myself."

"I do. And if you insist that we have to break up, I will accept it if you feel that is what it takes. But I still would like to see that clipping." He had not answered her one way or another. Then she asked about school. Velma and some of the parents were trying to keep his room going. As she was ready to leave, he ran upstairs and came back and handed her the envelope. If he was no better till Tuesday, the doctor wanted him to go to the hospital where he could work more closely with him.

*   *   *   *

She came in during the night. When John Mark opened his eyes on Saturday morning, Lavina sat by his bedside and greeted him with a smile. A joy went through his whole being. Maybe it was just a bad dream that he couldn't love Lavina anymore. He smiled and her smile brightened more yet. But was this Lavina? It looked like her smile. He couldn't remember where he was.

He asked, "Have you come?"

"Yes, why do you look so puzzled?" Lavina asked.

"I was trying to remember, were you sick?" John Mark asked.

"I haven't been hungry," she admitted. "I guess I lost weight."

"Why are you here?" he asked. "Shouldn't I be going to school?" But then he felt weak and he started recalling he was in the hospital. The whole gloomy present loomed before him. Everyone was disappointed in him.

As if reading his thoughts, Lavina laid her hand on his and said, "I came in because the doctor told me to. You were very sick yesterday. Do you remember?"

"Yes, I remember again. I wish I wouldn't have to wake up; disturbing thoughts chase each other as soon as I get awake."

"Things will change again. The doctors are trying to help you, but they cannot until you believe things are better. You have to get strong and fight those thoughts. You have to master them. They are running freely, and I want to help you build a fence. They might still at times come now and then to see if they can get through, but once they know that the fence will not give, they won't try so often."

"Do you think there is medication that can do that?" he asked, watching her intently.

"I think so," Lavina said fumbling around in her handbag. There was a rustling of paper and then she said, "I have something to share with you. You remember that clipping you gave me?"

"Is that why you weren't eating? I didn't want to give it to you, but you insisted," he reasoned.

"No, I wasn't hungry because I knew how sick you were. I read the clipping that you gave to me, but I didn't read anything in it that I could compare with you; the situation was all so different, I put it in safekeeping to think about. And I prayed that I might be given wisdom to help you overcome your fear that is mastering you. That night at three o'clock I suddenly awoke and felt slept out. I was so wide awake and my concerns turned to you. I ached to help you but my heart was too full to pray. I had prayed so much already, then I got up quietly and tiptoed downstairs to get that clipping. I wanted to read it again.

"When I came back up, I was stunned to see I had also picked up another paper with the clipping from a paper that I had often searched for already and couldn't remember where I had put it. I looked in that drawer quite a few times; I thought I had lost it." Lavina wiped a tear from her eye that was getting misty. She cleared her throat and continued.

"Maybe I never told you, but after you were keeping my company awhile, your mother gave me a paper that she wanted me to have. I understand it was with your grandmother's things and when she died, they gave it to your mother."

John Mark sat up in bed in anxious interest asking, "What paper?"

"I think your mother said it was when you joined church; the day you got baptized an overwhelming feeling came over you when the bishop begged your hand and told you to rise to a new life and a new beginning. Your tears flowed over in joy and your grandmother asked you about it, and she thought it was too soon for joy, then you explained to her what a wonderful feeling it was for you to realize that it was a new life, a new beginning. You now had the chance everyone else had. It didn't matter that you were adopted or whatever. It was a new start, a new life, all the same in Christ. Your grandmother wrote down the message as she felt you might need those words someday since they were revealed to you." Lavina looked up to the sound of John Mark softly crying. Tears of pent up feeling were being released.

He dabbed his eyes and blew his nose and his words were muffled as he said, "I haven't thought of that for a long time; I should have remembered."

Lavina continued and said, "Satan is mighty; he can convince us of many things if we start fearing, but God is Almighty."

"I could have saved myself a lot of turmoil if I would have talked to you about it before it got me so down."

"That's a privilege we have. That's why you are coming on Sunday evenings. Just because it was an adopted person, you grew a fear like in that story I talked about. One lady thought it wasn't safe for any girl to be alone anywhere and the other lady thought it was no wonder the girl got in trouble. We have to study the circumstances."

John Mark blew his nose and cleared his throat saying, "May I come again if I feel able to after trying to deny you?"

"I'm looking forward to the time when you can come again. I didn't blame you. You felt guilty and you felt breaking up our courting would help. You were desperate to do something, but I doubt that it would have brought the results you thought."

At that time the nurse came in with the breakfast tray and John Mark reached for his orange juice glass and drank all of its contents.

The nurse looked at him and said, "Are you hungry this morning? I'll refill the glass for you."

After the nurse returned with the glass of orange juice, Lavina said, "I'll go get something to eat too. I'll go down to the cafeteria."

The breakfast tasted really good to John Mark, more taste than it had for a long time.

Long after he had finished eating, John Mark walked out in the hall wondering if maybe Lavina had gone home. He walked down the hall a little. He saw a nurse go through a door into a small room, and as the door opened, he saw Lavina in the room talking with one of his doctors.

He was back in his room looking out the window when Lavina returned. She joined him at the window and pulled up chairs for both of them. She continued visiting and while talking about the seasons changing, autumn fading, and winter knocking soon, she said, "I guess you realize that the wedding will be canceled for the time being. Until you are stronger again." John Mark nodded his head.

Silently, he thought in his mind all plans were canceled, but he wasn't sure any more. Out loud he said, "There is still time." Lavina lingered awhile visiting until John Mark's parents came. Then she said she would be leaving. The doctors had come in and rejoiced at seeing him feel better.

Later in the day Wilmer came to see him. John Mark was so surprised. Wilmer didn't say much while John Mark's parents were there. But when his parents left, John Mark shared his surprise of seeing him in here.

Wilmer said, "Mom encouraged me to come."

"Ellen?" John Mark questioned.

"Yes, Mom," he said so submissively. "That's Mom," he said wiping his hands over his brow and shifting his weight from one foot to the other saying, "I still remember how much I dreaded having another mother and how you gave me so much hope. It was just like you said; it was worth all the adjustments."

"I would have even encouraged you more if you had told me who your mother was going to be. Ellen helped me a lot," John Mark said.

Wilmer went on to say, "I don't know if she was a good teacher but she is a good mother. I don't know what we would do without her. To think how much I hoped it would not happen. If it had not been for your encouragement, I likely would have run away from it, or made it miserable enough that they would have sent me away." John Mark looked at the lanky boy who had grown from a difficult schoolboy into a respectful young man.

"When I heard things looked dark for you, I told Dad how you had encouraged me and he must have told Mom. She questioned me about it and sent me over and said I should tell it to you just as I told it to her."

"You know, that was a long time ago. I hardly know what I told you, probably what Dad told me years ago. I thought what he said would always help me about the trials not worthy to compare with the good that will be revealed, but when a trial came this time, I simply couldn't fight it. But I am just finding out what good friends I have. You are the third unexpected person who came to me with comfort. I am learning things I wouldn't have ever found out if I hadn't gone through this. I am beginning to realize the value of friends. I hadn't realized that people care so much. I learned things that would never have been explained to me if I hadn't been brought this low. It makes it seem like there was something I had to go through. I often wondered how you found life. I am glad to hear that your father's marriage to Ellen was a blessing. Ellen had also done so much good in getting me prepared to be a teacher. Without her help, I likely wouldn't have ever found my pound of talent."

*   *   *   *

When the December air began to chill the countryside, John Mark found himself back in the schoolroom with Velma and Lois helping until he adjusted. The familiar routine of the schoolroom helped him adjust to normal life again.

He was grateful that God had directed and led him back to recovery without losing Lavina. He was shown how much he needed her, a lot more weighty matters than opening a cleanser can. They had planned that in March they would unite in marriage and walk together.

275

Chapter Thirty-One

It had rained during the night but the clouds were parting this early March morning and patches of blue were coming through here and there as John Mark drove over to Nevin Ringler's. The guests and workers started arriving. All his friends and cousins and neighbors came with their wives, and Paul Ray and Matilda were getting married next week. Warren and Rhoda had done so much for them that he chose them to be witness on his side since Delores hadn't joined the young folks yet.

He asked Lavina, "Who is that man I saw outside, the one a little on the older side. I thought I knew all your uncles who were coming." Lavina thought a moment and then said, "Oh, you mean the minister. I forgot to tell you last evening, neighbor Ivan's walked over here with a few men who had been visiting there from Michigan. We invited them to the wedding. They seemed interested when they heard there was a wedding here today. The minister's name is Paul Landis."

As the guests were all seated and the song had started, John Mark followed Lavina down the stairway to the two empty chairs in the center where the living room and bedrooms connected. It had not been in vain that they waited until March to get married, as Paul Landis wouldn't have been a guest. And he wasn't only a guest today. When the singing died down, Paul Landis stood up and cleared his throat and looked the congregation over for a moment. Paul was past middle age. His hair hadn't thinned much nor faded in color much yet, but his bent, stooped back and wrinkles showed that many a year rested on him already. His callused hands showed that they had been used to toil over a lot of years.

276

But he was still quite spry and his motions were swift as he started saying, "I wish God's rich blessings and grace to you all in this morning hour as we have gathered here in the brother and sister's house. I really don't know why I'm here," he said throwing out his hands and shaking his head from side to side and pausing as if he was waiting for someone to answer. Then as an afterthought he quickly added, "I was supposed to be home by now, but through some kind of misunderstanding, we missed the bus yesterday afternoon, and we walked up here last evening to visit. Then we got invited to the wedding today so we didn't go after the bus this morning as planned. Now I am asked to minister the admonishing and comfort of God's Word to people I don't know. My mind is so full this morning. I don't know if I can share this all with you.

"I haven't had time to think over the message or read much Scripture. I was so empty this morning and since I was here early, I walked around on the farm and there was an overflowing message revealed to me. The spirit is so—oh—full, overflowing, like I say, I haven't had time to think over and get it in order. I don't know if I can share it all with you, but I'll pour it all out as it was given to me. Why this message is needed, I don't know. As far as I can see, this is a young boy and girl taking the step. Nothing reveals to me that this has come about wading through difficult and stormy paths, but I'm getting ahead of myself.

"Like I was saying, I was here early this morning and so I walked a little over the farm and that is when the spirit opened its rich streams, deeply stirring in my heart. Where do I start? The spirit is so pressing. I don't know if I can cover every part in order. Maybe more of you noticed or maybe the people who live here weren't even aware. Because I have owned an orchard all my life, I naturally noticed trees, and they interest me. Therefore, I noticed the apple tree in back of the house. I don't know what its life story is. Maybe a rabbit gnawed at it when it was only a young shoot. Or it could be that a little boy drove against it with his little wagon. Whatever, it doesn't matter."

He went on and John Mark heard Lavina taking a deep breath. He could just about know what she was thinking. Something like,

"Surely I won't have to hear about that tree even at my wedding!" Lavina's father shifted his legs in his nervous way, looking straight ahead. Without being fully aware, John Mark moved his foot over nearer to Lavina's assuring her it was all right and she wasn't alone.

Paul was talking rapidly, "But what matters is that tree turned my mind to an article I read years ago. I don't know why the spirit directs this to a wedding sermon. I'm not here to question it, only to bring it forth. I saw that even if something had hindered the tree's roots at first, it had also strengthened the roots. You can see the roots on one side of the tree are stronger and thicker even if they are deformed and scarred. They had to grow stronger to keep hold or reroot. This tree has thicker roots than the other trees that seem to be about the same age. And I thought of an article. I wish I could have read over it, but the copy is at home. I trust what I need of it will unfold.

"The article was about a man. The way I understand it, he was a minister and a doctor. He came to visit a woman who had been missing from the church services for a while. When he got there, the woman said she was laid up with her foot broken.

"She said to him, 'Likely you say it's a judgment against me for not coming to church regularly.' I understand she failed to come to church regularly even before she broke her leg.

"The doctor said, 'I missed you and I hope you are recovering fast.'

"She corrected him saying, 'Slowly, not fast, and I can't stand it. I'm so bored when I'm not doing things. I have so many things to do right now, but I must sit here six weeks. It's all a waste of time,' she fretted.

"The doctor changed the subject and said, 'Your lilies are beautiful. What tall, straight stalks and wonderful blossoms!' Then the doctor laughed and said, 'Someone brought me a jar like that with water and pebbles and bulbs putting out green shoots. I stood there in the sunshine and rejoiced in the quick growth until someone told me that unless I let them root in the dark, they would never have strength enough to flower.'

"Then she asked him, 'Did you put the bulbs in the dark then?'

"He said, 'I kept them in the dark until the white roots climbed the pebbles in every direction. The roots didn't grow in the dark, but when they came into sunlight again, they leapt into a flower because they had strength behind them. But,' he said, 'my blossoms were weak compared with yours. I had waited too long to strike roots, you see.'

"The woman looked at the lilies and back to his face asking, 'Is that a parable?'

"Then from his pocket he drew a worn testament and opened it at Ephesians and read, 'That ye being rooted and grounded in love might be filled with all the fullness of God. In all things which is the head even Christ.' You can read those verses in Ephesians 3:17-19. Quite a long way for even the best of us to grow, isn't it?'

"'And you say we can't do it without roots? And roots have to grow in the dark?' the woman asked.

"'The sunshine often keeps us too busy to grow roots,' he said. The woman said it made a good parable.

"'Rooted in love means God, I suppose. Rooted in love,' she mused. 'That means drawing all our strength from Him doesn't it? I don't believe I know Him well enough,' the woman admitted. He told the woman he saw her Bible on the bookshelf and that he would go get it for her.

"The woman said, 'I've been too busy to read it lately, but if I am put in the dark to grow roots, I'd better begin, hadn't I?'

"The minister looked at the lilies and said, 'With roots like that, think what flowers you will carry.' And that's what I thought of when I saw that strong thick-rooted tree behind the house. Just think of the storms it will be able to withstand! But it was put in the dark first to grow those roots. It had been hindered, then it gave stronger roots. Like further in the article it says the sunshine often keeps us too busy to grow roots. If things always go well for us, our roots don't grow so deep. They don't get exercise. Rooted in love, it's a fitting wedding scripture. If it is love that rooted you, the marriage will be able to stand. I don't know this young couple. I don't know what the circumstances were that led you together or what you endured to get together.

"Sometimes young people experience heartbreak and trials and sometimes hard-tried patience until God makes His will known. And sometimes, young people can easily glide together and fulfill God's will. I do not know, but God knows. But the spirit seems to speak so strongly 'with roots like that, think of the flowers you will carry.' I trust you know about those roots. Have you been kept in the dark to grow roots and when they came to light again, they leapt into flowers because they have strength behind them? I can feel the sympathy or oneness or closeness of the people present here, that there have been memories stirred up. I don't know what memories; the Spirit knows. He has been speaking through me, things I hadn't at all planned to say. I can feel these young trees have been rooted in love and kept in the dark enough to have grown strength behind them. And I trust that when they are brought out to the light, they will flower. Too often we act quickly to work our way out of the dark and miss our chance to get deep roots. But I will not take away more from the bishop who has further to lead."

The bishop wiped his eyes and blew his nose. Dad shed some tears on his suit coat; Mother was holding her handkerchief to her cheek. Warren had gotten his handkerchief out a few times during the sermon. John Mark heard Lavina trying to swallow unshed tears. John Mark himself was too spellbound to feel sad. The man had given reason for all his struggles. It needed to be so. Had he known all this before, things would have been easier. The few people who had known the wedding had been canceled were the ones whose memories stirred tears. It had been hard for the bishop. Only Warren and Rhoda knew about the patience and testing that was endured until they were led together, the time they were set in the dark to grow roots. But the whole congregation knew that John Mark had been depressed in October.

The bishop touched a little on the minister's parable, acknowledging its truth without going into detail. He admonished John Mark and Lavina in the worth and truth of staying steadfast, for the crown is not at the beginning, or in the middle, but at the end. He reminded them there would still be times the plant would be set in the dark to strengthen the roots. The bishop said he was glad that the time was up, the setting in the dark was fulfilled.

"Though no flowers are seen yet, we can see only the roots and plants; buds are pushing; flowers will come later. But I can testify with such roots, I think the flowers will come forth if the plant keeps growing. Not flowers for you just enjoying together, your home is to be a living plant in the neighborhood and church school and wherever. And now I will turn to the text to use for wedding ceremonies."

Later in the day, John Mark asked Lavina if she wasn't glad that her goats tormented the little tree, and that the man missed his bus, or they might never have known what these dark days were for.

"But I am more grateful that I hadn't known how to open the cleanser can," he added.

"Did you think of that when we were asked if we could say that God led us together?" she teased.

"No, I didn't, because it wasn't really the cleanser can. It was God's leading, for remember how many mysterious ways it took until we got to the cleanser can?"

"What are you referring to?" she asked. "Well, Priscilla was supposed to be teaching that day and I was going to stay at the wedding for supper. Sometimes it still amazes me."

"Maybe we could write a book." Lavina laughed saying, "First we have to live the chapters. I suppose this is the preface."

"If we would live happily ever after, we wouldn't need deep roots," John Mark added.

Chapter Thirty-Two

John Mark had borrowed a ladder from Dad and when he hitched up to return it, Lavina went along for the drive.

On the way home, Lavina asked, "Was something keeping you and your dad so long outside? I was about ready to go check if everything was all right or if you even remembered I was along."

John Mark chuckled, "I didn't forget you yet; but seriously, Dad has to talk at times. I keep forgetting the weight he has since I am not home so much any more."

"Oh, church problems?" she questioned.

"Yes, problems and concerns, discussions and whatever. He was sharing about Titus Kilmer, son of Elias. They are having a problem in the home between father and son. Titus has stayed with uncles at times, but it hasn't been working out so well. The parents have come to the church for help or advice. Elias got a little bitter toward the church then. Instead of taking their advice, he thinks they were picking on him. When the church tried to talk to Titus, he sort of made a mockery of it; you see, he didn't join the church yet. So they don't have much hold on him, but they tried to reason with him."

John Mark shared about different things Dad talked about. As they came into the kitchen and lit the lamp, Lavina rather carelessly said, "Maybe that's who we need—Titus to paint the buildings on the outside this summer."

"You mean he and Edgar?" John Mark laughed. "Weren't you talking about having Edgar to run errands this summer?" John Mark reminded her.

The next morning when Lavina awoke, John Mark was sitting on the rocker in the bedroom, wide awake and dressed to go, with his head resting in the palm of his hands. Lavina asked him what he was doing.

"I am thinking," he said.

"How come you got up to do it? It's only 4:30."

"I was restless. I didn't want to disturb you."

"So what are you thinking?"

"Were you serious about Titus?"

"Titus?" she questioned, "You mean to work here? Why not? You won't get the painting done."

"I have been doing a lot of thinking."

"But how much are you going to be here this summer? I'm not so anxious to be here alone with him when you're at school meetings and errands and shopping, etc."

"Well, you wouldn't be alone with him if Edgar was here. Maybe I could arrange my errands for one day a week and have him go elsewhere that day."

"Sounds good."

*   *   *   *

The little farmette along Triple Bridge Road became home to four people. When John Mark asked Lavina if she was satisfied and happy, she said, "Well, it's more worthwhile to cook and since I get water ready to wash, I may as well wash enough clothing to make it worthwhile."

Edgar was good company for Titus. Edgar kept exclaiming what all Titus knew and what all he was able to do and that gave Titus the important feelings he needed. Edgar talked a lot with Titus while Titus painted, and at times John Mark saw that Titus allowed Edgar a chance to paint some. When Edgar was mowing yard Titus came and took a turn to give Edgar a rest. It cheered them both.

There were days when Titus was gloomy and silent and wouldn't talk about what was troubling him, but it was usually Edgar who popped out something that made him loosen up again. John Mark had taught Edgar how to play some games that they played in the evenings before bed and it had interested Titus. He often watched how John Mark tried to teach Edgar games and finally succeeded. Soon Titus and Edgar were playing games and at times Titus came up with other games and got Edgar interested in playing them.

When school started, Edgar went back to school, although he would be about old enough to quit. He enjoyed school. It gave him something to do. Titus had by now done most of the painting and had taken jobs at the neighbor's, helping husk corn. He was still boarding at John Mark's, but he ate dinner at the neighbor's.

There were evenings when Titus was rebellious when he came home. It seemed he had a problem getting along with people and now he had more to get along with. He was quite upset at times. On those evenings, John Mark talked with him, reasoning and convincing, and pleading with him, while Lavina went on to bed.

Then there were days when Titus found out about a clock somewhere in the neighborhood that didn't work and he spent hours concentrating and working on it. He never got frustrated. He used some clock tools that he had gotten years ago.

As the autumn went on and the corn husking was about completed, John Mark advertised clock repairing for Titus and it was no wild goose chase because people kept bringing clocks. As the weather turned colder, Titus was contentedly occupied. Often John Mark became involved, just seeing Titus's interest. They had emptied the small room downstairs that had been a catchall and allowed Titus to have that room with his tools spread out so that he did not need to clear everything away when it was mealtime.

On a December evening after Titus had retired for the night, John Mark and Lavina were about to retire for the night but were still sitting in the kitchen relaxing, when John Mark asked, "Well, I would be ready to go to sleep. Aren't you ready to go to bed?"

"I really don't feel tired yet."

"Is something disturbing you?" John Mark asked, quite concerned. "You have been staring at the wall for quite a while."

"I have been thinking. Oh, I wish we could help Allen's Vera. I often think about her. You know, first she broke up with Eugene, and it was such a struggle for her and she was so depressed, she couldn't do her work properly. Now she lost her job, which doesn't

284

make it better. They are doctoring, but the doctor is talking about putting her in the hospital."

"And what have you been thinking about?"

"The poor girl. If there was any way to help her."

"Do you mean like giving her a home and work?" John Mark asked.

"She has a home and I suppose work if she could only have an urge."

"She does have a home, but at times it helps to be in different surroundings to forget memories and rebuild others," John Mark reminded her.

"Oh, do you mean we could ask her to come?" Lavina asked, relieved.

"I don't know if it would work. Do you think you could take such stress now?" John Mark asked, his voice filled with concern.

"Oh, I was thinking maybe we could help her recover. Then she could help us when we need help."

"But what are you going to occupy her with until that time? I hardly think she would want to help Titus with clocks."

"Oh, that's right. We have Titus, but you know, I have been helping him some with getting mail ready and the like. And you know, Miss High here, our neighbor, was disappointed that I couldn't wash her windows for her this fall again and there's more cleaning to do in that house than she can do. I haven't helped her as much as she would have liked."

"Well, maybe we could ask Vera to come and you could go with her to Miss High's and get her started. She could be here for most of the meals and the nights, as you know that would work up Miss High too much to try and make a proper meal for someone."

"Of course she would eat here. Then till she would have Miss High's house in order, we would have more work for her."

In the next weeks as the days continued, when John Mark came home from Just More Worthy he noticed that Vera was becoming more cheerful and more talkative. At first she was sullen and, well, she just had no desire to continue. She was living just because it was her duty. But now, often Vera and Lavina were talking about things Miss High showed them or things she had talked about.

After they were in bed, John Mark asked Lavina how long they were over there that Miss High could talk about all that, or what they were working on that they could visit so much. Then Lavina explained that she had gone along with Vera over to Miss High's and got Vera started in washing out cupboards and then she had come home while Vera stayed. Vera said Miss High rested awhile and then came into the kitchen and was visiting while she finished washing out the cupboards. Then Miss High wasn't done talking yet, so she gave Vera a chance to rest. She visited on. "I guess she was reminiscing over her school-teaching days. I gather Vera was interested. Vera shared different things she asked Miss High. I have a feeling it did as much good for Miss High as it did for Vera. Vera was saying she wants to go to Miss High's tomorrow to clean a carpet." Lavina looked at John Mark knowingly. He suddenly understood why Lavina had said it in such an interesting manner.

"Oh, you mean it was nothing less than a miracle that Vera had an urge to talk about 'tomorrow'?"

"Right! I was beginning to feel she was a hopeless case. She just had no urge. It seemed like it was a trial for her to live the day out and as if she desired it would be her last day. I have a feeling that maybe Vera poured out to Miss High, too. Just by things Vera said that Miss High said. They must have been talking about Vera's life." There was just a hint of tears in her eyes.

"It was like I was tending a special plant, watering it carefully, coaxing it to grow, and was on the verge of thinking it was dying. Now I see a little green speck; maybe it's the plant."

"I know what you're talking about. That is what I have been working with at school when I work so hard and finally se a light dawn in their eyes. Maybe we could soon have a Just More Worthy here at home!

"Maybe we could."

"What do you mean? We have it already."

"But I'm not helping."

"Sure you are helping," Lavina said. "You are helping with Titus."

"I know, but I'm gone all day. I would enjoy being here with the family."

"Well, sometimes it would be good if someone was here to help Titus. The clock repair shop is really growing."

"I know," John Mark said, wistfully. "I never thought I would want to do anything else except teach children in school. But the more I help Titus in the evening with repairing clocks and meeting his customers, the more I think I could learn to like it. It's work that does not hinder my weak leg."

"But do you think Titus will keep the business here? He could move away some day."

"If he'd move away far enough, we could both be busy."

"But first he has to stay long enough for you to learn it. You are just his little boy, aren't you?"

"That's right!" John Mark laughed softly, "I feel like I'm in first grade when I'm in the clock shop, and I don't know if I'll succeed in qualifying for second grade. Maybe I'll have to repeat first grade for being absent too many times."

The next evening, Titus asked as they lingered at the supper table, "What are you going to call the clock shop?"

"What do you mean, call it?" John Mark asked.

And Titus said, "There is trouble in mailing things. Some people call it clock shop, some clock repair, then some of it goes to the clock shop in town. When I make a business order, they ask my name and I say Titus Kilmer and they ask, 'What's your shop name?'"

"You could put the name of the road on it for the mail," John Mark suggested.

"You mean Triple Bridge Clock Repair?"

"Oh, I thought just in the address, but that's an idea. We could call it that. Then we both can own and work on it. And write checks."

"That would be a good idea. You know as well as I that you are paying all the parts and advertising. I am only working for you for labor."

*   *   *   *

287

"What are you going to call your son?" Lavina asked as John Mark stood looking at the bundle lying in bed. He was all bundled up except for his round red face and a thick layer of hair covering the little head.

"I wasn't thinking of a name," John Mark said as he looked up sort of in a daze. "I was thinking of many things . . . " John Mark added.

"I could tell. I wonder like what?" Lavina asked.

"I was thinking of my real parents and well, I was thinking— oh, I wonder what the baby will grow up to be."

"I guess what we influence him to be. But what are you going to call him?" Lavina reminded him.

"Do fathers name their babies?" John Mark asked.

"Not necessarily, but I know what I would call my daughter."

"And what's that?"

"I'd call her Kathleen," Lavina said rather excited in a thrilling way.

"Why?" he asked.

"Because look what Kathleen has done for me!"

"What would you call your son then?"

"Oh, let me see," Lavina said as if thinking wildly. "Maybe John David for you and your grandfather, or John Edgar."

"Does it have to be after a relation?" John Mark asked.

"Well, no. Why?"

"I was just wondering." John Mark was thinking deeply of people who influenced him or did good deeds for him. He was thinking over his life, how Warren and Rhoda helped bring him and Lavina together, but then he remembered the cleanser can. His thoughts ran on how they did come together. How they almost parted and how Lavina had been led to help him stand up again after his deep depression. There was no other way anybody influenced him more in life than Lavina had. Well, Dad had done a great thing for making a future for him and helping him when he was depressed in his younger years. Then he thought of the day he and Lavina were united.

Suddenly he said, "Now I know!"

"You know what?" Lavina asked.

"The name. He'll be Paul Landis!"

Lavina looked at him for a moment, half smiling and asked, "Were you thinking about our wedding?" John Mark nodded.

"But we can't choose the last names."

"What do you mean, we can't choose the second name? You said John David."

"That minister from Michigan's last name was Landis like yours is Wenger."

John Mark gasped, "Oh, but Landis is also a first name," he reminded her.

"Well, yes it is, on second thought, but with Paul it sounds like a last name, since we learned to know Paul like that."

"But this is a different person. He'll grow up being Paul Landis Wenger!"

Lavina repeated it a few times and said, "Since Paul is such a short name we could easily use it in Paul Landis."

"So that's what it shall be then."

Vera became a busy person, keeping meals prepared and diapers washed out, the house clean and the laundry done. And she was still running over to Miss High's trying to keep her house in order. Miss High had fallen and was quite stiff and sore, so she needed help with the regular housework. And Paul Landis was quite confused as to which was day and which was night. At times it seemed the baby was on the night shift.

Chapter Thirty-Three

The family along Triple Bridge Road came into a routine again. Paul Landis was a happy baby and learned to sleep at night time. John Mark came home from school and greeted his chubby, smiling, three-month-old son and shared the day's happenings with his faithful wife and listened as she shared the activities of her day at home.

Then John Mark joined Titus in the clock repair shop until supper. After supper it still seemed like something was missing since Vera was now busy with Miss High. Miss High had the flu and had gotten so weak she couldn't do her everyday work anymore. Titus worked on the clock repair shop's paperwork with John Mark getting quite involved if he didn't have any schoolwork to catch up on.

One day after supper Lavina asked John Mark if he had looked at the mail.

"Oh yes, I did," John Mark finally remembered.

Lavina looked at him rather strangely and asked, "Were you surprised?"

"Surprised at what? You mean with three bills?" he asked.

"Didn't you read the letter?"

"No, I didn't read it. Did she have anything new to write about? Is she getting married maybe?" he questioned.

"Who? Oh, you mean Annie. That letter isn't from my Michigan pen pal. You better read that letter." Lavina wasn't going to tell him, so he got up and fetched the letter and pulled it out of the envelope and unfolded the sheet. In doing so, a paper fell out. He picked it up and saw it was a $50.00 check. Maybe it was for some clock repair, but he didn't know they sent any clocks to Michigan. It was his job to get the UPS orders ready. He started reading the letter and gasped and looked at the check again. It was from the minister Paul Landis from Michigan. He found out they had a baby named after him and used his full name. So he sent $50.00 to start a savings account for the little fellow.

Don't strange happenings ever come to an end? John Mark wondered in silence as he finished reading the letter.

*   *   *   *

When the school months ended, Edgar came to their home again to help with errands and such, since at home there were a lot of others to run errands and here he felt more needed. He brought along two of his setting hens. He had much interest in the little chicks, watching and managing them.

In July, the community people came asking if John Mark could try giving Simeon Hoover's Carl a home. He was somewhat retarded and rather hard to handle. Simeon wasn't well and Mrs. Hoover alone couldn't make out too well with him. At times he cooperated better in unfamiliar surroundings than in his own family.

"They asked as if we are some kind of home for the retarded," John Mark told Lavina unbelieving.

"I don't care to give it a try if you stay at home instead of going back to school." Since Titus couldn't keep up with the clock repair, it would be a good opportunity. They had been refusing some clock repairs. Karen Good agreed to take his place teaching at Just More Worthy.

As autumn continued, John Mark was getting acquainted with Carl, taking him to different places in the neighborhood, helping with odd jobs, working with him to get a little bit of an idea what work he could handle. Carl had taken some interest in Edgar's chicks and hens, but he had taken more interest in the dozen or more chickens they had for their own egg use. He would fetch eggs quite often in a day and clean them regardless if it was necessary or not. Sometimes he would wash them twice.

John Mark made arrangements and took him over to Luke Fox's where they had a large laying hen house and helped Carl get started in gathering eggs. Carl had also cleaned two baskets and helped pack eggs. Once a day John Mark and Carl went over there and helped with the eggs. As John Mark watched Carl's interest and joy, a thought started churning in his mind. Why couldn't they put chickens in that shed where Grandpa Ringler had had pigs in the lower part and feed and storage in the upper part. They had been using the lower part for storing the lawn mower, bicycles, and step ladders, etc. Someone would need eggs and if not, they could take them to market. So with Carl's help John Mark prepared the building for chickens.

After the building was ready, John mark put 125 chicks in the lower part and seventy-five in the upper part, plus the dozen they had for regular use. Then Edgar had the small chick house all to himself for his chick raising. Edgar also had an interest in egg gathering and packing eggs.

Often Edgar and Carl went together gathering eggs, and Carl enjoyed Edgar and his help even more at cleaning them. Carl knew the number of eggs they laid each day and since John Mark was being paid for giving Carl a home, he left Carl have a little bit of income from the eggs which sparked an interest in Carl that John Mark hadn't known he had.

As spring came, John Mark moved Edgar's setting hens to the top part of the horse stable when he got a batch of baby chicks to replace some of the chickens and enlarge the flock some. Between Carl and Edgar, John Mark didn't need to take care of the chicks, only check them every so often and give instructions. In fact, it seemed that's the only thing he did everywhere. The teachers at school, Karen and Alta, depended on him to make decisions as to what books and things to use and what pupils to accept and when to open the next room. And he was still ordering the school supplies. In the clock repair shop Titus went ahead but depended on him to manage the financial matters and ordering and mailing. Sometimes he helped Titus if there was a certain deadline.

Sometimes John Mark wasn't sure he was working anything. Titus ran the clock shop, the teachers kept the school running, and Edgar and Carl were taking care of the chickens. He found himself with stacks of paperwork belonging to the business, ordering clock parts, keeping track of income and expenses of the chickens, and seeing about markets for eggs. By now Titus had joined the church and developed into a decent, level-headed boy, working for Triple Bridge Clock Shop that he started up, but John Mark owned it.

Paul Landis was now running around mostly taking care of himself, so Lavina also had time to help with the clock mail and paperwork. Thus she didn't panic when they were asked if they could board little Lillian Martin. She was starting first grade in Just More Worthy on account of her hearing disability which caused her to be a slow learner. Her parents lived too far away from the school, and they couldn't find transportation to get her back and forth twice daily, so she stayed at John Mark's from Monday evenings to Friday mornings. She was a good playmate for Paul Landis.

It was on a Sunday that John Mark's parents had been with them for dinner that Dad talked about Elmer Horning's Julia. She was having problems. She wasn't as talented and knowledgeable as many people are, but she was able to mingle with the young folks and the parents had work for her.

But now her younger sisters were married and it seemed to depress her realizing she would be different. And it was causing problems. She lost interest in everything. She had no confidence in herself. As John Mark was telling Lavina about it in the evening, Lavina suggested maybe she could come help butcher some of the old chickens and help more at Miss High's since Vera got another job. The neighbor girls were trying to fill in, but things weren't going so well. So with John Mark and Lavina's persuasion, Julia's parents let Julia come to the home on Triple Bridge Road, filling the vacancy Vera left since she had moved home again. Miss High was glad that Lavina and her helper could help again as the neighbor girls were always in a hurry to move on again.

Julia was rather sullen and quiet when butchering chickens, but took an interest in playing with Paul Landis. And she was a bit more cheerful when they worked for Miss High a few days in a row. But no wonder, Miss High always praised them so much and Julia didn't mind sitting down and listening while Miss High told her stories of bygone days. Little by little, Lavina sent Julia over to do jobs alone for Miss High. Then at times she went over to see if the jobs were done satisfactorily.

Lavina became aware that they talked a lot more than they worked, but Julia usually could do the jobs well enough for Miss High. It gave Julia a feeling of satisfaction that she was doing something, but there were days when Julia was quiet and moody and even the visits over to Miss High's home didn't help. It was usually an act from Paul Landis or Lillian that brought Julia out of her brooding world. She loved children and Lavina guessed her quiet times were caused by wishing to have a friend instead of keeping house at Miss High's.

During the summer, Lavina's father agreed to let them build a few rooms onto the house. It was crowded at times now with Julia there. Lavina at times used the extra eggs up by making noodles. In fact, it was becoming a weekly task. The bulk food store wanted all the noodles they could make.

The number at the house on Triple Bridge Road increased again when Lillian came back for another tern. Also, Baby Warren came to join his brother Paul Landis, who was two and one-half years old.

Lavina was grateful for Julia. She was familiar with their schedule and things went smoothly. When the activity of the day quieted down and the family had all scattered to their beds, John Mark was deep in thought.

"Is something bothering you?" Lavina asked when he didn't make any preparations to get ready for bed when they went in the bedroom.

"It's not bothering me. I can't say how it makes me feel, but Titus told me that he had been dating Vera for a few weeks already."

"Vera and Titus dating! Surely not our children!" she exclaimed.

"You are about as shocked as I was, but Titus has come a long way. Vera had just been depressed giving up her steady and had to adjust to starting over in life."

"Then you think Titus will continue doing so well?"

"For sure with Vera. Now, depending on who he would be-friend, I would feel a little anxious, but that he is interested in Vera tells me a lot."

*   *   *   *

One evening in December, Lavina was straightening up the kitchen and then reading some while trying to settle Warren down for the night. John Mark sat at his desk writing and scratching his head. After the clock struck ten, John Mark looked up when Lavina came and silently stood beside him, looking at his paper he was bent over.

He smiled at her puzzled look when she said, "Doesn't look much like numbers to me."

"Just wait. I'm almost done," he said covering the last half of the paper with his hand to tease her.

A few minutes later he handed her a large piece of paper on which he had written down "John Mark and Lavina Wenger's Home Stead." Each first letter of a word he had written big and then beside each letter he wrote a word beside the letters. Beside J for John he wrote "joy," beside M for Mark he wrote "mercy," and beside L for Lavina he wrote "love," beside W for Wenger he wrote "we," and beside H for home he wrote "here," and finally, beside S for stead he wrote "share": Joy, Mercy, and Love We Here Share.

He was writing down the expense and income of keeping the children and then other income on a separate account to try and keep it straightened out as he put it under the name of "Joy, Mercy, and Love We Here Share." He wanted to have Lavina's name included as she was doing half of the work of it. Just More Worthy didn't in-clude Lavina. Now her name helped form the message. For short, people started calling it "Joy, Mercy, and Love Home."

A few evenings later, as they were lingering at the supper table, there was a knock at the door. They opened it to a dressed-up Mennonite man. John Mark invited him in.

He didn't have a name for him, but Lavina exclaimed, "Paul Landis!" Paul Landis, who was almost three years old, looked up startled, wondering why his mother called him so urgently. Then the man laughed, and John Mark recognized the minister, Paul Landis. He said he couldn't stay long as they had to move on and he wanted to start soon. He had come with some others on church work and the others were making a call elsewhere.

"But my," Paul Landis said, ruffling his hand through his hair, "you age me faster yet, if this is all your family." He waved his hand among the children round the table who were getting up.

John Mark pointed to the paper Julia had made and put on the wall above the kitchen sink with the instructions of their homestead. John Mark explained quickly that one stays here to go to special education school, one is Lavina's brother, one is helping us to take care of an aging neighbor lady, one runs the clock repair shop for him, and one is here to tend the laying hens and eggs for them. They all belonged together.

"Titus here got me started on clock repairing so I could quit teaching school and be home with the family." Paul asked some more questions. Edgar and Carl decided to go hunt the eggs, and Titus went to the clock shop. Lillian picked up Warren who was dissatisfied, while Julia remembered to go over and see what needed to be done for Miss High for the evening.

The older man looked from one to the other and said, "You must have had deep roots with such flowers coming forth when set in light. Some with strength behind them. Rooted in love," he added as an afterthought.

They had an interesting little visit and when Paul was about ready to leave, he grabbed little Paul Landis and kissed him, which drove the child almost to tears. Then Minister Paul quickly got a balloon out of his pocket and blew it up and gave it to him, which put a shy smile back on the little child's face. But he still only half trusted the man.

After Minister Paul left, John Mark confided to Lavina, "Titus and Vera are what I call the flowers coming forth. The work has strength behind it and when it is brought to light we can see flowers."

"Do you remember the days or years when we were set in the dark for the roots to get strength? In December before our wedding?" Lavina asked.

"I don't really remember. It's just like a dream that can't be recollected. It's not, well, oh, like Dad said, 'It's not worthy to compare with the joy.'" John Mark looked up the verse to see really what it said. "For I reckon that the sufferings of this present time are not worthy to be compared with the glory which shall be revealed in us (Romans 8:18)." Yes, it was not worthy to compare with the glory!

The End